QUARTERDECK

A **KYDD** SEA ADVENTURE

JULIAN STOCKWIN

QUARTERDECK
A **KYDD** SEA ADVENTURE

McBooks Press, Inc.
Ithaca, New York

Published by McBooks Press 2005
Copyright © 2004 by Julian Stockwin
First published in Great Britain in 2004 by Hodder and Stoughton
A division of Hodder Headline

Cover painting by Geoff Hunt
Cover and interior designed by Panda Musgrove

Library of Congress Cataloging-in-Publication Data

Stockwin, Julian.
  Quarterdeck : a Kydd sea adventure / by Julian Stockwin.
    p. cm.
  ISBN 1-59013-115-0 (hc. : alk. paper)
  978-1-59013-128-2, 1-59013-128-2 (trade pbk : alk. paper)
  1. Kydd, Thomas (Fictitious character)—Fiction. 2. Great Britain—
History, Naval—18th century—Fiction. 3. Seafaring life—Fiction. 4.
Sailors—Fiction. I. Title.
  PR6119.T66Q37 2005
  823'.92—dc22   2005010741

Distributed to the trade by National Book Network, Inc.,
15200 NBN Way, Blue Ridge Summit, PA 17214
800-462-6420

In recent memory of Lieutenant Chris Walklett, RN
A true heart of oak

Prologue

A CLOCK TICKED LOUDLY IN THE SILENCE. The three commissioners, experienced sea captains all, stared implacably at the candidate, waiting for his answer.

Acting Lieutenant Thomas Kydd had every reason to feel the terror that froze his bowels: failure at this examination would see him stripped of his temporary rank and returned ingloriously to his old shipmates.

"Er, well, I would—"

"Come, come, sir! An easy enough question—your certificate of service claims sea-time in *Artemis,* a crack frigate as ever I've seen. You must have seen a flying moor above a dozen times."

It was unfair: here in this august Navy Office board-room he was being asked to describe one of the most risky manoeuvres, dropping anchor at speed and sailing on to the full scope of the cable, then letting go another before falling back on the two anchors. Black Jack Powlett of the *Artemis* would never have chanced his vessel so, Kydd thought indignantly, then took a deep breath. "Coming boldly up t' the anchorage, I, er, would range both cables out on the gun-deck—veering parties double-banked, o' course—an' at m' furthest on, let go th' best bower. Then—"

"You do not feel it prudent to double bitt your cable first, sir?" the first commissioner interjected.

Then the second came in: "And we have heard nothing of setting this bower a-cockbill in readiness."

"That is, if your ship has not yet a trick stopper or similar," the first added smugly.

Kydd forced his mind to an icy resolve. "Aye, sir—I may have omitted t' say that in getting the anchor off the bows it is first necessary . . ."

It seemed to satisfy. He dared a glance at the third member of the board, who sat hard-faced and silent, Captain Essington, the captain of *Triumph* in which he had served at the bloody battle of Camperdown.

"Passing to navigation," the first commissioner said flatly.

Kydd's anxieties returned: he had learned his skills at the hands of a merchant-service sailing master who had taught him a plain yet solid understanding of his craft, but Kydd knew that the Navy liked arcane descriptions and definitions.

"We'll begin with basic understanding, Mr Kydd. What is your conceiving of a great circle?"

"Er, the plane o' the equator when projected fr'm the centre on to a tangent plane becomes a straight line—"

"Thank you. The workings of an azimuth altitude will be familiar enough to you, no doubt—then clarify for me the correction of the right ascension of the mean sun, if you please."

Kydd struggled, but could see frowns settling, glances exchanged. Failure was now more than a possibility and a cold dread stole over him. If only they would ask—

"Mr Kydd, you are aboard a two-decker." It was Essington, leaning forward. Kydd shifted position to face him directly. There was no trace of compassion in the man's eyes. "Shall we say in the Caribbean? You are scudding before a regular-going hurricane and you sight land—dead to loo'ard. You throw out both bowers." The other commissioners looked at Essington with curiosity. "They carry away, one after the other. Only a sheet anchor is left to you to prevent the ship being cast ashore. Detail your actions, if you will, sir, to forestall a wreck and grievous loss of life." He leaned back, unnerving Kydd with his stare. His fellow captains held back in surprise as Essington finished acidly, "And shall we have a coral bottom?"

Kydd cast about for something to say, the right action to take in such an extreme situation—but then it dawned on him: he had been in exactly this plight in the old *Trajan,* and himself had been the one to pass keckling to preserve their last anchor, called as lee helmsman by the master himself. "Aye, sir," he said crisply. "First we need t' ride out the blow. A coral bottom means we'll have to pass a deal of keckling aroun' the first two or three fathom of cable above the anchor clinch, and then . . ." Those desperate hours off the unknown island were burned into his consciousness: that endless night, the screaming hurricane, the cold dawn and the fearful danger of their action in clawing off. It steadied him, the simple recounting of fine seamanship. "But to make an offing will be hard, an' we must wait f'r the wind to shift a point or two, but then we must take our chance, and only one chance it is. Show small canvas, and at th' right time cut the cable an' run f'r the open sea."

The commissioners nodded, expressionless. "I think that's enough, gentlemen, do you not?" Essington said.

Kydd held his breath. There was mumbled conferring, more frowns. Was it possibly more than coincidence that Essington had brought forward that particular circumstance? As if he had particular knowledge of his past and . . .

"Where are your certificates?"

They were asking for attestations to his "Sobriety, Obedience, Diligence and Skill in the Profession of a Seaman." Kydd handed over the journals and documents in a floodtide of hope: if he had failed, why would they be wasting time on the formalities?

The journals were leafed through, but they had been meticulously kept for years and it seemed the certificates of age and rated service appeared acceptable. His heart leaped: the last hurdle was being overcome.

"If my reckoning is correct, we have a difficulty." One of the commissioners held the original, if somewhat crumpled, certificate of service from Kydd's first ship, *Duke William*. "From this, it does seem that Mr Kydd is, according to regulations, one year short of the requirement for sea-time."

Kydd had known of this deficiency, but had prayed that the regulations would not be applied rigorously. Horatio Nelson himself had been promoted to lieutenant before time, but if a commissioner of the board wished to make an issue of it little could be done.

Essington took the paper, then looked up with a tigerish smile. "Yes—but this is worthless! It is in error! I distinctly recollect when Captain Caldwell was removed from *Royal Billy* to *Culloden*. I rather fancy we would get a different date were we to ask him directly. As it is, Captain Caldwell is now in the West Indies, admiral of the Leeward Squadron if my memory serves. I doubt he is to be troubled on this trivial matter."

His manner quelled all discussion. The other commissioners gathered up the papers and returned them to Kydd. "Well, it seems we are of one mind. Our recommendation will go forward to the Navy Office that for the good of the service you shall be confirmed in rank to lieutenant. Good day to you, sir."

CHAPTER 1

THE PORTSMOUTH MAIL MADE GOOD SPEED on the highway south from London. Inside, it smelt pungently of leather and old dust, but Thomas Kydd did not care: it would take a great deal more than this to subdue his growing excitement.

After the examination, Kydd had spent some days in Yarmouth, where *Tenacious* had been taken out of commission for battle repairs, and had prevailed upon the naval outfitter in the matter of a splendid lieutenant's uniform, determined to go home on leave in a handsome manner.

He stared out at the tranquil winter country scene of soft meadows and gnarled oak trees. This was England at last, his hearth and home after so many years away. The postillion's long horn blared, and he leaned out of the window. It was Cobham—Guildford was not far away. He glanced at his friend sitting next to him. "An hour, Nicholas—an hour only, an' I'll be seein' m' folks again!"

Renzi had been quiet since London, his withdrawn, ascetic expression discouraging talk. He nodded politely and smiled, then looked away.

Heaven only knew what he was thinking about. Their years together had been full of perils and adventure, but Renzi's friendship had brought Kydd an insight into learning, and respect for the riches of the mind. And now they were returning to where their long adventure had started.

Yet again Kydd brought to memory how he had last left home, when he and Renzi had stolen away back to sea, to *Artemis,* the famous frigate, after founding a school to secure his family's livelihood. There had been a world voyage that had ended in shipwreck, rousing times in the Caribbean, adventures in the Mediterranean. It seemed half a lifetime, but it was only four years or so. Here he was, just twenty-five, and . . .

The coach jerked to a stop, and the horses were changed for the last stage to Guildford. The door swung open, and a young lady was handed up, her tall bonnet catching on the roof sill. She settled opposite in a rustle of pale-blue silk, her eyes downcast.

An older gentleman followed, acknowledged Kydd and Renzi, then sat beside her. The ostler offered a hot brick in worn serge, which the man manoeuvred under the young lady's feet. "Thank you, dear Papa," she said demurely, snuggling her hands into a muff.

The man favoured a belly-warmer, which he settled inside his long coat. "Uncommon cold for this time o' year!" he grunted.

Long inured to conditions far worse, Kydd caught Renzi's amused but discreet sideways glance. "Er, I'm sure y'r right."

The girl looked up, and noticed their uniforms. "Oh!" she said prettily, her hand at her mouth. "You're sailors!"

The man coughed irritably. "They're officers, m'dear, naval officers, not sailors, d'ye see?"

"It is what I meant to say, Papa. Pray, sirs, were you in that dreadful battle of Camperdown? I have heard that it was quite the most shocking fight this age!"

The man clicked his tongue in exasperation, but Kydd's heart swelled with pride. Their coach still bore laurel branches from the helter-skelter celebrations of only a week or so ago.

"Indeed, this is so, Miss, and you will understand how truly

weary we are, that we yearn for the blessings of peace and solitude for a period . . ." Renzi said quietly.

"Of course, sir, please do forgive me." Her eyes rested briefly on
Kydd. Then she turned determinedly to stare out of the window.

Kydd felt a pang of irritation, but understood that Renzi was
sparing him idle chat so that he could enjoy the anticipation of
his homecoming.

The mention of Camperdown, his first big fleet action,
brought back emotions that were still too raw and recent, images
of the nightmare of the great mutiny at the Nore and its sequel;
his mind shied away from them and instead concentrated on the
incredible fact that he had been promoted on the field of battle
and officially confirmed. He was now Lieutenant Kydd! It was
still too heady a thought, so he let his mind return to the excitement of his homecoming.

The coach jolted over the infamous potholes at Abbotswood:
Guildford Town was now minutes away. Almost too quickly, the
square, grey-stone Elizabethan grammar school passed on the
left, and the town proper began, familiar buildings at the top of
the high street. The post-horn's baying echoed off the almshouse
opposite Holy Trinity, drawing mildly curious glances from the
townsfolk.

Clattering over the old cobbled road, they passed under the
big clock, and the driver tooled the mail-coach through the narrow black and white half-timbered entrance of the Angel posting-
house.

Kydd and Renzi left their bags with the obsequious landlord,
then emerged on to the high street and turned left, past shops
and alleys well known to Kydd. The reek and colour of the town,
the bustle and shouts, the passing tide of people all seemed to advance like a dream.

Some glanced curiously at the two men, others with admiration. Self-conscious, Kydd waited for someone to recognise him,

but perhaps the dark blue, white and gold of his handsome uniform put paid to that. He saw Betty, the fishmonger's attractive daughter, who stopped and stared in shock at the sight of him. Kydd doffed his brand-new cocked hat.

They reached the red-brick church of Holy Trinity, and turned off past the glebe cottages to Schoolhouse Lane, as it was now known. There was no mistaking the little naval school ahead: a huge blue ensign floated above for all the world to see—the flag under which Kydd had fought at Camperdown. And as they drew near they could hear a muffled chanting on the air: ". . . three sevens are twenty-one, four sevens are twenty-eight, five sevens . . ."

They stepped into the tiny quadrangle, two King's officers returned from the sea. A youngster emerged at the run from a classroom and teetered to a halt. He whipped off his cap and shrilled, "I'll fetch th' bo'sun, if y' please, sir!"

Jabez Perrott emerged out of the building and stumped importantly towards them. His eyes widened, and he gasped, "Be buggered! It's Master Kydd, be gob!"

Kydd opened his mouth, but Perrott, reddening with pleasure, grabbed for his silver call and emitted a piercing blast. Then, in a lower-deck bellow that had not softened with the years, he roared, "*Aaaaall* the hands! *Haaaands* to muster—clear lower deck, ye swabs! *Haaaands* to muster!"

Children boiled out of the classrooms, screeching in delight at the antics of their strict boatswain.

"Mr Perrott! *Mr Perrott!* What *are* you doing?"

Kydd recognised the voice and, holding back tears, advanced to meet his mother.

"Oh! Tom! It's you! M' darling boy, it's you! And you've . . ." The rest was lost in a fierce embrace that went on and on, knocking his hat askew.

"Mother! So long . . ."

Kydd's father had aged: his form was stooped and his eyes sightless. Nevertheless, he bore himself nobly in the black breeches of a headmaster. "Er, is that you, son?"

"It is, Walter!" his mother said, as the old man moved uncertainly towards Kydd, holding out his hand. Kydd took it, then hugged him.

"Walter, Tom is an officer!" She looked anxiously to Kydd for confirmation—the idea was so enormous.

"Aye, Mother, it's 'Lieutenant Kydd, Royal Navy' you must call me now, or I'll clap ye all in irons!" He spoke loudly so his father would make no mistake about what he was hearing.

"Carry on, sir?" Perrott said to Kydd, touching his hat.

"Er, please do," said Kydd.

"Ship's comp'ny, ahoy! I'll have yez in two lines afore the mast—let's be havin' ye!" he bawled at the children. They shuffled eagerly into line. "Now, we dips our colours t' a pair o' 'eroes 'oo has jus' come back 'ome fr'm such a battle as never was, an' we're going t' show how much we admires 'em!"

Lieutenants Kydd and Renzi stood solemnly to attention as "God Save The King" and "Rule Britannia" were sung enthusiastically by the wide-eyed youngsters.

A piercing squeal on the boatswain's call brought quiet, and the colours were dipped reverently to half staff. With great dignity Perrott turned to face Kydd, removing his hat. Taken by surprise, Kydd raised his own cocked hat, at which the colours rose again.

"Silence!" Perrott thundered at the awed children. "Now, Lootenant Kydd will talk t' you about y'r dooty."

Kydd managed to splutter a few words: "Y'r duty is . . . steadfast in all weathers . . . courage at the cannon's mouth . . . King and country."

It seemed to be enough. An eager child broke ranks and held up his hand. "Please, sir, I want t' be a sailor—how do I be a sailor?"

Soon a pink-faced Kydd was mobbed by shouting boys.

"Pipe down, y' scurvy crew, 'n' listen to the l'tenant!" growled Perrott happily.

Kydd glanced across at his mother, who was bursting with pride, and knew there was only one thing to do. He turned to his father and touched his hat. "Cap'n, sir, permission f'r liberty ashore t' both watches!"

"Oh, er, liberty?" his father stuttered. "Yes, yes, er, Lieutenant Kydd. A half-holiday to, er, all hands!" The children screamed with delight and poured out of the school, leaving a dazed, happy Kydd family standing in the quadrangle.

"I shall withdraw at this point, if I may," Renzi said quietly.

"No, no, Mr Renzi," Mrs Kydd insisted. "You must stay an' tell us where you have been on the sea—you'll both have such tales, I do declare!" She turned to Kydd. "Now, I'll ask Mr Partington to spare us his room for you—he can stay with his friend Jonathan. For Mr Renzi . . ." She trailed off. Then she resumed stiffly: "But, then, now Thomas has a reputation, he'll want t' have his own establishment."

His mother's words could not hide the essence of the matter, the brutal truth, and Kydd felt a chill at the passing of his simple life. He saw her colouring: she had understood that her son was no longer hers. From now on, society events and invitations would firmly distinguish between the Kydds.

"We shall stay at the Angel," Renzi said softly. "Then we will take modest lodgings in town."

Kydd mumbled agreement.

"Well, then, that's settled," his mother said bravely. "It's for the best, o' course. Come inside an' take a posset—you must be frozen after y'r journey."

• • •

As he cradled a mug of hot curdled milk at the kitchen table Kydd listened to the flow of prattle from his mother, felt the quiet presence of his father and caught the curious flash of the maid's eyes. His own kept straying down to his uniform, the blue and gold so striking. Who could guess what the future might hold now? A deep sigh escaped him.

He heard the approaching *tap, tap* of footsteps. His mother smiled. "Ah, that must be Cecilia—she'll be so surprised to see you!"

The last time he had seen his sister was in a wrecked boat in the Caribbean. He recalled her mortal terror as they had fought for their lives against the sharks. What would she think of him now?

"She's done very well with Lord an' Lady Stanhope, Thomas. Quite the lady companion she is now," Mrs Kydd said proudly. "And don't go quarrellin' with her, if y' please, you know how it upsets your father."

The outside door rattled, and Cecilia's voice echoed down the passageway. "Father—what *is* going on? I saw quantities of your boys on the street and . . ." Her voice died away as the two men rose to their feet. She looked from face to face, incredulous. "Thomas? You . . . you . . ."

Kydd awkwardly held out his hands. "Ye're doin' well, Mother says—"

Suddenly her expression softened to a deep tenderness, and she seized her brother in a fierce hug. "Oh, Thomas! I've so missed you!"

He felt her body heaving, and when she looked at him again he saw the sparkle of tears. His own voice was gruff with emotion as he said, "Sis—y' remember in th' boat—"

She stopped him with a finger on his lips and whispered, "Mother!" Then she let him go, crossed to Renzi and placed a generous kiss on both his cheeks. "Dear Nicholas! How are you? You're still so thin, you know."

Renzi replied politely, and Cecilia turned back to her brother. "Thomas and Nicholas are going to take chocolate with me at Murchison's and tell me all their adventures, while you, Mother, prepare such a welcome for this wandering pair!" she announced. Her eyes widened. "Gracious me—and if I'm not mistaken in the particulars—Thomas, you're a . . ."

"L'tenant Kydd it is now, Cec," he said happily.

The evening meal was a roaring success. Kydd became hoarse with talking and Renzi was quite undone by the warmth of his welcome. Cecilia could not get enough of Kydd's descriptions of the Venice of Casanova, even above his protestations that the danger of their mission meant he was hardly in a position to discourse on the republic's attractions.

Distant thumps and a sudden crackle sounded outside. Cecilia clapped her hands. "The fireworks—I nearly forgot! Tonight we'll see your Admiral Onslow—he is to be a baronet, and is now resting at Clandon with his brother the earl. It's said he'll make an address from the balcony of the town hall! Gentlemen—I wish to attend! I shall be with you presently." She swept away imperiously to appear shortly afterwards in a pelisse at the height of fashion: lemon silk, lined and faced with blue. She looked at them both with the suspicion of a pout. "And who will be my gentleman escort?"

Kydd hesitated, but instantly Renzi bowed deeply and offered his arm. "May I observe that I find Mademoiselle is in looks tonight?" he said, with the utmost courtly grace.

Cecilia inclined her head and accepted his arm. They went outside and, without a backward glance at Kydd, moved off down the lane, Cecilia's laughter tinkling at Renzi's sallies.

Kydd watched them helplessly. His sister had changed. There

was not a trace of childhood chubbiness left: her strong features had developed into strikingly dark good looks and a languorous elegance. Her position with Lady Stanhope had allowed her to find an easy confidence and elegance of speech that he could only envy; he followed them, trying to look unconcerned.

Crowds pressed everywhere, while excited chatter and the smell of fireworks hung on the air. People held back respectfully. Kydd was not sure whether it was in recognition of them as gentlefolk or because of the Navy uniform. Closer to the torch-lit balcony the throng was tightly packed and they had to remain some distance back.

Cecilia kept Renzi's arm, but pulled Kydd forward, attracting envious looks from other ladies. "Oh, I'm so proud of you!" she exclaimed, her voice raised above the excited babble of the crowd. She smiled at them both, and Kydd felt better.

"It was th' admiral gave me m' step, Cec—there in th' great cabin o' *Monarch*." Kydd paused, remembering the scene. "But it were Cap'n Essington put me forward."

A deep thumping came from the other side, further down the high street: the Royal Surreys called out to do duty on this naval occasion. Thin sounds of fife and trumpet rose above the hubbub, strengthening as they approached. Then, with a pair of loud double thumps on the bass drum, it ceased.

The crowd surged below the balcony and settled into a tense expectation. Torchlight illuminated upturned faces, caught the sparkle of eyes, the glitter of gold lace. At the signs of indistinct movement within, a rustle of anticipation arose and the mayor emerged on to the balcony in his best scarlet gown and tricorne, resplendent with his chain of office. "M' lords, ladies an' gennelmen! Pray silence for the mighty victor o' the great battle o' Camperdown, our own—Adm'ral Onslow!"

The genial sea officer Kydd remembered stepped out on to the balcony. A furious storm of cheering met him, a roar of wholehearted and patriotic acclaim. Onslow, in his full-dress admiral's uniform, sword and decorations, bared his head and bowed this way and that, manifestly affected by the welcome.

Kydd watched him turn again and again to face all parts of the crowd. At one point he thought he had caught the admiral's eye, and wondered if he should wave back, but there was no sign of recognition.

The noise subsided, and Onslow moved to the front of the balcony. He fumbled in his coat, and withdrew a paper. He hesitated, then put the paper back, straightening to a quarterdeck brace. "M' lord mayor an' lady—citizens of Guildford!" he began. "I thank ye for your fine and loyal address followin' the action off Camperdown. But I must make something very clear to ye. An admiral doesn't win battles, the seamen do. An' I cannot stand here tonight without I acknowledge this before you all! Over there t' larb'd! Yes, those two men, ahoy! Be s' good as to join me and show y'selves! These are two of your true victors o' Camperdown!"

"Thomas—go!" Cecilia squealed, when it became obvious whom the admiral had singled out. The crowd shuffled and fell back.

Onslow was waiting for them and shook their hands warmly. "A fine thing t' see ye both," he rumbled, his keen eyes taking in their new uniforms. "Let's out an' give 'em a sight, then you'll honour me with y'r presence at the presentation."

They emerged together on the balcony to a roar, Kydd waving awkwardly, Renzi bowing. Kydd's eyes searched out Cecilia. She was shouting something to him, waving furiously, and his heart swelled.

"A capital choice," Renzi said, removing his coat and standing in waistcoat and breeches. "It seems we shall be waiting out

Tenacious's repair in a tolerable degree of comfort." He settled into a substantial high-backed chair.

Kydd rubbed his hands before the fire. The agent had left, and they had taken on this half-mansion below the castle for a reasonable sum. The owner had apparently instructed that officers in His Majesty's service could rely on his patriotic duty in the matter of a lease. Not only that but, agreeably, they could share the services of domestic staff with the adjoining residence, which, as it was inhabited by an old lady, should be no trial.

Kydd looked around him with growing satisfaction, albeit tinged with trepidation. The rooms were not large, but were bigger than anything he had lived in before. He'd always known that the heart of the home was the kitchen, but here it seemed that this elegant room had taken its place.

The walls were a soft sage colour, the broad, generous sash windows were hung with muslin and festoon curtains, and stout druggets lay beneath his feet instead of oiled floorcloths. The furniture was reassuringly old-fashioned and sturdy. He turned again to the fire with its plain but well-proportioned marble surround and mantelpiece, and felt an unstoppable surge of happiness. "Two or three months, d'ye suppose?" he mused, recalling the savage wounds *Tenacious* had suffered.

"I would think so." Renzi sat sprawled, his eyes closed.

"Nicholas, th' sun is not yet above th' foreyard, but I have a desire t' toast our fortune!"

Renzi half opened his eyes. "Please do. You will not find me shy of acknowledging that it is these same fates that determine whether one should die of a loathsome disease or—"

"Clap a stopper on it, brother!" Kydd laughed. "I'll go 'n' rouse out somethin' we c'n—"

"I think not."

"Why—"

"Pray touch the bell for the servant."

"Aye, Nicholas," Kydd said humbly. He found the well-worn but highly polished silver bell and rang it self-consciously.

"Sir?" A manservant in blue, with a plain bob wig, appeared.

Renzi pulled himself upright. "Should you unlock my grey valise you will find a brace of cognac. Pray be so good as to open one for us."

"Certainly, sir," the man said, with a short bow, and withdrew.

Kydd tried to look unconcerned and toasted his rear until the servant returned bearing a gilt tray.

"À votre santé," Renzi said.

"À votter sonday," Kydd echoed awkwardly. The brandy burned a passage to his empty stomach.

Renzi stood up, raising his glass to Kydd. "Our present fortune. May this indeed be a true augury of our future."

"Aye, an' may we never find th' need t' deny our past ever," Kydd responded. "Nicholas. M' true friend." He looked sideways at Renzi and, seeing he was attending politely, pressed on: "I've been a-thinkin'—you don't care if I say my mind?"

"My dear fellow! If it were any other I would feel betrayed."

"Well, Nicholas, this is all more'n I could ever hope for, somethin' that can only happen if—if y'r destiny is written somewhere, I reckon. So I'm takin' this chance wi' both hands! I'll give it m' rousin' best copper-bottomed, double-barrelled, bevel-edged try, I will!"

Renzi nodded. "Of course, brother."

"So this is what I have t' do." Kydd took a determined pull on his brandy. "I've seen y'r tarpaulin officer come aft through the hawse, a right taut son o' Neptune. Ye sees him on watch on th' quarterdeck an' it puts y'r heart at ease. But, Nicholas, I

don't want t' be a tarpaulin officer. They're stayin' l'tenants all
their days, fine messmates I'm sure, but who should say—plain
in their habits. The other officers step ashore t'gether while they
stays aboard 'n' makes friends wi' a bottle."

He glanced down at the glass in his hands. "I want t' be a
reg'lar-built King's officer and gentleman, Nicholas, an' I asks
you what I c'n do to be one o' them."

Renzi's half-smile appeared. "If this is your wish, Tom—yet
I'll have you know there is no shame in being one of nature's
gentlemen . . ."

"If y' will—"

"Ah. All in good time, dear fellow. This does require a mort
of reflection . . ."

It was all very well for Kydd to ask this of him, even if what he
said was perfectly reasonable—but in truth the job was nigh impossible. Renzi's eye covertly took in Kydd's figure: instead of a
fine-drawn, willowy courtliness there were strong shoulders and
slim hips standing four-square; rather than a distinguished slen-
der curve to the leg, his knee-breeches betrayed sculpted mus-
culature. And in place of a fashionably cool, pale countenance
there was a hearty oaken one, whose open good humour was not
designed for societal discretion. And yet he was undoubtedly intelligent: Renzi had seen his quick wits at work. But Kydd would
have to learn to value politeness and convention—not his strongest suit. Then there was his speech—Renzi squirmed to think of
the sport others would make of him behind his back. The probable course of events, then, would be for Kydd to retreat into the
comfort of bluff sea-doggery, and thereby exclude himself from
gentle-born society. But this was his particular friend: he could
not refuse him.

"Mr Kydd, as now I must call you, this is what I propose."
He fixed him with a stare. "Should you choose this path then I

must warn you that the way is arduous. There's many a chance to stumble. Are you prepared for a hard beat to wind'd?"

"I am."

"And there are, er, matters you must accept without question, which are not, on the face of it, either reasonable or explicable. Do you undertake that you will accept from me their necessity without question?"

Kydd paused. "Aye."

"Very well. I will give you my full assistance in your worthy endeavour, and if you stay the course, for you may indeed wish to yield the race at any point—"

"Never!"

"—then I in turn agree to assist in your elevation into society."

Kydd flushed. "I won't shame ye to y'r friends, if that is y'r meaning."

"That was not my meaning, but let us make a start." He reached for the cognac and filled Kydd's glass. "There is a beginning to everything, and in this it is the understanding that for a gentleman it is appearances that define. Politeness, the courtesies due to a lady, these are held at a value far above that of courage out on a yard, true saltwater seamanship. It is unfair, but it is the world. Now, in the matter of the courtesies, we have . . ."

Kydd persevered. He was aware that Renzi's precepts were introductory only and that there lay ahead a challenge of insight and understanding far different from anything he had encountered before. The morning lengthened, and by the time Renzi had reached the proper use of euphemisms Kydd was flagging.

They heard the rap of the front-door knocker. "I'll go," Kydd said, rising.

"You shall not!" Renzi's words stopped him, and he subsided into his chair.

The manservant entered with a small silver tray in his gloved hands and went pointedly to Renzi. "Are you at home, sir?"

Renzi picked up a card. "I am to this young lady, thank you."

"Very well, sir."

As the servant left, Renzi shot to his feet. "Square away, Tom—it's your sister!"

Cecilia entered the sitting room, eyes darting around. "Er, you're welcome, Cec," Kydd said, trying vainly to remember his morning exercises in civilities.

She acknowledged Renzi with a shy bob. "Mother said—such a silly—that men are not to be trusted on their own in a domestic situation. How insulting to you!"

"I do apologise, Miss Kydd, that we are not dressed to receive. I hope you understand."

"Nicholas?" Cecilia said, puzzled, but then her expression cleared. "But of course—you're standing on ceremony for Thomas's sake." She looked at her brother fondly.

Kydd smouldered.

Cecilia, ignoring him, crossed to a candlestand and delicately sniffed the nearest. "Well, it's none of my business, but I can't help observing that unless you have means beyond the ordinary, beeswax candles must, sadly, be accounted an extravagance. Tallow will be sufficient—unless, of course, you have visitors." She crossed to the windows and made play of freeing the shutters. "You will be aware how vital it is to preserve furniture from the sun."

"We c'n manage," Kydd growled. "An' I'll thank ye to keep y'r household suggestions to y'rself."

"Thomas! I came only out of concern for your—"

"Cec, Nicholas is tellin' me the right lay t' be a gentleman. Please t' leave us to it."

"Indeed!"

"Dear Miss Kydd, your kindness in enquiring after our situation is handsomely done," said Renzi, "yet I feel it is probably a man's place to impart to another the graces of a gentleman."

Cecilia hesitated. "That's as maybe, Mr Renzi, but there is another purpose to my visit. You appear to have forgotten that a naval uniform will not answer in all appearances in polite society. I came merely to offer my services in a visit to the tailor."

At the tailor's Cecilia was not to be dissuaded. She quickly disposed of Kydd's initial preferences. A yellow waistcoat, while undoubtedly fetching, was apparently irredeemably vulgar: dark green, double-breasted was more the thing; she conceded on the gold piping at the pockets. Buff breeches, a rust-coloured coat, and for half-dress, a *bon de Paris* with discreet gold frogging would be of the highest *ton*—she was not sure about the lace.

"An' what's the reckonin' so far?" Kydd had done well in prize money in the Caribbean, and after Camperdown there would be more, but this must be costing a shocking sum.

Cecilia pressed on relentlessly. A dark blue frock coat was essential, in the new style with cut-away skirts that ended in split tails for an elegant fall while horse-riding—it seemed frivolous to Kydd, who was more used to a sensible full-skirted warmth. A quantity of linen shirts was put in train, and material for a cravat was purchased that Cecilia insisted only she might be trusted to make.

Kydd rebelled at pantaloons, long breeches that could be tucked into boots. Knee breeches were what he would be seen in—no one would mistake him for a damned macaroni.

The tailor, gratified at patronage by those so recently in the public eye, promised that he would bend his best efforts to have them delivered soon. Kydd was then escorted to the bootmaker and, finally, to the premises of Henry Tidmarsh, hosier, hatter and glover, where he found for himself a dashing light-grey brimmed hat with a silver buckle.

As Kydd tried on hats, Renzi came up beside Cecilia. "Quite a transformation," he murmured.

"Yes, Nicholas," agreed Cecilia, keeping her voice low, "but I fear he will be thought a coxcomb if his dress is not matched by his manners."

She turned to him, her hand on his arm. "Dear Nicholas, I know you are trying your best, but Thomas can be very stubborn if he chooses. Do bear him with patience, I pray."

"Of course. But the hardest for him will undoubtedly be his articulations—his speech damns him at once."

Cecilia touched his arm. "Is there anything, perhaps, that I can do?"

Renzi's thoughts had taken quite another course. She was no longer the ingenuous girl-child he had known from before. Cecilia was a desirable, self-possessed woman, who would be an ornament to any social gathering. "Er, this is possibly something we could discuss together, should you be at leisure." He felt a flush rising at the implication of the words.

"Why, Nicholas!" Cecilia said gaily. "If I didn't know you more, I'd be obliged to consider you importunate." She flashed him a smile, and turned her attention to her brother's fancy in hats.

Although he was now entitled to do so, Kydd could not indulge in the wigs that he had learned to make in his apprenticeship: the comet, the royal bird, the long bob—even the striking Cadogan puff—were now no longer fashionable. He would wear nothing, simply a neat black ribbon to hold back his hair at the nape of the neck. Hair-powder was taxed, so it would be quite understood if he left his hair as nature intended.

True to his word, the tailor delivered his work in only three days, and Kydd stood before the full-length bedroom mirror, regarding himself doubtfully. A generous cut on the waistcoat avoided any tense wrinkling resulting from muscle-play beneath, but the buff breeches seemed to cling indecently close. However, if he had to appear in public, this was not a bad beginning, he thought. He gazed down approvingly at the white stockings and buckled shoes, then whirled once about.

"Glad to see you in spirits, brother," came from behind him.

"Aye, what must be . . ." said Kydd, adjusting a cuff. "Are ye ready, Nicholas?"

"Ah!" Renzi waved a finger.

"What? Oh! I meant t' say, are you prepared, Mr Renzi?"

"Then let us sally forth on the world."

Renzi was in brown, a complete dark brown, with breeches, coat and even waistcoat in the colour, relieved only by the cream gush of his cravat and the stockings. In the manner of a Romantic he sported a broad-brimmed dark hat worn at a rakish angle.

It was the first time Kydd had used an ebony cane. As they passed along Chapel Street it felt awkward to the hand, whether he swung it at each pace to click on the ground or twirled it about. He fought down a sense of fakery, but after the second time a passer-by made way respectfully for him he felt happier.

They passed under the big clock in the high street—the beadle outside the town hall touched his hat to them—turned down a side-street and entered a dingy doorway.

"Might I present M'sieur Jupon? He is engaged to be your dancing master." A short but fierce-eyed man swept down in the most extravagant leg to Kydd, then straightened, fixing him with a challenging stare.

"Er, pleased t' meet ye," Kydd stuttered, and essayed a jerky bow. Jupon and Renzi exchanged glances.

"M'sieur Jupon will instruct you in the graces of movement and courtesy, and you will attend here for one hour daily until you have mastered the elements."

"Ah, Mr Kydd, you're not boardin' your ship now, sir. Do try a little *grace* in y'r movements." The voice of the lady horse-master carried effortlessly across the ring. She could well be relied on to hail the foreyard from the quarterdeck in a blow, Kydd thought.

The horse, however, had sensed his innocence, swishing its tail and playing with its bit. Its eyes rolled in anticipation while Kydd struggled to heave himself up, staggering one-footed in a circle.

Renzi dismounted and came across. He checked the girth and yanked on the stirrup. "Ah, the stablehand is having his amusement. You'd have your knees round your ears with this! We'll ease away—so." The stirrups descended, the horse quieter under Renzi's firm hand. He slapped the horse familiarly on the rump. "Look, here's a tip. Make a fist, and touch the stirrup bar up here. Now swing the iron up under your arm, and the right length for you will be when it just touches the body."

Kydd swung up nervously into the saddle, suddenly finding himself at a great height. The horse snorted and tossed its head. He felt that it was biding its time before wreaking some terrible revenge.

"So we seem t' have made up our mind to go ridin' at last." A sarcastic bellow came across the ring to him. "We start wi' the walk."

The horse plodded in a circle, and Kydd's confidence grew.

"Back straight, Mr Kydd." He forced his spine to rigidity and completed another circle. "Jehosaphat Moses! Keep y'r back supple, Mr Kydd. Let y'r hips rock *with* the horse, sir!"

The trot was more to his liking with its brisk motion, but the horse whinnied with frustration at the tight rein and Kydd eased it a little.

A gate was opened into a larger field, and Renzi began to canter. Kydd followed behind, feeling the thud of hoofs through the animal's frame and hearing snorts of effort coming from the great beast beneath him. It was exhilarating, and he relaxed into it. The horse seemed to sense this and responded with a more fluid, faster motion.

"Well done, Mr Kydd!" he heard. "'Collected an' light in hand,' we say."

As he turned he saw the woman pull out a large fob watch. "To me!" she demanded impatiently.

Kydd felt the horse respond to his signals with knee and reins and suddenly was reluctant to finish for the morning. Impulsively, he clapped his knees to the beast's barrel-like sides. After a brief hesitation the horse responded and broke into a gallop. Instinctively Kydd acted as he would aloft, his standing crouch that of a topman leaning forward to hand a billowing sail. The horse stretched out down the length of the field. Now wildly excited, Kydd caught a glimpse of figures staring at him as he thundered past. The wind tore through his hair, the din of hoofs and the animal's rhythmic movements beat on his senses.

A gnarled wooden fence spread across his vision. As they hurtled towards it, Kydd considered an emergency turn to larboard. Far behind him a faint bellow sounded: "Bridge y'r reins! Bridge your *reins!*" but he was too far gone. The horse threw itself at the rails. There was a momentary muscular tensing, a lunge into space, then all was quiet for a heartbeat before the beast landed with a mighty thud and a jerk.

Kydd stayed aboard as the horse raced away through nondescript winter-brown bracken and into the woods beyond. It hesitated in mid-stride, then swerved on to a woodland path, Kydd ducking to avoid whip-like branches.

He became aware of hoofbeats out of synchrony with his own, and indistinct shouting. He guessed it would be Renzi following, but dared not look behind. He shot past a gaping greenwood forager, then reached a more substantial lane across their path.

The horse skidded as it negotiated a random turn, but the mud slowed it, and the gallop became less frantic. It panted heavily as it slowed to a trot. Renzi caught up and grasped the reins. "How are you, brother?"

Kydd flashed a wide grin. "Spankin' fine time, Nicholas, s' help me," he said breathlessly, his face red with exertion.

Renzi hid a grin. "And what has happened to your decorum, sir?"

"Oh? Aye, yes. Er, a capital experience, sir."

They rode together for a space. The lane widened and a small cottage came into view ahead. "Do dismount, old fellow, and ask directions back," Renzi suggested. Gingerly, Kydd leaned forward to bring his leg across the saddle, but in a flash he had toppled backwards into the black winter mud, still with one foot in a stirrup.

The horse stamped and rolled its eyes as Kydd got ruefully to his feet and trudged down the garden path to the door.

It was answered by a stooped old man with alert bright eyes. Before Kydd could speak, he smiled. "Ah, Master Kydd, I do believe? Thomas Kydd?"

"Aye, y'r in the right of it," Kydd said. "That is t' say, you have th' advantage of me, sir."

The man feigned disappointment. Kydd's face cleared. "O' course! Parson Deane!" It seemed so long ago that, as a boy, he had taken delight in going to the lakeside with the old man and his dog after duck. "I hope I find you in health, sir," he said. The parson glanced up at Renzi, who was still mounted. "Oh, sir, this is Mr Renzi, my particular friend. Mr Renzi, this is the Rev'nd Deane."

Renzi inclined his head. "My honour, sir. Our apologies at this intrusion, we merely seek a more expedient way back to our *manège*."

Deane's face creased in pleasure. "I shall tell you, should you come inside and accept a dish of tea while Thomas tells me where he's been spending his days."

They left the horses to crop grass outside the garden fence and went into the parson's house. Deane looked at Kydd keenly, clearly enjoying his sparse recital of his impressment and subsequent adventures. "So now you're an officer?"

Kydd grinned boyishly. "L'tenant Kydd!" he said, with swelling pride.

"Then you are now, in the eyes of the whole world, a gentleman. Is this not so?"

It seemed appropriate to bow wordlessly.

Deane contemplated Kydd for a long moment. "Do you stop me if I appear impertinent," he said, "yet I would later remember this moment with shame were I not to share with you now my thoughts concerning your station."

"It would be f'r my advantage, Mr Deane." He couldn't resist a quick glance of triumph at Renzi—after all, he had remembered the polite words—but Renzi responded with a frown. Obediently Kydd turned all his attention to the old man.

"It seems to me that the essence of a gentleman is to be found in his good breeding, his impeccable civility to all, including his servants. 'Manners maketh man,' as the Good Book teaches us. Outer manners reflect inner virtue."

Renzi nodded slowly. "The worthy Locke is insistent on this point," he murmured.

"It is never quite easy for the young to acquire the civil virtues," the parson continued. "'*Quo semel est imbuta recens, servabit oderem testa diu,*' was Horace's view, and by this you should understand . . ."

• • •

Kydd stirred restlessly in his armchair. "Gettin' to be a gallows' sight more'n a man c'n take, Cec, all this'n."

Cecilia affected not to hear. Kydd glanced at her irritably. "I mean, how much o' this is going to stand by me at sea?"

"That's better," Cecilia said demurely, but laid down her book. "Now I'm sure the other officers will be polite and well bred, so you must be the same."

Kydd snorted.

Renzi sighed. "You have still three issues of the *Gentleman's Magazine* to digest, to my certain knowledge," he said accusingly.

"And a *Spectator*," Cecilia chimed in. "How can you keep a lady entertained at table without you have small-talk to share?"

She looked at Renzi in mock despair, then brightened. "Mr Renzi, have you seen our castle? The merest ruin, I'll grant, but of an age indeed. Mama will be persuaded to come—she knows all the history."

"I'm wore out," said Mrs Kydd, finding a wooden bench overlooking what remained of the castle keep. "You two have a good look roun' by y'rselves."

Cecilia was agreeable, and Renzi took her on his arm for the stony path winding about the castle mound. The winter sun had a fragile brilliance, contrasting colour bright with grey and brown tints.

"It grieves me to say it, but Thomas did not shine at the tea-party in any wise," he opened. He was uncomfortably aware of her touch—it had been long years since last he had enjoyed polite female company, and Cecilia was now a beauty.

"Yes—the silly boy, sitting there like a stuffed goose while the ladies made sport of him. I despair, Nicholas, I really do."

Renzi assisted Cecilia past a perilous rock. She flashed him a look of gratitude, then dropped her eyes, but her hold on his arm tightened.

"Miss Kydd . . ." began Renzi thickly, then stopped. With his own feelings about her far from clear was it fair—was it honourable?—to engage her affections?

"Yes, Nicholas?" she said, smiling up at him.

He pulled himself up. "I was . . . Your mother confides that you have secured the liveliest trust in your position with Lady Stanhope."

"I have been very fortunate," she said gravely. Then a smile broke through. "You've no idea how many of the highest in the land I've seen. Lady Stanhope requires I attend her at all her routs and I'm sure it's only to find me a husband."

"And—"

"Don't be a silly, Nicholas. I'm sensible of my fortune in this and, I do declare, I'm not ready to forsake it all now for the tedium of domestic life." She tossed her head, eyes sparkling.

After another few paces she turned to him with a troubled expression. "Thomas—he . . ."

He knew what concerned her: her brother would find himself first ridiculed and later shunned if he could not hold his own in company. "Time is short, I agree. Do you not think that we are obligated to press him to enter in upon society in a more formal degree?"

Cecilia bit her lip, then decided. "A dinner party! Now, let me see . . . We have the pick of Guildford, of course, a hostess would die to entertain a brace of heroes from Camperdown, but I rather feel that at this stage Thomas would not welcome the public eye too warmly." She thought for a moment, then said, "I know—I'll speak with Mrs Crawford, advise her that after such a dreadful battle Thomas relishes nothing better than a small, intimate gathering. I'll be seeing her on Thursday and shall speak to her then."

"Splendid," responded Renzi. It would indeed be a suitable occasion for Kydd, if he could overcome his timidity in august surroundings. He beamed approval at Cecilia.

"Er, Nicholas," she said off-handedly, "something that I keep forgetting to ask. It's just my ill-bred curiosity, but you've never mentioned your own people." She stopped to admire a singularly gnarled small tree.

"My own? Well . . . shall I say they're just an Old Country family of Wiltshire whom I haven't attended as assiduously as I might?"

Kydd sat motionless at the bare table, listening while Cecilia explained and cautioned, his expression hard but in control.

"No, Thomas, it just will not do. We do not enter like a herd of goats to feed. First to take their places are the ladies, and they will occupy one end of the table. When they are seated the gentlemen proceed—but, mark this, in strict order. They will be placed at the table in the same succession."

Cecilia's eyes flicked once to Renzi, then turned back to Kydd.

Kydd's face tightened, but he kept his silence.

"Now, Mrs Crawford always dines *à la française,* as you know, Thomas, and allows promiscuous seating so a man may sit next to a lady, though some find this too racy for the English taste, and in this . . ."

Renzi's sympathy was all too transparent. "I do rather think that Tom is more a man of daring and action, dear sister. This posturing must be a disagreeable strain for such a one."

"Nevertheless, he shall require his manners wherever he may be," Cecilia said coldly. "A gentleman does not put aside his breeding simply for the perils of the moment. Now, please attend, Thomas."

• • •

"Miss Cecilia Kydd, Mr Thomas Kydd and Mr Nicholas Renzi!" blared the footman.

The babble of conversations faded: it was common knowledge that the two guests now arrived had suffered in the legendary October clash off the Dutch coast, and it had been said that they had chosen tonight to resume their place in polite society. There were many curious rumours about these officers, but no doubt before the night was over the details would have been made clear.

A wave of determined females advanced, led by the hostess, and the groups dissolved in a flurry of introductions.

"Enchanted," said Mr Kydd, making a creditable but somewhat individual leg to a gratified Mrs Crawford.

"Do say if you become too fatigued, Mr Kydd," she said, eyeing his broad shoulders. "You'll find us in the utmost sympathy with your time of trial."

"That is most kind in ye, dear Mrs Crawford," the handsome sailor-officer replied gravely.

She turned reluctantly to the other one, a sensitive-looking, rather more austere gentleman, and, reclaimed by her duty, murmured politely.

They sat down to dinner under the golden glitter of chandelier and crystal, to polite approbation at the first remove.

"May I help you t' a portion of this fine shott, Miss Tuffs?" said Mr Kydd, politely. The young lady on his left, nearly overcome at being noticed by one of the principal guests, could only stutter her thanks, tinged with alarm at the resulting pile of roast piglet generously heaped to occupy the whole plate.

"Sir, this toothsome venison demands your immediate attention. Might I . . ." The red-faced gentleman to the right would not be denied, and placed a satisfying amount on Mr Kydd's plate.

"Your servant, sir," said Mr Kydd, inclining his head.

It was clear that the middle-aged woman across from him was

set on securing his attention. "The weather seems uncommon blowy for the time of year," she said.

Mr Kydd thought for a moment, and replied politely, "It's a saying ashore only, Mrs Wood, 'When the wind is in the east, 'tis no good to man nor beast.' And by this is meant that in the winter season we often shiver in th' winds o' Tartary from the east. Now, at sea we bless this wind, Mrs Wood, for it is a fair wind for our ships down-channel and . . ."

Fully satisfied in the matter of explanations, Mrs Wood retired to contemplate, at which Mr Kydd turned his attention to the red-faced gentleman. "*Gentleman's Magazine*'s interestin' this week—says about your electric fluid invented by Mr Volta all comes from frog legs in the end," he remarked bravely.

The man shook his head slowly in amazement. "Now, that's something I never knew," he said at length. A look of barely concealed satisfaction suffused Mr Kydd's face as he looked up the table to where Mr Renzi sat quietly, nodding slowly.

A footman obliged with claret. "Wine with you, sir!" Mr Kydd said happily, with all the joyous relief to be expected of one having passed through a personal trial and not been found wanting. "I give you Lady Fortune, an' may she always be one!"

CHAPTER 2

"AYE, 'ERE SHE COMES, CAPTING," the inn porter said, indicating the gig under sail coming around Garrison Point. He held out his hand for a promised sixpence and left them to it, their chests and other impedimenta in a pile on Sheerness public jetty while they waited for the boat from *Tenacious.*

Kydd's heart bumped. This was the day he had been looking forward to these several months while *Tenacious* was under repair, the most important day of his life, the day he joined his ship confirmed in his rank, a King's officer. The day or so aboard after Camperdown didn't really count—he could hardly remember anything of the brute chaos and towering weariness in the wounded ship limping back to Sheerness.

The coxswain, a midshipman, cautiously rounded into the wind twenty yards off. Two seamen brailed up and secured the sail for a pull under oars the final distance to the jetty steps. It was not what Kydd would have done: the breeze, although fluky, was reliable enough for an approach under sail alone.

As the boat glided alongside, the sailors smacked the oars across their thighs and levered them aloft in one easy movement, just as Kydd had done in the not so distant past. His eyes passed over the boat and the four seamen, as he recalled the old saying,

"You can always tell a ship by her boats." Was caution a feature of this ship, he wondered.

The sailors seemed capable, long-service able seamen economically securing the sea-chests and striking them into the centre of the boat, but Kydd sensed darting eyes behind his back as they took the measure of the new officers.

He and Renzi assumed their places in the sternsheets, at leisure while the midshipman took the tiller. The boat bobbed in the grey North Sea chop and Kydd's new uniform was sprinkled with its first saltwater. He tried to keep his face blank against surging excitement as they rounded the point to open up the view of the Nore anchorage—and his ship.

She was one of a straggling line of vessels of varying sizes moored in this transitory anchorage to await different destinies. A wisp of memory brushed his consciousness: it was at the Nore that he had been taken as a bitter victim of the press gang, so long ago now, it seemed.

He glanced back to the scatter of dockyard buildings, the low fort, the hulks, and a pang of feeling returned for Kitty Malkin, who had stood with him during the dark days of the Nore mutiny. She had uncannily foretold his elevation, and that she would not be a part of it. Other memories of the time came too, dark and emotional. The red flag of mutiny, the spiralling madness that had ended in savage retribution and shame. Memories he had fought hard to dim.

Kydd crushed the thoughts. He would look forward, not back, take his good fortune and move into the future with it. The phantoms began to fade.

"She's storing," Renzi said, as if reading something in his face.

"Er, yes, those are powder hoys alongside, she's ready t' sail," Kydd muttered, his eyes fixed on the approaching bulk of *Tenacious*. The foretopmast was still on deck for some reason but her long commissioning pennant flew from her masthead. Repairs complete, she now stood ready in the service of her country.

A faint bellow from the ship sounded over the plash of the bow wave. The bowman cupped his hand and bawled back, "Aye, aye!" warning *Tenacious* that her boat was bearing naval officers, who would expect to be received as the custom of the sea demanded.

The midshipman again doused sail and shipped oars for the last stretch. Kydd resolved to attend to the young gentleman's seamanship when the opportunity arose. The boat bumped against the stout sides and the bowman hooked on. Kydd held back as Renzi seized the handropes and left the boat. Although their commissions bore the same date, he was appointed fourth lieutenant aboard, and Kydd, as fifth, would always be first in the boat and last out.

The ship's sides were fresh painted, the thick wales black, with the lines of guns set in natural timber, smart in a bright preparation of turpentine and rosin. A strong wafting of the scent mixed pleasingly with that of salt spray.

Above, a boatswain's call pierced the clean, winter air. Kydd was being piped aboard a man-o'-war! He mounted the side-steps: his eyes passed above the deck line to the boatswain's mate with his pipe on one side and two midshipmen as sideboys on the other. He touched his hat to the quarterdeck when he made the deck, and approached the waiting officer-of-the-watch. "Lieutenant Kydd, sir, appointed fifth l'tenant."

For a moment he feared this officer would accuse him of being an impostor, but the man merely smiled bleakly. "Cutting it a trifle fine, don't you think?" he said, then turned to the duty quartermaster and ordered the chests swayed inboard. Renzi came to stand with Kydd.

"Captain Houghton will want to see you immediately, I should think," the officer-of-the-watch said.

"Aye aye, sir," Kydd replied carefully, conscious of eyes on him from all over the busy decks. He remembered little of her from the exhausted hours he had spent aboard after the battle, fighting to bring the damaged vessel to safe harbour, but all ships had similar main features. He turned and went into the cabin spaces aft.

Renzi reported first. There was a rumble of voices; then the door opened. "Seems pleasant enough," he whispered to Kydd.

Kydd knocked and entered. The captain sat behind his desk facing him, taking advantage of the wan light coming through the stern windows. He was glowering at a paper.

"L'tenant Kydd come aboard t' join, sir."

"Don't sit," the captain said heavily. "You're to hold yourself ready to go ashore again."

"But, sir, why?"

"You are owed an explanation, I believe," Houghton said, looking at Kydd directly. "I've been given to understand that your origins are the lower deck, that is to say you have come aft through the hawse, as the expression goes."

"Er—aye, sir."

"Then this must be to your great credit, and shows evidence, no doubt, of sterling qualities of some kind. However . . ." He leaned back in his chair, still fixing Kydd with hard, grey eyes. ". . . I am determined that *Tenacious* under my command shall have a loyal band of officers of breeding, who will be able to represent the ship with, um, distinction, and who may be relied upon in the matter of courtesy and gentle conduct.

"You should understand that it is no reflection on yourself personally, when I say that I am applying to the commissioner to have you replaced with a more suitable officer for this vessel. There is no question in my mind that your services will be far more valuable to the service perhaps in a sloop or gunboat, not in a sail-of-the-line." He stood. "In the meantime you may wish to avail yourself of the conveniences of the wardroom. Carry on, please."

Kydd stuttered an acknowledgement and left. He felt numb: the swing from exhilaration to the bleakness of rejection was as savage as it was unexpected.

The mate-of-the-watch waited on the open deck. "Sir?" Kydd's chest and personal possessions lay in a small heap.

"Leave 'em for now." Kydd felt every eye on him as he went below to the wardroom. The only inhabitant was a marine captain sitting at the table, pencilling in an order book. He looked up. "Some sort o' mistake," Kydd mumbled. "I'm t' be replaced."

"Oh, bad luck, old trout."

Kydd took off his coat and sat at the other end of the table. As desolation built, he tried to subdue the feeling of homelessness, of not belonging in this select community. He got up abruptly and, pulling himself together, stepped out on deck. He had seen Renzi with a party forward getting the topmast a-taunt. Renzi would have no problems of breeding with this captain, and later he must find his friend and bid him farewell.

The officer-of-the-watch caught sight of Kydd and turned with a frown. Some waiting seamen looked at him with open amusement. Face burning, Kydd returned to the wardroom. It was half-way through the afternoon and the marine captain had left. A young wardroom servant was cleaning the table. "Ah, sorry, sir, I'll leave," he said, collecting his rags.

"No, younker, carry on," Kydd said. Any company was better than none.

He looked about. It was a surprisingly neat and snug space with louvred cabin doors looking inward to the long table along the centreline and the fat girth of the mizzen mast at one end. The bulkheads and doors were darkly polished rich mahogany, and at the other end there was plenty of light from the broad stern windows—even the privacy of a pair of officers' quarter galleries. She would be an agreeable ship for far voyaging.

This old class of 64s were surprisingly numerous—still probably near thirty left in service—and were known for their usefulness. As convoy escorts they could easily crush any predatory frigate, yet at a pinch could stand in the line of battle. In home waters the mainstay of the major battle fleets was the 74, but overseas, vessels like *Tenacious* were the squadron heavyweights.

Kydd's depression deepened as he wandered about the wardroom. On the rudder head he found a well-thumbed book, *The Sermons of Mr Yorick*. Raising his eyebrows in surprise he found that it was instead a novel by a Laurence Sterne, and he sat to read. Half-way into the first chapter and not concentrating, he heard a piping of the side and guessed that the captain had returned with news of his replacement.

Word was not long in coming. A midshipman pelted down and knocked sharply. "Lootenant Kydd? Sir, cap'n desires you wait on him."

On deck the officer-of-the-watch looked at him accusingly. His chest and bags, obviously a hindrance, had been moved to the base of the mainmast. "Be getting rid o' them soon," Kydd said defiantly, and went inside to see the captain.

This time Houghton stood up. "I won't waste our time. We're under notice for sea, and there's no officer replacement readily at hand. I see you will be accompanying us after all, Mr Kydd."

A leaping exultation filled Kydd's thoughts. Then a cooler voice told him that the explanation for his change of fortune was probably the inability of the commissioner's office to change the paperwork in time—an officer's commission was to a particular ship rather than the Navy as a whole, and could not easily be put aside.

"I'll not pretend that this is to my liking, Mr Kydd," the captain continued, "but I'm sure you'll do your duty as you see it to the best of your ability." He stared hard at Kydd. "You are the most junior officer aboard, and I need not remind you that if you fail me then, most assuredly, you will be landed at the first opportunity."

"I will not fail ye, sir."

"Umm. Quite so. Well, perhaps I'd better welcome you aboard as the fifth of *Tenacious,* Mr Kydd." He held out his hand, but his eyes remained bleak. "Show your commission and certificates to my clerk, and he will perform the needful. My first lieutenant has your watch details and you will oblige me by presenting yourself on deck tomorrow morning for duty."

Excitement stole back to seize Kydd as he stood in the wardroom supervising his gear being carried down. His cabin was the furthest forward of four on the larboard side, and he opened the door with trepidation: only a short time ago this had been officers' private territory.

It was small. He would be sharing his night-time thoughts with a gleaming black eighteen-pounder below, and his cot, triced up to the deckhead for now, ensured that he could never stand upright. He would have to find room for his chest, cocked-hat box, sword, personal oddments and books. A cunningly designed desk occupied the forward width, taking advantage of the outward curve of the ship's side. He pulled at its little drawers and wondered which dead officer had unintentionally left it behind for others.

The gunport was open. At sea it would be closed and then the cabin would be a diminutive place indeed, but he had been in smaller. He tried the chair at the desk. It was tiny, but well crafted to fit into such a space, tightly but comfortably enfolding his thighs. He eased into it and looked around. Spartan it might be, but it was the first true privacy he had ever experienced aboard ship. His eyes followed the line of intersection where the bulkhead met the overhead beams. The thin panels were slot-ted: at "beat to quarters" this entire cabin would be dismantled and struck down in the hold below. Over the door he noticed a ragged line of colour, where a curtain had once been fastened to cover the door space; he could have the door open and still retain a modicum of privacy.

It was adequate, it was darkly snug—and it was his. He went to his chest and rummaged around. Carefully stored at the bottom was his commission. Undoing the red silk ribbon he unfolded the crackling parchment and read it yet again.

By the Commissioners for executing the Office of Lord High Admiral of Great Britain . . . Lieutenant Thomas Kydd . . . we do appoint you Lieutenant of His Majesty's Ship the Tenacious . . . strictly charging the Officers and all the Ship's Company . . . all due Respect and Obedience unto you their said Lieutenant . . .

Kydd savoured the noble words.
It concluded sombrely:

Hereof nor you nor any of you may fail as you will answer to the contrary at your peril. And for so doing this shall be your Warrant . . .

It was signed Evan Nepean, secretary to the Admiralty, and the date of seniority, 20 January 1798, with the scarlet Admiralty seal embossed to the left. This single document would figure prominently for the rest of Kydd's life, defining station and position, rank and pay, authority and rule. He creased it carefully and put it away. A deep breath turned into a sigh, which he held for a long time.

He turned and found himself confronting a black man. "Tysoe, sir, James Tysoe, your servant," he said, in a well-spoken tone.

Kydd was taken aback, not that Tysoe was black but at the realisation that here was proof positive of the status he had now achieved. "Ah, yes." He had had a servant in the gunroom before, but this was altogether different: then it had been a knowing old marine shared with all the others; here the man was his personal valet. "Do carry on, if y' please," Kydd said carefully.

Tysoe hesitated. "I think it were best, sir, should I stow your cabin."

"Thank ye, no, I'll take care of it," Kydd said, with a smile. There was nothing too personal in his possessions, but the thought of a stranger invading his privacy was an alien notion.

"Sir, I can do it," Tysoe said softly. Something in his voice told Kydd that he should let the man go about his business. Then he realised that, of course, Tysoe needed to know the location of everything if he was to keep his master well clothed and fettled.

"Well, just be steady with the octant," Kydd admonished him.

"Lieutenant Kydd, I believe!" Renzi chuckled as he entered the wardroom.

Kydd's heart was full, but he was still unsettled by his unfortunate welcome to the ship and could only manage, "Aye, do I see Lieutenant Renzi before me?"

Renzi dumped a number of well-used order books on the

table. "Well, my friend, it does seem this is a task it would be prudent to begin immediately, if not earlier."

Regulations. Orders. Directions. Covering every possible situation. Each in careful phrasing ensuring that every subordinate in the chain of command would be in no doubt that if any disagreeable situation arose it would not be the fault of his superior.

From the Admiralty:

Article: *The Captain is to demand from the Clerk of the Survey a book, with the inventory of the stores committed to the charge of the Boatswain and Carpenter...*

Article: *If any be heard to curse or blaspheme the name of God, the Captain is strictly required to punish them for every offence by causing them to wear a wooden collar...*

Article: *The Lieutenant is expected that he do provide himself with the necessary instruments, maps and books of navigation, and he is to keep a journal according to the form set down and at the end of the voyage shall deliver copies thereof signed by himself into the Admiralty and Navy Offices...*

Article: *No commander shall inflict any punishment upon a seaman beyond twelve lashes upon his bare back with a cat of nine tails, according to the ancient practice of the sea...*

The commander in chief of the North Sea Fleet had his own instructions—from the timing of the evening gun when at anchor, to conduct when in sight of the enemy—all in all a dizzying succession of domestic detail, mixed with grave admonitions to duty.

Kydd sensed movement outside.

"Well, now, if I'm not mistook, here's our fourth and fifth lootenants!" It was a pleasant-faced young officer, rubbing his hands with cold.

"Ah, Thomas Kydd, sir, at your service."

"Well, then, my dear sir, I am your humble and obedient Gervase Adams, third of this barky—was junior luff in *Raven*, sadly no more." Kydd shook hands, grateful for the friendliness.

Adams turned to Renzi. "Give you joy of your step, Renzi," he said formally, holding out his hand. Renzi had served for a small time in *Tenacious* as master's mate: he'd been part of the ship's company at Camperdown. Kydd realised that they assumed his origins to be a senior midshipman promoted, not someone from forward, as he was.

Adams looked over Kydd's shoulder at the books. "This is what you should be boning up on, m' boy." He tapped one marked "Captain's Orders." "This owner is new to me, but if he's running to form he'll expect you to have it by heart in a day—'This is the word of the Lord: hear ye and obey!'"

There was a knock at the door and Adams crossed to answer it. "L'tenant Kydd! Seems first luff has need of the solace of your company at this time."

Kydd hesitated, partly out of concern for the reception he would receive from the captain's deputy, partly out of confusion as to where to go. He knew the first lieutenant's cabin would be here in the wardroom, the largest one to starboard and right in the stern, but it was unoccupied.

"In harbour he sets up shop in the coach next to the captain's cabin, you'll find." Adams paused. "Bryant the Beatific. The men call him Bull—last ship a frigate, and he wants his own command so bad it stinks. I'd steer small with him, Kydd, to be sure."

"Sit, sir." Bryant finished his scrawling. "So, Mr Kydd, you're the fifth and junior. I've put you with Mr Bampton as second officer-of-the-watch until you can prove yourself. And I'll have you know, sir, that if you don't—and that damn soon—I'll see you broke. That I promise. Understand?"

"Sir."

He consulted his paper. "And you'll take the afterguard, where you're under my eye." He looked up. "Heard you came aft the hard way—and heard else—you'll not be shy in a fight an' I like that. Now, you bat square with me, and you'll do. Right?"

"Aye, sir." Kydd was not sure what he was implying, and answered cautiously. The man, with his aggressive, out-thrust jaw and direct, almost angry manner, unsettled him.

"Ah, yes—and you'll be signal lootenant, o' course."

"But, sir, I—"

"Then you'll learn, damn it, like we all did!" Bryant snapped. "You've got a signal midshipman, Rawson, and two steady hands on the bunting. Do y' want a wet nurse as well?"

"I'll do m' duty right enough." Kydd felt himself reddening.

Bryant eased back in his chair. "Let's see. You were entered as a landman in 'ninety-three, then shipped in *Artemis* frigate around the world, did a few years in the Caribbean and came back a master's mate. Earned their lordships' approbation in the late mutiny at the Nore, and didn't disgrace yourself at Camperdown." He slapped the papers back into their pack. "I'm sure you'll do your duty, Mr Kydd." He rose. "Now, keep station on me—it's a new wardroom, we need to make our number to each other."

The long table was laid with a starched white cloth and silver was much in evidence. It was close on four o'clock, supper time; aboard ship it was always taken considerably earlier than on land.

Kydd lost Bryant in a swirl of officers as old friends warmly greeted each other and new ones respectfully made themselves known. Renzi was deep in conversation with a plainly dressed man who had a curiously neat and sensitive face. Kydd made to cross to him, but a glass was thrust into his hand, and Adams's pleasant face appeared. "A tincture with you, m' friend," he said, leaning back while a seaman politely plied a bottle. The wine was deep and red, and eased Kydd's trepidation.

"Your very good health, sir," Kydd said. Adams smiled, then turned to an older lieutenant, but before he could speak, Bryant, attended by a steward, took the head of the table, his back to the stern windows.

"We sit now," warned Adams, and led Kydd quickly to the opposite end of the table, to one side of the thickness of the mizzen mast growing up at the end. Then he swung round deftly and sat opposite.

A buzz of talk arose. Bryant roared down the table, "Wine with you, Mr Kydd!"

The table fell quiet and Kydd caught covert glances in his direction. He tried to gather his wits. "C-confusion to the French!" he called, raising his glass to Bryant. The words seemed weak and theatrical after the hearty oaths of seamen.

The marine captain raised his glass and declaimed drily, "And to ourselves—as no one else is likely to concern themselves with our welfare."

"Damn right!" Bryant said vigorously, and drank deeply, then held up his empty glass. Talk began again, but Bryant banged a spoon on the table. "Gentlemen!" he demanded loudly. "Today sees *Tenacious* with her company of officers complete. We're in commission, and we'll be rejoining the North Sea Fleet very shortly. I believe it's not too soon to make our acquaintance of each other."

Kydd could hear a bottle being opened out of sight as he positioned his glass. He was grateful to the wine for settling his apprehensions.

"I'm your premier. My last ship was *Thetis*, thirty-eight, in the Indian Ocean, where we saw not much o' the French worth a spit. I hope to see some better sport before long." He pitched his voice to the older lieutenant. "Now you, sir."

"Bampton, second luff, only officer surviving after Camperdown. Served two years with the North Sea Fleet in *Tenacious* before," he added drily.

"Ah, was you at the Nore mutiny?" the marine wanted to know.

"Yes." Kydd froze. "And no. I was set ashore by the mutinous villains—but had the pleasure later of seeing 'em at a yardarm." He gave a thin smile and sipped his wine.

Bryant's gaze slipped to Adams, who took up his cue. "Gentlemen, you see before you one Gervase Adams, relict of the *Raven*, eighteen, fir-built and cast ashore. Take heed all ye who would place Baltic fir before good British oak . . ."

"And?"

Renzi's manner was perfect: his easy affability brought approving grunts from around the table. He raised his glass in Kydd's direction. "Might I bring forward my particular friend Thomas Kydd, whom you see before you as junior aboard, but whose shining parts his modesty forbids him to mention. His actions in thwarting a fearful case of barratry while still a child of the sea is well remarked, and I owe my continued existence to his acting forcefully in a curious circumstance on an island in the Great South Sea. He it is who conned the longboat in the Caribbean that preserved Lord Stanhope, and in all, gentlemen, we must conclude that Mr Kydd be truly accounted a favoured son of Neptune!"

Bryant rumbled loudly, "Hear him!"

Kydd reddened, and mumbled something. The table remained silent.

"That may be so," exclaimed Adams, "but be advised, Kydd, it's the custom of the service that if you've been around the Cape of Good Hope you're entitled to one foot on the table. If you've doubled Cape Horn, both feet on the table, but nothing entitles you to spit to wind'd!"

There was warmth in the easy laughter that followed the old saw. Kydd had no idea that there was such a fraternity in the officers in their wardroom, and he longed to be truly one of them.

Introductions continued. The marine turned out to be a Captain Pringle, with a well-polished line in wardroom wit. It seemed that later a brand-new lieutenant of marines would also grace the ship.

Renzi's new friend was a Mr Peake, a quietly spoken and erudite gentleman who would be their chaplain, and completing the company, further along, was one not in uniform but wearing a comfortable green-striped waistcoat. He announced himself laconically as Pybus, the ship's surgeon.

The wardroom dissolved into talk and laughter, and a violin out of sight behind the mizzen mast began a soft piece Kydd did not recognise. At the same time the smell of onion soup filled the air, and silently a bowl appeared before him. Simultaneously, a number of covered dishes arrived.

"Kydd, dear fellow, may I assist you to some of these fresh chops?" Adams said, as Kydd finished his soup. "Sadly, we shan't see their like again, I fear, before we next make port."

Behind the chair of each officer stood a seaman or marine to wait at table; Tysoe was at the back of Kydd. Adams waited until he had withdrawn to see to Kydd's glass. "That old blackamoor you have there, come down in the world since he was *valet de chambre* to Codrington, who, you might recollect, died of an apoplexy in our very great cabin." He leaned forward. "You don't have to stay with the old fellow—ask Pringle for a marine, they know the sea service."

Kydd looked round at the other servants. There was none who appeared to be above thirty; Tysoe had substantial grey in his bushy hair. Having seen the scrimmages that sometimes took place as servants jostled to see their masters' needs met first, he had his doubts that Tysoe would hold his own. But something about the man's quiet dignity touched Kydd. There were advantages to youth, but different ones with maturity and, besides, were they not both outsiders? "Er, no, I'll keep Tysoe," Kydd answered.

He saw the glow of contentment in the others as his eye roved over the animated officers. Eddying talk rose and fell, then lulled. He heard Bampton call down to him, his voice studied and casual: "Kydd, something or other tells me you're no stranger to the lower deck. Can this be right?"

Bryant frowned. The table fell quiet, and faces turned to Kydd.

He took a deep breath. "True, very true, sir. I was untimely taken up as a pressed man and, unable t' run, I find myself still here."

Awkward grins surfaced, and Pringle murmured to the table in general, "That won't please the owner—not by half, it won't."

Bampton persisted: "Was this not alarming? For your family is what I mean."

"Damn it all!" Bryant exploded, glaring at Bampton. "We were promised figgy duff—where the devil is it?"

It was a pearly calm winter's day when Kydd appeared for duty on the deck of the man-o'-war, a King's officer. After their pressed men had been claimed and come aboard, the ship's company would be mustered by open list into divisions and Kydd would see his men for the first time.

A hoy from the receiving ship came alongside in a flurry of flapping canvas and shouted orders. Kydd continued to pace the quarterdeck, the arrival of pressed men not his concern. Out of sight, in the waist below, the first lieutenant would be setting up to receive them, rating the seamen by their skills and consigning the rest—landmen—to the drudgery of brute labour.

Kydd felt contentment at the thought that within a week or so this deck would be alive and heeling to the stern winds of the open ocean.

Renzi fell into step beside him.

"Nicholas! How did y' sleep?" Kydd's own experience had not been of the best. Alone in the dark, he had tried to keep the thoughts that surged through him under control. The cot, a square-sided canvas frame suspended from the deckhead, was comfortable, but he had not realised that bedding was his own responsibility, and were it not for Tysoe's silent intercession, he would have gone without.

"Well, it must certainly be admitted, our elevation to society in this watery world has its distinct attractions." Renzi wore an indulgent smile, which triggered a jet of frustration in Kydd. After his own experiences, it was galling to see Renzi take to his new life so easily.

"It is agreeable, perhaps, but today we get th' measure of our men," he said impatiently. Adams was on the opposite side of the deck, deep in conversation with a master's mate, and also appeared anxious to be started.

"Mr Kydd?"

He turned to see a dignified older man in plain uniform. The man touched his hat. "Hambly, sir, sailing master."

"Good morning, Mr Hambly," Kydd replied. A full master, Royal Navy, paying his respects, the highest professional being in Kydd's universe before. The man's steady look had a quality of appraisal, cool judgement.

"Thought I'd make y'r acquaintance, sir." Before Kydd could speak, he continued, "Mr Jarman is m' friend."

Kydd remembered the master of the topsail cutter *Seaflower*, who had patiently taught him the elements of navigation and whose octant he now used, pressed on him after his famed open-boat voyage.

"A fine man, Mr Hambly," Kydd said sincerely. "I owe him much."

The master smiled slowly, touched his hat to Kydd, then Renzi, and left.

A double strike on the bell sounded forward: this was the time for the officers to repair to the great cabin where the shape of things to come would now become apparent.

"Gentlemen, be seated." The captain remained standing, staring out of the stern windows. "I won't keep you long," he said. "It is my intention to conclude the fitting of this vessel for sea as soon as possible. I desire that today you shall muster the people by open list, and prove your divisions. The first lieutenant has assured me he has now a complete watch and station bill."

Bryant nodded emphatically, then glanced around at the officers meaningfully. There had been frantic work by his writer and clerks the previous night.

Houghton continued sternly, "He wishes that this shall be advised to all hands—with a view to shifting to sea routine within a small space of days. The quarters bill will be posted this evening, I am assured." He withdrew a silver watch. "Shall we say, divisions at five bells?"

"Mr Lawes?" Kydd addressed the only master's mate among the group of about twenty men.

"Aye, sir."

"Pleased t' see you," Kydd said, touching his own hat at Lawes's salute. He turned to survey the men drawn up on the poop-deck. Most of his division, the able seamen, landmen and idlers, would still be below for these first proceedings. "Our petty officers, Mr Lawes?"

"Sir."

These men were the hard centre of his division, the ones in local charge of the seamen at masts, yards and guns. They would also be at his right hand when his division was tasked for special duty, whether the boarding of a prize or the cutting out of an enemy—and they would be looking directly to him for their lead.

"This is Mr Rawson, signal midshipman." It was the previous day's coxswain of the ship's boat, Kydd remembered.

"And Mr Chamberlain, midshipman." He was absurdly youthful, thought Kydd, observing his curls and slight build, yet he knew this boy had a status and duties that placed him well above the hardiest able seaman.

"Samuel Laffin, bo'sun's mate . . ." Dark-featured and oddly neat in his appearance, on his hat he wore a ribbon with *"Tenacious"* in gold lettering.

"Henry Soulter, quartermaster." Kydd recognised a natural deep-sea mariner, and warmed to his softly spoken ways.

And there were others, whom he knew he should remember— petty officers of the fighting tops, quarter gunners, petty officer of the afterguard—and rarer birds, such as captain of the hold, yeoman of the powder room and the carpenter's mates. In all, he would have a fair proportioning of the five hundred-odd of *Tenacious*'s company, such that most of the skills of a man-o'-war would be at hand if Mr Kydd's division was called away as a unit.

Kydd stepped forward and braced himself to address them: they would be expecting some words to set the tone. "Ye'll find that I play fair, but I expect the same from you all. You know I come fr'm before the mast, that's no secret, but chalk this in y'r log—I know the tricks, an' if I see any of 'em, I'll be down on ye like thunder.

"I like a taut ship. If y' see an Irish pennant, send a hand t' secure it. If the job's not finished b' end of watch, stay until it's done. And look after y'r men! If I see you warm 'n' dry on watch while a man has a wet shirt, I'll have ye exchange with him."

He felt their eyes on him, and he knew what they were thinking: how would all this translate to action, or was it mere words?
Would he leave it to them, the senior hands, to deal with things
on the spot so long as the objective was achieved, to administer
justice in the time-honoured ways of the sea? In effect, would
their status be properly acknowledged?

"Y' have your lists?" Each petty officer would have the watch
and station details of every man he was responsible for, and
Lawes would have a master list. After today there would be no
excuse for any seaman not to know where he should be in every
circumstance foreseeable by experience and necessity.

"Mr Lawes, I shall inspect my division in one bell."

The territory allotted for mustering Mr Kydd's division was the
after end of the main deck. His men assembled in order, three
rows on each side facing inboard, their ditty bags of clothing at
their feet. There was controlled bedlam as watch and stations
were explained, noted and learned, friendships discovered between those of like watch and part-of-ship, and new-rated petty
officers got to grips with their duties.

Kydd paced quietly down the middle. He could leave it to
Lawes to muster the men and report when ready while he eyed
them surreptitiously.

A Royal Navy warship was divided into as many divisions as
there were officers. In this way each man could claim the ear of
his own officer for complaint, requests and someone to speak for
him at a court-martial. It was a humane custom of the Navy, but
it required that the officer was familiar with his men.

But the men had other allegiances. Apart from the specialist
artisans, the idlers, the crew was divided into two watches for
routine working of the ship—starboard and larboard watches.
These would in turn be divided into parts-of-ship—the fo'c'sle,

maintop, afterguard on the quarterdeck and so on. As officer-of-the-watch, Kydd would therefore be certain to meet his men in another guise.

If there was a break in routine, as when a ship came to her anchor or took in sail for a storm, each man had his own particular post of duty, his station. Whether this was up at the main yard fisting canvas, or veering anchor cable when "hands for mooring ship" was piped, he had to close up at his station or risk the direst punishment.

Now, before *Tenacious* faced the open sea, was the time to establish that the ship's company was primed and ready for their duty.

"Sir, division ready f'r your inspection," said Lawes cautiously. He was an older master's mate and Kydd suspected that his origins were also from before the mast.

They stepped forward together to the front row. The sailors looked ahead vaguely, but Kydd knew he was under close scrutiny. In the future he could be leading them into the hell of a boarding, the deadly tensions of a night attack in boats—or seeing them spreadeagled on a grating under the lash.

"You, sir, what's your name?" The grog-blotched skin, rheumy eyes and flaccid ditty bag were a giveaway.

"Isaac Hannaford, s' please yer, sir."

"And?"

The man's eyes shifted uneasily. "Can't rightly recolleck," he finally answered.

"First o' starb'd, sir, afterguard," Lawes said heavily.

"Let's see y'r clothing, then, Hannaford," Kydd said. The ditty bag was upended to reveal a forlorn, unclean assortment. "Mr Lawes, what's in this man's list?"

"Sir, shirts, two, stockings, four." Hannaford was an old hand and knew the ropes—but he had sold his clothing for illicit grog.

"Come, now, Hannaford, you're an old haulbowlings. Can't

you see, without kit, you're not going t' be much use to the barky?" There was no use waiting for an answer, and he rounded on Lawes. "To see th' purser for slops, t' make up his list." It would be stopped out of his pay; whether that would have any effect was doubtful. "And each Sunday t' prove his kit to the petty officer of his watch."

As Lawes scrawled in his notebook Kydd passed to the next man. "Thorn, sir." Kydd nodded and moved on.

He stopped at a fine-looking seaman, so tall that he stood stooped under the deckhead. "Haven't I seen you afore now? Was it . . . *Bacchante,* the Med?"

"'Twas, right enough, sir," the man said, with a surprised smile. "But you was master's mate then—no, I tell a lie, quartermaster as was. Saw yez step ashore in Venice, I remembers." At Kydd's expression he hurried to add, "An' it's William Poulden, waist, sir, second o' larb'd."

Kydd decided he would see if he could get this good hand changed from the drudgery of being in the waist with the landmen to something more rewarding.

He stopped at a shy-looking youngster with a stye on one eye. "What's y'r station for reefing at th' fore?"

"Ah—fore t' gallant sheets 'n' clewlines, sir," the boy said, after some thinking.

"Hmmm." This was a topman—he should have been quicker to respond. "And mooring ship?"

"T' attend buoy an' fish tackle," he said instantly. Kydd knew that the quick reply was a guess. No topman would be left on the fo'c'sle while taking in sail. "Mr Lawes, this man c'n claim his tot only when he knows his stations. And he sees the doctor about his eye."

The rest of his division seemed capable. He noted the odd character eyeing him warily—but he would see their quality soon enough when he stood his first watch.

A distant call sounded from forward, a single long note, the "still." The captain was beginning his rounds.

"Straighten up, then! Mr Lawes, see they toe the line properly, if you please." The rows shuffled into line, to Kydd's eyes their alert and loose-limbed bearing infinitely preferable to the perfect rigidity of a line of soldiers.

He saw the captain approach, accompanied by the first lieutenant, looking under pressure, with the captain's clerk and Pringle. Kydd whipped off his hat and prepared for inspection, but the captain managed only a rapid glance, a nod at Kydd and a few words with Lawes before he passed to the gun-deck below.

The officers assembled for sail drill had no indication of the captain's mind when he appeared from his cabin. His fixed expression could mean disappointment at the quality of the men he had seen earlier or satisfaction with the relative ease with which *Tenacious* had been manned.

In any event, now would be the time that reputations were won or lost, weakness and strengths revealed, not least of which would be that of the captain himself, as he reacted to the success or otherwise of the morning's evolutions.

Kydd felt the tension. His eyes met Renzi's and provoked a slow half-smile as both turned to face their captain.

"Loose and furl by mast and watch. I shall not want to exercise further today—but if we are not striking topmasts within the space of three days . . ."

Already at his station on the quarterdeck, Kydd watched the other officers move to the fo'c'sle, main deck and forward of the mainmast.

"Larb'd watch o' the hands—*haaaands* to stations for making sail!"

Two hundred seamen raced to their stations, the fore, main and mizzen shrouds black with men heading for the tops; others ran to the pin rails at the ship's side and the massive square bitts at the base of each mast, around which hung a complex maze of ropes.

Along the deck men hurried to the belaying points for important lines running aloft, braces, halliards, sheets. Petty officers pushed and bullied the hapless landmen into their places, showing no mercy to the slow-witted. It all seemed so straightforward now, but Kydd recalled his first daunting experiences at tailing on to a rope, in the old 98-gun *Duke William* in these very waters.

When the muttering, cursing and murmuring had settled, the captain lifted his speaking trumpet. "Foremast, loose all sail to a bowline."

Adams, clearly tense and waiting for the start, instantly lifted his head and blared up, "Lay aloft, royal yardmen! Lay aloft . . ."

"Belay that!" Houghton's face was red with anger, and the hard edge in his voice carried forward. "Brace around, damn it, lay the yard first, you fool!"

Adams's command had been a mistake. Firmly anchored, and with but one mast with sail abroad, there was no opportunity to use another mast, with sails backing, to balance the forces. His order would have seen the ship move ahead and strain at her moorings.

Crimson-faced, Adams stood down his men at the halliards, shifting them to the forebraces, and brought the yards round, as he should have done before sending the men aloft to set the sail.

Kydd knew his turn would come.

The exercise went on. At the foremast, sail cascaded down at the volley of commands, to hang limply forward. Minutes later, men returned to the yards, this time to furl the sail to a seaman-like stow. Houghton said nothing, his furrowed brow evidence of the direction of his thoughts.

"Mainmast, loose all sail to a bowline," Houghton ordered. He was staying with the larboard watch and moving along the masts: Kydd, at the mizzen, would be facing his test so much the earlier. Would his petty officers be reliable enough on the job, up there on the mizzen top? There was no chance that he himself would ever again be up there with them, to see their work, intervene if needed, chase down laggards . . . It took an effort of will to remain aloof and outside the real action, merely to direct in general—but at the same time the responsibility was his alone.

"Mizzen, loose all sail to a bowline!"

Kydd turned instantly.

"Lay aloft an' loose mizzen tops'l!"

No point in going through the orders in detail from the deck, when the captain of the mizzen top was perfectly capable of taking charge on the spot. Kydd wheeled around and snapped, "Let go brails and vangs—man the clew outhaul and out spanker!" The mizzen did not have a course spread on the cro'jack to worry about, but it did have a mighty fore and aft sail, the spanker, and this with not only a lower boom but a substantial gaff that had to be bodily raised apeak.

"Get those men movin', the maudling old women!" he threw irritably at the petty officer of the afterguard in charge of the halliard crew on deck. This was no time to be cautious, here directly under the captain's eye.

The mizzen topsail yard was nearly hoisted. Kydd bit his lip, but the sail came tumbling down at just the right time. He had been right to trust the men in the top.

"Lay aloft—loose t' garns'l!" Men swarmed up the higher shrouds, while below the topsail was settled. With the sail hanging down limply as it was, Kydd had foreseen the need to haul out the foot forward, and used the old trick of untoggling the top bowlines from their bridles and shifting them to a buntline cringle.

He stole a quick glance at Houghton. The captain stood impassive, waiting.

The topgallant set, it was then just the mizzen royal—and the gaskets came off smartly at just the time the spanker gaff reached its final position. Kydd judged that there would be no need on this occasion for play with a jigger at the spanker outhaul, and simply waited for the motion to cease.

"Start the halliards b' a foot or two," he warned the afterguard—they had unwisely belayed fully before the order.

Sheepishly they threw off the turns, but Kydd was startled by a blast of annoyance from the captain. "What the devil are you about, Mr Kydd? Not yet finished?"

The sprightly sound of "Roast Beef of Old England" on fife and drum echoed up from the main deck. The men had already taken their issue of grog and gone below for the high point of their noonday meal, leaving the deck to the officers and indispensables of the watch. As they returned to work, to part-of-ship for cleaning, Kydd thankfully answered the call and made his way to the wardroom.

The table was spread, wine was uncorked and splashing into glasses; expressions were easing after the morning's tensions. Laughter erupted at one end of the table and the fragrance of roast pork agreeably filled the air.

"Your good health, brother!" Renzi grinned at Kydd over his glass: he had done tolerably well at the mainmast that morning, avoiding the captain's wrath at the last moment by quick-thinking at the braces.

"Thank ye—and yours, old friend," Kydd replied. There was a lot to think about, not the least of which was his standing in this world, so utterly different from that of the seaman.

An insistent tinkling intruded into his thoughts. It was the second lieutenant, tapping his glass with a spoon. "Gentlemen, may I have your attention?" He waited until the talk died. "I don't have to tell you that we shall soon be rejoining the fleet, which means, of course, that we shall need to provision against some months at sea."

He looked pointedly at Kydd. "There are some who are victualled 'bare Navy' but have nevertheless seen fit to accept the hospitality of this mess." Mystified, Kydd turned to Adams, who merely raised his eyebrows. "This is neither fair nor honourable. But be that as it may, in my humble post as mess caterer, I have calculated that we shall need to consider the sum of fifty pounds per annum as a minimum subscription."

"Preposterous! That's more'n five poun' a head!" Bryant's glass trembled in mid-air. "What do we get for that?"

Bampton heaved a theatrical sigh. "The mess commensal wine by quarter cask is half a pint a day, captain to dinner once a month. We lay in the usual cheeses, barrel oysters, tea and raisins, other conveniences for the pantry, such as cloves, pickles, ginger and the like, and when we consider breakages in glasses and dishes . . ."

Kydd thought of the seaman's broadside mess, with its square wooden plates and pewter tankards, the men using their own knives. There was little that could be considered breakable, and even the petty officers carried few crockery items in their mess racks. He decided to lie low while discussions raged about the mess subscription. He himself was not pressed for money and he had taken the precaution of appointing an agent. The Caribbean prizes had long yielded their bounty, but Camperdown was promising not only a medal but gun money in surprising degree.

"That's settled, then." Bampton made a pencil note and sat back. "We agree to subscribe the sum of five guineas per head. The officers' wine store is near empty, and with the usual allowance I believe you shall find room for four dozen apiece—you will be laying in your own cabin stores, of course.

"Now, it is usual to empower the mess caterer to go ashore on the wardroom's behalf. I shall do so in Yarmouth, and will expect one guinea in advance from each officer."

CHAPTER 3

OVER THE NEXT FEW DAYS THE RUMBLE and squeak of gun trucks was a never-ending background to shipboard life. Not content with exercising the company of *Tenacious* at ship drill, their captain had a quarter gunner and his four gun crews in turn hard at work from dawn to dusk.

Houghton had been on a gun-deck in the long-drawn-out battle of the Glorious First of June. "Different ships, different long-splices," was the saying before the mast: some captains were particularly keen on appearances, others favoured the niceties of seamanship. With this one it was gunnery, Kydd had realised quickly.

Then the awaited sailing orders came. Within minutes Houghton had summoned his officers to his cabin. "I have here the Admiralty's instructions—and I have to say, they are not what I was expecting." Houghton lifted his eyes from the paper, enjoying the suspense. "Indeed not. It would seem that their lordships believe that after Camperdown the North Sea Fleet may be safely reduced, and therefore we are to be sent to join the North American station."

Excited talk broke out. "Sir, if we should fit foreign, then . . ." The first lieutenant needed details. Not only did there have to be a wholesale hold-restowing but there would, no doubt, be official impositions, from carrying mails to chests of specie for a garrison, to prickly passengers and returning prisoners.

"Now where in Hades do we find real foul-weather gear in Sheerness?" Pringle muttered. "Gets cold as charity in Halifax."

"Quite," agreed Houghton, "but we shall touch at Falmouth for a convoy. If my memory serves, there is adequate chandlery servicing the Atlantic packets. I'd advise you all to wait and procure your cabin stores there."

"You've been to Halifax, sir?"

"I have. But not since His Highness took up his post."

"Sir?"

"His Royal Highness Prince Edward. Our only overseas possession to boast a prince of the blood. Quite turned society on its head, I've heard." Houghton stood up. "Gentlemen, may I remind you there is not a moment to be lost? The first lieutenant will provide a list of actions that will result, I trust, in our being under way for the Downs in two days."

"*Haaaands* to unmoor ship! *Aaaall* the hands! All hands on deck!" Although expected, the order brought a rush of excitement at the first move in putting to sea for a voyage of who knew how long.

A smack poled away from the sides of the ship, the tender now released from its workaday fetching and carrying. Her crew waved up at the big two-decker flying the Blue Peter at the fore masthead. She was outward bound to foreign parts, to mysterious worlds across the oceans, while they remained at home.

Kydd stood easy on the fo'c'sle, waiting with his party to bring the anchors to final sea stowage. Decks below, in the fetid gloom, the capstans would be manned and the fearsome job of winning her anchors would be acted out. Thankfully, this was not his concern.

The soft green of the land held a tinge of melancholy: how long before he would see these shores again? What adventures lay waiting? Just a brief stop in Falmouth to pick up the convoy, then he might be looking on his native England for the last time—deaths by disease and accident far exceeded those from enemy action.

Kydd's thoughts were interrupted by a swirl of muttering from his men as they watched a fishing-boat putting out from the shore. Under every stitch of sail, and heeled to her gunwales, it was making directly for *Tenacious*. Kydd went to the deck-edge and saw it come to clumsily at the side-steps. A redcoat stood up, swaying, and started waving and shouting.

The man obviously wished to board, but the side-ropes were no longer rigged. Kydd could hear shouting as a number of sailors gathered at the ship's side. A rope was flung down, knocking the man to his knees. The fishermen fashioned a bowline on a bight and passed it under the man's arms and, to barely muffled laughter, he was hoisted spinning and kicking aboard *Tenacious*. His baggage followed quickly. This would be the long-expected junior marine officer, Kydd guessed, but when he looked next, both marine and baggage had disappeared.

He glanced up. The men aloft were at their place—the cast would be to larboard, and his men deployed accordingly. Bampton waited at the gangway, watching Kydd with disdain. But with a clear hawse and the tide not yet on the make, Kydd was confident he knew what to do.

Over the bow, the starboard cable curved down into the grey-brown sea, the anchor buoy bobbing jauntily seventy feet ahead. From the low hawse hole the twenty-two-inch cable gradually tautened, a heavy shuddering settling to a steady passing inboard.

Checking yet again that the cat and fish falls were led properly along the deck, Kydd watched the anchor buoy inching towards the ship until the buoy boat grappled it. The process grew slower the steeper the angle of cable, until at last it was up and down.

"Short stay," he growled at a seaman, who whipped up a white flag. The quarterdeck at the other end of the ship now knew that the anchor was ready to be tripped from the sea-bed. It would be essential to loose sail the instant this happened, the ship under way and therefore under control immediately; otherwise she would simply drift with the wind.

All waited in a tense silence. Kydd looked over the fat beakhead. The cable had stopped passing in, and he could imagine the savage struggle taking place at the capstan.

Suddenly the cable resumed its movement and Kydd sensed the ship feel her freedom. "She's a-trip," he snapped. The man's arm came down. With anchor aweigh *Tenacious* was now no longer tethered to the land. She was at sea.

Houghton's voice sounded through the speaking trumpet. Sail dropped from yards and staysails jerked aloft. He was taking a chance that the remainder of the cable would be heaved in and the anchor duly catted by the powerful tackle before the ship got too much way on. Kydd looked over his shoulder down the deck; when he saw Houghton's challenging figure, he knew he must not fail.

The first ripple of water appeared about the stem at the same time as the inches-thick anchor ring broke surface. "Stoppers!" roared Kydd. It was now a race to uncouple the anchor from the cable and heave it clear of the water before the wake of the ship established itself. "Hook on!" He leaned over the side to see. Men were furiously passing the stoppers on the cable, which would then be ready for hauling in at the hawse. He wheeled round, and cannoned into the second lieutenant, winding him.

"Have a care, damn you, sir!" Bampton said venomously.

"Aye, sir." Kydd burned; the officer had no right to be there in a difficult operation for which he had no responsibility. The situation was well in hand: on hearing the "hook on" the quick-witted fo'c'sle party had, without orders, taken the strain and begun hauling vigorously on the big cat-fall. Kydd had seen Poulden's leadership in this and blessed his recommendation to have the seaman transferred from the waist.

The squealing of sheaves stopped as the anchor rose to the projecting cathead. "Well there, the cat." It had done its duty by hoisting the anchor out of the sea. He turned back to the side and called down: "Pass th' ring-painter—get that stopper on fast!" The three and a half tons of forged black iron was now being buffeted by passing waves.

There was a problem with the stoppering, the ropes passed to restrain the great weight of the cable. A hundred pounds in every six feet, it was a slithering monster if it worked free. Another fo'c'sleman swung round the beakhead to help, but with the vessel now under way and a frothy bow-wave mounting, the situation was getting out of control.

"Poulden!" Kydd barked. "Get down an' get the fish-tackle on." The tall seaman dropped to the swaying anchor and, balancing on its arms like a circus acrobat, took the fish-tackle and applied it firmly below the inner fluke.

Kydd's early intervention enabled the anchor to be hauled up sideways out of the race of water while the crossed turns at the cable were cleared away.

"Walk away with the fish, y' sluggards!" Kydd ordered, satisfied. He had been right: *Tenacious* was a sea-kindly ship, her regular heave on the open sea reminiscent of a large frigate, even if there was more of the decorum of the mature lady about her.

Kydd lingered on the fo'c'sle after the party had secured. The hypnotic lift and crunch of the bows was soothing and he closed his eyes for a moment in contentment—but when he opened them again he saw four seamen looking at him resentfully.

Straightening, he took off his hat, the sign that he was there but not on duty, and left; it was their fo'c'sle and the men off watch had every right to their relaxation. He no longer belonged there: he had left their world and entered a higher one, but in its place did he now have anything that could provide the warmth and companionship he had enjoyed before?

On the way back, as he passed the belfry, there was a sharp clang: seven bells of the forenoon watch. Until safely anchored once again there would always be, for every hour of the day or night, a full complement of hands taking care of the ship, keeping watch and ward over their little community in the endless wastes of ocean.

Kydd was due to go on duty with Mr Bampton as officer-of-the-watch and himself as second. He made his way to the quarterdeck, where the captain held conference with the first lieutenant. They paced along the weather side, deep in conversation, while Kydd waited respectfully on the leeward.

At ten minutes before the hour Bampton mounted the main companion to the deck. He was in comfortably faded sea rig, with the modest gold lace allowed a lieutenant bleached to silver. A few months at sea would have Kydd's brand-new blues in the same way. Kydd was at his post early, and he said peevishly, "I thought to see you below, Mr Kydd."

"Sir." Kydd touched his hat.

"No matter. Pray keep station on me, and don't trouble to interrupt, if you please." Bampton waited impatiently for the captain to notice him. "Sir, to take the deck, if you please." Kydd heard the captain's wishes passed—course and sail set, special orders.

"I have the ship, sir," Bampton said formally, and thereby became commander *pro tem* of HMS *Tenacious*. His eyes flickered to Kydd, then he turned to the mate-of-the-watch. "I'll take a pull at the lee forebrace," he said, "and the same at the main."

He looked up, considering. "Send a hand to secure that main t'gallant buntline—and I mean to have all fore 'n' aft sail sheeted home in a proper seamanlike manner, if you please."

He turned on his heel and paced away down the deck. Kydd didn't know whether to follow or stay at attention. He compromised by taking a sudden interest in the slate of course details stowed in the binnacle. "Nobbut a jib 'n' stays'l jack," he overheard the quartermaster's low growl to his mate, and saw no reason to correct the observation.

It was a hard beat down Channel, a relentless westerly heading them and the brood of merchant shipping that was taking advantage of the company of a ship of force. They clawed their way tack by tack, driven by the need to make Falmouth and the convoy on time.

The wind strengthened, then fell and eased southerly, allowing a tired ship's company to shape course past the Eddystone, albeit in an endless succession of rain squalls.

The master put up the helm and bore away for Falmouth. As the yards came round and the wind and seas came in on the quarter—a pleasant lift and pirouette for him, a lurching trial for the landmen—Kydd looked ahead. He'd never been to Falmouth, the legendary harbour tucked away in the craggy granite coast of Cornwall. It would be the last stop in England before the vastness of the Atlantic Ocean.

The master stood hunched and still, raindrops whipping from his dark oilskins and plain black hat. This man held a repository of seamanship experiences and knowledge that even the longest-serving seaman aboard could not come close to: he could bring meaning and order into storm, calms and the unseen perils of rock and shoal.

Kydd moved up and stood next to him. "My first visit t' Falmouth, Mr Hambly," he said. "I'd be obliged should you tell me something of the place."

The head turned slowly, eyes cool and appraising. "Your first, Mr Kydd? I dare say it won't be y'r last while this war keeps on." He resumed his gaze forward. "A fine harbour, Falmouth, in the lee of the Lizard, and big enough for a fleet. At the beginning o' last year, you may recollect the great storm—'twas then four hundred sail sheltered f'r three weeks in Falmouth without we lost one. Fine port, Mr Kydd."

"Then why doesn't we have the Channel Fleet there instead of Plymouth?"

The master's expression cracked into a smile. "Why, now, sir, that's a question can't concern an old shellback like me."

"Th' hazards?"

"No hazards, sir, we have nine mile o' ten-fathom water inside, Carrick Roads, and no current more'n a knot or two . . ."

The coast firmed out of the clearing grey rain, a repelling blue-black only now showing here and there a tinge of green. To larboard of them the great promontory of the Lizard thrust into the Channel. The hurrying seas had changed direction and were now heading in the same direction as *Tenacious*.

Hambly pointed to a jumble of broken coastline: "The Manacles." Kydd had heard of their reputation. "An' here is where you'll find the great sea wrack and th' bloody sea dock," Hambly added. "Seaweed, in course."

"The bottom?"

"Grey sand, mixed wi' bits o' shell and brown gravel, but as soon as y' finds barley beards or cornets, think t' turn up th' hands an' shorten sail." When approaching a coast in fog or other murk the only indication of its proximity was a change in the appearance of what was brought up in the hollow base of the hand lead-line armed with tallow. To Kydd this was singular— these tiny sea mites had been born and died deep in the bosom of the sea. The first time they met the light of this world was when they were hauled up by a seaman, to convey the means of preserving the life of half a thousand souls. Held in thrall, Kydd stared over the grey seascape.

"And it's here you'll fin' the sea grampus—an' the baskin' shark, o' course. As big as y'r longboat, he is, but as harmless as a sucking shrimp—"

"Mr Hambly," Bampton cut in sharply from behind. "Be so kind as to attend your duties—we're but a league from St Anthony's."

"Aye aye, sir," Hambly said calmly, and crossed to the binnacle in front of the wheel. He picked up the traverse board and deliberately matched the march of its pegs with the scrawled chalk of the slate log, then looked up at the impassive quartermaster. "Very good, son," he said, and resumed his vigil forward.

An occluding head of land opened to an indentation and the smaller sail accompanying them began to converge on the same place. "St Anthony's," Hambly murmured, as the headland, fringed with white, pulled back to reveal an opening in the lowering coastline no more than a mile wide. On the western side was the stark, squat, greyish-white of a broad castle turret. "Pendennis, an' Falmouth lies beyond."

He turned to the officer-of-the-watch. "Tops'ls will suffice, sir."

By this time the captain had appeared on deck, but he made no attempt to relieve the officer-of-the-watch.

"Bo'sun, all hands on deck, pipe hands to shorten sail." Kydd wondered at Bampton's order: to his eyes there was no urgency—the watch on deck were quite capable of taking in the courses one by one.

The calls pealed out and men tumbled up from below to take in the big lower sails. "Keep the men on deck, if you please," Bampton ordered.

"You'll beware Black Rock," Hambly warned Bampton. "A

pile o' broken rocks squatting athwart th' entrance, right in our course." He pointed to a flurry of white around a mound of black right in the centre of the harbour entrance.

"Which side, Mr Hambly?" Bampton asked.

"The eastern, sir, deepest channel."

"A point to starboard," snapped Bampton. The quartermaster spoke quietly to the helmsman, who set the bowsprit pointing off to starboard of the gloomy black whaleback.

"Not as you'd say difficult," Hambly said. "You sees Black Rock at half-tide, and on th' overflow you c'n be sure there's three fathom over the bar within."

A coastal brig, sailing at the same rate, converged on the eastern passage with *Tenacious*. Both vessels were before the wind; they drew closer. The smaller vessel seemed to ignore their presence.

The captain snatched up the speaking trumpet from its bracket. "The brig ahoy, sheer off. Bear away, this instant!" A ship-of-the-line was far too ponderous to play games.

"He means to head us through," Houghton exclaimed in disbelief. "You villains! Bear off! You must give way to a King's ship, damn you!"

Houghton stalked forward, eyeing the menace of Black Rock ahead. "Give him a gun, forrard!" he roared. A six-pounder on the fo'c'sle banged out. The gunsmoke was borne away in a body through the entrance, but the brig paid no heed, her main yard dipping and swaying closer and closer to their own lower rigging. "We take the eastern channel, let that villain choose the west," Houghton snapped. The brig's shallower draught would allow him the passage.

"Aye aye, sir. Lay Black Rock close to larb'd, and hold your course," Bampton acknowledged.

Just two hundred yards from Black Rock the brig diverged to the other side of the danger. The seaweed-covered rocks were now in close detail. All eyes followed the rogue vessel still under full sail plunging past the hazard.

"Sir!" the helmsman called urgently. Unable to release the wheel he indicated vigorously with his head. With all attention on the brig they had not noticed two fishing smacks close-hauled under fore and aft sail, crossing their bows to leave harbour. They shot into view from behind St Anthony's Head to starboard. Seeing the brig they changed their minds and tried to go about, floundering in stays dead ahead.

Bampton's mouth opened—but closed again. The channel was only a few hundred yards wide, with Black Rock to one side and the high headland of St Anthony to the other. It didn't take much imagination to see that, running downwind as they were, backing or dousing sail to stop their way was impossible—even if this was achieved *Tenacious* would probably slew helplessly round to cast up on shore. The smacks were doomed.

"Helm a-larb'd," Hambly calmly told the man at the wheel. "Keep with th' land a cable or so."

"No . . ." Bampton hesitated. He could not utter the words of contradiction that would firmly sheet home to him responsibility for the next few minutes.

The master kept his eyes ahead, his face tranquil. *Tenacious's* bows slowly paid off towards the rain-dark coast towering so near to starboard. Individual tumbling rock formations could be made out, seagulls perched on them watching the big ship curiously. The swash of their wake, the slat and creak of shipboard noises were loud in the silence.

They'd avoided the smacks, but another danger presented. Sprawled across their track was a new headland, with a round castle prominent on its heights, but Hambly kept his course.

"Should you—"

Hambly did not deign to notice Bampton.

Kydd saw the problem. If they could not come hard round

their only other action to starboard was to head ignominiously into a creek just opening up. He held his breath, then felt the first puff of a playful easterly coming down the creek . . . Depth of water close to, local winds—the master had known!

The edge of their sails shivered and Hambly said, over his shoulder, "We'll brace up, I believe."

As they did so, Kydd saw that, without any movement at the helm, the ship's bow swung safely away from the shore.

"Aye, the set of th' ebb," Hambly said and, unexpectedly, smiled. HMS *Tenacious* found her course again and came to anchor in the spacious expanse of Carrick Roads and Falmouth.

Kydd hugged his boat-cloak around him as the officers' gig left the shelter of the ship's side, sails to a single reef. He pulled his hat tighter and smiled weakly at Renzi through spats of spray. A straggle of low buildings along the shoreline, Falmouth was a small town tucked away just inside the western headland, around from the ruined Pendennis Castle.

Inside the harbour, clusters of smaller ships were moored close before the town, but the majority of shipping, assembling for the convoy, crowded into Carrick Roads—a mass of merchant ships of all kinds and destinations, with boats under sail or oar criss-crossing the waters.

"Fish Strand," Renzi told the coxswain, as they approached the town. The gig headed past the anchored vessels for the tiny quay. "Return before dusk, if you please," he ordered, and the two friends stepped ashore.

"If you should desire a restorative . . ." The First and Last on Market Street seemed to meet the bill—with a jolly tavern-keeper and roaring fire in the taproom to accompany their hot spiced rum.

"Fish Strand?" Kydd said, cupping his toddy.

"Indeed. Mr Pringle assures us that somewhere about here we'll find all we need to preserve the soul in the wilderness of Nova Scotia." Renzi pulled a battered guinea from his pocket. "And it seems that I should return with a proof suitable for a diminutive midshipman against Boreas's worst."

Lieutenants did no watches in harbour: this was a duty for master's mates and midshipmen. Kydd acknowledged that it was very satisfactory to be free to go ashore as the spirit moved, and he was privately relieved to be away from the atmosphere in the wardroom.

A grey-haired man of some quality entered the alehouse. He saw the two naval officers and inclined his head, then signalled to the pot-boy and came across. "Good afternoon, gentlemen. Do I see officers of that fine two-decker in the roads?"

"You do, sir," Renzi answered. "Lieutenants Kydd and Renzi of His Majesty's Ship *Tenacious,* at your service."

"Greaves, Lawrence Greaves. And your noble vessel is bound for North America?"

"She is."

"Ah! Then you will be our guardian angel, our protector of this 'trade,' perhaps?" Greaves was clearly no stranger to sea passages—a "trade" was the common maritime term for a convoy. "May I sit with you?" he asked. "My wife and I will be embarked on the *City of Sydney* for Halifax." The pot-boy hovered. "The same? Or would you prefer wine?" The grey was confined to his side-whiskers, and his eyes were genial. "Your first visit?"

"It will be," Kydd admitted, "but I'll wager this is not *your* first, sir."

"No indeed. I'm commissioner for lands in Halifax, as it happens, returning to my post."

"Then, sir, it puzzles me t' know why you don't take the packet service—it's much the faster," Kydd said, seeing a smart brigantine with the Blue Peter at her masthead through the tavern window.

"No mystery, my friend. My wife is no sailor and insists on the conveniences of a larger vessel, and for me, I much prefer the comforting presence of one of His Majesty's men-o'-war about me. Do you know much of these packets?"

"Not a great deal, sir, but that they do carry inviolable protections against the press," said Renzi.

"Well, then, the post-office packet, small but fast, the mails of the kingdom are entrusted to these, and not only that but passengers and specie—bullion for treasury interchange. They risk tempest and privateers to make a fast passage, and I ask you to conceive of the value to a merchant of receiving his letter-of-credit by reply within fifteen weeks of consigning his petition to an Atlantic crossing."

Kydd murmured an appreciation, but Greaves leaned forward. "A nest of villains, sir! They carry the King's mails, but should they spy a prize, they will not scruple to attack at risk of their cargo—and worse! Even under the strictest post-office contract, they weigh down their vessel with private freight to their common advantage. And should this not be enough, it is commonly known that while the post office will recompense them for a loss at sea to an enemy, profit may just as readily be won from the insurances."

A crack of gunfire drew their attention to the brigantine. Her Blue Peter was jerking down, with vigorous activity at her foredeck windlass. "Ah, yes, she'll be in Halifax two weeks before us—if the privateers let her . . ."

Kydd put down his glass. "Mr Greaves, have you any suggestions f'r preserving body 'n' soul in Halifax? We've heard it can be grievous cold at times."

"Why, yes, but you'll be paying over the odds here, you'll find. Pray wait until Halifax and you will quickly acquire an embarrassment of stout gear. Shall we raise a glass to the success of our voyage?"

"Just curious," Kydd said, as they strolled down the sea-smelling streets of Falmouth, the keening herring gulls raucous along the seafront, clouds of them swooping on the boats landing fresh-caught fish.

"Then if you must, here is one such." With a pang, Kydd reflected that this was like the old days, when he and Renzi had been carefree sailors wandering together in sea-ports around the world.

Outside the shop a large signboard announced, "The Falmouth Bazaar, Prop. James Philp: Stationer, Perfumer, Patent Medicines and Dealer in Fancy Goods to the Falmouth Packet Service."

The interior was odorous with soaps and perfumery, an Aladdin's cave of massed fabrics, baubles and necessaries, the tawdry and the sublime; no passenger facing the prospect of more than a month at sea would lack for suggestions of what to include in their baggage.

The shopkeeper approached them. "If I c'n be of service to you gennelmen?" he said, gripping his lapels.

"You have a fine range o' stock," Kydd said, fingering a lace shift of unusual stoutness.

"We have indeed," said the shopkeeper. "And what, may I en-quire, might interest you?"

Further into the store Kydd saw a couple looking curiously their way. "What do y' have for the run t' Halifax?" he asked.

"Leather an' velvet reticules, purse-springs, clarionets o' su-perior tone, dissected maps, Pope Joan boards wi' genuine pearl fish, ivory walkin' stick with sword—"

"Aye, that will do," said Kydd, ignoring the ingratiating tone. "I'll think on it."

The two left, then turned on to Killigrew Street where they came across Bampton. Kydd lifted his hat politely.

"Mr Kydd," he responded archly. "I admire your *sangfroid*."

"Sir?"

"There is a convoy assembling to sail tolerably soon, and you see fit to linger ashore at your pleasure, when as signal lieutenant you know there is a convoy conference to conduct. You must be confident it will not sail this age."

"Convoy conference?"

"Why, of course! A signal lieutenant, do you not read your standing orders?" His sniff of disdain incensed Kydd. "Flagship of the escort, and the first lieutenant has not a staff for signals? I shouldn't wonder that at this moment he has the ship in a moil, looking for her signal lieutenant."

Hardly a flagship, thought Kydd, as he left the first lieutenant's cabin. Just two men-o'-war: the ship-sloop *Trompeuse* and the six-pounder brig *Viper,* both near hidden by the increasing numbers of merchant ships assembling in Carrick Roads.

Bryant had not been searching for him. He seemed mildly surprised that the new signal lieutenant had cut short his run ashore to hurry back on board. Papers for the ship's masters had not yet been completed, and in any event Houghton had not yet indicated his wishes in the matter of the signal codes to be used in the convoy.

Loyally, Renzi had returned on board with Kydd, and joined his friend as he headed for the upper deck. "Are we to panic, do you think?" he murmured.

"Not as who should say. But t' play the ignoramus does not sit well wi' me."

"What are—"

"You'll see!"

• • •

With a bored look on his face, the duty master's mate was standing by the main shrouds with his telescope of office. He was clearly taken with the idea Kydd put to him. "Bo'sun's mate! Desire midshipman Rawson to present himself on the quarter-deck."

"Mr Rawson," said Kydd, to the wary youth, "your boat-handling, I'm sorry t' say, is not of the standard we expect aboard a sail-o'-the-line, and a flagship, at that."

Rawson mumbled something, but Kydd clapped him on the shoulder. "But don't ye worry, lad, today you an' I will go a-sailing together and you could learn something t' your advantage."

Renzi looked at him curiously, but Kydd went on, "An' then you shall show me what y' know of signals."

For the rest of the forenoon Kydd took away the twenty-five-foot gig and a boat's crew, and in his turn Rawson discovered what it was to sail. Under Kydd's patient direction, and in the brisk winds of the roads, the lug foresail and mizzen were dipped and backed, brailed and reefed while Rawson found how to read a wind, to give best to a squall and when to ship washstrakes.

While the boat plunged between the anchored merchantmen, Kydd hid his apprehension: before long he would have to stand alone on the quarterdeck taking command as a full officer-of-the-watch in a major warship.

The afternoon saw a changed Rawson, respectful, increasingly confident and ready to fall in with Kydd's wishes.

"We shall rig for signalling, if y' please."

"Sir?"

"For exercise, hands to stations f'r signalling," Kydd repeated firmly.

"Aye aye, sir," Rawson said hastily. It took some time to find the other signal midshipman and four seamen, and just as long to find the little table for the signal log.

"Are we ready?" Kydd checked on his signals crew—Rawson and three of the seamen at the flag-locker, and his own midshipman messenger with another.

"Sir."

"Then we shall begin. Mr Rawson, please t' change places with y'r young friend, I want you on hand. Now, ye see *Trompeuse* lying there fine t' larboard. We're senior, and will want to have her responding to our motions. I've spoken with her commander, he is persuaded t' exercise his own signals crew, so we will play the admiral."

The flag-locker was set snugly across the taffrail, right at the after end of the raised poop-deck, handy for the mizzen peak signal halliards. The locker had dozens of neat miniature doors, each with a brightly painted image of a flag.

"Have you a list of these, b' chance?" Kydd asked casually.

Rawson brought over a dog-eared pocket book. "This belonged to the last signal l'tenant—he didn't survive Camperdown—and now it's yours." It was a handwritten notebook of useful information gleaned from the *Fighting Instructions* and other sources.

"Sir, in the front here we have our flags. This is the code of Admiral Howe that we carry, and it's just numbers—'ought to nine. We have some others, the 'affirmative,' the 'preparative' an' that, but it's best you see 'em in action. All we do is look in this part of the signal book and we have codes for two hundred and sixty signals, spelled out by number."

He glanced at Kydd doubtfully, and continued, "So if we want to tell our ships 'Break through the enemy line and engage 'em from the other side,' then we look up in the headings, find the signal, and it's twenty-seven, which we hoist."

"Seems clear enough—but what if we want t' tell them to

stay about all together? How do we let 'em know when t' put the helm down?"

"Ah, that's easy. The order is hoisted up so all c'n see it. Then when they all say they're ready, we pull it down sharply, which is the signal. Or we can use the preparative flag if the admiral wants to give us time t' get ready."

"But what if we want t' do something that doesn't have a code in the book? What do we then?"

Rawson scratched his head. "Can't send it," he admitted. So that was the reason, Kydd realised, for the many occasions he had known when his ship had laboriously come up within hail of a senior, and the two ships had rolled along together while angry communications took place by speaking trumpet.

He tried not to think of the impossibility of doing this in the smoke and violence of battle and took up the little signal book again. "So, let's amuse *Trompeuse*. I see here I can order her to open fire on th' closest enemy—so let's be having it. I find the code here . . ."

"Er, begging your pardon, Mr Kydd, but we hoists *Trompeuse*'s pennant first so he knows the signal is for him, which we finds here."

At the flag-locker a yellow and blue pennant was taken, deftly toggled to the signal halliard, then sent soaring aloft. On another halliard the two-flag code was hoisted close up.

Kydd waited for a reaction. A red and white pennant jerked aloft from the brig. "The answering pennant," crowed Rawson. "They see and will obey!"

Their own signal brought down, one made its way up the mast of the little ship. Rawson dived for the book. "Nine-seven-one— 'I have to report there has been undue mortality in my rats.'" At Kydd's expression he explained gleefully: "It's a sign means they could have fever aboard!"

• • •

The evening grog issue cut short their sport, and Kydd went below with the signal book. The system seemed rational enough but he could foresee problems. What if the wind was gusting *towards* them from a ship? It would set her flags end-on. And in any kind of battle, with its vast amount of powder-smoke, flags would be invisible.

"So signals is the life for you?" Adams said.

"Seems t' be all plain sailing to me. And is a mort better than chokin' on smoke in the gun-deck!"

Adams adjusted his cravat. It was an open secret that a certain landlady was bestowing her favours liberally, under certain expectations not unconnected with Adams's solitary visits ashore. "Pray don't be too cocksure, dear chap," he said, with feeling. "A reputation can be destroyed by false bunting just as easily as putting a ship ashore."

Kydd smiled, but closed the book. He felt reasonably secure in his knowledge of signals and, despite Bampton's acid words, surely there could not be much more to add that he needed to say to a crowd of merchant seamen. With the ship about to sail, it made sense to sup on the fat of the land while they could. "Nicholas! I have a fancy to step ashore again, are you interested?"

"Falmouth?" Renzi ruminated, hiding a smile. "This is the Valubia of Virgil—you have probably overlooked that passage in *The Aeneid* describing Falmouth. Let me see: '*Est in recessu longo lo cus; insula portum . . .*' it goes, as I remember. You will recognise the Dryden too: 'Where vale with sea doth join into its purer hands; 'twixt which, to ships commodious Port is shown—'"

"Sir!" It was a small midshipman at the door. "The captain, sir, desires Mr Kydd to attend on him before he lands, should it be convenient."

"The convoy instructions have arrived, Mr Kydd," Houghton

grunted. His clerk scratched away to one side, a sizeable pile of paper mounting beside him.

"Sir."

"And the convoy will sail in two days." Houghton looked up at him. "I am senior officer and I will be calling a conference of ships' masters for tomorrow afternoon at two. You will attend, of course, and will probably wish to prepare. My clerk, when he's finished, will disclose to you my private signals and wishes in respect of the escorts.

"Mark my words, I mean to brook no insolence from the master of any merchant vessel, and I will have obedience. I want you to make this quite plain."

"Aye aye, sir," Kydd said, turning to go. "And may I have a convoy signal list?"

Houghton started in annoyance. "Of course not! Have you forgotten they are secret? The losing of just one such can lead our convoy into ambuscade, the loss of millions, disgrace to our flag. All are accounted for, sir, and are now under guard—I'm surprised you see fit to ask such a thing."

It was a shock: first, the level of secrecy to which he was now privy, but second, that he had not given it much thought. Simple courage and seamanship were no longer the only things that would matter in the future.

Houghton grunted. "Very well. You may study a signal list in the lobby while Mr Shepheard is working. Any notes you take will be kept by him also. That is all, Mr Kydd."

His heart sank; the mass of detail about fleet signals was exhaustive. Once under way and at sea each ship would be an island, unreachable except for these signals. Kydd leafed through the orders for distinguishing signals and vanes, then the instructions on to the formation of the convoy; it would apparently be a multi-column square advancing over the ocean. The name of each ship was filled in and assigned a number, which turned out to be its column and row position, and the three escorts were positioned around them, *Tenacious,* with a tiny flag added to her name, in the van.

The bulk of the details however, was taken up with resolving problems before they occurred. He turned more pages in dismay. Even putting to sea in good order required special flags to be hung out from odd places about the ship. A red and white weft at the mizzen peak indicated that a ship wished to speak, probably for some urgent concern; a signal of 492 required the unfortunate ship concerned to hoist a yellow flag and steer straight for an enemy in a warlike manner, imitating the action of a warship.

It went on: Kydd's eyes glazed. He began to resent the implied assumption that a naval officer could do anything at a moment's notice, and tried not to think of what he had to face in less than a day. Was it possible to get to grips with so much in that time?

Marines at the landing pier clashed to present arms when Captain Houghton stepped out of the boat, and more lined the way along Arwenack Street to the Customs House where the conference was due to take place.

With their marine guard Kydd paced along stoically behind Houghton and his first lieutenant, lugging the padlocked bag of signal instructions and trying to ignore the curious glances of the townsfolk. At the Customs House, a big, square-looking stone building with a brace of captured French cannon at the entrance, they were met by a prosperous-looking individual wearing an old-fashioned tricorne hat. "Cap'n Houghton? Raddles, Collector o' Customs. Welcome to Falmouth, an' your convoy gentlemen are a-waitin' within." They passed inside along a musty-smelling passage. "Been here before, sir?" Without waiting for an answer he went on, "The long room is where they meets mostly."

They entered a large room with barn-style beams and imposing, floor-length windows. It was noisy, as some hundreds of plainly dressed and weatherworn seamen were present. The babble died as they entered, and those standing in groups moved to take chairs.

Kydd followed Houghton up the aisle to the front, conscious of heads turning. There was a small lectern, a chalkboard and a table. Just three chairs, facing the hundreds seated, waited.

Houghton took the centre chair and Kydd the left. Bryant was on the right. The talking died away. The collector introduced the officers briefly with a bow and a gesture, then left.

The captain wasted no time. He stepped up to the lectern and fixed his glare on the audience. "I am senior officer of the escorts. On this voyage you will have ships of force with you, and need fear nothing from the French, as long as you sail agreeable to the plan. Runners will not be tolerated unless arrangements are in hand. Do I make myself clear?"

Kydd knew that runners were individual ships that tired of the slower speeds of a convoy and struck out ahead alone. They were taking a chance and were on their own, but stood to gain a lot when theirs was the first cargo landed.

"We have a favourable wind and I intend to proceed tomorrow forenoon with the tide. If you have any objections to the sailing plan you may see me in *Tenacious* up to six hours before we weigh. Otherwise I will take it that you agree to its provisions and will abide by them." He gripped the sides of the lectern. "Have you any questions? No?" A restless stirring went through the meeting. Houghton relaxed his stance. "Lieutenant Kydd here will present the sailing plan and explain the signals." Kydd felt a moment of panic, but remembered to nod and smile under the scrutiny of so many eyes. He had a deep sense of responsibility that so many merchant seamen were putting their trust in the Navy.

"Then it is only left for me to wish you fair winds and a successful voyage. Good day, gentlemen."

To Kydd's relief, Houghton and the first lieutenant strode together down the aisle and left. He had no wish for his performance to be seen by anyone from *Tenacious*. Aware of a rustle of expectation he moved to the lectern and stood before the sea of stony faces. "L'tenant Kydd, signal lieutenant in *Tenacious*."

His voice came out thin and unconvincing. "I want t' talk to you about our convoy to Halifax an' Newfoundland," he said, trying to toughen his tone. "And especially the conduct o' your ships when given direction by th' escorts. My captain has particularly asked me to—"

"So what if we can't agree wi' your *direction,* young feller?" A hard-faced man towards the front had risen to his feet. "The King's service knows aught o' what worries us, so why should we do *everythin'* you tell us? Eh?"

Kydd stuttered a weak reply.

Another master got up, more to the back, but his voice boomed out effortlessly. "Tell us, Mr Lootenant Kydd, truly now, have ye ever crossed the Atlantic in a blow? Come on, son, don' be shy! When it's blowin' great guns 'n' muskets, squalls comin' marchin' in a-weather, lee gunnels under half th' time. Have ye?"

"Er, myself, I'm no stranger t' foul weather."

"Good. Then you'll be able t' tell us how in Hades we c'n spy all your flags an' numbers in a fresh blow an' all!" The two captains sat down to a murmur of agreement.

In front of him were experienced seamen who had been to sea before he was born and whose sea wisdom cast his own into pale insignificance. Kydd saw that Bryant had returned, and was standing at the end of the hall, listening to him. "Should ye not make out our signal, y' keep the answering pennant at the dip," he went on hesitantly. He saw some leaning forward, straining to hear. "If th' weather—"

Bryant marched up the aisle, grim-faced. Kydd yielded the lectern to him.

"I'm L'tenant Bryant, first o' the *Tenacious*," he began, challenging them with his tone and glowering at them individually. "L'tenant Kydd is my assistant." He flashed a dispassionate glance at Kydd. "Now we have a convoy to get under way afore noon tomorrow, so no more nonsense, if y' please. Any who wants to argue with a King's ship knows what to expect."

He took a wad of instructions and held them up. "As you all know, this is how we conduct our convoy. As usual I'll start at th' beginning, remembering all you've been told about keepin' this under lock 'n' key.

"Convoy assembles in Falmouth Roads, outside the harbour. Each ship t' rig their coloured vane to fly at the fore or main, accordin' to the instructions, not forgetting your number good and plain on each stern-quarter. Order o' sailing and first rendezvous, you should have by you, before we leave."

Bryant leaned forward on the lectern. "Now, here's a thing. My captain's a right Tartar, he is, a hard horse driver who's always on our necks. He's your senior officer now, so I advise you all t' spread what canvas you need to keep the convoy closed up an' all together." He allowed that to sink in, then went on, "Signal code for the convoy is in two parts, and provision is made . . ."

The presentation continued. Kydd stood awkwardly beside Bryant, resentful yet admiring of his easy competence.

Then the conference drew to a close and a line of merchant captains came forward to sign the register and take custody of their convoy instructions. They left to return to their ships; the Blue Peter would soon be at each masthead.

Kydd picked up his gear, avoiding Bryant's eye. He was startled to hear him give a quiet laugh. "They falls out o' the line of
sailin', you know what we do? Give 'em a shot in the guts! Sets
'em into a more co-operative frame of mind, it does."

Bryant helped Kydd heap paper rubbish into the bag; this
would later be burned. "But the biggest threat we can use is to
report 'em to Lloyds," he continued. "They show stubborn, we
tell Lloyds, an' then they have to explain to their owners why
their insurance premiums just doubled." Before Kydd could say
anything, Bryant had consulted his watch and stalked off.

Chapter 4

"God blast his eyes!" Houghton's fists were clenched and he shook with fury. "I'll see this rogue roast in hell! Hoist his number on the lee fore halliard and give him another gun."

The signal for "lie to, and await orders before proceeding" still flew from *Tenacious*'s mizzen peak together with *Lady Ann*'s distinguishing number. It was inconceivable that the shabby timber ship could not understand the need to form up the convoy properly before their voyage began. She seemed intent on heading off into the general distance, vaguely bound for the west, despite the plain sight of so many other ships hove to with brailed-up canvas waiting for the remainder of the convoy to issue out from the inner anchorage.

Kydd marvelled at the sight in front of him: 148 ships, large and small, a vast mass of vessels filling the wide bay. Bustling between them were the two smaller escorts. The whole scene was an expression of economic strength—and vulnerability. If Britain could preserve this great stream of trade goods arriving and leaving the kingdom, her survival was assured. If not, the end of this cataclysmic war would not be far off.

At last *Lady Ann* slewed and hove to, but her actions had meant *Tenacious* had moved well out of station and had to heave round back to the assembly points. Her captain was fuming, his officers on edge and the ship's company thoroughly bad-tempered.

The last of the joiners came through the harbour entrance, past Black Rock and into the open sea. "Convoy will proceed," roared Houghton, glaring at his signal lieutenant as though it was all his fault.

Kydd found the place in the signal book, and hastily shouted the hoist to those at the taffrail flag-locker. Flags were bent on, soaring up the halliards as the thump of their fo'c'sle gun drew attention to them.

"Have they acknowledged yet?" snapped Houghton.

Kydd had his telescope up, trying to locate *Trompeuse* and *Viper,* just two sail among so many.

"Well?"

Kydd saw the three gunboats of the port's standing force, which had been detached to see the convoy to sea and were temporarily under Houghton's command, but he could not spot the low, half-decked, two-masted craft.

"Good God! Do I have to—"

"*Viper* acknowledges, sir." It was Bampton at the officer-of-the-watch's telescope.

"And *Trompeuse,*" Kydd added, finding the small ship-sloop. Then he spotted the vessel sliding into the line of sight from behind a bulky salt-carrier, a red and white pennant at her signal halliards. "A gunboat answers, sir."

Houghton took a deep breath. "Then hoist and execute for pennant ships, damn your eyes!"

Rawson already had the signal bent on and swooping up the rigging where it fluttered gaily for several minutes then jerked down. One by one, from random places in the milling ships, trusted merchant vessels followed the lead of *Tenacious* and hoisted a yellow triangular flag above an unmistakable red and white square—the Halifax convoy.

First *Tenacious,* then the pennant ships marking leading positions in the convoy purposefully set their bowsprits to the open Atlantic, and a pattern formed after them. Ship after ship fell into column, jockeying with shortened sail into their order of sailing; men-o'-war chivvied and snapped at the heels of the laggardly, and the vast fleet headed away from the land. The gunboats returned to port.

Well before they had left the outer Falmouth Roads and laid the deadly Manacles to starboard, the signal for escorts to take station was made. *Tenacious* led the convoy, she and her consorts on the windward side of the mass of shipping—the best position to drop down quickly on any of their charges if they were attacked.

"*Viper* to leave the stragglers and come up to station," Houghton ordered testily. "Never know what's waiting for us out there." The inevitable late starters would have to catch up as best they could. One lumbering merchantman was caught flat aback when avoiding another, and Kydd could see its helpless gyration through his glass as it gathered stern-way and turned in reverse in obedience to the last helm order.

A grey-white wall of drizzle approached silently. In the westerly wind the craggy loom of the peninsula to starboard was no threat. But when they reached its end, the notorious Lizard, they would leave its shelter and face whatever the Atlantic Ocean could bring.

"Damn!" Bampton cursed. The light rain had reached them and was beginning a damp assault. While Houghton kept the deck no one dared go below, and all had to suffer coats heavy with wet and rivulets of cold water wriggling down their necks. The captain stood aggressively as the rain ran down his face. Kydd's crew shivered and clutched their coats but none dared ask to leave the deck.

Suddenly Houghton started. "Who has the watch?"

"I, sir," responded Bampton.

"I shall be in my cabin." Houghton wheeled round and left. Other officers followed his example and went below, but Kydd knew he must stay so he moved down from the exposed poop-deck. Bampton called for his watch-coat and Kydd his oilskins, but then the rain ceased and the wind resumed a chill buffeting.

Kydd used his signals telescope to survey the slow-moving convoy. Once they made the open sea beyond the Lizard they would spread more sail for best speed, but if the stragglers could not make up the distance before they met the friendless ocean they would be in trouble.

In the main they were closing manfully, but a small gaggle were now miles astern locked together. Kydd shuddered with the cold and lowered the telescope. But something made him raise it again. The larger of the stopped vessels had one corner of her main course drawn up to the yard, a peculiar action at sea. He steadied the glass, leaning back with his elbow braced on his chest to see better. There was activity, but it was not co-ordinated.

Straining to make it out, he waited for a spasm of shivering to subside and concentrated on the other vessel. Something about her—she was not low in the water. "Sir!" he said loudly. "Seems the stragglers are being taken!"

"What?" said Bampton incredulously. He brought up his big telescope. "Are you mad? That's nothing but a parcel of lubberly merchantmen got in a tangle!"

"But the main course! It's up to—"

"What are you babbling about, Mr Kydd? She still flies her pennant. The other vessel has her vane a-fly—leave them to it, I say."

"Sir, should we not send *Viper* down to 'em?"

"And put her to loo'ard and having to beat back just when we make the open sea? I'm surprised at your suggestion, Mr Kydd, and can only ascribe it to your, er, lack of experience in these waters."

The captain appeared from the cabin spaces. "Ah, Mr Bampton. All's well?"

"Yes sir."

"Th' stragglers are bein' snapped up f'r prizes!" Kydd blurted out.

"What? Give me that," said Houghton, taking Kydd's telescope.

"I'm sorry, sir—Mr Kydd's enthusiasm sometimes exceeds his experience and—"

"Why do you say that?" Houghton snapped at Kydd.

"Main course. It's goosewings now, but that would be so if they only had time to haul one clew up to the yard, not both, and if the lubbers hadn't yet loaded the signal guns or shipped aprons against the rain, they—"

Bampton broke in, "What are you wittering about, Kydd? Those vessels have their numbers hoisted. They have not hauled down their colours or signalled distress—they're in a god-awful mess. I've seen it many times before, and so will you."

Houghton's telescope steadied. "*Viper* and *Trompeuse* to close and investigate," he bawled to the poop-deck.

He rounded on Bampton. "Mr Kydd knows his signals—'Haul up your main course and two guns to weather' is the signal for the approach of strange sail. They must have been caught napping by some damned privateer disguised as one of our ships, who knows our procedures and that our attention is all ahead."

Trompeuse hurried back along the convoy, keeping to the windward edge. *Viper* angled off downwind.

The master came up to watch developments but remained silent.

"What *is* that idiot in *Viper* up to?" Bampton said.

Kydd had his own ideas about why the gun-brig had clapped on all sail away to the east, well to leeward of the action, but kept his silence.

Tysoe arrived with Kydd's oilskins and a warm jersey, which Kydd struggled into under his waterproofs.

"*Sail hoooo!*" The masthead lookout's hand was flung out to seaward. As the Lizard opened up to the westward a respectable-sized frigate under easy sail close inshore came into view.

"No colours," growled Houghton, "but we know what she's up to. Quarters, Mr Bampton."

Then *Tenacious* heard the heart-stopping thunder of the drums in anger for the first time this voyage. Kydd's post in battle was at the signals; he had but to send for his sword and see to the lead-lined bag ready for sinking secret material should the need arise.

"She thinks t' fall on the convoy while the escorts are to loo'ard dealing with the brig—they wouldn't guess a ship o' force was waiting for 'em," the master said. With grim satisfaction Kydd spared a glance astern.

The enemy must have seen events swing against them, for both the hapless goosewinged merchantman and the anonymous brig loosed sail hurriedly and swung about—but it was too late. The reason for *Viper*'s move had become clear. She was now squarely between the enemy and his escape.

"Spankin' good sailin'!" Kydd burst out. With *Trompeuse* now coming down fast from one direction and *Viper* well placed in the other, the end was not really in doubt.

The smoke of a challenging shot eddied up from *Viper*, the ball skipping past the enemy and her prize. The two came briefly together, probably to recover crew, before one broke out French colours and crammed on all sail to try to make off, leaving the other with ropes slashed and drifting helplessly. So close to Falmouth there would be no trouble recovering the abandoned prize.

As the brig attempted to pass *Viper,* she made a perfect target for raking fire and *Viper* did not waste it. When the smoke of her broadside cleared, the brig had already struck her colours. Jubilation rang out on *Tenacious* from the deck below, and satisfied smiles were to be seen on the quarterdeck.

But as *Tenacious* thrust towards her, the frigate shied away and bore south-east, towards the distant French coast. When she had drawn away, and *Tenacious* stood down from quarters, Kydd saw that the convoy was now much closer together, and in impeccable formation.

As one, the argosy rounded the Lizard, taking Atlantic rollers on the bow in explosions of white, hauling their wind for the south-west, the wanly setting sun and the thousands of miles that lay ahead.

"Your health, Mr Kydd!" The surgeon leaned forward, as usual in his accustomed evening-wear of a worn green waistcoat. He had an odd, detached way of regarding people, part earnest, part sardonic.

"Thank ye, Mr Pybus," Kydd answered, "It's always a pleasure t' have a doctor wishing me good health."

The wardroom was abuzz with chatter. Besides the charge of anticipation that a new voyage always brought, there was the tension of getting the convoy to sea—and their first brush with the enemy.

"Sharp of His Nibs to spot the wolf among the sheep," said Pringle, helping himself to another cutlet.

Adams leaned across for the asparagus. "Did hear that you helped him to a conclusion, Kydd?" he said, and when his eyes flicked towards the head of the table, Kydd guessed that the story of his *contretemps* with Bampton was now common knowledge.

"Always like t' help when I can," he said cautiously. Bampton was talking with the purser, but Kydd occasionally caught his eyes straying to himself.

Louder, Adams went on, "To the devil with modesty, old fellow, tell us, what put you on to him?"

"Er, his lee clew t' the course was—"

"Speak up, dear chap, we're working to wind'd!" To make her offing of Wolf's Rock in the night, the ship's taut rigging was causing the length of her hull to creak in noisy protest.

"I said, with only one clew to the yard an' the chance her guns were yet not primed, she'd be tryin' t' let us know she was in trouble and could not. If she had her vanes an' colours correct, seems to me she was surprised, and then th' boarders let all stand to make us think she was a vessel retirin' back to Falmouth."

He grinned. "But then I thought t' take a look at her draught— a brig, outward bound, an' sittin' high in th' water! Stands to reason—"

"You didn't tell me that!" Bampton's voice cut through the talk, which quickly died away. "If I'd known what you saw!"

It was on the tip of his tongue to remark that with his bigger telescope Bampton was better placed to see the same thing, but Kydd remained guarded. "Ah, in fact, there was not really time enough t' tell it."

Bampton held rigid.

The next morning the land was gone. There was just empty sea and the convoy. In loose columns, they bucketed through the long heaving swells from the west, substantial Hudson Bay traders with fine passenger cabins, hardy vessels headed for the Newfoundland cod fishery, slab-sided timber ships that would return with precious masts for the dockyards of the kingdom. And impoverished immigrants crammed among supplies for the settlements.

The night-time shortening of sail now became a resetting of

plain sail to reach maximum speed of the slowest. A tedious schedule of hauling and loosing was necessary to adjust speeds; the leading-edge ships had to be reined in while slower ones, which had slipped to the back during the night, were bullied into lengthening their stride.

Routine was only re-established mid-morning when *Tenacious* was free to go to quarters for exercise of the great guns. After an hour or more of hard work the welcome sound of the tune "Nancy Dawson" drifted up from the main deck, announcing grog and dinner for the hands.

But first, on an open deck nearly deserted of seamen, the officers gathered on the quarterdeck for the noon-day sight. Every officer performed the duty, including the midshipmen, but only the "workings" of the lieutenants were pooled for reliability.

This would be Kydd's first occasion as an officer, for although since those years in the Caribbean he had known how, it was now that his contribution would be a valid element in the navigation of a King's ship.

He readied his octant, an old but fine brass and ebony instrument, by setting the expected latitude down to the tangent screw. This would shorten the time needed to do a fine adjustment in the precious seconds of a meridian altitude. Next, he took the precaution of finding his "height-of-eye" on the quarterdeck. There was an appreciable correction to be made—from there the distance to the horizon of a ship-of-the-line was a full seven miles.

Cradling his instrument Kydd took his place, feeling the long swell come in fine on the bow in a heave down the length of the ship. He estimated it at no more than twelve feet, which meant another correction to height-of-eye. Then, like the others, he trialled the sun—close, but some minutes to go.

He was aware of the helmsman behind him, silently flicking

the wheel to catch a wave, glancing up at the weather leech of a sail, then resuming his blank stare ahead. Kydd knew what he was thinking—the wielding of sextants, the consulting of mysterious figures in the almanac marked out an officer from a common seaman.

He lifted the octant again: the reflected lower edge of the sun was getting near the horizon. Kydd waited patiently, shifting the vernier with delicate twists of the tangent screw. Then it was time, the sun was at its highest altitude: reflected by the octant, its image kissed the line of the horizon.

"Stop," he called, his voice mingling with the others. The time to a second was recorded by a master's mate: this was the exact instant of local noon along this line of longitude, the meridian. By the elevation of the sun above the earth, the distance along that line from the equator, the latitude, could be found, and where the two intersected would be the ship's position.

He lowered his instrument and, through habit, glanced into the binnacle: at noon on the meridian the sun was exactly due south so this was a good time to check the compass.

In the wardroom the table filled quickly with paper and books. Kydd jotted down his octant reading, returned the instrument to its case, and found his *Moore's Nautical Almanac*. In practised sequence he entered the tables, applied the corrections and neatly summarised his workings, his final latitude and longitude boldly there for all to see.

"Thank you, gentlemen," the master said, collecting the workings. They agreed within a minute or so, but Kydd's was the closest of all to Hambly's own.

"Mr Kydd." The captain was standing on the weather side of the quarterdeck.

"Aye, sir," Kydd replied, moving quickly to him.

"As you must be aware," he said gruffly, "with four watch-keeping officers, having a second officer-of-the-watch forces them to watch on, watch off. The first lieutenant has asked that the ship's officers now move to single watches."

"Sir."

"Therefore you will oblige me by assuming your own watch," he said drily. "Should you feel unsure in *any* situation, you will call me at once. Do you understand?"

"Instantly, sir."

"Carry on, please, Mr Kydd."

The last dog-watch was nearly over when Kydd appeared by the wheel to take the next watch. In the early night-darkness the men stood about quietly, their faces eerily lit from beneath by the dim light of the binnacle lamp.

"Mr Bampton," Kydd said in greeting.

The second lieutenant grunted, and turned to look at Kydd. "Course sou'west b' south, courses are in to topsails one reef, last cast of the log five and a half knots." He glanced once at the dark, near invisible sea, speckled prettily with golden pricks of lanthorn light where the convoy sailed on quietly through the night.

"Convoy still seems to be with us, carpenter reports nine inches in the well, we have two in the bilboes." These unfortunates would spend all night in leg irons until hauled before the captain in the morning, but it was necessary to pass on the information. In the event that the ship was in danger of foundering they must be released.

"You have the ship, I'm going below. If you get into a pother, *don't* call me. Good night."

It was done. A momentary rush of panic, then exultation. The man standing on the quarterdeck in command, around whom the world that was HMS *Tenacious* would revolve, was Thomas Paine Kydd.

A duty quartermaster held out the chalk log. The watch always started with a clean slate and Kydd took it, his notations of course and sail now holy writ to be transcribed later to the master's log. He heard the quartermaster murmur the heading to the new hand on the wheel, then saw him squint at the compass before returning to report, "Sou'west b' south, Brown on the wheel, sir." Much as Kydd himself had done not so very long ago.

The figures dispersed, leaving the new watch in possession of the deck. Kydd's midshipman messenger was behind him, and the mate-of-the-watch with his boatswain's mate stood to leeward, waiting for orders. The rest of the watch were at different positions around the deck under their station captains, for now Kydd, as an officer, could never treat with them directly.

Eight bells clanged forward. It was the first watch, and in accordance with practice, the ship went to evening quarters. Messdecks were transformed as ditty bags were taken down, benches stowed below, mess-traps placed in racks and the hinged table removed. Once again the broad space reverted to its true purpose—a gun-deck with martial rows of heavy cannons.

At the guns, the fighting tops and in the waist of the ship, men stood ready. It was a time to muster them, to ensure they knew their place in combat intimately, and also it was an opportunity for the seamen to learn about those in authority over them. But this did not concern Kydd, who maintained his watch from on high over them all.

Quarters over, the men were released. Hammocks were piped down from their stowage in the nettings around the bulwarks and slung below. In the same hour the space passed from a dining room to a ship of war and then a dormitory. The ship changed from a busy working place to a darkened domain of slumber.

It was a clear night with the wind steady on the beam. Kydd stepped inside the cabin spaces to the lobby, where a small table bore a chart. It was now his duty to think of the bigger picture. A seaman before the mast simply accepted that a course was set to a compass heading. Beyond that, it was of no interest to someone who could have no say in his destiny, but who at the same time did not have to worry about it.

Kydd lowered the dim lanthorn so its soft golden light was enough to see their pencilled course pricked out. They were heading mainly south with the Canary current to avoid the strong trade westerlies, and to pick up later the countervailing seasonal north-easterlies in a swing across the width of the ocean.

Kydd stepped out on deck again. He had been in countless night watches and been comforted by the nocturnal sounds: the slaps and dings of ropes against masts, sails occasionally cracking with a high-spirited flourish, the never-ceasing spreading groan and creak of timbers, the ghost-like susurrus of wind in the lines from aloft—all had been a soothing backdrop before. Now its character had changed. Any number of hazards might lie in wait to challenge his still untutored judgement, a started strake even now spurting black water into the depths of the hold, a wrung topgallant mast tumbling to sudden ruin, a sleepy merchant ship yawing across their bows . . .

"Lawes, prove the lookouts!" It sounded more urgent than he meant.

In response to his mate-of-the-watch's hail came answering cries of "Aye aye!" from around the deck.

Kydd moved along the weather gangway, thumping on ropes. If they gave a satisfying hard thrum they were well taut, but a dead feel under his fist meant a job for the watch on deck. He returned by the lee gangway, looking up at the pale expanse of sail. They drew well, but there was no compelling need for speed, locked in as they were to the speed of the convoy. He had no wish to be known as a "jib and staysail jack," always trimming yards and canvas to the annoyance of the night watch.

Back on the quarterdeck, the ship's easy motion was reassuring, the stolid presence of the helmsman and quartermaster companionable, and his tense wariness subsided.

The master-at-arms came aft from the main hatchway with a midshipman and corporal. "All's well, sir, an' lights out below," he reported.

"Very good. Carry on, please," Kydd said, echoing the words of the countless officers-of-the-watch he had known. The master-at-arms touched his hat, leaving them to their solitude.

The accustomed tranquillity of a night watch began to settle—bringing a disengagement of mind from body, a pleasant feeling of consciousness being borne timelessly to reverie and memories.

Kydd pulled himself together. This was not the way an officer-of-the-watch should be, with all his responsibility. He turned and paced firmly to the mainmast and back, glaring about.

The night wore on. It was easy sailing: he could hear the monotone of one of the watch on deck forward spinning a yarn. There was a falsetto hoot and sudden laughter, but for him there would be no more companionable yarns in the anonymous darkness.

He spun on his heel and paced slowly back towards the binnacle, catching the flash of eyes in the dimness nearby as the quartermaster weighed the chances of a bored officer-of-the-watch picking fault with his helmsman. Reaching the binnacle Kydd glanced inside to the soft gold of the compass light. Their course was true. All along the decks, lines bowsed taut. What could go wrong?

His imagination replied with a multitude of possible emergencies. He forced them away and tried to remain calm, pacing slowly to one side of the deck. Low talk began around the wheel. It stopped when he approached again. Could they be discussing him? Years of his own time at the wheel told him that they were—

and anything else that might pass the hours of a night watch.

Oddly comforted, he made play of going to the ship's side and inspecting the wake as if he was expecting something, but his senses suddenly pricked to full alertness—there were sounds that did not fit. He spun round. An indistinct group of men lurched into view from the main hatchway. Even in the semi-darkness he could see that two were supporting a third, slumped between them. Another followed behind.

He recognised the voice of the boatswain but not those of the other men, who were moaning and arguing. Kydd hurried to the light of the binnacle. "Yes, Mr Pearce?" he snapped at the boatswain.

The moaning man was lowered to the deck in a sprawl. "Fetch the corporal with a night-lanthorn," Kydd snapped, "and ask the doctor to—"

"Sir," Pearce began heavily, "Ord'nary Seaman Lamb, sir, taken in drink in th' orlop."

"What's this, y' useless skulker? Think t' swill out o' sight, do you?" Kydd spat venomously.

The violence of his anger shocked him and he knew he had overreacted. He pulled himself together. "What's y'r division?"

"L'tenant Adams, sir," Lamb said thickly, touching his forelock in fear.

"Said it's his birthday, sir."

The white face of the offender stared up at Kydd from the deck. Lamb struggled to stand but fell back.

Kydd could easily picture what had happened. With typical generosity his messmates had plied him with illicitly hoarded rum in celebration. He had staggered down to the orlop to sleep it off, then had the misfortune to encounter the boatswain on his rounds.

Kydd's sympathies swung to the lad. Life on the lower deck in the cold north Atlantic was not pleasant and seamen looked for any kind of release—generally rum.

But there was no real escape. A ship of war that might in minutes find itself yardarm to yardarm with an enemy was no place for a drunken hand at the guns. Kydd's duty was plain. "Sleeps it off in irons, t' front the captain in the forenoon." Houghton would have no mercy and tomorrow there would be pain and suffering at the gangway.

Kydd turned his back and paced away. He had no stomach for any scenes of pitiful begging but there were only muffled gasps and grunting as the young sailor was hauled away.

"Bring him forward." Houghton stood rigid, his lips clamped to a thin line, his hands behind his back as Lamb was brought before the lectern.

"Take orf that hat!" growled the master-at-arms. The youth's thatch of hair ruffled in the wind that buffeted down over the half-deck. His open face was set and pale, but he carried himself with dignity.

On one side of the captain Kydd attended for the prosecution, on the other was Adams. "Well?" snapped the captain, turning to Kydd.

"Sir, Ordinary Seaman Lamb. Last night at six bells o' the first watch the boatswain haled this man before me under suspicion o' drink." Caught by the boatswain, prostrate with drink before the officer-of-the-watch, there was not the slightest chance of denial. But the grim ritual of the trial must be completed.

"And was he?"

Kydd's answer would be the boy's condemnation. "He—he was incapable." He had had as much chance of avoiding those words as Lamb had of escaping the lash.

"I see. Mr Adams?"

"Sir. This lad is young. It was his birthday and his shipmates plied him with grog in celebration but, sir, in his youth and in-experience he was unable to resist their cajolery. It's nothing but youth and warm spirits—"

"This is of no account! At sea there is no excusing a man-o'-war's man being found beastly drunk at any hour, when paid by the King to hold himself in readiness to defend his country! Have you anything to add as witness to his character?"

"Er, Lamb is a willing hand. His ropework is admired by all in the maintop. And, er, he volunteered into *Tenacious* and is always forward in his duty . . ."

The captain glanced once at Adams, then fixed Lamb with a terrible stare. "Have you anything to say for yourself, you rogue?"

Lamb shook his head and bit his lip. "Then I find you guilty as charged. Two dozen!" Lamb went white. This was savage medicine, quite apart from the theoretical limit of a dozen strokes allowed a captain at sea.

"*Haaands* lay aft to witness punishment—*aaaall* the hands." Boatswain's mates strode about above and below decks with their piercing silver calls, summoning witnesses to justice. As would be the way of it from now on, Kydd remained out of sight below in the wardroom, avoiding conversation until the word was passed down for the final ceremony.

"Officers t' muster!" squeaked a messenger at last. Solemnly, the officers left the wardroom and made their way up to the quar-terdeck. There, the gratings were rigged, one lashed upright to the half-deck bulkhead and one to stand on. The ship's company were mustered ready, a space of open deck, then a sea of faces stretching forward. Kydd avoided their gaze, moving quickly up the ladder to the poop-deck.

The captain stalked forward to the poop-rail, much as Kydd

had seen so many times before from the opposite side, looking up as a foremast hand. Now, with the other officers, he stood squarely behind him, seeing only the back of his head. Blackly, he saw that his view of proceedings was obscured by the break of the poop, and that therefore on all those occasions before, the officers must have seen nothing of the lashes and the agony.

Marines stood to attention at the rails, a drummer-boy at the ready. Lamb stood before his captain, flanked by the powerful figures of two boatswain's mates. A brief rattle of the drum brought a subdued quiet.

"Articles of War!" barked Houghton. His clerk passed them across. "'Article two: All persons in or belonging to His Majesty's ships or vessels of war, being guilty of drunkenness, uncleanness or other scandalous actions, in derogation of God's honour, shall incur such punishment . . . as the nature and degree of their offence shall deserve.'"

He closed the little book. "Carry on, boatswain's mate."

The prisoner was led over to the gratings and out of sight, but Kydd—flogged himself once—needed no prompting to know what was going on. Stripped and lashed up by the thumbs, Lamb would be in a whirl of fear and shame and, above all, desperately lonely. In minutes his universe would narrow to one of pounding, never-ending torment.

Kydd had seen floggings by the score since his own, but this one particularly affected him.

The drum thundered away, then stopped. Kydd's skin crawled in anticipation of that first, shocking impact. In the breathless quiet he heard the unmistakable hiss of the cat, then the vicious meaty smack and thud as the body was driven against the gratings. A muffled, choking sob was all that escaped—Lamb was going to take it like a man.

There was a further volleying of the drum; again the sudden quiet and the sound of the lash. There was no sound from Lamb.

It went on and on. One part of Kydd's mind cried out—but another countered with cold reason: no-one had yet found a better system of punishment that was a powerful deterrent yet allowed the offender to return to work. Ashore it was far worse: prison and whipping at the cart's tail for a like offence—even children could face the gallows for little more.

The lashing went on.

The noon sight complete, the officers entered the wardroom for their meal. "Your man took his two dozen well, Gervase," Pringle said to Adams, as they sat down. He tasted his wine. "Quite a tolerable claret."

Adams helped himself to a biscuit. "I wonder if Canada rides to hounds—'t would be most gratifying to have some decent sport awaiting our return from a cruise. They've quite fine horseflesh in Nova Scotia, I've heard."

"Be satisfied by the society, old chap. Not often we get a chance at a royal court, if that's your bag."

"Society? I spent all winter with my cousin at his pile in Wiltshire. Plenty of your county gentry, but perilously short of female company for my taste."

Conversation ebbed and flowed around Kydd. As usual, he kept his silence, feeling unable to contribute, although Renzi had by degrees been drawn up the table and was now entertaining Bryant with a scandalous story about a visit to the London of bagnios and discreet villas. Pringle flashed Kydd a single veiled glance and went on to invite Bampton to recount a Barbados interlude, leaving him only the dry purser as dinner companion.

The afternoon stretched ahead. Kydd knew that Renzi had come to look forward to dispute metaphysics with the erudite chaplain and had not the heart to intervene. Having the first dog-watch, he took an early supper alone and snapped at Tysoe for lingering. Melancholy was never far away these days.

He went up on deck early, and approached the master. "Good day to ye, Mr Hambly."

"An' you too, sir."

"Er, do you think this nor' easterly will stay by us?"

"It will, sir. These are the trades, o' course." Hambly was polite but preoccupied.

"I've heard y' can get ice this time o' the year."

The master hesitated. "Sir, I have t' write up the reckonings." He touched his hat to Kydd and left.

At four he relieved Bampton, who disappeared after a brief handover. Once more he took possession of the quarterdeck and the ship, and was left alone with his thoughts.

An hour later Renzi appeared. "Just thought I'd take a constitutional before I turn in," he said, "if it does not inconvenience." He sniffed the air. "Kydd, dear fellow, have you ever considered the eternal paradox of free will? Your Oriental philosopher would have much to say, should he consider your tyrannous position at the pinnacle of lordship in our little world . . ."

Kydd's spirits rose. There had been little opportunity so far to renew their old friendship, and he valued the far-ranging talks that had livened many a watch in the past. "Shall ye not have authority, and allow a false freedom to reign in bedlam?" he said, with a grin, falling into pace next to Renzi.

"Quite so, but Mr Peake advances an interesting notion concerning the co-existence of free will in the ruled that requires my disabusing the gentleman of his patently absurd views." He stared out pensively to leeward.

Kydd stopped dead. Bitterness welled and took focus. Renzi stopped, concerned. "What is it, brother? Are you—"

"Nothing!" Kydd growled, but did not resume his walk.

"May I—"

"Your ven'rable Peake is waiting—go and dispute with him if it gives you s' much pleasure!" Kydd said bitterly.

Renzi said softly, "There is something that ails you. I should be honoured were you to lay it before me, my friend."

It was not the time or place—but Kydd darted a glance around the quarterdeck. No one was watching. He looked across to the conn team at the wheel and caught the quartermaster's eye, then pointed with his telescope up the ladder to the poop-deck. The man nodded, and Kydd made his way with Renzi up on to the small deck, the furthest aft of all. It was not a popular place, dominated as it was by the big spanker boom ranging out from the mizzen mast and sometimes activity in the flag-lockers at the taffrail. They were alone.

Kydd stared out over the wake astern, a ragged white line dissolving to nothing in the distance, ever renewed by their steady motion and the noisy tumbling foam under their counter. His dark thoughts were full but refused to take solid form, and he hesitated. "Nicholas. How c'n I say this? Here I stand, an officer. *A King's officer!* More'n I could dare t' dream of before. And it's—it's not as it should be . . ."

Renzi waited patiently, gazing astern.

Kydd continued weakly, "Y' see, I don't *feel* an officer—it's as if I was playin' a role, dressin' up for the part like a common actor." The frustrations boiled up and he gulped with emotion. "I know th' seamanship, the orders an' things but—Nicholas, look at me! When the others talk t' each other, they're talkin' to the squire, the gentry—their father is lord o' the manor of some fine family, they talk of ridin' with the hounds, calling on the duke in London, what's the latest gossip . . ." His voice thickened. "And me, what can I talk about at table without I open m' mouth and be damned a yokel?"

Renzi murmured encouragement. Paradoxically, this made it all the worse for Kydd, and his frustration took a new path. "It's easy enough f'r you. You've been born into it," he said bitterly, "lived that way all y'r life. This is why you can talk y'r horses an' estates 'n' politics with the others. And have you thought how it is f'r me? I sit there sad as a gib cat, hearin' all this jabber and feelin' as out of it as—"

The carpenter interrupted them with his report and Kydd processed the information mechanically. Twenty-four inches in the well: if he left it, the night watch would have to deal with it, manning the big chain pump with all its creaking and banging, rendering sleep impossible for the watch below. He'd see to it before he left the deck.

Renzi spoke quietly: "Tom, do you consider awhile. We all have had to learn the graces, the manners and ways of a gentleman. It's just that we've had much longer than you to learn. You see? You *will* learn in time, then—"

"Be damned!" Kydd choked. "Do ye take me f'r a performing monkey? Learn more tricks and bring 'em out in company? Is this how to be a gentleman?"

Renzi's face set. "You're being obnoxious, my friend," he said softly.

"An' I'm gettin' sick o' your word-grubbin' ways! You're no frien' if all you can say is—"

Renzi turned on his heel. "Nicholas! I—I didn't mean t' say . . ." Renzi stopped. Kydd's hand strayed to his friend's shoulder but there was no response: Renzi merely turned, folded his arms and looked coldly at him. "I've been thinkin' a lot, Nicholas. About who I am, is the short of it." He lifted his chin obstinately. "Afore now I've been proud t' be a man-o'-war's man. Life f'r me has been simple an' true. Now I've gone aft it's all gone ahoo. I've lost m' bearings—an' all my friends."

"Do I take it that you still wish to be an officer?"

Kydd looked away for long moments. "Nicholas, you may account me proud or stubborn—but I will not be a tarpaulin to pity f'r his plain ways. An officer left t' one side when it comes to society an' promotion. Gentlemen officers laugh at the poor sot behind his back—gets a-fuddle wi' drink ashore 'cos he don't know what t' say. I'd rather be cream o' the shit than shit o' the cream, damn it."

Renzi winced. "You may regret turning your back on fortune."

"Did I say I was? I just don't know, is all."

Renzi coughed gently. "Possibly I am in no small measure to blame in this, dear fellow, but still I feel there is only one logical course, and one you seem to have already rejected. For as long as it will take, you must apply your best and most sincere endeavours to fitting yourself out for a gentleman officer—in look, word and deed. Then, and only then, you may take your rightful place in society, my friend."

At Kydd's moody silence Renzi insisted on an answer. "I'll think on it," was all he could achieve.

They were heading north to where the Labrador current from the icy fastness of the polar region met the unseen river of warm water driving up from the Caribbean, the Gulf Stream. Such a confluence was highly likely to result in the navigator's nightmare: fog.

Ahead there were several days of slow sailing across the mouth of the great St Lawrence before they made the shallower waters of the Grand Banks, then the doubling of Cape Race for St John's and landfall.

The Halifax-bound leaver division of the convoy had parted, and now the convoy was mainly smaller ships, bringing out supplies for the important cod fishery, with some larger vessels who would touch at St John's before making south for the United States. Kydd knew them all by sight now, and it would be strange after a month and a half of ocean travelling when their familiar presence was no longer there.

With the wind dropping all the time, the seas lost their busy ruckling of the long, easy swell. There was hardly a gurgle or a splash from the ships' languorous sliding through the grey water. Quite different from the fetid heat and glassy calms of the doldrums, this was simply the removal of energy from the sea's motion.

A sudden cry came from the masthead lookout. "*Saaail hoooo!* Sail t' the nor'ard, standin' towards!"

A distinct stir of interest livened the decks. This was much too early for the sloops and gunboats of St John's they were to meet, and a single sail would be bold to challenge a ship-of-the-line.

"My duty to the captain, and I would be happy to see him on deck," the officer-of-the-watch, Adams, told his messenger, but it was not necessary. Houghton strode on to the quarterdeck, grim-faced.

"You'd oblige me, Mr Kydd, should you go aloft and let me know what you see."

Kydd accepted a telescope from Adams and swung up into the rigging, feeling every eye on him. His cocked hat fell to the deck as he went round the futtock shrouds—he would remember to go without it next time—and to the main topmast top, joining the lookout who politely made room for him.

"Where away?" Kydd asked, controlling his panting. Breaking the even line of the horizon was a tiny smudge of paleness against the grey—right in their path. He brought up the telescope. It was difficult to control: even in the calm sea the slow roll at this height was sufficient to throw off the sighting. He wedged himself against the topgallant mast, feet braced against the cross-trees, then got his first good look at the pale pyramid of sail head on. His heart jumped. The glass wandered and the small image blurred across.

"What do you see?" Houghton bellowed from below.

Kydd swept the telescope to each side of the pyramid. Nothing. Tantalisingly he caught brief glimpses of it, now getting sharper and larger, but there was never enough time to fix on it. He prepared to lean over to hail the deck, then noticed wan sunlight shafting down close to it. He would give it one last try.

A glitter of light moved across the sea towards it. He raised his telescope—and saw it transformed. "Deck *hooo!* An ice island!"

The whole incident had gone unnoticed by the convoy, for the height-of-eye of *Tenacious*'s lofty masts ensured she saw it well before any other, but all were able to take their fill of the majestic sight as they passed hours later. Up close, it was not all pure white: there were startling pale blues, greens and dirty blotches— and such a size! There was an awed silence along the decks as men came up to stare at the silent monster from the frozen north.

The wind died, leaving a lethargic swell and the ship creaking and groaning under a dull, pearly sky. While Houghton paced up and down in frustration, Kydd noticed one of the larger vessels of the convoy far to the leeward edge. As with all ships, her sails hung lifeless from her yards but for some reason she had none on her foremast, not even headsails. "Odd," he mused to the master. Then a signal jerked hastily aloft from her mizzen peak halliards. Without wind to spread the flags it was impossible to make out the message, but there was clearly activity on deck.

"Damn the fellow!" Houghton snapped. Virtually dead in the water, there was little *Tenacious* could do to investigate further.

"I thought so," the master said, seeing the dead white of a fogbank advancing stealthily in eddying wreaths that hugged the sea surface and eventually engulfed the ship in a blank whiteness. The muffled crump of two guns sounded from somewhere within the white barrier; in conjunction with the flags this was the agreed signal for distress.

Houghton stopped. All eyes turned towards him. They could not lie idle if there were souls in need of them.

"Away launch, if you please, Mr Pearce." He paused to consider. "A bo'sun's mate and ten men, and we'll have two carpenter's mates in with 'em—and pass the word for the surgeon."

He looked about the deck and caught Kydd's eye. "See what all the fuss is about, Mr Kydd. If the ship is at hazard of foundering and our men can save her, do so. Otherwise advise her master in the strongest terms that a King's ship is not to be troubled in this way." Kydd knew perfectly well why he had been selected for this duty—as the most junior officer, he would be the least missed if he were lost in the fog.

As the yardarm stay tackles were hooked on to the boat Houghton added, "Take an arms chest too, Mr Kydd." Some of the ships carried convicts for the defensive works in St John's.

Kydd went to his cabin and found his sword, part of the uniform and authority of a naval officer when boarding a strange vessel. Tysoe helped fasten the cross strap and buckle on his scabbard sling. "Nothing but a merchantman all ahoo." Kydd chuckled at the sight of his grave expression.

"Get a boat compass," Kydd told Rawson, as he came back on deck. Seamen tumbled into the big launch, then helped sway down the arms chest; there was no point in shipping mast and sails in the flat calm.

Rawson returned with a small wooden box with a four-inch compass set in gimbals. Kydd had the bearing of the hapless vessel and checked that the indication with the boat compass was good. This was handed down, and he watched Rawson go aboard the launch, correctly wearing his midshipman's dirk. Kydd then went down the side, last to board.

"Take the tiller, if y' please," Kydd told Rawson, taking his place in the sternsheets. The surgeon sat patiently on the opposite side. "Why, Mr Pybus, you haven't any medicines?" he said, seeing no bag or chest.

"Oh? You know what it is then I must treat? Wounds, inflamed callibisters, one of a dozen poxes? I tried to persuade these brave fellows to load aboard my dispensary entire but . . ."

Houghton called down loudly from the ship's side: "I'll thank you to lose no time, Mr Kydd!"

"Aye aye, sir," Kydd threw back. "Get moving!" he muttered to Rawson.

"Fend off forrard," Rawson ordered. "Out oars—give way, together." Kydd gently wedged the compass into the bottom of the boat, careful to ensure there was no iron near. Their lives might depend on it.

The men stretched out. It was a good three miles to pull but conditions were ideal: not any kind of sea and the air was cool and dry—it might be different in the fogbank. Kydd saw that Thorn, the stroke oar, was pulling well, long and strong and leaning into it. He was a steady hand with a fine gift for ropework. Further forward was Poulden, who, Kydd vowed to himself, he would see as a petty officer in *Tenacious*.

Rawson stood with the tiller at his side, his eyes ahead. "Mr Rawson," Kydd said quietly, "you haven't checked your back bearing this last quarter-mile."

The youth flashed an enquiring glance astern at the diminishing bulk of *Tenacious*, and looked back puzzled.

Kydd continued mildly, "If we're runnin' down a steady line o' bearing, then we should fin' that where we came from bears exactly astern. If it doesn't, then . . ." At the baffled response Kydd finished, "Means that we're takin' a current from somewheres abeam. Then we have t' allow for it if we want to get back, cuffin." He had been checking surreptitiously for this very reason.

The white blankness of the fogbank approached and suddenly

they left a world with a horizon, a pale sun and scattered ships, and entered an impenetrably white one, where the sun's disc was no longer visible, its light wholly diffused and reduced to a weak twilight. Men's voices were muffled and a dank moisture lay on everything as a tiny beading of slippery droplets.

They pulled through the wreathing fog-smoke, Kydd making certain of their course—its reciprocal would lead them back to their ship. Paradoxically the heavy breathing of the men at the oars sounded both near yet far in the unpleasant atmosphere that was weighing heavy on his sleeves and coat and trickling down his neck from his hat.

"Sir?" Poulden cocked his head intently on one side. "Sir! I c'n hear a boat!"

"Oars!" snapped Kydd. The men ceased pulling. "Still! Absolute silence in the boat!" They lay quietly, rocking slightly. It was long minutes of waiting, with the cheerful gurgle and slap of water along the waterline an irritating intrusion. Men sat rigid, avoiding eyes, listening.

Then there *was* something. A distinct random thump, a bang of wood against wood and a barely synchronised squeaking, which could only be several oars in thole pins or rowlocks—and close.

It was probably innocent, but what boat would be abroad in these conditions without good reason? The sound faded, but just as Kydd was about to break the silence it started again somewhat fainter—but where? The swirling clammy white was a baffling sound trap, absorbing and reflecting, making guesses of direction impossible.

Kydd felt a stab of apprehension. "Break out the arms—I'll take th' tiller. Quickly!" he hissed.

The wooden chest emptied quickly. Cutlasses were handed along with a metallic slither, one or two tomahawks, six boarding pistols. Kydd saw that they were ready flinted and prayed that the gunner's party had them loaded. He drew his sword. The fine-edged weapon, which had seemed so elegant, now felt flimsy and insubstantial beside the familiar broad grey steel of a cutlass.

He laid the naked blade across his knees and experimentally worked the tiller. Rawson fingered his dirk nervously, but the surgeon lolled back with a bored expression. He had no weapon and, in reply to Kydd's raised eyebrows, gave a cynical smile.

Waiting for the men to settle their blades safely along the side, Kydd held up his hands for quiet once more. In the breathless silence, a drip of water from oars, the rustle of waves and an occasional creak were deafening. Kydd concentrated with every nerve. Nothing.

He waited a little longer, automatically checking that their heading remained true, then ordered quietly, "Oars, give way, together." The men swung into it and the bluff-bowed launch got under way again.

In one heart-stopping instant a boat burst into view, headed directly for them. In the same moment Kydd registered that it was hostile, that it was a French chaloupe, and that it had a small swivel gun in its bow.

His instincts took over. "Down!" he yelled, and pulled the tiller hard over. The swivel cracked loudly—Kydd heard two shrieks and felt the wind of a missile before the bow of the enemy boat thumped heavily into their own swinging forepart. French sailors, their faces distorted with hatred, took up their weapons and rose to their feet in a rush to board.

The launch swayed as the British responded, snarls and curses overlaid with challenging bellows as they reached for their own weapons in a tangle of oars and blood. Pistols banged, smoke hung in the still air. One Frenchman collapsed floppily, his face covered with blood and grey matter; another squealed and dropped his pistol as he folded over.

It was the worst form of sea warfare, boat against boat, nothing but rage and butchery until one side faltered.

An arm came out to grasp the French gunwale and pull it alongside. A tomahawk thudded across the fingers, which tumbled obscenely away. "Get th' bastards!" Kydd roared, waving his sword towards the enemy.

The boats came together, oars splintering and gouging, enemy opponents within reach. The furious clash and bite of steel echoed in the fog. Kydd's sword faced a red-faced matelot flailing a curved North African weapon. The smash of the blade against his sword numbed Kydd's wrist, but the man triumphantly swept it up for a final blow, leaving his armpit exposed. Kydd's lighter steel flashed forward and sank into the soft body. The man dropped with an animal howl.

There was an enraged bellow and a large dark-jowled man shouldered his way into his place, a plain but heavy cutlass in his hand. His face was a rictus of hatred and his first lunge was a venomous stab straight to the eyes. Kydd parried, but the weight of the man's weapon told, and Kydd took a ringing blow to the side of the head.

The man drew back for another strike. He held his weapon expertly, leaving no opening for Kydd. The next blow came, smashing across, and Kydd's awkward defence did not stop a bruising hit above his hip. He felt cold fear—the next strike might be mortal.

As the man stepped on to the gunwale he cunningly swept a low straight-arm stab at Kydd's groin and, at his hasty defence, jerked the blade up for a lethal blow to Kydd's head. Kydd's sword flew up to meet it, an anvil-like ringing and brutish force resulting in the weapon's deflection—and a sudden lightness in his hand.

Kydd looked down. His sword had broken a couple of inches from the hilt. The man gave a roar of triumph and jumped into the launch. Kydd backed away, flinging the useless remnant at him. Jostled by another fighting pair the man stumbled before he could land his final stroke. Kydd cast about in desperation and saw a bloodied cutlass lying in the bottom of the boat.

He wrenched it up, in the process taking a stroke from the Frenchman aimed again at the head, but Kydd's blade was now a satisfying weight in his hand and he'd kept the blow from landing. Fury building, he swung to face his assailant. The man paused, taken aback by Kydd's intensity.

Kydd went on to the attack with the familiar weapon. He smashed aside the man's strikes, landing solid, clanging hits. In the confined space it could not last. As he thrust the broad blade straight for the belly, Kydd brought one foot forward to the other. The man's cautious defence was what he wanted. As the man readied his own thrust, the spring in Kydd's heel enabled him to lunge forward inside the man's own blade, the cutlass drawing a savage line of blood on one side of his head.

The man recoiled, but met the side of the boat and fell against it. Mercilessly Kydd slashed out, his blade slithering along the top of his opponent's to end on the man's forearm. The Frenchman's cutlass fell as he clutched at his bloody wound.

"*Je me rends!*" he shouted hoarsely. Kydd's blade hovered at the man's throat, death an instant away. Then he lowered it.

"Down!" he snarled, gesturing. "Lie down!" The man obeyed. The blood mist cleared from Kydd's brain and he snatched a glance around him. As quickly as it had started the brutal fight was ending. In the launch the three or four Frenchmen who had boarded were dead or giving up, and the bulk of the British were in the chaloupe, forcing back the remainder. The end was not far away.

"Tell 'em t' lie down!" he yelled. "Don't let the bastards move an inch!"

High-pitched shouts came from the French boat; they were yielding. Kydd felt reason slowly return to cool his passions. He took a deep breath. "Secure the boats t'gether," he ordered, the bloodstained cutlass still in his hands.

His body trembled and he had an overpowering urge to rest, but the men looked to him for orders. He forced his mind to work. "Poulden, into th' Frogs' boat and load the swivel." The petty-officer gunner was nowhere to be seen—he'd probably not survived.

While Poulden clambered over the thwarts and found powder and shot, Kydd looked around. There was blood everywhere, but he was experienced enough in combat to know that just a pint looked mortal. The wounded men were being laid together in the widest part of the launch as Pybus climbed back in. When he caught Kydd's eyes on him, he defiantly handed over a toma-hawk—bloodied, Kydd noted.

At Poulden's call, the French were herded weaponless back into their chaloupe and the swivel brought round inside to men-ace the boat point-blank. "Hey, you, Mongseer!" Kydd's exasper-ated shout was lost on the sullen men in the boat. He turned to his own boat. "Any o' you men speak French?"

The baffled silence meant he would have to lose dignity in pantomime, but then he turned to the midshipman. "Rawson! Tell 'em they'll be hove overside if they make any kind o' false move." Let him make a fool of himself.

Kydd realised he was still clutching his cutlass, and laid it down, sitting again at the tiller. His hip throbbed and his head gave intermittent blinding stabs of pain; it was time to return to *Tenacious* and blessed rest. He would secure the Frenchy with a short towline; they could then row themselves close behind un-der the muzzle of the swivel. He would send another three men to stand by Poulden.

Pybus was busy with the men in the bottom of the boat. "So, we go home," Kydd said, searching around for the compass. "Now do ye remember what course . . ."

Ashen-faced, Rawson held out a splintered box and the ruins of a compass card. With an icy heart Kydd saw that their future was damned. The wall of dull white fog pressed dense and featureless wherever he looked, no hazy disc of sun, no more than a ripple to betray wave direction. All sense of direction had been lost in the fight and there was now not a single navigation indicator of even the most elementary form to ensure they did not lose themselves in the vast wastes of the Atlantic or end a broken wreck on the cold, lonely Newfoundland cliffs.

Kydd saw the hostility in the expressions of his men: they knew the chances of choosing the one and only safe course. He turned to Rawson. "Get aboard an' find the Frenchy's compass," he said savagely.

The midshipman pulled the boats together and clambered into the chaloupe. In the sternsheets the man Kydd had bested held up the compass. Rawson raised his hand in acknowledgement, and made his way aft. Then, staring over the distance at Kydd with a terrible intensity, the Frenchman deliberately dropped the compass box into the water just before Rawson reached him.

Disbelieving gasps were followed by roars of fury, and the launch rocked as men scrambled to their feet in rage. "We'll scrag the fucker! Get 'im!" Poulden fingered the swivel nervously: if they boarded he would no longer have a clear field of fire.

"Stand down, y' mewling lubbers!" Kydd roared. "Poulden! No one allowed t' board the Frenchy." He spotted Soulter, the quartermaster, sitting on the small transverse windlass forward. "Soulter, that's your division forrard," he said loudly, encompassing half the men with a wave. "You're responsible t' me they're in good fightin' order, not bitchin' like a parcel of old women."

"Sir?" The dark-featured Laffin levered himself above the level of the thwarts from the bottom boards where he had been treated for a neck wound.

"Thank 'ee, Laffin," Kydd said, trying to hide his gratitude. If it came to an ugly situation the boatswain's mate would prove invaluable.

"We'll square away now, I believe. All useless lumber over the side, wounded t' Mr Pybus." Smashed oars, splintered gratings and other bits splashed into the water.

"Dead men, sir?" There was a tremor in Rawson's voice.

Kydd's face went tight. "We're still at quarters. They go over." If they met another hostile boat, corpses would impede the struggle.

After a pause, the first man slithered over the side in a dull splash. His still body drifted silently away. It was the British way in the heat of battle: the French always kept the bodies aboard in the ballast shingle. Another followed; the floating corpse stayed with them and did not help Kydd to concentrate on a way out of their danger. The fog swirled pitilessly around them.

"Is there any been on th' Grand Banks before?" Kydd called, keeping his desperation hidden.

There was a sullen stirring in the boat and mutterings about an officer's helplessness in a situation, but one man rose. "I bin in the cod fishery once," he said defensively. Kydd noted the absence of "sir."

"Report, if y' please." The man scrambled over the thwarts. "This fog. How long does it last?"

The man shrugged. "Hours, days—weeks mebbe." No use, then, in waiting it out. "Gets a bit less after dark, but don't yez count on it," he added.

"What depth o' water have we got hereabouts?" It might be possible to cobble together a hand lead for sounding, or to get information on the sea-bed. He vaguely remembered seeing on the chart that grey sand with black flecks turned more brown with white pebbles closer to the Newfoundland coast.

"Ah, depends where we is—fifty, hunnerd fathoms, who knows?"

There was nowhere near that amount of line to be found in the boat. Kydd could feel the situation closing in on him. "Er, do you ever get t' see th' sun?"

"No. Never do—like this all th' time." The man leaned back, regarding Kydd dispassionately. It was not his problem. "Y' c'n see the moon sometimes in th' night," he offered cynically.

The moon was never used for navigation, to Kydd's knowledge, and in any case he had no tables. There was no avoiding the stark fact that they were lost. There were now only two choices left: to drift and wait, or stake all on rowing in a random direction. The penalty on either was a cold and lengthy death.

"We got oars, we get out o' this," muttered one sailor to stroke oar. There were sufficient undamaged oars to row four a side, more than needed; but the comment crystallised Kydd's thinking.

"Hold y'r gabble," Kydd snapped. "We wait." He wasn't prepared to explain his reasons, but at the very least waiting would buy time.

The fog took on a dimmer cast: dusk must be drawing in. Now they had no option but to wait out the night. Danger would come when the cold worked with the damp of the fog and it became unendurable simply to sit there.

In the chaloupe the French sat tensely, exchanging staccato bursts of jabber—were they plotting to rise in the night? And now in the launch his men were talking among themselves, low and urgent.

He could order silence but as the dark set in it would be unenforceable. And it might cross their minds to wait until it was fully dark, then fall upon Kydd and the others, claiming they had been killed in the fight. The choices available to Kydd were narrowing to nothing. He gripped the tiller, his glare challenging others.

For some reason the weight of his pocket watch took his notice. He'd bought it in Falmouth, taken by the watchmaker's claims of accuracy, which had been largely confirmed by the voyage so far. He took it out, squinting in the fading dusk light. Nearly seven by last local noon. As he put it back he saw derisive looks, openly mocking now.

Night was stealing in—the fog diffused all light and dimmed it, accelerating the transition, and soon they sat in rapidly increasing darkness.

"All's well!" Laffin hailed loyally.

"Poulden?" Kydd called.

"Sir." The man was fast becoming indistinct in the dimness.

As if to pour on the irony the dull silver glow of a half-moon became distinguishable as the fog thinned a little upward towards the night sky. If only . . .

Then two facts edged from his unconscious meshed together in one tenuous idea, so fragile he was almost afraid to pursue it. But it was a chance. Feverishly he reviewed his reasoning—yes, it might be possible. "Rawson," he hissed. "Listen to this. See if you c'n see a fault in m' reckoning."

There was discussion of southing, meridians and "the day of her age" and even some awkward arithmetic—but the lost seamen heard voices grow animated with hope. Finally Kydd stood exultant. "Out oars! We're on our way back, lads."

They broke free of the fogbank to find the convoy still becalmed, and away over the moonlit sea the silhouette of a 64-gun ship-of-the-line that could only be *Tenacious*.

A mystified officer-of-the-watch saw two man-o'-war boats

hook on as the missing Kydd came aboard. At the noise, the captain came out on deck. "God bless my soul!" Houghton said, taking in Kydd's wounds and empty sword scabbard.

"Brush with th' enemy, sir," Kydd said, as calmly as he could. "Compass knocked t' flinders, had to find some other way back."

"In fog, and at night? I'd be interested to learn what you did, Mr Kydd."

"Caused us quite some puzzling, sir, but I'll stake m' life that Mr Rawson here would be very pleased to explain th' reasoning."

Rawson started, then said smugly, "Oh, well, sir, we all knows that f'r any given line o' longitude—the meridian, I mean—the moon will cross just forty-nine minutes after the sun does, and falls back this time for every day. After that it's easy."

"Get on with it, then."

"Well, sir, we can find the moon's southing on any day by taking the day of her age since new, and multiplying this by that forty-nine. If we then divide by sixty we get our answer—the time in hours an' minutes after noon when she's dead in the south, which for us was close t' eight o' clock. Then we just picked up our course again near enough and—"

Houghton grunted. "It's as well Mr Kydd had such a fine navigator with him. You shall take one of my best clarets to the midshipmen's berth." Unexpectedly, the captain smiled. "While Mr Kydd entertains me in my cabin with his account of this *rencontre*."

CHAPTER 5

THE NEWFOUNDLAND CONVOY was now safely handed over off St John's, along with *Viper* and *Trompeuse,* the ship signalling distress in the fog missing, presumed lost. *Tenacious* hauled her wind to sail south alone to land her French prisoners and join the fleet of the North American station in Halifax.

As they approached there was a marked drop in temperature; chunks of broken ice were riding the deep Atlantic green of the sea and there was a bitter edge to the wind. Thick watch-coats, able to preserve an inner retreat of warmth in the raw blasts of an English winter, seemed insubstantial.

Landfall was made on a low, dark land. It soon resolved to a vast black carpeting of forest, barely relieved by stretches of grey rock and blotches of brown, a hard, cold aspect. Kydd had studied the charts and knew the offshore dangers of the heavily indented rock-bound coast flanking the entrance to Halifax.

"I'm advising a pilot, sir," the master said to the captain.

"But have you not sailed here before?" Houghton's voice was muffled by his grego hood, but his impatience was plain: a pilot would incur costs and possibly delay.

Hambly stood firm. "I have, enough times t' make me very respectful. May I bring to mind, sir, that it's less'n six months past we lost *Tribune,* thirty-four, within sight o' Halifax—terrible night, only a dozen or so saved of three hundred souls . . ."

While *Tenacious* lay to off Chebucto Head, waiting for her pilot, Kydd took in the prospect of land after so many weeks at sea. The shore, a barren, bleached, grey-white granite, sombre under the sunless sky, appeared anything but welcoming. Further into the broad opening there was a complexity of islands, and then, no doubt, Halifax itself.

The pilot boarded and looked around curiously. "Admiral's in Bermuda still," he said, in a pleasant colonial drawl. "Newfy convoy arrived and he not here, he'll be in a right taking."

Houghton drew himself up. "Follow the motions of the pilot," he instructed the quartermaster of the conn.

With a south-easterly fair for entry, HMS *Tenacious* passed into a broad entrance channel and the pilot took time to point out the sights. "Chebucto Head—the whole place was called Chebucto in the old days." The ship gathered way. "Over yonder," he indicated a hill beyond the foreshore, "that's what we're callin' Camperdown Hill, after your mighty victory. Right handy for taking a line of bearing from here straight into town."

Running down the bearing, he drew their attention to the graveyard of *Tribune*. Up on rising ground they saw the raw newness of a massive fortification. "York Redoubt—and over to starb'd we have Mr McNab's Island, where the ladies love t' picnic in summer."

The passage narrowed and they passed a curious spit of land, then emerged beyond the island to a fine harbour several miles long and as big as Falmouth. Kydd saw that, as there, a southerly wind would be foul for putting to sea, but at more than half a mile wide and with an ebb tide it would not be insuperable.

Tenacious rounded to at the inner end of the town, there to join scores of other ships. Her anchors plummeted into the sea, formally marking the end of her voyage.

• • •

"Gentlemen," Houghton began, "be apprised that this is the demesne of Prince Edward, of the Blood Royal. I go now to pay my respects to His Royal Highness. I desire you hold yourselves ready, and when the time comes, I expect my officers to comport themselves with all the grace and civility to be expected of a King's officer in attendance on the civil power."

The wardroom took the orders with relish. Every port had its duties of paying and returning calls; some were more onerous than others, with entertainments that varied from worthy to spirited, but this promised to be above the usual expectation.

For Kydd it would be high society as he had never dreamed of. Receptions, royal dinners, lofty conversations. All grand and unforgettable. But would he be able to carry it through like a true gentleman? Just how could *he* strut around as though born to it? It was daunting—impossible.

Soon the wardroom and spaces outside became a beehive of activity with servants blacking shoes, boning sword scabbards, polishing decorations, and distracted officers finding deficiencies in their ceremonials. The ship, however, lay claim to attention first: dockyard stores brought from England were hoisted aboard lighters and taken in charge, and a detachment of the 7th Royal Fusiliers came aboard to escort the regimental pay-chest ashore.

Fore and aft, *Tenacious* was thoroughly cleaned down, then put in prime order: the cable tiers were lime whitewashed, brick-dust and rags were taken to the brasswork, and cannon were blackened to a gloss with a mixture of lamp-black, beeswax and turpentine. Bryant took a boat away and pulled slowly round the ship, bawling up instructions that had the yards squared across exactly, one above the other.

Then the first invitations came. The captain disappeared quickly, and Pringle, who had old friends in Halifax, vanished as soon as he was decently able, accompanied by Lieutenant Best. The others prepared to find their own way ashore.

"Spit it out, man!" Adams demanded. The note handed in by a messenger was addressed to Renzi, who gravely announced to the wardroom that it seemed both himself and Lieutenant Kydd were invited to the home of the commissioner for lands, Mr Lawrence Greaves.

"Ah, as this eminent gentleman no doubt wishes to honour *Tenacious* in the proper form," said Adams smoothly, "it would be seemly, therefore, that a more senior officer be present. As it happens, gentlemen, I shall be at leisure . . ."

The boat landed them next to the careening wharf where a carriage waited. The stone steps of the landing-place were reasonably dry, but when they moved forward the hems of their boat-cloaks brushed the snow-mush.

On leaving the dockyard area they turned north, away from the town, and had their first glimpses of a new land. Kydd marvelled at the rugged appeal of the snow-patched raw slopes, the countless spruce and jack-pine—and the silence.

At their destination a gravel track led to a mansion, and as they drew up their Falmouth acquaintance came to the door. "This is most kind in you," Renzi said, with a bow. "May I present Lieutenant Gervase Adams, sir, who cannot be denied in his desire to learn more of your remarkable realm."

Greaves acknowledged him with a bow and slight smile. "Calm seas and a prosperous voyage indeed, gentlemen. Your brisk action at the outset of our voyage has been particularly remarked."

They settled inside by the large fire. "Calibogus?" Greaves offered. At the puzzled looks he smiled, "A Nova Scotian cure for the wind's chill—spruce beer stiffened with rum. I believe we will have King's calibogus, which is taken hot, and is a sovereign remedy."

Mrs Greaves joined them. "To an English eye, our country

may appear outlandish, gentlemen, but to us it is an Arcadia indeed," she said proudly.

"With the fisheries to bring wealth and substance to your being," Renzi replied.

"The cod kingdom you will find in the north, in Newfoundland. Here we glory in trade—you have seen our convoys, hundreds of ships and sailing almost every month . . ."

"Such a crowd of shipping—all from Nova Scotia?" Adams asked, puzzled.

"Ah, no, sir," Greaves said. "This is the trade of the North American continent—not only Canada but the United States as well. The seas are alive with privateers and other vermin, and without a navy of their own Cousin Jonathan likes to consign his goods here for safe passage across the ocean."

Renzi rubbed his hands as the generous pinewood fire blazed, warming and cheering. "This is spring," he ventured. "I believe in truth it may be said your winter is worse?"

"It can be a sad trial at times," Greaves replied, "but when the snows come and the great St Lawrence freezes a hundred miles from bank to bank, Halifax with its fine harbour is always free for navigation."

His wife added gravely, "Last winter was dreadful, very severe. Our roads were impossible with ice and snow and we ran uncommonly short of the daily necessaries—the Army could get no beef and the common people were being found frozen in the street! Goodness knows how the maroons survive."

In his surprise Kydd forgot himself and interjected, "Maroons—you mean black men fr'm Jamaica?"

"Yes! Can you conceive? They were in rebellion and given settlement here. It quite touches my heart to see their poor dark faces among all the snow and icy winds." Kydd remembered his times in the West Indies as Master of the King's Negroes. Could even the noble and powerful Juba have survived in this wilderness?

"To be sure, m' dear!" Greaves said. "Yet in their Maroon Hall you will see some of our best workers, and you remember that when they were offered passage back to Africa, only a few accepted. In my opinion they're much to be preferred to that homeless riff-raff on the waterfront."

Adams stirred restlessly and leaned forward. "The Prince. How do you find having a prince o' the blood among you all?"

"A fine man. He has done much for Halifax, I believe."

"Did not King George, his father, send him here into exile, and is he not now living in sin with his mistress Julie?"

"We do not speak of such matters," Greaves said coldly. "When His Royal Highness arrived, this place was raw and contemptible. Now it has stature and grace, with buildings worthy of a new civilisation, and is strong enough I fancy to secure all Canada from a descent."

"Sir, I didn't mean . . ."

"Do you care to see the town, perhaps? We have time to make a visit and return for dinner."

"You are very obliging, sir."

Halifax consisted of one vast rampart, an imposing hill overlooking the harbour. It sloped down to the shoreline, with a massive fortification dominating the crest—the citadel with its enormous flag. There, the party stepped out to admire the view. Greaves had provided fur coats against the chill bluster of the winds, which under lead-coloured skies intermittently drove icy spicules of snow against Kydd's skin. He shivered at the raw cold.

Around them was broad open ground, cleared to give the citadel a good field of fire. The vegetation emerging from snow-melt was bleached a drab light-brown and mud splashes showed where others had walked before. But the view was impressive: the expanse of harbour below stretched out in the distance, the sea a sombre dark grey. Model-like ships lay at anchor, black and still. And the rugged country, blanketed by the monotonous low black-green of subarctic forest, extended like a dark shadow as far as the eye could see.

Kydd caught Renzi's eye. His friend was rapt: "This is a land like no other!" he breathed. "One we might say is in perpetual thrall to the kingdom of the north. There is an unknown boreal fastness here that lies for countless miles to the interior, which has its own bleak beauty that dares men . . ."

Greaves smiled as they tramped back to the carriage. "You could not be visiting us at a worse time of the year," he said, "after the snow, and before the green-up. You may find it hardly credible, but in no more than a month there will be delicate blooms of wild pear, and trees all along Argyle Street that will surprise you with the green of old England."

Just below the citadel the first buildings began, substantial, stone structures that would not have been out of place in England. The air was chill and raw but smoky from countless fires that promised warmth and company. "Now, there's a sight!" Adams said, with satisfaction, as they reached the town proper. Houses, shops, people, all the evidence of civilised living. The streets were rivers of mud and horse-dung but everywhere there were boardwalks to protect pedestrians' feet.

After weeks of familiar faces at sea, the variety of passersby seemed exotic: ladies with cloaks and muffs picking their way delicately, escorted by their gentlemen; a muffin man shuffling along in sharp contrast to a pig-tailed ranger, half-Indian, with cradled long rifle and bundle. To Kydd's surprise sedan chairs toiled up the steep slope, a sight he had not seen since his youth.

"We do tolerably well in the matter of entertainments," Greaves murmured. "May I mention the Pontac, a popular coffee-house with quite admirable mutton pies, or Merkel's, if tea and plum cake is more to your taste?" At Adams's expression he added drily, "And, of course, there is Manning's tavern, which is well remarked for its ale and respectability."

"Sir, there is a service you may do us," Renzi said. "If you could indicate a chandlery or such that is able to outfit us in the article of cold-weather clothing . . ."

"That I can certainly do, and close by, at Forman's—you shall need my advice, I suspect." The emporium in question was well patronised, and they were met with curious looks from weather-worn men and capable-looking women. An overpowering smell lay on the air.

"Sea gear, if you please," Greaves told the assistant.

"Goin' north?" The broad Canadian twang was noticeable against Greaves's more English tones.

"He means to Newfoundland and the Arctic. Would this be so, do you think?"

"Not in a sail-of-the-line, I believe."

"Well, Capting, here in Forman's we has somethin' fer all hands. Aloft, it's tarred canvas th' best, but there's many prefers their rig less stiff sort o' thing, uses boiled linseed oil instead. An' regular seamen on watch always takes heavy greased home-spun under their gear as well."

He swung out a set of what seemed to be heavy dark leather gear. "Norsky fishermen swear by this'n." Selecting an impossibly sized mitten, he added, "Boiled wool, then felted—you don't fear fish-hooks in the dark wi' this!"

Watching their faces for a reaction, he chose another garment. "Er, you gents are goin' to be more satisfied wi' these, I guess." The jacket was of heavy cloth, but much more flexible. However, with every proud flourish he made, a rank animal miasma arose, catching at the back of the throat. "See here," the assistant said, opening the garment and revealing pale, yellowish smears along the seams. "This is guaranteed t' keep you warm 'n' dry. Prime bear grease!"

Forewarned by *Lady Jane* schooner, Halifax prepared for the arrival of the North American Squadron from its winter quarters in Bermuda. As if in ironic welcome, the morning's pale sun withdrew, lowering grey clouds layered the sky with bleak threat and tiny flakes appeared, whirling about the ship. Kydd shuddered. Obliged to wear outer uniform he had done his best to cram anything he could find beneath it, but the spiteful westerly chilled him to the bone.

Long before the squadron hove in sight, regular thuds from the outer fortresses marked its approach. Six ships in perfect line finally emerged around the low hump of George's Island, indifferent to the weather.

"*Resolution,* seventy-four," someone said, pointing to the leading ship's admiral's flag floating high on the mast. The rest of the conversation was lost in the concussion and smoke of saluting guns as the two biggest ships present, *Resolution* and *Tenacious,* acknowledged each other's presence, then deigned to notice the citadel's grand flag.

Just as her first anchor plunged into the sea the flagship's launch smacked into the water, and sails on all three masts vanished as one, drawing admiring comments from *Tenacious*'s quarterdeck.

Kydd tensed, aware of a warning glance from Bryant standing next to the captain, but he was ready. In *Resolution,* the white ensign at her mizzen peak descended; simultaneously, in *Tenacious,* the huge red ensign of an independent ship on its forty-foot staff aft dipped. In its place, in time with the flagship, a vast pristine white ensign arose, signifying the formal accession of the 64 to the North American Squadron.

The snow thickened, large flakes drifting down endlessly and obscuring Kydd's sight of the flagship. If he should miss anything . . .

A three-flag hoist shot up *Resolution*'s main; Kydd anxiously pulled out his signal book, but Rawson knew without looking. "'All captains!'" he sang out gleefully, almost cherubic in his many layers of clothing.

Kydd hurried down to the quarterdeck but Houghton had anticipated the summons and was waiting at the entry port, resplendent in full dress and sword. His barge hooked on below the side-steps and, snowflakes glistening on his boat-cloak, he vanished over the side.

Duty done, *Tenacious* settled back to harbour routine. The snow began to settle. Deck fitments and spars, brightwork and blacked cannon, all were now topped with a damp white.

As expected, "All officers" was signalled at eleven. Boats put off from every English man-o'-war in the harbour to converge on the flagship; the officers were in full dress and sword, with a white ensign to denote their presence.

It was the pomp and majesty of a naval occasion, which Kydd had seen many times before but from the outside. He stood nervously with the others as they were welcomed cordially by the flag-lieutenant on the quarterdeck and shown below by a serious-faced midshipman.

The great cabin of *Resolution* extended the whole width of the deck; inside a large, polished table was set for dinner with crystal and silver. Kydd, overawed by the finery, took an end chair.

Next to him a lieutenant nodded amiably, and Kydd mumbled

a polite acknowledgement. The hum of conversation slackened and stopped as Vice Admiral of the White, George Vandeput, commander-in-chief of the North American Squadron, came into the cabin.

The massed scraping of chairs was deafening as the officers rose, murmuring a salutation. "D'ye sit, gentlemen," he called, finding the central chair. He whirled the skirts of his frock coat around it as he sank into it, and beamed at the company.

"I'd be obliged at y'r opinion of this Rhenish," he said affably, as decanters and glasses made their appearance.

Kydd's glass was filled with a golden wine that glittered darkly in the lanthorn light. He tasted it: a harder, mineral flavour lay beneath the flowery scent. Unsure, he sipped it again.

Vandeput looked down the table but most officers remained prudently noncommittal. Renzi sat three places along, holding his glass up to the light and sniffing appreciatively. "A fine workmanlike Rheingau," he said, "or possibly a Palatinate, though not as who should say a Spätlese."

The cabin fell quiet as several commanders and a dozen senior lieutenants held their breath at a junior lieutenant offering an opinion on his admiral's taste in wine, but Vandeput merely grunted. "Ah, yes. I feel inclined t' agree—a *trocken* it is not, but you'll excuse me in th' matter of taste. Its origin is a Danish prize whose owner seemed not t' value the more southerly whites."

Renzi nodded and the admiral shot him an intent look, then steepled his fingers. "Gentlemen, f'r those newly arrived for the season, a welcome." He held attention while he gazed around the cabin, recognising some, politely acknowledging others. "We have some fresh blood here following our famous victory at Camperdown so I'm taking the opportunity t' meet you all. The North American Squadron—often overlooked these days, but of crucial importance, I declare. The convoy of our mast-ships alone justifies our being. Where would the sea service be without its masts and spars? An' half the world's trade flows through this port, including the West Indies, of course."

Kydd was transfixed by the glitter of the admiral's jewelled star, the gold facings of his coat, the crimson sash, which were grand and intimidating, but Vandeput's pleasant manner and avuncular shock of white hair set him almost at his ease.

"Therefore our chief interest is in the protection of this trade. I rather fancy we won't be troubled overmuch by French men-o'-war—rather, it's these damn privateers that try my patience. Yet I would not have you lose sight of the fact that we are a fleet—to this end I require that every ship under my command acts together as one, concentrating our force when ordered, and for so doing you signal lieutenants shall be my very nerves."

A rustle of amusement passed around the table: the flagship's smartness was well marked and life would not be easy for these junior officers.

"We shall be exercising at sea in company as opportunities arise. I commend my signal instructions to you, with particular attention to be given to the signification of manoeuvres. My flag-lieutenant will be happy to attend to any questions later.

"I wish you well of your appointment to the North American Squadron, gentlemen, and ask that you enjoy the entertainment."

A buzz of talk began as the doors swung wide and dishes of food were brought in. Kydd was about to help himself to the potted shrimps when the stout officer next to him half stood over the biggest salver as its cover was removed. "Aha! The roast cod. This is worth any man's hungering. Shall you try it, sir?"

The fish was splendid—buttery collops of tender white, and Kydd forgot his duty until the officer introduced himself: "Robertson, second of the *Acorn*. Damn fine cook our admiral has, don't y' know?"

"Kydd, fifth o' *Tenacious*." He hesitated, but Robertson was more concerned with his fish, which was vanishing fast. "*Acorn*—the nine-pounder lying alongside?"

"Is her," Robertson agreed. "I suggest only the chicken pie afore the main, by the way. Ol' Georgie always serves caribou, an' I mean to show my appreciation in spades."

"May I?" Kydd had noticed the disappearing fish and was pleased to have remembered his manners so far as to help him to a handsome-sized slice of cold chicken pie. The Rheingau was perfectly attuned to the cold food and his reserve melted a little. "Nine-pounder frigate—hard livin' indeed."

"Aye," Robertson said, his mouth full, "but better'n a ship-of-the-line."

"And how so?"

"Prize money, o' course. Ol' Georgie's no fool—sends us out all the days God gives after anything that floats, French, Spanish, Scowegian—even American, if we can prove she has a cargo bound for the enemy. If it's condemned in court, cargo 'n' all, then shares all round."

The rumours of caribou were correct, and to the accompaniment of a good Margaux, the dark flesh was tender with an extraordinary sweet wild meat flavour. Kydd sat back, satiated. Renzi was toying with a breast of spruce partridge while deep in serious talk with an older, lean-faced officer.

Kydd stole a look at the admiral: he was genially in conversation with a hard-looking officer to his left. Kydd wondered at the simple fact that he himself was sharing a meal with such august company.

"Wine with you, sir!" It was the officer opposite, who had not said much before.

Kydd held his glass forward. "Prize money b' the bucketful!" he toasted.

The other seemed restless. "That would be fine, sir, but while we're topping it the sybarite, others are fighting. And by that I mean winning the glory. There's no promotion to be gained by lying comfortably at two anchors in some quiet harbour—only in a right bloody battle." He held up his wine to the light and studied it gloomily. "To think it—we've been thrown out of the Med since last year, there've been descents on Ireland, and at home I hear Pitt has admitted the collapse and destruction of the coalition and none else in sight. We stand quite alone. Can things be much worse? I doubt it."

Kydd said stoutly, "I'm come fr'm the Caribbee and I can tell you, we've been takin' the French islands one b' one, and now the Spanish Main is ours. And who c'n doubt? The Mongseers have reached their limits, baled up in Europe tight as a drum. To the Royal Navy, gaol-keeper! And may she lose the keys!" But the officer remained grave and quiet. Kydd frowned. "Do ye doubt it, sir?" The wine was bringing a flush, but he didn't care; he seemed to be holding his own in this particular conversation.

With a weary smile the officer put down his glass. "I cannot conceive where you have been this last half-year that you have not in the least understood the motions of the French Directory—intrigues at the highest, or at the point of a bayonet, they have now secured the subjugation or acquiescence of the whole of the civilised world.

"They are arrogant, they care not who they antagonise, for in every battle they triumph, whole nations kneel at their bidding, and for what purpose? While these lie beaten, they have a mighty general, Buonaparte, who is ready to venture forth on the world! Mark my words, before this year's end there will be such a bursting forth by the French as will make the world stare!"

He leaned back in his chair and resumed his wine, looking reprovingly at Kydd. Deliberately, Kydd turned back to Robertson, who was now engrossed with the task of picking at a pretty corner dish. "Sweetbreads?" he mumbled, and offered the dish.

Kydd took one and tried to think of an intelligent remark to make. "The Americans'll be amused at our troubles wi' the French," he said hopefully.

Robertson raised his eyebrows. "Ah, not really, I think." He looked at Kydd curiously. "You must know they've done handsomely out o' this war—being neutral an' all, I mean. Can trade with any and all, if they can get away with it, o' course."

Kydd's blank look made him pause. "How long've you been made up, then?" he asked directly.

"Just this January," Kydd answered warily.

"Then I'd clap on more sail an' get as much o' this business hoisted aboard as you can. You're boarding officer an' take in a fat merchantman that the court decides is innocent, expect to explain yourself to the judge in damages!" He grinned broadly and turned to a pyramid of syllabubs.

The warm glow of the wine fell away. These men were of a different origin, brought up from the cradle with discernment, education, the talk of politics continually around them. How could he conceivably claim to be one of them? Kydd stole a look at Renzi, holding forth elegantly on some exemplary Greek, then at the admiral, listening with his head politely inclined to a fine story from a young lieutenant, and finally at the officer opposite, who was now yarning with his neighbour.

Kydd closed the door of his cabin. There was nobody in the wardroom, but the way he felt he did not want to see another face. His experience of the previous night had left him heartsick, unable to deny any longer that trying his hardest was not enough: he just did not belong in this society. He was a deep-sea sailor, true, but as an officer he was a fish out of water; talk of fox hunting and the Season was beyond him, the implications for his acceptance by them only too clear.

He knew well what was in store: others who had "come aft by the hawse" had found their place—as a tarpaulin officer. Known in the Navy as characters, they were bluff, hard on the men they knew so well and had no pretensions to gentility or learning. Utterly reliable at sea, they were outcasts in polite social situations, and usually took refuge in hearty drinking. As for promotion and ambition, improbable.

Was this his fate? He had tasted the sweets of a higher life with Renzi—their leisurely talking of philosophers and logic under a tropic moon, the dream-like times in Venice; the dinner with Renzi's brother in Jamaica had been a taste of what should be, but now . . .

Thought of his friend brought with it a wave of desolation. Renzi was in his element now, clearly headed for the highest levels and thoroughly enjoying his change of fortune. He had aided Kydd as much as he could, teaching him the forms and appearances, but there was no help for it. This was not a matter of learning the ropes, it was breeding.

His depression deepened: logic would say—and Renzi was a servant to logic—that in truth his friend no longer needed a sea companion to lighten his intellectual existence and ease his self-imposed exile. Now Renzi had the chaplain to dispute with whenever he felt inclined, Kydd thought bitterly. All told, perhaps it would have been more merciful if Kydd had never known another existence—had never encountered Renzi, even.

He felt despair and flung open the door for Tysoe. When his servant did not immediately appear he roared his name.

Tysoe arrived, his hands showing evidence that he had been at work boning Kydd's best shoes. He wore a perfectly composed expression. "Sir?"

"Fetch me one o' my clarets."

Tysoe's eyes flickered. "Will that be two glasses, sir?"

Kydd coloured. "No, damn y'r eyes—just th' one!"

When it came, he snatched bottle and glass, slammed his door, then splashed the wine into the glass, hands shaking with emotion. He drank hard, and it steadied him. He stared morosely at the ship's side in his tiny cabin, forcing himself to be calm. "Tysoe! Another bottle an' you can turn in f'r the night," he shouted.

It was obvious now. There was only one cause for his despondency: loneliness. An outsider in the wardroom, he was cut off from the rough, warm camaraderie before the mast that he knew so well. Now he had no one. And Renzi would be moving on soon, probably taken up as a flag-lieutenant.

The second bottle was half-empty already, but Kydd's pain was easing. He allowed the warm memory of Kitty to return: she had stood by him during the terrible days of the Nore mutiny—she had a strength he'd rarely seen in a woman. With her, he might have . . . There was a lump in his throat and he gulped another glass. If only she were here, if only . . .

He stared at the glass in his hand. Already he was turning into what he dreaded to be—a tarpaulin officer. Through self-pity he was sliding down the same slope as they all must have: to find acceptance they had turned themselves into a patronised caricature, then found a steady friend in the bottle.

"God rot me, but I'll not be one." His harsh croak in the confined space startled him. He seized the bottle and pushed it away. So shameful was the thought that he lurched to his feet and threw open the door, clutching the bottle by its neck. The wardroom was still deserted, all others no doubt gone ashore together.

"Tysoe!" he called. The man came quickly and silently and Kydd knew why: he had conceived it his duty to stand by his master while he got helplessly drunk, then tumble him into his cot.

The realisation hurt Kydd: it bore on his spirit that others would now be making allowances for him, and he stiffened. "If ye'd like the res' o' the wine . . ." He awkwardly held out the bottle. "I shan't need any more."

Renzi was not at breakfast but Kydd found him later in the day in his cabin. "The admiral plans to visit his realm in Newfoundland," he said, "and for some unaccountable reason he wishes me to accompany him. A vexation—if you remember I planned to join the Shiptons for whist." He seemed preoccupied. "There will be no sea exercises with the admiral in Newfoundland counting his cod, dear fellow. If you can bear to leave your signal books, why do you not see more of the country? You really should get away more."

Kydd murmured something, watching his friend rummaging in his chest.

Renzi looked up, shamefaced. "I'd be obliged should you lend me a shirt or two, Tom—there will be a quantity of social occasions in Newfoundland, I've heard." A surge of feeling surprised Kydd with its intensity as he fetched them, but he said nothing. A stubborn pride still remained, which would not allow him to burden Renzi with the problem.

Renzi left with a hasty wave. Pringle emerged from his cabin the picture of military splendour, a pair of pigskin gloves in one hand, a swagger stick in the other. He noticed Kydd, gave a noncommittal grunt, then he, too, strode away. Servants came to clear the afternoon clutter, looking at Kydd warily. There was nothing for it but to retire to his cabin.

Pride would not let him inveigle himself into another's invitation—besides, he might find himself in a situation that would end in his making a spectacle of himself again. He burned with embarrassment at the recollection of his conversation at table. What could they think of an officer as crassly ignorant as any foremast hand?

The wardroom was clear again; he paced about, morose. A book lay on the rudder-head. He wandered over idly and pulled it out: *Observations on the Current War, by an Officer of Rank.* It was full of maps and diagrams, painstakingly hatched with tiny lines and minuscule lettering. It covered in great detail every military campaign of the war so far.

He had never had an interest in the interminable toing and froing that seemed to be the lot of the Army, but this book had an introductory treatment for each theatre of war, which sounded robust and useful. His spirits rose a little. This at least was something constructive he could do—learn some facts to ward off assumptions of ignorance.

It was a workmanlike book, and the treatment was clear and direct but, even so, talk of why the Duke of York had considered the Austrian Netherlands worth a hopeless campaign was baffling, mainly because it assumed a degree of familiarity with the political background that he did not have.

He persevered, going to each introduction in turn and stitching together a basic understanding on which he could hang his facts. Yet as he did so, he found his attention held by the implications of what he was reading: armies and trade—expressions of a nation's economic strength, but vulnerable to the quixotic twists of fate and man's plotting.

It was a new experience for Kydd. He read on until a fundamental realisation stole over him. He set down the book and stared into space. Until now he had unconsciously thought of his ship as a boundary to his world. He could step ashore in foreign parts and see sights impossible for most, but he could always return to his snug little world and sail away. There, the dangers of the sea and the malice of the enemy were reality.

Now it was all changed. Events in one part of the world could reach out and touch an officer, have grave military and legal consequences if a wrong decision was made. They might conceivably damn his career or even cause an international incident. In essence, an officer dealt with the wider world; the common seaman did not.

"Mr Kydd!" Bryant's bellow reached effortlessly from the quarterdeck to the fo'c'sle where Kydd had taken refuge from the marines drilling loudly on the poop-deck under an enthusiastic Lieutenant Best.

Hastily Kydd made his way aft. "I've been called away, damn it, an' just when we're due a parcel o' new men. Should be coming aboard this hour. Bring 'em aboard, if y' please, and take all the able-bodied but, mark this, send all the rubbish back—we don't want 'em, right?"

"Aye aye, sir. Are they pressed men?"

"Not all. We've got a press warrant out, but most o' these are merchant jacks, tired of winterin', and odd sods off the streets. We can be satisfied with a dozen. I'll rate 'em when I get back this afternoon." Bryant jammed on his hat and stalked off.

Kydd warned off a duty midshipman to desire the surgeon to hold himself in readiness, the purser to his slops and the boatswain to provide a holding crew. It was a well-worn routine: the need for men in any man-o'-war was crucial. Even if the ship was in first-class shape, battle-ready and stored, it was all a waste without men to work her. Kydd had no misgivings about what had to be done to achieve this.

"A King's Yard boat, sir," Rawson reported. The dockyard launch made its way out to them and, as it neared, Kydd leaned over the side to see what was being brought. Looking up at him were a scatter of winter-pale faces, some listless, others alert, some sunk in dejection. A stock collection—the seamen among them would show immediately: they would have no trouble with the side-steps and bulwark.

The mate-of-the-watch took charge. It would not be seemly

for Kydd to appear until the men were inboard and assembled; he disappeared into the lobby.

It seemed so long ago, but into his mind, as clear as the day it had happened, came his own going aboard the old battleship *Duke William* as a pressed man, the misery, homesickness, utter strangeness. Now these men would face the same.

"New men mustered, sir."

Kydd tugged on his hat and emerged on to the quarterdeck, aware of all eyes on him. They were bunched together in a forlorn group near the mainmast. "Get them in a line, Mr Lawes," he ordered.

A more odd assortment of dress was difficult to imagine. Bearskin hats and well-worn animal-hide jackets, greasy-grey oily woollens and ragged trousers, even two with moccasins. More than one was stooped by ill-nourishment or age. Some, the ones standing alert and wary, with blank faces, carried well-lashed seaman's bags.

"I'll speak t' them now, Mr Lawes."

The shuffling and murmuring stopped. He stepped across to stand easily in front of them, waiting until he had their eyes. "My name's L'tenant Kydd. This is HMS *Tenacious*. We're a ship-of-the-line an' we're part of the North American Squadron, Admiral Vandeput."

Stony stares met him. The men were clearly resigned to a fate known to some, unknown to others.

"C'n I see the hands o' the volunteers?" A scatter of men signified. "You men get th' bounty in coin today, an' liberty later t' spend it. The rest . . ." Kydd continued: "When this war started, I was a pressed man, same as you." He paused for effect. It startled some, others remained wary. "Rated landman in a second rate. An' since then I've been t' the South Seas in a frigate, the Caribbean in a cutter and the Mediterranean in a xebec. I've got a handsome amount o' prize money and now I'm a King's officer.

So who's going t' say to me the Navy can't be th' place to be for a thorough-going seaman who wants t' better himself?

"Now, think on it. Should y' decide to serve King George and y'r country you could end up th' same. Give your names t' the first lieutenant as a volunteer this afternoon and tell him y' want to do well in the sea service o' the King and he'll give ye a good chance."

Kydd turned to Lawes. "Carry on, these men. Stand fast that one an' the two at the pinrail—we'll send 'em back. Rest go below to see the doctor." The men still had their eyes on Kydd, one in particular, a thick-set seaman, who lingered after the others.

"Good haul, I think." It was Bryant, watching them leave. "Surly-looking brute, the last. Shouldn't wonder if he's shipped for some very good reason."

The sun at last became visible through a pale cloud cover, a perceptible warmth on the skin, and Kydd's spirits rose. Ashore, he could make out a different green from the sombre green-black of the boreal forest, and he thought that the country might seem quite another in summer.

The captain left with the first lieutenant to call on the officers of York Redoubt, and a young lady whom Adams had taken up with demanded his constant presence. For now, Kydd decided, he would continue his acquaintance with war's wider canvas.

This time he prepared to take notes. Sitting at the wardroom table, his back to the stern windows, he picked up his book and resumed reading. He discovered that the thousand-year republic of Venice had been sacrificed in a cynical exchange between France and Austria and that the Corsican Napoleon Buonaparte must now be considered England's chief opponent.

It was truly astonishing how much of momentous significance to the world had happened since he had gone to sea—and to think that he had been unknowingly at the heart of these events. The evening drew in, the light faded, but he had found another book, more dog-eared and harder-going, which purported to be a treatment of the economic consequences of a world at war, and he set to.

He felt a small but growing satisfaction: this was one positive course he could take, and it was shaping into a workable aspiration in life. If he could not be a natural-born officer, at least he would be an informed one.

He became aware of a figure standing and looked up. It was Tysoe, cupping a small peg lamp that glowed softly with a clear, bright flame. "Thank 'ee, Tysoe—but does Mr Hambly know I have his lamp?" It was charged with spermaceti oil and used only for painstaking work at the charts.

"Sir, he will be informed of his generous assistance to you when he returns aboard."

Kydd inclined his head to hear better. "Er, what seems t' be afoot on the upper deck?" There had been odd thumpings and occasional cries, but nothing the mate-of-the-watch could not be relied on to deal with.

Tysoe bent to trim the lamp. "The hands, sir. They wish to dance and skylark." Kydd nodded. There were men aboard, visiting from other ships, the weather was clear and it would be odd if there was not some kind of glee going in the fo'c'sle. He laid down his book. Perhaps he should cast an eye over the proceedings.

Darkness had fallen, but it was easy to make out activity on the foredeck by the light of lanthorns hung in the rigging. A hornpipe was being performed beside the jeer bitts of the foremast. Kydd wandered forward unnoticed. The seaman was skilled, his feet flashing forward to slap back rhythmically, the rigid body twirling in perfect time, while his upper body, arms folded, remained perfectly rigid and his face expressionless.

The fiddler finished with a deft upward note and, with a laugh, took a pull at his beer. "Ben Backstay!" The call was taken up around the deck, and eventually a fine-looking seaman from another ship stepped into the golden light and struck a pose.

When we sail, with a fresh'ning breeze,
And landmen all grow sick, sir;
The sailor lolls with his mind at ease,
And the song and can go quick, sir.
Laughing here,
Quaffing there,
Steadily, readily,
Cheerily, merrily,
Still from care and thinking free
Is a sailor's life for me!

The violin gaily extemporised as cheers and roars delayed the next verse. There was no problem here: these were the core seamen of *Tenacious,* deep-sea sailors whose profession was the sea. They were the heart and soul of the ship, not pressed men or the refuse of gaols.

With a further burst of hilarity the singer withdrew to receive his due in a dripping oak tankard, and Kydd turned to go. Then a plaintive chord floated out, it hung—and a woman's voice sounded above the lessening chatter. "Sweet Sally, an' how her true love Billy Bowling was torn fr'm her arms an' pressed." A blonde woman, standing tall and proud, continued, "Sally's heart's near broken, she can't bear t' be parted—so she disguises as a foremast jack 'n' goes aboard that very night." Kydd moved closer: the woman resembled his lost Kitty.

Aboard my true love's ship I'll go,
And brave each blowing gale;
I'll splice, I'll tack, I'll reef, I'll row,

And haul with him the sail;
In jacket blue, and trousers too,
With him I'll cruise afar,
There shall not be a smarter hand
Aboard a man-o'-war.

Her voice was warm and passionate. Talk died away as she sang on. Kydd's mind took him back to other ships, other ports—and evenings such as this with his shipmates—when he'd had not a care in his heart.

She finished, but the memories she had aroused came on him in full flood, stinging his eyes. He became aware that faces were turned towards him, conversations dying away. A woman moved protectively towards her man and the expressions became dark, resentful.

Poulden came across. "Sir?" he demanded suspiciously.

These men had every right to their territory, little enough in a ship of war. And he had no right—he did not belong. "Er, just came t' hear the songs," he said weakly. "Rattlin' good singing, lads," he added, but it fell into a silence. "Please carry on," he said, louder.

The men looked at each other, then the seaman who had sung "Ben Backstay" got to his feet and stood purposefully under the lanthorns. He muttered an aside to the violinist and clutching a tankard launched loudly into:

To our noble Commander
His Honour and Wealth,
May he drown and be damn'd—

Singer and violinist stopped precisely in mid-note and looked at Kydd. Their point made, the duo continued:

—that refuses the Health;
Here's to thee Billy, honest an' true;
Thanks to the men who calls them his crew
An' while one is drinking, the other shall fill!

A girl sprang into the pool of light. "A sarabande!" she called. But Kydd had left.

CHAPTER 6

"WELL, I WISH YOU JOY of your voyage, gentlemen—unhappily I have a court-martial to attend and therefore shall not be with you." There was no mistaking the smug satisfaction in Bampton's tone. In the normal run of events the inbound convoy would have been met by one or two of the hard-working frigates, but this one was transporting the lieutenant-governor of New Brunswick and his family to take up his post and *Tenacious* had been deemed more suitable.

It seemed to Kydd that he was the only one looking forward to the sea-time. The weather had been miserable these past few days, cold and blustery, and although they would only be out a day or so at most, the general consensus was that it was an ideal time to snug down in harbour until better conditions returned.

Kydd had long ago realised that he was a "foul-weather jack"—one of those who revelled in the exhilaration and spectacle of stormy seas, racing clouds and the life-intensifying charge of danger. In this short voyage he knew they would probably not face a full-blown tempest but the thought of a lively experience at sea lifted his spirits.

Tenacious and *Ceres*, a 32-gun frigate belonging to the Newfoundland Squadron, proceeded to sea together. With the cliffs of Chebucto Head abeam, they braced up for the hard easterly beat to rendezvous with the convoy.

The weather was freshening: their bows met foam-streaked waves at an angle, dipping before them, then rearing up to smash them apart in explosions of white. Standing aft, Kydd felt the sheeting spray in his teeth. With canvas taut as a drum, weather rigging harping to the wind's bluster, and, far on their beam, *Ceres* swooping and seething along under small sail, he was happier than he had been for some time. There would be no problems with the enemy—any rational privateer would have long since scuttled southwards until the weather improved. No prize could be boarded in this.

By afternoon they had not sighted the convoy; almost certainly it had been delayed by the poor weather. Houghton, on the quarterdeck in oilskins slick with spray, obviously had no plans to return to port and at the end of the day they shortened sail and kept enough way on the ship to head the easterly. It showed signs of veering, which had the master muttering anxiously to Houghton. At midnight they wore to the south and at the end of the middle watch took the third leg of a triangle to approximate their dusk position again.

A cold dawn brought no improvement in the weather, just the same streaming fresh gale and lively decks a-swill with water. There was no sign of the convoy but *Ceres* had stayed with them and by mid-morning there was a flutter of colour at her peak halliards: the convoy had been sighted.

Widely scattered, the ships were struggling to stay together—it was a miracle that they were even within sight of each other after so many thousands of miles of ocean. Without a convoy plan Kydd had no idea how many there should be, but a quick count enabled him to report what must be a sizeable proportion to the captain when he appeared on deck.

"We're looking for *Lord Woolmer,* she's carrying the new

lieutenant-governor," Houghton said brusquely, "an ex-Indiaman. Be so good as to apprise the lookouts and report to me when she's in sight."

Ships of all kinds laboured past, converging on the rendezvous position; some showed obvious signs of storm damage. Towards the rear a battered sloop appeared, oddly out of shape with a truncated foretopmast, but bent on coming up with *Tenacious*.

"Heave to, please," Houghton ordered, as he took the officer-of-the-watch's speaking trumpet and waited. The sloop barrelled up to leeward and backed her headsails. Close by, the little vessel's appalling motion was only too apparent—she was bucking in deep, jerky movements, bursts of spray sheeting over the small huddle at the wheel.

"Where—is—*Lord—Woolmer?*" Houghton called.

A figure in the sloop made his way to the shiny wet shrouds and aimed a speaking trumpet. Kydd could hear thin sounds from it, but not make out what was said. The sloop showed canvas enough for it to ease in, its exaggerated bucketing so much the more pitiable as it lurched closer alongside.

"*Woolmer*—sprung mainmast—left her at fifty-five twenty west—running down forty-three north . . ."

At that longitude she was considerably to eastward of her course; somewhere in the stormy grey of the Atlantic she had encountered a squall that had nearly taken her mainmast by the board. She would have fished the mast with capstan bars and anything to hand, then been grateful for the easterly, which at least would have her heading slowly but surely for Halifax.

Looking down from the deck of *Tenacious*, Kydd felt for the sloop commander. Without a soul to ease the decision out there in the lonely ocean he had needed to weigh the consequences of standing by the injured vessel with her important cargo or resume his watch over the convoy. His presence was proof of the hard resolution he had made: to him the value to England of the merchant ships had outweighed that of one big ship and her passenger.

The sloop sheeted home and thrashed away after her convoy. Houghton turned to the master. "Mr Hambly, all sail conformable to weather. I believe we shall lay on the larb'd tack initially, with a view to returning to starb'd and intersecting our forty-three north line of latitude somewhere about fifty-seven west longitude."

Much depended on the weather. *Lord Woolmer* was heading westwards as close as she could stay to a known line of latitude. If *Tenacious* sailed along the same line in the opposite direction they should meet. The problem was that the wind was dead foul from the east—in difficult conditions *Tenacious* would need to tack twice to intersect the line at the probable furthest on of the other ship. And *Woolmer* herself would be finding it hard to be sure of her latitude without sight of the sun for days at a time.

Kydd went below to find a dry shirt. He was watch-on-deck for the last dog-watch and wanted to be as comfortable as possible; there would be no going below later. As he came back up the companionway he saw the master, face set grimly, entering his tiny sea cabin. "Do ye think th' easterly will hold?" Kydd asked, wedging himself against the door for balance. The hanging lanthorn cast moving shadows in the gloom.

"See this?" Hambly tapped the barometer, its vertical case on gimbals also a-swing. His face seemed old and more lined in the dim light. "Twenty-nine 'n' three fourths. These waters, as soon as we gets a drop more'n a tenth of an inch below our mean f'r the season, stand by. An' we've had a drop o' two tenths since this morning."

He checked the chart again and straightened. "North Atlantic, even at this time o' year, it's folly to trust. It wouldn't surprise me t' see it veer more southerly, an' if that's with a further drop we're in for a hammering."

Kydd turned to go, then asked, "You'll be about tonight, Mr Hambly?"

"I will, sir," said the master, with a tired smile.

In the last of the light the foretop lookout sighted strange sail. It was *Lord Woolmer* with no fore and aft canvas from the main or anything above her course. She put up her helm to run down on *Tenacious,* and Kydd could imagine the relief and joy aboard. With luck they would be safe in Halifax harbour in two or three days and the story of their crossing would be told in the warmth and safety of their homes for months to come.

By the time the ship had come up with *Tenacious* it was too dark for manoeuvres, so they waited until the big, somewhat ungainly merchantman pulled ahead then fell in astern, three lanthorns at her foreyard to comfort the other ship, whose stern lanthorns were plainly visible.

The morning brought the south-easterly that the master had feared; the wind had strengthened and the barometer dropped. It was time for even a well-found ship like *Tenacious* to take the weather seriously.

Houghton did not waste time. "Mr Pearce, Mr Renzi, we'll have the t'gallant masts on deck." The jibboom was brought in forward. Aloft, all rigging that could possibly carry away to disaster was doubled up, preventer braces, rolling tackles put on the yards, slings, trusses—nothing could be trusted to hold in the great forces unleashed in a storm.

Anchors were stowed outboard—they would be of crucial importance should land be seen to leeward—and were secured against the smash of seas on the bows with tough double ring painters and lashing along the length of the stock.

The rudder, too, was vital to safeguard: a relieving tackle was rigged in the wardroom and a spare tiller brought out. It would need fast work to ship a new one—Rawson could be trusted in this, or to rouse out a portable compass and align its lubber-line to the ship's head for use if the tiller ropes from the wheel on deck broke. The relieving tackle would then be used to steer.

On each deck a hatchway forward and aft ventilated the space through gratings. These now were covered with strong canvas and fastened securely with battens nailed around the coaming. Seas breaking aboard might otherwise send tons of water into the ship's bowels.

The most feared event in a storm was a gun breaking loose: a big cannon might smash through the ship's side. The gun-ner and his party worked from forward and secured them; each muzzle seized like an ox to the ringbolt above the closed gunport, with double breechings and side frappings. Finally, on deck, lifelines were rigged fore and aft on each side of the masts, and on the weather mizzen shrouds a canvas cloth was spread to break the blast for the helm crew.

Tenacious was now snugged for a blow. Kydd hoped that the same was true for the merchantman. What would probably be of most concern to her captain was the state of his noble passengers. However splendid their appointments, their cabins would now be a hell on earth: the motion would be such that the only movement possible would be hand to hand, their only rest taken tied into a wildly moving cot, their world confined to a box shaken into a malodorous, seasick chaos.

The ships plunged on into the angry seas. Aboard, muscles wearying of the continual bracing and staggering along the deck, eyes salt-sore in the raw cold and the streaming wet, Kydd made a circuit of the deck looking for anything that could conceivably fret itself into a rapidly spiralling danger. He checked little things, that the drain-holes of the boats were kept open, their deck-gripes bar-taut, spare spars under them lashed into immobility. When he stripped off in the damp fug

of the wardroom, he could see his own concern reflected in others' eyes, and Renzi wore a taut expression.

He pulled on wool: long undergarments, loose pullovers.
Anything to keep out the sapping cold of the streaming wind.

This was no longer an exhilarating contest with Neptune, but
something sinister. The first feelings of anxiety stole over Kydd—
there was a point in every storm when the elements turned from
hard boisterousness to malevolence, a sign that mankind was an
interloper in something bigger than himself, where lives counted
for nothing.

Back on deck Kydd had no need to check the compass to see
that the wind had veered further: the angle of the treble-reefed
topsails was now much sharper. If it continued much past south
they stood to be headed, prevented from making for Nova Scotia
to the west, no more than two days away.

Kydd could just make out a few words as he approached
Houghton, who was talking to the master under the half-deck
near the wheel: ". . . or lie to, sir." Hambly pointed out over the
foam-streaked seas. Beneath the wind-scoured waves a swell,
long and massive, was surging up. And it came from the south-
west, a portent of the great storm that had sent it.

Kydd glanced at the merchantman. They were but two days
from port. So near, yet—Houghton had no authority over her
and, indeed, if he had it was difficult to see how any meaningful
signal could be made.

"The monster crosses our way, sir, and I'm not sanguine of
th' chances of a wounded ship in a real North Atlantic storm,"
continued the master.

"We stay with *Lord Woolmer*. That must be our duty,"
Houghton said abruptly.

Within the hour *Woolmer* began to turn—away from the wind.

"She's scudding!" said Houghton.

"No, sir, I do believe she wears." The ship continued round, slowly and uncomfortably, until she had come up on the opposite, starboard tack where she held a-try about four points from the wind.

"I thought so!" Hambly said, against the bluster of the wind at the edges of the half-deck. "He's seen enough of the western ocean t' know that if there's a turn f'r the worse, the shift will come out of somewheres close to th' north, and wants to get his staying about over with now." It also meant that *Woolmer* had given up hope of making it through to Halifax and now lay to under storm canvas, going very slowly ahead, waiting out the storm. Kydd's heart went out to the passengers, who must be near to despair: storms could last weeks.

Tenacious was set to edging round to conform, and together the two vessels endured. By midday the seas had worsened and the wind's sullen moan had keened to a higher pitch, a dismal drone with whistling overtones. The swell had increased and the depth between each crest became a dismaying plunge and rise.

Kydd had experienced Caribbean hurricanes, but this was of a different quality: the cold at its heart gave it a unique dark malice. Like the other officers, Kydd stayed on deck. At noon they took stale bread and cold tongue, biscuit and anchovies, then resumed their vigil.

Suddenly, a mass of panic-stricken men burst up from the after hatchway, spilling on to the deck, falling over themselves to be out. A chill stabbed at Kydd. A seaman shouted hoarsely, "Gotta loose gun!"

Bryant dropped his food and raced for the hatchway, shouting to Kydd, "A dozen micks—now!"

Because of the weather the hammocks had all been stowed below in the lowest deck. Kydd stood in the hatchway, snatching a dozen men to a halt. "Down t' the orlop—we'll go under." He plunged recklessly down the hatchway, praying they would follow. As he passed the level of the gun-deck he had a brief glimpse of a squat black creature crouching for the kill. He hurried on.

Finally in the orlop he paused to allow his eyes to adjust; then he set the men to work. In the wildly heaving gloom hammocks were passed up while Kydd cautiously entered the deserted gundeck. The gun stood out brazenly from the ship's side. The muzzle lashing had pulled its ringbolt from rotten wood and some weighty motion of the ship had subsequently caused the iron forging of the breeching tackle on one side to give way. The big cannon had swung out and, held by a few stranded ropes, was all but free.

Bryant stood to one side with a crew of seamen armed with handspikes. Kydd signalled to the first men to come up.

"Stand your ground!" the first lieutenant roared, at the men hesitating at his back. The whites of their eyes showed as they fearfully hefted their handspikes and waited for the order. When Kydd's men had temporarily stopped the beast with hammocks thrown in its path, Bryant's would hurl themselves on it with the handspikes in an attempt to overturn it.

Tenacious rose to a wave and fell to starboard. It was all that was needed; the remaining ropes parted with a dull *twang* and the twenty-four-pounder trundled across the deck, accelerating as it went. The men threw themselves back at the sight of the unrestrained rampage while the cannon hurtled at the opposite side. Then the deck heaved the other way. The gun slowed and stopped, trickling back and forth in a grotesque parody of a bullfight as the ship hesitated at the top of a roll. The next headlong charge might be the last.

"Er, can we help?" Lieutenant Best, accompanied by half a dozen marines, stood uncomprehending and hesitating at the hatchway.

"No! Get 'em away." Kydd appreciated his courage but a crowd was not needed—only a handful of daring, active seamen. He glanced behind him: Chamberlain, the midshipman, with the agility of youth, Lamb, a spry topman, Thorn, steady and quick—he had enough.

"Each a mick, an' follow me—rest, wait until we has it cornered, then move in fast." He seized a trussed hammock for himself and moved forward, feeling the eyes of Bryant's crew on him.

Tenacious's bows rose to a comber. The deck canted up and the cannon suddenly rolled—towards him. Kydd threw the hammock before it and flung himself to one side. It thrust by, skidding on the hammock and fetched up against the mainmast with a splintering crash.

"Chamberlain—here! Lamb 'n' Thorn, get in behind it!" He spotted Best, still hovering. "Get out of it," he snarled, and pushed the crestfallen officer away.

They must close in at whatever risk: Bryant's crew could do nothing until the beast was stopped and then they had seconds only. The next few minutes would see heroes—or death. Warily he approached the cannon, trying to gauge the seas outside.

The bows began to rise again and he tensed, but the downward motion of the cannon abruptly changed course as the wave angled under her keel, and it rumbled headlong towards the ship's side and where Best stood, paralysed with horror.

It happened very quickly: a fatal wavering and the two-ton monster caught him, snatched him along, and slammed against another—a choking squeal and a brief image of spurting blood, limbs and white bone. Best's body was flung to the deck.

Yet his sacrifice was the saving of the ship. Caught in the gun's small wheels his body caused the cannon to slew and stop. Kydd hurled his hammock in its path. Others threw themselves at it, Bryant's crew with handspikes levering furiously, frantically.

They had won.

• • •

Shaken, Kydd needed the open decks. *Lord Woolmer* lay to a mile or so away, taking seas on her bows in explosions of white, pitching and rolling under her scraps of sail.

Hambly was standing by the main shrouds, looking up at the racing dark clouds and the torn seascape. On seeing Kydd, he shouted, "We're takin' it more from the west, I fear." The rest of his words were snatched away by the wind's blast.

"And this means?" Kydd had not heard Houghton approach behind them. Hambly wheeled round, then respectfully accompanied them to the shelter of the half-deck.

"Sir, it means the centre o' the storm is placin' itself right in our path. We'll be down t' bare poles at this rate—we should really bear away an' scud instead of lyin' to. There's no hope this storm is goin' to blow itself out, sir."

Kydd wondered whether the real reason *Woolmer* was hanging on was the reluctance of her captain to deny his passengers hope of a harbour and surcease. To scud was to abandon all attempts even to hold a position and simply fly before the violence, but this was to turn about and be blown back over the miles they had won at such cost.

"I understand, Mr Hambly, but we stay with them."

Conditions were deteriorating and it was hard to keep them in sight: the air was filled with stinging spray, the motion of the ship becoming a shuddering heave as the seas grew more confused.

The hours wore on. Kydd imagined what it must be like for the people of *Woolmer:* an indescribable nightmare, endlessly protracted.

After midday *Woolmer* finally submitted to fate and made the decision to scud. It would be touch and go: the swells issuing from the storm centre were now more than forty feet high, higher even than the lower yards, and clawed into white streaks by the pitiless wind. They had left it perilously late. To fall off the wind, then run before it they must first pass through the most dangerous time of all—broadside to the powerful seas.

Tenacious stood by while *Woolmer* began to turn, all aboard holding their breath. Her captain had clearly planned his turn away from the wind, for the small sail left on main and mizzen vanished at exactly the same time as her headsails mounted. The leverage told, and the ship, plunging and rocking like a fractious horse, began putting her bow downwind, faster and faster. A rampaging comber burst on her side, checking her movement, but with the appearance of square sail on her fore—loosed by some heroic topmen aloft—*Woolmer* completed her turn. Rolling drunkenly at first she settled to her new track.

"A princely piece of seamanship as ever I've seen, and with an injured mast!" exclaimed Houghton. Kydd quietly agreed: it had been well done indeed.

"At least they has no worry o' being pooped," said Hambly, eyeing the stately East Indiaman's high stern. With a following sea there was always the danger of a giant wave overtaking and crowding on to her deck to sweep everything before it.

"That's not m' worry," Kydd said—seared on his memory was fighting the helm of a similar-sized vessel in the Great Southern Ocean, the frigate *Artemis* on her way round Cape Horn.

Hambly looked at him, troubled. "What's that, sir?"

"No matter." Kydd could not voice the fears that had been triggered by the memory.

Houghton broke in decisively: "I'm going to scud under fore-topmast stays'l and a close-reefed fore tops'l. Mr Hambly?"

"Aye, sir." Hands went to their stations, Kydd on the poop at the mizzen. The reefed driver was brought in and all sail aft disappeared, released seamen sent to the main deck. *Tenacious* began her turn, experiencing the same vertiginous rolls before she, too, was round with the hard wind at her stern.

Barely set on her course, *Tenacious*'s fore topsail split and was instantly transformed to streaming ribbons. "I'll have a quick-saver on that," Houghton shouted at the hurrying boatswain, ordering the replacement topsail and a pair of ropes to be crossed over the sail to prevent it ballooning forward.

Then, there were cries of horror. No more than half a mile away, Kydd saw *Woolmer,* her silhouette dark against the white of the spindrift, strangely misshapen. Her weakened mainmast had given way under the wind pressure: it had splintered and fallen in ruin over the side.

While *Tenacious* watched, agonised, the inevitable happened. The crew were unable to cut away the substantial wreckage in time and it acted as a drag to one side. *Woolmer* yawed. Pulled to one side she was at the mercy of the onrushing water, which pushed her further broadside. Kydd's fears had come to pass: with no ability to come back on course she was forced right over on her beam ends, and the giant seas fell on the helpless vessel. *Lord Woolmer* capsized in a smother of wreckage, her long hull a glistening whale-like rock for a time before she disappeared altogether; lords, ladies and common seamen gone for ever.

"Mr Hambly," said Houghton, in an unnatural voice, "the best course for us?"

Hambly tore his eyes away from the scene and pulled himself together. "Er, to the suth'ard would keep us fr'm the centre . . . We scuds afore the westerly, that's undoubted, until we can show canvas and come about—there's nothing more we c'n do, sir."

Alone, *Tenacious* fought the sea, men moving silently in a pall of disbelief, senses battered by the hammering wind. For all of twenty hours the ship ran before the tempest until, in the early hours of the next day, the master judged it possible to set square sail on the main and thereby edge closer to the wind. By evening the winds had moderated to the extent that at last *Tenacious* could ease round more westward, towards the now distant Halifax.

But the storm had one last trial for the old ship. By degrees the wind shifted north and the temperature fell. The first whirling snowflakes came, then snow squalls that marched across the seas with dark, brassy interiors bringing intense cold.

It got worse. Ice covered shrouds, sails, decks, freezing exposed faces. It stiffened wet ropes to bars that seamen, with frozen fingers in wet gloves and feet in agony with the cold, had to wrestle with to coil.

Even breathing was painful: Kydd bound a cloth round his face but it soon clogged with ice as moisture froze. Below, the wardroom stank of damp wool, bear-grease and the hides used in foul-weather gear. No one spoke: it was too much effort. Renzi sat with his head in his hands.

On Kydd's watch the wind moan increased, the pitiless blast buffeting him with its fearsome chill. He hugged himself, grateful for his moose-hide jacket, and thought of the hapless men in the fo'c'sle. In the scrappiest clothing against the numbing chill they had to muster on watch day and night, working, enduring.

Hambly came over. "Shall have t' take in the main tops'l," he said, looking significantly at Kydd. They had been fortunate until now that they carried the same square sail, close reefed fore and main topsails, but the wind had increased again.

Kydd stared up at the straining sail. There was no question, the ship was over-pressed in these conditions and must be relieved—he could feel it in her laboured response to the helm. He was officer-of-the-watch and the responsibility was his, not the master's.

But there was the deadly glitter of ice on the shrouds, in the tops and along the yards: how could he send men aloft in the almost certain knowledge that for some there would be a cry, a fall and death?

His eyes met Hambly's: there was understanding but no compassion. Without a word Kydd turned and made his way down to the main deck where the watch on deck shivered, hunkered down in the lee of the weather bulwarks.

They looked up as he descended, their faces dull, fatigued, and pinched with cold. He paused. How could he order them to go aloft into a howling icy hell? Perhaps some rousing speech to the effect that the ship, they themselves even, depended on them taking their lives into their hands and going aloft? No. Kydd had been in their place and knew what was needed.

His face hardened. "Off y'r rumps, y' lazy swabs. I want th' main tops'l handed, now." They pulled themselves slowly to their feet. Their weary, stooped figures and bloodshot eyes wrung his heart.

"Lay aloft!" he roared. Every man obeyed. Kydd allowed a grim smile to surface. "An' there'll be a stiff tot f'r every man jack waiting for ye when you get back. Get moving!"

For two hours, ninety feet above Kydd's head, the men fisted the stiff sail in a violently moving, lethal world. Fingernails split and canvas was stained with blood, tired muscles slipped on icy wood and scrabbled for a hold, minds retreating into a state of numbed endurance.

And for two hours, Kydd stood beneath, his fists balled in his pockets, willing them on, feeling for them, agonising. That day he discovered that there was only one thing of more heroism than going aloft in such a hell: the moral courage to order others to do it.

For two more days *Tenacious* fought her way clear of the storm, which eventually headed north, increasing in malevolence as it went. On the third day the Sambro light was raised—and, after a night of standing off and on, HMS *Tenacious* entered harbour.

CHAPTER 7

"DAMN! THAT CURSED TAILOR will hound me to my grave," groaned Pringle. The mail-boat had arrived back from the dockyard and the wardroom sat about the table opening letters and savouring news from home.

Adams, clutching six, retired to his cabin but Bampton slipped his into a pocket and sipped his brandy, balefully watching the animation of the others.

Kydd was trying to make sense of his borrowed *Essays on Politesse Among Nations,* despairing of the turgid phraseology; his restraint in matters social, and sudden access of interest in literature, was generally held to be owing to some obscure improving impulse, and he was mostly left to it.

"You don't care for letters, Mr Kydd," Pybus said, with acerbity. He had received none himself, but was still scratching away lazily with his quill.

Kydd looked up and saw that there was indeed one letter left on the table. "For me?" He picked it up. "From m' sister, Doctor," he said. She wrote closely, and as usual had turned the page and written again at right-angles through the first to be frugal in the postage.

"Well?" demanded Pybus.

But Kydd was not listening.

Dear Thomas—or should I say Nicholas as well? I do hope you are keeping well, my dears, and wrapping up warm. The willows are budding early along the Wey here in Guildford and . . .

The words rushed on, and Kydd smiled to picture Cecilia at her task. Her evident concern for them both warmed him but her admiration for him as an officer in the King's Navy sparked melancholy.

A hurried paragraph concluded the letter:

. . . and Father says that it would be of service to him should you enquire after his brother Matthew. You remember they came to some sort of a misunderstanding an age ago, and his brother sailed to Philadelphia? Papa says that was in 1763. Since then we have heard nothing of him, except that in the War for Independence he was a loyalist and went north with the others to Halifax in about 1782. Thomas, it would so please Papa to know that he is alive and well—do see if you can find him!

Of course, his uncle: an adventurer in this wilderness land, carving a future for himself—or perhaps he was a successful trader, even a shipowner in the profitable Atlantic trade routes.

"News?" Pybus said drily.

"Oh, aye. Seems it could be m' uncle is here, Doctor, in Halifax. Who would credit it?" A Kydd ashore, possibly one who had achieved eminence in society and was highly thought of in the community. For the first time in a long while he felt a rush of excitement. "I do believe I'm t' visit him today."

"Kydd—Mr Matthew Kydd." It was strange uttering the words. There were not so many Kydds in the world that it felt anything other than his own name.

The man he had stopped considered for a moment. "Can't say as I've heard of the gentleman, sir," he said finally. "You may wish to try Linnard's the tailors. You'll understand they know all the gentry hereabouts." But Kydd was tiring of the chase. It was becoming clear that his uncle was far from being a notable in Halifax. It had been foolish of him to imagine that one of modest origins could have pretences at high office—but this did not mean that he had not secured a lesser, well-respected place in society.

He toiled up the street, a curious mix of fine stone edifices and shoddy clapboard buildings, but it was not practical to think of entering and asking at random: there had to be a more efficient way. An idea came to him. He would contact Mr Greaves, the commissioner for lands. If his uncle was in any form a landowner he would know him. Kydd brightened as he savoured the effect on his uncle of receiving a card out of the blue from a Lieutenant Kydd shortly about to call.

The land registry was a stiff walk well to the south, and Kydd set out along Barrington Street, past the elegance of St Paul's Church. A line of soldiers was marching up and down on the large open area to his right, and when Kydd approached, the young officer in command halted his men and brought them to attention, then wheeled about and saluted. Kydd lifted his hat to him, which seemed to satisfy. With a further flourish of orders the soldiers resumed their marching.

Then an unwelcome thought struck. Supposing his uncle had fallen on hard times or was still a humble tradesman? It would make no difference to him—but if Greaves thought he was of lowly origins it might prove embarrassing . . . He would move cautiously and find out first.

"To be sure, a Kydd," murmured the clerk, at the desk of the weathered timber structure near the old burying ground. "There was one such, resident of Sackville Street, I seem to recall, but that was some years ago. Let me see . . ." He polished his spectacles and opened a register. "Ah—we have here one Matthew Kydd, bachelor, established as trader and landowner in the year 1782, property on Sackville Street . . . Hmmm—here we have a contribution to the Sambro light, er, the usual taxation receipts . . ."

It was certainly his uncle. At last! How would he greet him? He had never met the man: he had sailed from England well before Kydd had been born. Should it be "Uncle Matthew" or perhaps a more formal salutation?

". . . which means, sir, we have nothing later than the year 1791."

Kydd's face dropped. "So—"

"We find no evidence at all for his continued existence after then. I'm sorry."

"None?"

"No, sir. You may wish to consult the parish books of St Paul's for record of his decease—there was fever here at the time, you understand."

"Thank ye, sir." Kydd made to leave, but another clerk was hovering nearby.

"Sir, you may be interested in this . . ." They moved to the other end of the office. "My wife admired Mr Kydd's work," he said, "which is why she bought this for me." It was a handsomely carved horn of plenty, taking bold advantage of the twisted grain of the wood, and supported at the base by a pair of birds. "You will understand that time is on our hands in the winter. Mr Kydd used to occupy his in carving, which I think you will agree is in the highest possible taste . . ."

Kydd stroked the polished wood, something his own near relative had created: it felt alive.

"Yes, those birds," the clerk mused. "I confess I have no knowledge of them at all—they're not to be seen in this part of Canada. But Mr Kydd always includes them in his work. It's a custom here, a species of signature for claiming fine work as your own."

"But I recognise it well enough," Kydd said. "This is y'r

Cornish chough, sir. And it's the bird you find in the coat-of-arms of our own Earl Onslow of Clandon and Guildford."

The man looked back at him with a bemused kindliness, but there was nothing more to learn here. Kydd emerged into the day: he was not yet due back aboard so his hunt would continue.

But at St Paul's there was no entry for Matthew Kydd, in births, deaths or marriages. A whole hour of searching in the gloom of the old church sacristy yielded only two entries in the tithe-book, and a smudged but tantalising reference to banns being called.

A mystery: at one time he had existed, now he did not. It was time to face the most unsatisfactory result of all: his uncle was not in Halifax but somewhere else in Canada—or, for that matter, he could be anywhere. And it explained why no one seemed to know of a Kydd in Halifax. He would regretfully conclude his search and write to his father accordingly.

"If you'd be so good, Tom . . ." Adams seemed anxious, but it did not take much imagination to grasp why he would want to absent himself from church that Sunday morning.

"I trust she's so charming you hold it of no account that you put your immortal soul to hazard?" Kydd said. The captain had made it plain that he wanted an officer from *Tenacious* at the morning service on Sundays, and it was Adams's turn.

Kydd had no strong feelings about religion, although he enjoyed the hearty singing of the grand old hymns. With his Methodist upbringing he was inured to sitting inactive for long periods.

Army officers with ladies on their arms swept into the church. Other ranks waited respectfully outside and would crowd in later. Kydd took off his hat and made his way inside, settling for an outside seat in a pew towards the front, nodding to the one or two other naval officers scattered about.

A pleasant-faced woman sat down next to him and flashed him an impish smile. "There, my dear," said the stern, stiffly dressed man by her, settling a rug about her knees.

"Thank you," she said, and as soon as it was seemly to do so, turned to Kydd and whispered, "I don't think I've seen you here, sir."

"Lieutenant Kydd of the *Tenacious*," he whispered back, unsure of the etiquette of the occasion.

"Mrs Cox. Your first visit to Halifax, Lieutenant?"

The church was filling fast but the front pew was still decorously empty.

"Yes, Mrs Cox. Er, a fine place f'r trade."

"Indeed. But when I was a little girl it was a horrid place, believe me, Lieutenant." She smiled again.

There was a damp, penetrating cold in the cavernous interior of the church, barely relieved by two fat-bellied stoves smoking in corners. Kydd shivered and wished he had brought a watch-coat.

Mrs Cox fumbled in her muff. "Here you are, Lieutenant," she said, proffering a silver flask. "Get some inside and you won't feel the cold." It was prime West Indian rum. At his ill-concealed astonishment she pressed it on him. "Go on—we all have to." Aghast at the thought of drinking in church, Kydd hesitated, then, red-faced, took a pull, but as he lowered the flask he saw an august personage and his lady sweeping up the aisle.

Crimson with embarrassment, Kydd froze. With a gracious inclination of her head, the woman smiled and continued. Kydd handed back the flask and settled for the service, trying not to notice the distracting stream of servants bringing hot bricks for the feet of the quality in the front row.

Outside, after the service, when they passed pleasantries, Kydd remembered that Mrs Cox had been born in Halifax. Impulsively he asked, "I wonder, Mrs Cox, can you remember

less'n ten years ago, a gentleman by the name of Kydd, Matthew
Kydd?"

She considered at length. "I can't say that I do, Lieutenant. A
relation?"

"My uncle—I'm tryin' to find him."

Mr Cox pulled his ear as if trying to recall something. "Er,
there was a gentleman by that name, I think—recollect he was in
corn and flour on Sackville Street. Fine-looking fellow."

"That's him," said Kydd.

A look of embarrassment flashed over Cox's face. "Ah." He gave
a warning glance to his wife, whose hand flew to her mouth.

"Then I'm truly sorry to tell you . . . he is no more," Cox said
quietly.

Kydd swallowed.

"Yes. In about the year 'ninety—or was it 'ninety-one?—he
went to Chignecto with his partner looking out prospects, but
unhappily was mortally injured by a bear."

"I remember. It was in the newspaper—such a dreadful thing,"
Mrs Cox added. "It never does to disturb them in their sleep, the
brutes."

Cox drew himself up. "I'm grieved that your search has led you
to this, sir. I do hope that the remainder of your time in Halifax
will be more felicitous. Good day to you, Lieutenant."

As was usual for officers in harbour, Kydd's duties were light and
he felt he owed it to his father to gather the circumstances of his
brother's demise. Possibly he had family, a widow. He would get
the details from the newspaper and pass them on.

The *Halifax Journal* office was on Barrington Street, not far
from Grand Parade, and the man inside was most obliging. "Yes,
indeed, I remember the story well. A fine man, come to such a
fate. Uncle, you say. I'll find the issue presently. If you would be
so good . . ."

On a table near the compositing desk Kydd learned the sad details of his uncle's death. He had gone to Chignecto, on the other side of Nova Scotia, exploring prospects in muskrat and beaver. His business partner, an Edward Gilman, had accompanied him, but of the two who had set out, only one returned: Gilman. He had buried his friend and partner at the edge of the wilderness by the sea, then brought back the news.

Judging by the upset expressed in the newspaper, Matthew Kydd had been a man of some substance and standing and was sorely missed. Kydd leafed idly through the rest of the paper.

Out in the street he determined that before he wrote to his father he would find Gilman, ask what kind of man his uncle was, find out something about his end.

Sackville Street was just round the corner, steep and colourful with timber dwellings and shops; some were worn and weathered, others painted brown and yellow or red and white. He found a corn factor with a faded sign telling him that this was Gilman's establishment. There was no mention of "Kydd."

He went into the dusty office, where he was met by a suspicious-looking clerk. "May I speak with Mr Gilman?" Kydd asked.

"Concernin' what?"

"That's my business," Kydd said.

The man hesitated, clearly baffled by Kydd's naval uniform. "Mr Gilman," he called. "Gennelman wants t' see you."

Kydd had the feeling of eyes on him. Eventually a hard-looking man appeared, his face showing distrust. "I'm Gilman. Yes?"

"I think y' knew Matthew Kydd?"

Gilman tensed but said nothing.

"You were with him when he was killed by a bear?"

"You're English," Gilman said slowly.

"He was m' uncle, came t' Canada in 'seventy-eight."

Gilman's expression altered slightly. "I weren't with him. That was my pap."

The man must have lost his youth early in this hard country, Kydd reflected. "I'd be much obliged if he could talk with me a little about m' uncle," he said.

"He can't." At Kydd's sharp look he added, "He's bin buried. In the Ol' Burying Ground."

"Do you remember Matthew Kydd?"

"No." It was flat and final.

Pybus was unsympathetic. "Chasing after long-lost relatives is seldom a profitable exercise. Now you have the task before you of communicating grief and loss where before there was harmless wondering. Well done, my boy."

Kydd sharpened his pen and addressed himself to the task. How to inform his father that his brother was no more, and had met his end in such a hideous way? The plain facts—simply a notification? Or should he spare his father by implying that his death was from natural causes? Kydd had never been one for letters and found the task heavy-going.

He decided to wait for Renzi's return. There was no urgency, and Renzi could readily find words for him, fine, elegant words that would meet the occasion. He put aside his paper and went up on deck.

The master had a telescope trained down the harbour. "D'ye see that schooner, sir? Country-built an' every bit as good as our own Devon craft."

Kydd took the telescope. "Aye, not as full in th' bow, an' has sweet lines on her."

He kept the glass on the vessel as Hambly added, "An' that's because of the ice up the St Lawrence, o' course. They'll ship a bowgrace in two or three weeks, when the ice really breaks up. Nasty t' take one o' them floes on the bow full tilt, like."

The approaching vessel stayed prettily and shortened sail

preparatory to anchoring, Kydd watching her. She was a new vessel, judging by the colour of her sails and running rigging. He
shifted the view to her trim forefoot, pausing to admire her figurehead—a Scottish lass holding what appeared to be a fistful of
heather, a striking figure in a streaming cloak with a pair of birds
at her feet.

Birds? He steadied the telescope and, holding his breath, peered
hard. He kept his glass on the schooner as she glided past. There
was no mistake, they were Cornish choughs.

"I'll be damned!" Kydd said softly. Then he swung on Hambly.
"Tell me," he said urgently, "do y' know which yard it was built
this'n?"

"Can't say as I does." Hambly seemed surprised at Kydd's sudden energy. "There's scores o' shipyards up 'n' down the coast,
most quite able t' build seagoin' craft o' this size."

It might be a coincidence—but Kydd felt in his heart it was not.
"The yawl ahoy," he hailed over the side to *Tenacious*'s boat's
crew, then turned back to Hambly. "I'm going t' see that schooner, Mr Hambly."

The master of the *Flora MacDonald* did not want to pass the
time of day with a lieutenant, Royal Navy. His cargo was to be
landed as soon as convenient, and although an impress warrant
was not current, who could trust the Navy? However, he did allow that the schooner was new and from St John's Island in the
great Gulf of St Lawrence, specifically, the yard of Arthur Owen
in New London.

Was it conceivable that his uncle had survived and was now
working as a ship-carver on an island somewhere on the other side
of Nova Scotia? It made no sense to Kydd. Why hadn't his uncle
returned to take up his business? It was coincidence, it had to be.

But he knew he would regret it if he did not follow up this tantalising sign. A quick glance at a chart showed St John's Island no

more than a couple of days' sail with a fair wind and if Canso strait was free of ice.

Although *Tenacious* was required in port by the absence of the admiral and his flagship, activity aboard was light, and there was no difficulty with his request for a week's leave.

It was probably only someone continuing his uncle's particular carving signature, but the expedition would be a welcome change and would give him a chance to see something of Canada. He asked Adams if he wished to come, and was not surprised at his regrets—his diary was full for weeks ahead. Kydd was going to adventure alone.

Vessels were making the run to the newly ice-free St John's Island with supplies after the winter and Kydd quickly found a berth, in a coastal schooner, the *Ethel May*. Wearing comfortable, plain clothes, he swung in his small sea-bag.

The beat up the coast was chill and wet, but the schooner's fore and aft rig allowed her to lie close to the north-easterly and she made good time; Cape Breton Island, the hilly passage of Canso strait, then the calmer waters in the gulf, and early in the morning of the second day they closed with St John's Island.

It was a flat, barely undulating coastline with red cliffs and contrasting pale beaches. The dark carpet of forest was blotched in places with clearings, and even before they gybed and passed the long narrow sandspit into New London Bay Kydd had seen signs of shipbuilding—gaunt ribs on slipways, timber stands, distant smoke from pitch fires.

In the sheltered waters the schooner glided towards a landing stage with a scatter of tidy weatherboard buildings beyond. "Where y' bound?"

"Owen's yard," Kydd answered.

The skipper pointed along the foreshore. "Around th' point,

one o' the oldest on St John's." He pronounced it "Sinjuns."

"Thank ye," Kydd said, feeling for coins to put into the man's outstretched hand. It had been a quick trip, and sleeping in a borrowed hammock in the tiny saloon was no imposition.

Kydd pushed past the crowd and the buckboard carts that had materialised on the schooner's arrival, hefted his sea-bag and set out.

The road was slush and red mud that the passing inhabitants seemed to ignore. Women wore old-fashioned bonnets and carried large bundles, their skirts long enough for modesty but revealing sturdy boots beneath. Men passed in every kind of dress; utility and warmth took first place over fashion. All looked at Kydd with curiosity—few strangers came to this out-of-the-way place.

The buildings were all of a style, mainly timbered, with high, steeply sloping roofs; the fields were wooden-fenced, not a stone wall in sight. English hamlets had lanes that meandered over the countryside; here there were bold straight lines in everything from settlements to roads.

The shipyard was not big: two slipways and a jetty, a blacksmith's shop and buildings presumably housing the workforce. Kydd tried to keep his hopes in check but he felt a thrill of anticipation as he approached one of the half-built hulls. "Is this Mr Owen's yard?" he hailed shipwrights at work high up on staging.

"It is," one called.

"Th' one that built the *Flora MacDonald?*"

"The very same."

"Could y' tell me if you've heard of a Mr Kydd—Matthew Kydd?" blurted Kydd.

"Can't say as we heard any o' that name on th' island, friend."

"I'd like t' meet the ship-carver who worked on her figurehead, if y' please," Kydd said.

"We don't do carvin' in this yard. Ye'll want Josh Ellis."

Ellis ran a small business in town. Kydd found the shop and a well-built man of about thirty came to the counter. "I'd like t' speak with Mr Ellis," Kydd said.

"That's me."

He was obviously not old enough to be his uncle; Kydd tried to hide his disappointment. "Did you work the figurehead o' the *Flora MacDonald,* Mr Ellis?"

"*Flora MacDonald?*" he reflected. "That's right, I remember now, pretty little schooner from Arthur Owen. Do ye wish one for y'self?"

"Fine work," Kydd answered carefully. "Did ye carve the birds an' all?"

"I did."

"What sort o' birds are they, then?"

"Well, I guess any ol' bird, nothin' special."

"Nobody told you how t' carve them?"

"What is it y' wants? Not a carving, I figure," Ellis said, defensive.

"I'm sorry if I offended—y' see, those birds are special, Cornish choughs. You only find 'em in England an' they're rare."

Ellis said nothing, watching Kydd.

"An' they remind me of m' uncle. You find 'em on the coat-of-arms of our earl, in Guildford." There was still no response. "I came here because I thought I'd find out somethin' of him—Kydd, Matthew Kydd."

"No one b' that name on the island, I c'n tell y' now." He folded his arms across his chest.

Kydd saw there was no point in continuing. The whole thing looked like coincidence, and if there was anything more he could not think why. "Well, it was only a fancy. I'll wish ye good day, sir."

• • •

He decided to head back to his ship. The landing-stage was close, but there were no vessels alongside and it was deserted. He hesitated, then made for the small general store in the main street to enquire about a passage back to Halifax.

"None I knows of t'day." The shopkeeper stroked his jaw. "Could be one's goin' t'morrow or the next—we don't have a reg'lar-goin' packet, only traders."

Kydd lumped his bag on the counter. "Seems I'm stranded . . . ye have an inn, b' chance?"

"No, sir," he said with amusement, "but y' might try Mrs Beckwith. Her husband were a seagoin' gentleman."

"Yes indeed," said Mrs Beckwith. "I have a room fit fer a adm'ral, bless ye. Stow yer dunnage an' tonight I'll bring alongside as fine a line o' vittles as'll stick t' yer ribs."

Kydd decided to walk off his expectations; the letter was waiting to be written when he returned to *Tenacious* and he was in no rush to begin it. Besides, the tranquillity of this strange land was appealing: tiny shoots of green were now appearing at the sunny edges of fields, even flowers peeping up through winter-bleached grass. The silence stretched away into the distance. It could not have been more remote from war and the striving of nations.

"So far fr'm the Old Country," Mrs Beckwith said, as the dinner was brought in by a well-built young man. "Oh—this is Mr Cunnable, he boards wi' me too."

"Er, yes. That is, it's a long way t' England."

"Mr Kydd, help y'self. This is our salt cod, an' we got a pile more o' them potatoes. Now, would ye mind tellin' me, how do th' ladies in London Town have their hair this year? Heard tell, high style well powdered 'n' greased over y'r pads is quite past."

"Thank you, Mrs Beckwith, salt cod will be fine with me.

Er, the ladies o' quality I think now are windin' it up and fixin' it to the top of their heads. This is damn fine fish even if I do say so. But these leaves, I can't recollect we have any of them in England."

"Sour dock an' sheep sorrel. Gives winter vittles a mort more flavour. So you're a Navy officer! Then y' must've been to some o' them great balls an' banquets with our Prince Edward! They do say they're goin' to change the name o' this island after him."

"We've only been here a short while, an' our admiral is away in Newfoundland, but I'm sure we'll be invited soon." Kydd lifted his glass; in it was a golden brown liquid, which he tasted gingerly. It was a species of ale, with an elusive tang of malt and spice.

"Seed-wheat wine—made it m'self. Tell me, Mr Kydd, in England do they . . ." She paused, frowning, at a knock on the door. "'Scuse me."

Kydd nibbled at what appeared to be a peppery-flavoured dried seaweed and listened to Mrs Beckwith's shrill voice rising, scolding, and another, quieter. She returned eventually, flushed and irritable. "It's very wrong t' disturb ye, Mr Kydd, but there's a woman here wants t' see you an' won't go away."

Kydd got up. "She's Irish," warned Mrs Beckwith. "If y' like, shall I ask Mr Cunnable t' set the dog on her?"

"No, no. I'll come."

A woman in a shawl hung back in the darkness and spoke quietly: "Good evenin' to yez, sorr—an' you're the gennelman just come ter the island an' asking after his uncle?"

"Yes, that's right."

"Then I'm t' tell ye, if tomorrow at noon y' comes with me, you'll meet someone as knows what happened t' him."

The next day, dressed economically, she was waiting motionless down the road. Kydd saw that, despite her lined face, she held herself proudly. Without a word she turned and walked away from the town.

Where the river shoreline came close she turned down a path. It led to the river and a birchbark canoe with an Indian standing silently by it. The woman muttered some words and the Indian turned his black eyes on Kydd and grunted.

The canoe was much bigger than he had imagined, twenty feet long at least, and made of birchbark strips. There were cedar ribs as a crude framework and seams sewn with a black root. It had half a dozen narrow thwarts and Kydd was surprised to see it quite dry.

In the middle part, a good five feet across, there was a mound of baggage. "If ye'd kindly get in like this, sorr," the woman said. She leaned across the canoe until she held both sides, then, transferring her weight, stepped in neatly and sat. "Be sure t' stand in th' very middle," she added.

Kydd did as he was told, sitting behind her in the front part. The Indian shoved off, swung in, and began to ply his paddle in a powerful rhythm that quickly had them out in the river and gliding along rapidly. He worked silently, his face set like stone, and the woman did not offer any conversation.

They left cleared land behind, dark green anonymous forest stretching away endlessly on both sides. Eventually the Indian ceased paddling, then spun the canoe round and grounded it at the forest's edge.

"Nearly there," the woman said. They left the Indian to follow with the baggage and took a footpath into the trees. Kydd felt as if the forest was closing in; with its hard green conifers uniformly shaped to shed snow, unknown cries and sudden snapping in the undergrowth, it was utterly different from the soft deciduous woodland of England. Kydd thought of his uncle, killed by a bear that had burst from the trees, and was afraid. Why had he agreed to this madness?

Suddenly he glimpsed the dark blue of water, and a grey spiral of smoke. "Here!" the woman said happily, as they came upon a cluster of log cabins in a patch of land leading down to the sea. She called, and a man appeared. He stood on the porch of one of the largest cabins, a big man, long-haired and with a deep chest; he wore moose-hide worked with porcupine quills.

"My husband Joseph Bourne, sorr."

The man shook hands with Kydd, looking at him keenly. Kydd felt the strength and hardness in his clasp. "I hear you knew my uncle, Matthew Kydd, Mr Bourne," Kydd said.

"Very close t' me, he were," Bourne said at length, in a deep Canadian burr. "Come inside, sit y'self down."

The cabin was snug and warm with a steeply sloping cedar-shingle roof; the logs chinked smoothly on the inside. Skins and two bear hams hung from the high beams. Woven Indian matting decorated the walls and a pair of long guns was crossed above the fire. It smelt pungently of smoke and human living.

Two rocking chairs faced the fire, and the men sat together. "M' wife got t' hear of you in town," he said, in a voice both soft and slow. "Thought I could help."

Kydd murmured something, conscious of the man's look.

"You're fr'm the Old Country," Bourne said. "Fr'm what part do ye hail?"

"Guildford, which is in Surrey."

"Very pretty, I heard."

"Mr Bourne, ye said you'd tell me of m' uncle Matthew," said Kydd.

"All in God's good time, friend," Bourne said, and leaned round his chair. "Colleen, c'n you fetch us a jug o' beer, darlin', and some moose jerky? Our guest's come a long way t' be here.

Now, y'r uncle Matthew." He collected a long pipe and tobacco pouch from the chimneypiece above the fire. "Need t' think," he said, as he stuffed the bowl and got a light from the fire. When he had it going to satisfaction, he started: "He came t' Nova Scotia fr'm the Colonies in 'seventy-eight—wanted no truck wi' revolutions an' that. Set himself up in business, an' did well for hisself. Then got destroyed by a bear in Chignecto country."

Kydd tried to hide his irritation—that much he already knew, and if the man simply wanted company . . . "Sir, it would oblige me greatly, should you—"

"His wife died in Halifax o' the fever. Had three bairns, all taken. That was in 'eighty-four." He drew long on his pipe, staring into the fire. "After that, well, I guess he took a diff'rent slant on life. Got inta business, corn tradin' an' such. Did well, laid out silver in the right place an' got him a gov'ment contract f'r the Army, set up in Sackville Street, noticed by th' governor . . . but never remarried."

"What kind o' man d'ye think he was?"

Bourne poured from a stone jug into colourful pottery tankards and offered one. From the woodsy taste, Kydd recognised it as spruce beer—it had a compelling bitterness and he decided it was an acquired taste.

"A straight arrow, I reckon. Hard worker but . . ."

"Mr Bourne?"

"But I'm thinkin' he weren't so happy, really." He lapsed again into an introspective silence.

Kydd coughed meaningfully and asked, "I have t' ask if you know anything about his bein' taken by the bear. Was it . . . quick?" His father would want details.

Bourne puffed once more, then said quietly, "Who wants t' know?"

"Why, he had an elder brother who's my papa. They parted

years afore I was born, some sort o' misunderstanding. M' father's gettin' frail an' hoped t' be reconciled. Now I have to write t' him, you understand."

Bourne got to his feet, crossed to the fire and knocked out his pipe on a log. He turned, but did not resume his chair, looking at Kydd with an unsettling intensity.

Then his gaze shifted; his wife was standing rigid behind Kydd, staring at her husband. His eyes returned to Kydd. "You're a smart lad. What d' they call ye?"

"I'm Thomas—Tom Kydd." He looked steadily at the older man. "An' do I call ye Uncle?" he added softly.

In the stillness the hardwood fire snapped and spat, sending up fountains of red sparks. For a long time Bourne held his silence, until Kydd thought he had not heard. Then he spoke. "I guess you do that," he said.

"Come, lass, sit by we," Kydd's uncle said, after composure had been regained and whiskey had been downed. She moved over and sat on the floor, close.

"I'm goin' t' tell ye the whole nine yards, Thomas—Tom. It's a long ways fr'm here to Guildford, so don't go makin' judgements before you've heard me out. I told ye no lie. About seven, eight year ago I weren't happy. Ye might say I was miserable. I got t' thinkin' about life 'n' all, and knew I was a-wastin' the years God gave me. So I did somethin' about it. Simple, really. I did a deal with m' partner—Ned Gilman, right true sort he were. I spelled out t' him that if he said I was took by a bear, an' let me start a new life, I'd let him have the business. We shook on it, an' I guess that's it—here I am."

"Just—gave him th' business?"

"I did. But he suffered for it!" His face wrinkled in amusement. "Folk said th' bear tale was all a story—that really he'd murthered me an' left me t' rot, while he came back alone 'n' claimed th' business."

Kydd remembered the hostility his enquiries had met and now understood. "Will ye leave y'r bones here, d'ye think?" It was a far, far place, England, where ancient churches and the old ways comforted, with graveyards, ceremony and mourning at life's end. What was there of that in this raw land?

"Tom, you don't know this land, y' never lived here. It's hard, break-y'r-heart bad at times, but it's beautiful—*because* it's so hard."

He stood up suddenly. "Come wi' me." He strode to the door and out into the gathering dusk. The sun was going down in a display of soft lilac and grey; a mist hung over the still waters and the peace was only broken by the secret sounds of nature.

"See there? It's a land so big we don't know how far it is t' the other side. It's new an' raw, open to all—the west an' the north is all waiting, mile on mile o' country without it's seen a man. But that's what I want, t' be at peace. M' heart is here, Tom, where I c'n live like God means me to."

Kydd saw his face light up as he spoke. "How d' ye live? Y'r carving?"

Turning to him the older man spoke quietly but firmly. "T' you, I'm a poor man. I ask ye to think of what I have here—all m' time is my own, all of it. This place is mine, I built it m'self as I want it. And yes, I carve—in winter y' has a lot o' time, an' what better than t' create with y'r own hands?"

He chuckled. "Y' saw the choughs. I didn't think t' see any-one fr'm old Guildford here. But it keeps me in coin enough t' meet m' needs." He threw open a door to a side cabin. In the gloom Kydd could see huge figures: griffins, mermaids, solemn aldermen and long, decorative side panels. The odour of fresh-carved timber chips was resinous and powerful. "The yards're startin' for th' year. They'll be wantin' the winter's work now."

They trudged back to the main cabin. A train-oil lamp was burning inside, intensifying the shadows, while the smell of beef pie and potatoes eddied about.

"Now, m' lad, how's about you tell me about Guildford an' y'r folks?"

Kydd talked of the Old Country, of the stirring changes that had resulted from this final great war with the French, the school they had bravely started, the appearance of various little ones in the family. At one point Kydd stopped, letting the stillness hang, then asked carefully, "We were told there was a misunderstanding with my papa, Uncle. Was it s' bad you remember it t' this day?"

His uncle guffawed loudly. "Was at first, but then I hears after, she married someone else anyhow. Didn't seem right t' start up writin' again so . . ."

The evening was a great success. Colleen brought out a hoarded jar of blueberry wine and, in its glow, stories of old times and old places were exchanged long into the dark night.

"So you've never regretted it?"

"Never!" His hand crept out to take hers. "In Halifax they'd never let an Irish woman in t' their society. I'd always be tryin'. Here we live content the same as man 'n' wife, an' here we stay."

The fire flared and crackled, the hours passed and the fire settled to embers. Eventually Kydd yawned. "Have t' return to m' ship tomorrow," he said, with real regret.

His uncle said nothing, staring into the fire. Then he took a deep breath. "Seems y' have a teaser on y'r hands, m' boy."

"A problem?"

"Yes, sir. Now, consider—you've seen me, alive 'n' well. You have t' decide now what ye say to y'r father. The world knows I was killed by a bear. Are you goin' to preserve m' secret an' let it stand, or will ye ease his human feelings 'n' say I'm here?"

"I—I have t' think on it," was all Kydd could find to say.

His uncle gave a slow smile. "I'm sure ye'll know what t' do."
His gaze on Kydd was long—and fond.

"Wait here," he said, and went outside.

While he was gone, Kydd's thoughts turned to his father.
Where was the mercy in telling him that, according to the world,
his brother was no more? Or, on the other hand, that his brother
was alive and well but had turned his back on society, preferring
a pariah woman and a vast wilderness?

There was just one course he could take that would be both
merciful and truthful. He would say that, according to the re-
cords, his uncle Matthew had lived in Halifax doing well until
1791 but had then moved somewhere else in the immense country of Canada. In this way at least his father would remain in
hope.

The door creaked open and his uncle returned with an object
wrapped in old sacking. "You're goin' to be the last Kydd I ever
sees," he said thickly, "an' I'm glad it were you. See here—" He
passed across the sacking. It contained something heavy, a single, undistinguished black rock. But, breaking through it in several places, Kydd saw a dull metallic gleam. Gold. Astonished,
Kydd took it, feeling its weight.

"Fell down a ravine years ago, goin' after a animal, an' there
it was. But it's no use t' me—I bring that t' town an' in a brace o'
shakes it'll be crawlin' with folks grubbin' up th' land an' fightin'.
Never bin back, leave th' rest in the good earth where it belongs.
But you take it—an' use it to get somethin' special, something
that'll always remind ye of y'r uncle Matthew in Canada."

Chapter 8

SEAMEN WERE HOISTING IN HEAVY STONE BOTTLES of spruce-beer essence. Admiral Vandeput considered the drink essential to the health of his squadron.

"I'll sweat the salt fr'm your rascally bones—sink me if I don't." The squeaky voice of a midshipman was unconvincing: he had a lot to learn about the handling of men, Kydd thought, and turned away irritably. He put his head inside the lobby. Adams had promised to relieve him, but was nowhere to be found. Kydd returned impatiently to the quarterdeck. The seamen had finished their work and all of the wicker-covered jars were below at last.

The last man of the work party was still on deck, slowly coiling down the yardarm tackle fall. There was something disquieting about this thick-set seaman: Kydd had seen him come aboard with the new men and several times he'd noticed the man looking his way with a significant cast.

Kydd paced forward. The man glanced over his shoulder at him and turned his back, busying himself with his task. When Kydd drew near he straightened and turned, touching his forelock. "Mr Kydd, sir," he said, his voice not much more than a low rasp.

Surprised, Kydd stopped.

"Sir, ye remembers me?"

There was an edge of slyness to his manner that Kydd did not like. Was he a sea-lawyer perhaps? But the man was only a little shorter than Kydd himself, powerfully built, with hard, muscular arms and a deep tattooed chest: he had no need of cozening ways on the mess-deck.

The man gave a cold smile. "Dobbie, petty officer o' the afterguard," he added, still in a low tone.

Kydd could not recall anyone by that name. The midshipman popped up out of the main-hatchway but saw them together and disappeared below again. "No, can't say as I do," Kydd replied. Unless the seaman had something of value to say to an officer he was sailing closer to the wind than a common sailor should. "I don't remember you, Dobbie—now be about y'r duties."

He turned to go, but Dobbie said quietly, "In *Sandwich*." Kydd stopped and turned. Dobbie stared back, his gaze holding Kydd's with a hard intensity. "Aye—when you was there. *I* remembers ye well . . . sir."

It had been less than a year ago but the *Sandwich* was a name Kydd had hoped never to hear again. She had been the mutineers' flagship and at the centre of the whirlwind of insurrection and violence at the Nore. It had climaxed in failure for the mutiny and an end to the high-minded attempt to complete the work begun at Spithead. Many sailors had paid with their lives. Kydd had joined the mutiny in good faith but had been carried along by events that had overwhelmed them all. But for mysterious appeals at the highest level he should have shared their fate.

"Dick Parker. Now there was a prime hand, don' ye think? Saw what was goin' on, but concerns hisself with the men, not th' gentry. Sorely missed, is he."

Kydd drew back. Was Dobbie simply trying to ingratiate himself, or was this a direct attempt at drawing Kydd into some crazy plot? Anxiety and foreboding flooded in. Either way this had to be stopped.

"Enough o' this nonsense. Where I came from before I went t' the quarterdeck is no concern o' yours, Dobbie. Pay y'r respects to an officer an' carry on." Even in his own ears it rang false, lacking in authority.

Dobbie looked relaxed, a lazy smile spreading across his face. Kydd glanced uneasily about; no one was within earshot. "Did ye not hear? I said—"

"Me mates said t' me, 'An' who's this officer then, new-rigged an' has the cut o' the jib of the fo'c'sle about 'im?' What c'n I say?" Dobbie was confident and as watchful as a snake. "I keeps m' silence, 'cos I knows you has t' keep discipline, an' if they catches on that you is th' Tom Kydd as was alongside Dick Parker all the time—"

"What is it ye want?" Kydd snapped.

Dobbie picked up the end of the fall and inspected its whipping, then squinted up at Kydd. "Ah, well. I was wonderin'—you was in deep. Not a delegate, but 'twas your scratch what was clapped on all them vittlin' papers, I saw yez. Now don't y' think it a mort strange that so many good men went t' the yardarm but Mr Tom Kydd gets a pardon? Rest gets the rope, you gets th' King's full pardon 'n' later the quarterdeck." The lazy smile turned cruel. "We gets t' sea, the gennelmen in the fo'c'sle hear about you, why, could go hard f'r a poxy spy . . ."

Kydd flushed.

Dobbie tossed aside the rope and folded his arms. "Your choice, Mr Tom Kydd. You makes m' life sweet aboard—I'm a-goin' t' be in your division—or the fo'c'sle hands are goin' to be getting some interestin' news."

"Damn you t' hell! I didn't—" But Dobbie turned and padded off forward.

Kydd burned with emotion. It was utterly beyond him to have

spied treacherously on his shipmates as they had fought together for their rights. He was incapable of such an act. But the men of the fo'c'sle would not know that. Dobbie was one of them, and he was claiming to have been with Kydd at the mutiny and to have the full story. Unable to defend himself in person, Kydd knew there was little doubt whom they would believe.

The consequences could not be more serious. He would not be able to command these men, that much was certain; the captain would quickly recognise this and he would be finished as an officer. But it might be worse: a dark night, quiet watch and a belaying pin to the head, then quickly overside . . .

And the wardroom—if they believed he owed his advancement to spying and betrayal, what future had he among them?

It was incredible how matters had reached such a stand so quickly. He would have to move fast, whatever his course. The obvious action was to submit. It had definite advantages. Nothing further would happen because it was in Dobbie's interest to keep his leverage intact. And it would be simple: Kydd as an officer could easily ensure Dobbie's comfortable existence.

The other tack would be to brazen it out. But Kydd knew this was hopeless: he would be left only with his pride at not yielding to blackmail, and that was no choice at all.

He yearned for Renzi's cool appraisal and logical options: he would find the answers. But he was in Newfoundland. Kydd was not close to Adams and the others: he would have to face it alone.

His solitary, haunted pacing about the upper deck did not seem to attract attention, and two hours had passed before he found his course of action.

Kydd knew the lower deck, its strengths and loyalties as well as its ignorance; its rough justice and depth of sentiment could move men's souls to achieve great things—or stir them to passionate vindictiveness. He would now put his trust in them, an unshakeable faith that he, even as an officer, could rely on their sense of honour, fairness and loyalty.

The afternoon ebbed to a pallid dusk, and the hands secured, then went below for grog and supper. Kydd waited until they were in full flow. Then he went down the after hatchway to the gun-deck and paused at the foot of the ladder.

The mess-tables were rigged and the usual warm conviviality of a meal-time, enlivened by rum, rose noisily from the tables between the rows of guns. A few curious looks came his way, but in the main seamen were more interested in the gossip of the day and he was ignored.

Methodically, he removed his cocked hat. Then he took off his lieutenant's uniform coat and laid it carefully over his arm. By this time he had the attention of the nearest, who looked at him in astonishment.

He paced forward slowly, and with terrible deliberation. One by one the tables lapsed into an amazed silence, which grew and spread until the whole gun-deck fell into an unnatural quiet and men craned forward for a better view.

Kydd continued his walk, his face set and grim, eyes fixed forward in an unblinking stare. He was either right to trust—or he had lost everything. He passed the great jeer capstan, the mighty trunk of the mainmast, the main hatch gratings, his measured tread now sounding clear and solemn.

He halted abreast the fore capstan, his eyes still fixed forward. Slowly his gaze turned to one side: Dobbie sat, transfixed, at the mess by number-five gun. Kydd marched over. Not a man moved. He held Dobbie with his eyes, dropping his words into the silence. "I'll be waiting for ye—the Mizzen tavern. At two, tomorrow." Then he wheeled about and began the long walk back down the silent gun-deck.

• • •

In the privacy of his cabin Kydd buried his face in his hands. As an officer there was no question of how to deal with a slur on one's honour: a duel was the inevitable result. Dobbie was not a gentleman, therefore Kydd could not demean himself in calling him out. But this was a matter for the lower deck: different rules applied. By now the news would be already around the ship. It was too late for him to back away—and also for Dobbie.

Dobbie was big and a bruiser, well used to a mill. Kydd could take care of himself, but this was another matter. Of a surety he would be the loser, in all probability suffering a battering and disfiguring injury. But the result would be worth it. Never more would any man question his honour or integrity: Dobbie's word would be hollow against that of a man who had set aside the power and privileges that were his by right to defend his honour in the traditional way.

Kydd had no fear of it coming to the ear of the captain—or any other officer, for that matter. It would be common currency on the mess-decks and every seaman and petty officer would know of it, but it was their business and, as with so many other things, the quarterdeck never would hear of it.

He slept well: there was little to be gained in brooding on hypothetical events of the next day and in any case there was nothing he could do about it now that events had been set in train.

As he moved about the ship there were surreptitious looks, curious stares and a few morbid chuckles. He went below to find his servant. "Er, Tysoe, there is something of a service I want you t' do for me."

"Sir, don't do it, sir, please, I beg," Tysoe said, with a low, troubled voice. "You're a gentleman, sir, you don't have to go mixing with those villains."

"I have to, an' that's an end to it."

Tysoe hesitated, then asked unhappily, "The service, sir?"

"Ah—I want you to find a fo'c'sle hand who c'n lend me a seaman's rig f'r this afternoon. Er, it'll be cleaned up after."

"Sir." But Tysoe did not leave, disconsolately shuffling his feet. "Sir, I'm coming with you."

"No." Kydd feared he would be instantly discovered and probably roughed up: he could not allow it. "No, but I thank ye for your concern."

There was a fitful cold drizzle when Kydd stepped into the boat, which gave him an excuse to wear a concealing oilskin. Poulden was stroke; he had gruffly volunteered to see Kydd through to the Mizzen tavern, but made determined efforts not to catch his eye as he pulled strongly at his oar.

They landed at King's Slip. Without a word, Kydd and Poulden stepped out and the boat shoved off. The waterfront was seething with activity and they pushed through firmly to Water Street.

It was lined with crude shanties and pothouses; raw weathered timbers abuzz with noise, sailors and women coming and going, the stink of old liquor and humanity in the air. A larger hostelry sported a miniature mast complete with upper yards, jutting out from a balcony. "The Fore, sir," said Poulden, self-consciously. "We has three inns; the Fore, the Main, 'n' the Mizzen, which, beggin' yer pardon, we understands t' be respectively the wildest, gayest an' lowest in Halifax." Hoisted on the Fore's mast was the sign of a red cockerel, a broad hint to the illiterate of the pleasures within.

Kydd's heart thudded, but he was angry with Dobbie—not so much for trying such a scheme but for the slur on Kydd's character. His anger focused: whatever the outcome of the next few hours he would see to it that he left marks on Dobbie.

They swung down a side-street to see a crowd of jostling men outside an entrance with a small mizzen mast. "Sir, gotta leave ye now." Poulden returned the way he came, leaving Kydd on his own. His mouth dried. Screeches of female laughter and roars of appreciation at some unseen drunken feat filled the air. As a young seaman he'd been in places like this, but he had forgotten how wild and lawless they were.

"There he is! Told yer so!" Heads turned and Kydd was engulfed with a human tide that jollied him inside, all red faces and happy anticipation. A black-leather can was shoved at him, its contents spilling down his front. "No, thank ye," he said quickly, thrusting it away.

Women on the stairs looked at him with frank curiosity, some with quickening interest at his strong, good looks. A hard-featured seaman and two others tried to push through. "Gangway, y' scrovy bastards, an' let a man see who it is then," he grumbled.

"Akins, Master o' the Ring. I have t' ask, are ye Lootenant Kydd an' no other?" The taphouse broke into excited expectancy at Kydd's reply. He recognised both of the others: Dean, boatswain's mate of *Tenacious,* standing with brutal anticipation, and Laffin, petty officer of the afterguard, wearing a pitying expression. There were others from *Tenacious,* their images barely registering on Kydd's preternaturally concentrated senses.

"Are ye willing t' stand agin Bill Dobbie, L'tenant, the fight t' be fair 'n' square accordin' t' the rules?" There was a breathy silence. Bare-knuckle fighting was brutal and hard, but there were rules—the Marquess of Queensberry had brought some kind of order to the bloody business.

"Aye, I'm willing."

The pothouse erupted. "Fight's on, be gob, an' me bung's on Dobbie."

This was going to be a legendary match to be talked of for years. The crush was stifling, but Laffin cleared the way with his fists and they passed through the damp sawdust and sweaty, shoving humanity to the sudden cool of the outside air. It was a small inner courtyard with rickety weathered buildings on all four sides. In the centre, sitting on a standard seaman's chest, was Dobbie.

Kydd stopped as the significance of the chest crowded in on him. This was not going to be a fight according to Queensberry's rules: this was a traditional way of the lower deck to settle the worst of grudges—across a sea-chest. They would sit facing each other over its length, lashed in place, to batter at each other until one yielded or dropped senseless.

To back away now was impossible. He had to go through with it. He took in Dobbie's deep chest and corded arms. His fists were massive and strapped up with darkened, well-used leather. There was no doubt that Kydd was in for heavy punishment.

The men and women in the courtyard were shouting obscene encouragement to Dobbie, urging him to take it out on an officer while he had the chance. A hoot of laughter started up at the back of the crowd and Kydd's servant was propelled to the front.

"Tysoe!"

"Sir, sir—" He had a bundle clutched to his chest, and his frightened eyes caught Kydd's. "I came, sir, I—I came—"

"He's come t' drag Tom Cutlass home after, like," chortled Dean. It was the first Kydd had heard of any lower-deck nickname—from the desperate time fighting in the boat when his sword had broken and he had taken up a familiar cutlass. Strangely, it strengthened his resolve.

"Don't worry, Tysoe, I'll see ye right!" Kydd said forcefully, above the crowd.

The laughter died as the men sensed the time had come. Kydd looked directly at Dobbie, who returned the look with a glittering-eyed malignity. "Get on wi' it, yer sluggards!" screamed one woman, her cries taken up by the baying circle of men. Scowling, Akins turned to Kydd. "Get y'r gear off, then, mate."

Kydd pulled off his shirt, feeling the icy cold wind playing on his bare torso. There was a stir of amazed comment as the stretched and distorted scars criss-crossing his back were recognised for what they were: a relic of the long-ago agony of lashes from a cat-of-nine-tails at a grating. The woman's screeches diminished and the crowd subsided.

Laffin produced cords and Kydd took his place at the other end of the chest, feeling the feral impact of Dobbie's presence, his heart racing at the carnage about to be wrought. The ropes cut into his legs, but his eyes rose to lock on Dobbie's.

"Are ye ready, gemmun?" Akins had no watch, no tools of a referee—this was going to be a smashing match. A thin, cold rain began, chilling Kydd's skin and running into his eyes, mixing with salt sweat, stinging and distracting. He raised his fists slowly, his heart hammering. Dobbie responded, holding his low for a first murderous punch, his pale, unblinking eyes locked on Kydd's.

Akins raised his arm, looking at each in turn. His eyes flickered once and the arm sliced down. "Fight!" he yelled and leaped aside.

For one split second, Dobbie held Kydd's eyes, then cut loose with a bellow. "No!" he roared, dropping his arms. "Be buggered! I'll not do it!"

The crowd fell into an astonished silence, staring at Dobbie. He thrust his head forward, his fists by his side. "Take a swing, mate—come on, make it a settler."

Kydd, shaken but suddenly understanding, obliged with a meaty smack to the jaw, which rocked Dobbie. Laffin came forward with his knife and severed the ropes. Dobbie got to his feet. He shook his head and turned to the rowdy crush. "Shipmates!

Y' came t' see a grudge fight, an' I'm sorry I can't give yez one. See, this 'ere is Tom Kydd as I remember fr'm the Nore—I saw 'im stand alongside Dick Parker 'n' them in the mutiny when others were runnin' like rats. But I thought as 'ow 'e got 'is pardon by sellin' out his mates, an' I told him so.

"Mates, if y' wants a lesson in honour, Mr Kydd's yer man. Won't stand fer anyone takin' 'im fer a villain without 'e stands up fer 'isself, an' that's why 'e sees me 'ere—a duel, like. An I 'ave ter say, I didn't reckon 'e'd 'ave the sand t' see it through, sling 'is mauley like a good 'un, 'im bein' an officer an' all."

He turned back to Kydd and touched his forehead. "I'd take it kindly in ye should y' shake m' hand, sir."

A roar of wild applause burst out, going on and on, until Dobbie held up his arms. "M' lads—I want yer t' unnerstand, this 'ere Kydd is one of us, but 'e's done good fer 'imself, an' that's no crime. An' I f'r one is going ter foller Lootenant Kydd."

"All bets 'r off, gennelmen!" bawled Akins.

The press of spectators broke into riotous commotion. Kydd's comprehension of events rapidly disintegrated—he was being slapped on the back and idolised by dozens of drunken seamen. An unwilling Tysoe was plied with beer; women's gleeful painted faces danced before him; and Dobbie, now the centre of a throng of seamen, was telling the story of the great mutiny of the Nore.

Admiral Vandeput and his squadron returned three days later, joining *Tenacious* at her anchorage. Kydd was in the boat returning from the flagship, and could see Renzi waiting on the quarterdeck of *Tenacious,* and dared a brief wave. It was good to see his friend and the clouds lifted from his spirit.

Clutching the precious pouch of despatches and confidential signal information, Kydd hauled himself up the side and took Renzi's hand. "I'd thought to see you flag-lieutenant b' now," he said.

"Flag-lieutenant? Not if the present incumbent can help it."
Renzi chuckled drily. "And while you've been in this Arcadia
resting, I've been privy to secrets concerning the cod fishery that
would stand you amazed, dear fellow."

"You'll tell me of y'r secrets this very afternoon. You get y'r
gear inboard while I get these t' Captain Houghton. I have it from
on high that the adm'ral will want t' have his squadron to sea f'r
exercises as soon as he's stored—that's t'morrow, I'll wager."

"If it were at all possible, a light walk ashore among the spring
blooms would be pleasant, Tom. Our admiral does not spare his
minions, you may believe."

The Dartmouth side of the harbour was speckled with green
shoots and the ground was firming. They paced it out in the hesi-
tant sunshine, feeling the country awake out of its winter retreat.

"A singular place, Newfoundland," Renzi said, at length. "At
times I believed that the island should be entirely covered by cur-
ing fish, were it not that room has to be made for the vats of that
monstrously malodorous fish oil."

"Your secrets?" Kydd wanted to know.

"Nothing, really. It's a turbulent place that requires the admiral to show firm on occasion—the fisher gentry from Devon have
it that Newfoundland is their personal fief, and deliver rough justice to those who say otherwise. You'd smile to hear the talk in an
assembly at St John's—you'd swear it was Exeter or Bideford on
market day."

They walked on companionably. "So, all has been uneventful
in the meantime?" Renzi enquired.

Kydd hesitated. Renzi was the soul of discretion, but that was
not the point at issue—his uncle had left the resolution of his
problem to him alone: Should he involve his friend in a matter of
family?

There was no question: he had been on his own for too long.

"Nicholas, the strangest thing—I met m' uncle f'r the first time not long since." His tone made Renzi look at him sharply.

"Yes—m' father's brother, here in Canada." Kydd went on to tell of his discovery and his quandary—and his decision neither to conform to the story of the bear nor to reveal his uncle's current whereabouts to his family.

"An admirable, even logical decision, Tom, and I honour you for it," Renzi said sincerely.

They strolled on in the quietness at the edge of the forest. "That's not all of the matter, is it, brother?" Renzi said, stopping and facing Kydd directly. "I'd be honoured to share whatever it is that lays its hands on my friend."

Kydd looked away, staring at the jack-pines carpeting the landscape, all seeming the same but when looked at separately every one an individual, uncountable thousands into the blue-grey distance. "Nicholas, it doesn't answer. I have t' face it. I'm not t' be one of y'r deep-dyed, gentleman officers who knows their fox-hunting an' Seasons. I know seamanship an' navigation, not dancin' and talking to ladies."

"Dear fellow, this—"

"When I got my step t' the quarterdeck it was hard t' believe. Then it seemed to me that there was no end t' it—captain of my own ship, even. But I know better than that now. The King's service needs l'tenants for sure, but only the *gentlemen* will find 'emselves promoted—an' I'm no gentleman, an' now I know it."

"No gentleman? What nonsense—"

"Spare me y'r comfortin' words, Nicholas," Kydd said bitterly. "For my own good, I have t' hoist this aboard an' stop pining f'r what can't be, and that's that."

"But it only requires you learn the marks of civility, the—"

"Is that *all* it is to be a gentleman, jus' know all the tricks? I don't think so." Kydd fell silent, morosely kicking a pine cone.

"Do you despise gentlemen?" Renzi asked quietly.

Kydd flashed him a suspicious look. "Not as who should say—they were born to it, that's their good luck . . . and yours," he added, with a sardonic smile.

They walked on for a space, then Kydd stopped again. "T' be honest, it sticks in m' gullet that I'm t' leave promotion to others—and I'm of a mind t' do something about it."

"What?"

"Well, in a merchant ship they have no care f'r gentle ways—a berth as mate in an Indiaman would suit me right handsomely, one voyage a year out east, an' my own freight . . ."

"Leave the Navy?"

"And why not?"

Kydd obstinately avoided Renzi's gaze as his friend stared at him.

In a brisk south-easterly early next morning the North American Squadron put to sea for one week's exercising in the waters between Nova Scotia and the United States, the 74-gun HMS *Resolution* as flagship in the van, the seven ships a picture of grace and might.

In *Tenacious,* at the rear, the picture was more apparent than real: the file of ships that stretched ahead to the flagship in perfect line also obscured her signals, and the little fleet could not stretch to the luxury of a repeating frigate.

Despairing, Kydd hung out from the rigging to weather, trying to steady his big telescope against the thrumming in the shrouds and bracing himself to catch the meaning of *Resolution*'s signal flags end-on. They were clawing their way out close-hauled; if they were to end on an easterly course passing south of the Thrumcap they would have to pass through the wind's eye.

It was the admiral's choice, to tack about or wear round, and with the Neverfail shoal waiting ahead and the same unforgiving rocks under their lee that had claimed *Tribune* so recently. Tack or wear—put the helm down or up—it all depended on the signal that would be thrown out to the fleet in the next few minutes.

Captain Houghton stumped up and down the quarterdeck, nervous midshipmen scuttling along behind him, the master keeping a respectful distance to his lee. It was impossible to send the men to their stations until it was known the action to be taken, and they stood about the decks in uneasy groups.

Devil's Island, the most seaward part of Halifax, lay abeam: now there was no reason why they could not bear up—and then there was a tiny flutter of bunting on *Resolution*'s poop.

Kydd concentrated with his glass. A quick refresh from his pocket book had shown him that there was only one flag in the two hoists that differentiated "tack" and "wear"—a yellow diagonal on a blue background—and this was number three, "tack." If he just glimpsed that flag, he could ignore the rest and they would gain a vital edge. Houghton stopped pacing and faced Kydd. Around the ship men followed suit, every face turning towards him.

There! A cluster of flags mounted swiftly in *Resolution*'s rigging, their fluttering edges making the hoist nearly impossible to read—but Kydd's straining eyes had spotted the distinctive number three as the flagship's signal crew bent it on as part of the hoist. Before the flags had reached the peak he roared triumphantly, "It's *tack!*"

Men raced to their stations; running gear was thumped on the deck and faked for running, afteryards manned by the starboard watch and headyards the larboard, double manning for the greatest speed. The signal jerked down aboard the flagship—execute!

The wheel spun as the quartermaster at the wheel and his mate threw themselves at the task and *Tenacious*'s bluff bow began to move. At the waist, ropes' ends were out as the petty officers ensured the foresheet was let go smartly and the lee brace

checked away. In growing excitement Kydd saw that of the file
of ships only *Tenacious* herself at the rear and the flagship at the
head had begun a swing round into the wind. His pride swelled
at the evidence of his enterprise—they were well into their tacking
about while in front, *Andromeda,* was still in line ahead.

"Helm's a-lee!" Big driving sails began shaking, the yards
bracing round while the foreyards took the wind aback to lever
her round. *"Mainsail haul!"* The ship passed slowly through the
eye of the wind and all hands heaved and hauled with all their
might to make the sails belly out comfortably on to the new tack.
It was neatly done.

"Sir!" It was Rawson, tugging on his sleeve urgently. Kydd
turned irritably. The midshipman pointed mutely at the line of
ships: *Resolution* had tacked about as fast as they, but all the rest
were still thrashing along on the old tack, not one even attempting to go about.

A feeling of growing apprehension crept over Kydd. Something
was wrong. *Resolution* was now in plain view to weather, her entire beam to *Tenacious* instead of her stern—and as they watched,
a flutter of bunting mounted at her main, the original signal. But
ominously, there for the whole fleet to see was *Tenacious*'s pennant climbing brazenly aloft. A gun thudded out peremptorily for
attention.

"What, in the name of God?" Houghton roared at Kydd. The
admiral was telling the world that HMS *Tenacious* had blundered
and should conform to his signal.

"It's tack, but *in succession,* sir," Rawson whispered urgently,
pointing to an entry in the signal book. It was the order to tack,
sure enough, but the maddening additional flag at the end indicated that instead of turning into line like a file of soldiers, the
admiral wanted the column of ships to reach a fixed point, then
wheel round to follow him, thereby preserving their line ahead
formation.

"Sir, the signal is 'tack in succession.' I—I'm sorry, sir . . ." Kydd's voice seemed thin and weak.

Houghton's chest swelled and his face reddened, but before the explosion another gun sounded impatiently from the flagship. There was nothing for it but public ignominy.

"*Haaands* to stations for staying!" *Tenacious* must obey the last order and come back to her original tack; her ship's company, feeling the shame and the entire fleet's eyes on them, took up their ropes again while Kydd stood mortified, face burning. *Tenacious* came ponderously about and tried to assume her old place at the end of the line—but by now the line itself was all but gone, preceding ships now having reached the fixed point and tacked round on to the new course.

Cursing, weary men picked up their ropes and prepared to haul round for the third time in a row. But when the due point was reached *Tenacious* had not picked up enough speed, and when the helm went down she headed up languidly into the wind—and stayed there, held in the wind's eye, in irons.

The master lunged over and took the helm, bawling at the men forward as the ship drifted astern, the hapless officer-of-the-watch nervously clutching his telescope and watching the captain, appalled. Kydd, with nothing to do, could only stand and suffer as the ship tried to regain her dignity.

Finally in her place at the rear of the line stretching away to the east, *Tenacious* settled down and Kydd turned to his captain, prepared for the worst—but yet another signal streamed out from *Resolution*. "Fleet will heave to," Kydd reported carefully. Main topsails were backed and way fell off. There had to be a reason why the whole squadron was coming to a stop.

"Flagship, sir—our pennant and, er, 'Send a lieutenant.'" The admiral wanted an official explanation from *Tenacious* for the recent display—and there would be no bets taken on who would go as the sacrifice . . .

• • •

Admiral Vandeput did not spare his squadron. Between Cape Sable and Cape Cod, seven ships sailed resolutely in formation, assuming tactical divisions by signal, running down invisible foes, shortening sail for battle. Curious fishing-boats were diverted by strings of flags run up the flagship's rigging, followed by instant animation aboard every vessel of the squadron—and the occasional gun for attention.

Kydd doggedly improved his acquaintance with the *Fighting Instructions* and attached signals, and when the squadron was ready to return to port several days later, he was fully prepared. "Sir, vessels in the squadron to retire in order of sailing." It was the return to Halifax. "Signal to wear, sir," Kydd added, as the flags broke at the masthead. This would see the ships turning on their heel and facing where they had been—but this time with *Tenacious* leading the squadron back to port.

Now was the time to show her breeding in the manoeuvre of going about completely, stern to wind. "Brace in the afteryards—up helm!" The mizzen topsail began shaking, the main just full and the fore up sharp. *Tenacious* started her swing, the line of ships ahead commenced their wheel about. "Lay y'r headyards square! Shift headsheets!" Her rotation brought the wind right aft, and the weather sheets were eased to become the lee. "Brace up headyards—haul aboard!" Men laboured to get the tack hard in forward and the sheets aft as she came on to her new heading. *Tenacious* responded with a willing surge.

"Draw jib!" It was the last order before she settled on her new course, the sheets hauled aft to bring the headsails to a full tautness. The fo'c'slemen responded heartily, the thought of safe haven in Halifax just hours away lending weight to their hauling.

A crack as loud as a three-pounder gun came from far forward. The crew on the jibsheets fell to the deck, others crouched down and looked about fearfully. It was impossible to see what was happening from aft as the clews of the big courses effectively shut out the scene.

"Can't 'old 'er, sir!" bawled the helmsman, as *Tenacious* immediately fell off the wind and inevitably out of line. An incomprehensible hail came from forward, amplified by a breathless messenger. "Lost our jibboom, sir!" he yelled, his voice cracking.

Houghton lifted his speaking trumpet. "Douse the fore t'gallant instantly, d'ye hear?" He wheeled round, his face set. A volley of orders brought sail in, and way off the vessel. "You know what to do, get forrard and bear a hand—now!" he snapped at Kydd. Rawson could be relied on to hoist the necessary "not-under-command" general signal that indicated *Tenacious* was no longer in a position to obey her captain.

Kydd hurried forward. This was Renzi's part-of-ship: Kydd would take orders from him without question. He arrived at the scene to see a tangle of rigging from aloft—and a truncated bowsprit. A thumping from the lee bow and men staring down showed where the failed spar was now.

"Poulden, do you clap on the t'gallant bowline as well." It was strange to hear the crack of authority in Renzi's voice, to see the gleam of hard purpose in his friend's eyes.

"Sir," Kydd reported to the fourth lieutenant.

Renzi flashed a brief smile. "Martingale stay parted, the jibboom carried away," he said, flicking his eyes up to watch the progress of the jib downhaul, which was clearly being readied to hoist the spar back aboard. "I'm sanguine we'll have it clear soon—it's to loo'ard, and I've taken the liberty to set the foretopmast stays'l to make a lee while we see to the jib."

The boatswain quickly had the experienced fo'c'slemen at work reeving a heel rope: the fifty feet of Danzig fir surging below was a formidable spar to recover aboard.

Renzi gazed intently at the descending downhaul. "Mr Kydd,

I'd be obliged if you'd inform the captain of our situation, that I've furled the fore t'gallant, but desire the fore t'gallant mast be struck."

Kydd touched his hat, then hastened back to the quarterdeck.

Houghton listened sourly, his eyes straying to the line of ships passing by, beginning the evolution to heave to. "Request Flag to pass within hail," he said. The signals soared up rapidly, but even as they did, *Resolution* had put down her helm and closed.

Briefly, Houghton passed details by speaking trumpet to the admiral. There was little to discuss: *Lynx,* a 16-gun ship-sloop, was detached to stand by them while they repaired; the remainder sailed on to Halifax.

It was not an easy repair: even with a spare spar fortunately to hand, the stump of the jibboom had to be extracted from the bowsprit cap and sea-hardened heel ropes cut away. It was sheer bad luck that the bee-block seating the new jibboom to the bowsprit needed reshaping, and now with jib-stay and fittings to apply there was no chance they would complete by dusk.

The hours passed uncomfortably. Without steadying sail on the open sea *Tenacious* wallowed glumly all night, Cape Cod forty miles under her lee. Kydd had the morning watch: red-eyed and tired, he observed a grey dawn approach with *Lynx* far out to the southward but stoutly clapping on all sail. Thick mist patches persisted to the north in the calm seas, wisps reaching out occasionally to *Tenacious* with their clammy embrace.

As soon as there was light enough, work began on the jibboom, and well before the wan sun had cleared the foreyard it was all but complete.

"What, in hell's name?" Houghton said, stopping his restless pacing. It was gunfire—to the north and not too distant, a distinct thud.

"At least twenty-fours, maybe thirty-twos," growled Bryant, puzzled. Another flurry of thumps in the mist were heard.

Houghton looked nonplussed. "This can only be the squadron—there's not another sail-o'-the-line at sea, unless . . ." He paused, then looked significantly at Bryant. "Send *Lynx* to investigate with all despatch." It was a disturbing mystery: guns of such weight of metal were only carried by line-of-battle ships.

Lynx disappeared into the light mist while *Tenacious* had her topsails set and drawing within minutes of her headsails being once more complete. As she began to gather way her mainsail was loosed and she picked up speed.

The royals of a ship showed above the mist, and *Lynx* burst into view, a signal at her main. "Enemy in sight!" shouted Kydd from the poop, but the signal had been recognised at once.

"Clear for action!"

For the first time on the American side of the Atlantic *Tenacious* made ready for battle. The mist cleared slightly—giving a tantalising view of two dark shapes before it closed round them once more.

The urgent rhythm of "Hearts of Oak" ceased as Bryant reported the ship cleared fore and aft; it was replaced by a long, solemn drum-roll. Quarters!

Kydd's sword banged against his legs as he raced up the poop-deck ladder—if this were a rogue enemy 74 and frigate escort they were in dire trouble.

"Make to *Lynx*, 'take position one mile to windward,' if you please," said Houghton. Small fry had no business in the line when big ships met in combat.

Tenacious glided into the trailing mist, the wind now only a dying breeze. The masthead lookout hailed the deck. "*Deck hoooo!* Two ships, two points t' larboard, near ter five mile off!"

At Houghton's command Kydd exchanged the heavy signal telescope for the more handy glass of the officer-of-the-watch and swung up into the shrouds. He was clear of the mist by the maintop; there was no need to go further—and over there to larboard, protruding through the rumpled white upper surface of the fog, were the upper masts and tops of two vessels—ship rigged, as the lookout had said.

Kydd held the telescope against an upper shroud and gazed intently. Both were under sail but were hove to at an angle to each other. He steadied the glass and found the tricolour of France hanging limply on one, he couldn't tell for the other; certainly they were not ships-of-the-line. He swept once around the horizon, noting that the mist was clearing to patches around the enemy, and bawled down his report, then clambered back to the deck.

"What the devil? You saw no other vessels at all?" Houghton barked. They had unmistakably heard the gunfire of a ship of force.

"Sir, is it—" the master began, then the obscuring mist lifted, and some four miles away almost dead to leeward they saw the enemy.

"Damn my eyes if that ain't a frigate!" Bryant said, in wonder.

"An' that looks like one o' our merchant ships, sir," interposed Hambly.

"Lay us to wind'd of the frigate, Mr Hambly," said Houghton shortly. "We'll look for that damned ship-o'-the-line later."

Adams came up to stand beside Kydd. "Can you just conceive," he said, with a boyish grin, "what discussions must be afoot on her quarterdeck? Just about to take a fat prize and a ship-o'-the-line, no less, sails out of the fog."

Houghton said, over his shoulder, "Mr Kydd, recall *Lynx*—

to take station astern." Aboard the Frenchman there would be something approaching panic: an additional ship in the equation, however small, meant double the worry for the unknown commander of the frigate, now making hasty sail.

"Stuns'ls, sir?" The south-easterly breeze was playful and light and they were bearing down slowly.

"No, Mr Hambly. We'll wait and see what he's going to try first." If the frigate bore away downwind there would be every reason for stuns'ls but if she moved off on the wind *Tenacious* could not follow until the awkward sails and their booms had been taken in.

With the rapt attention of the entire quarterdeck, the Frenchman's length foreshortened as her yards came round. "She's running large," said Bryant. It would be strange indeed if a frigate did not have the legs over a cumbersome ship-of-the-line in a stern chase and in a matter of hours she would be clean away.

The merchant ship, a large vessel with clean lines, ran up her colours as they approached. "American?" Bryant took off his hat and scratched his head, glancing up at their own ensign as if for reassurance.

"Cousin Jonathan is a neutral—what *is* the Frenchy up to?" Adams murmured, as they passed the cheering merchant ship under full sail.

"If y' please, sir . . ." began the master.

"Mr Hambly?"

"If I'm not wrong, sir, that's not a National Ship—she's a heavy privateer. Slight in the build, maybe over-sparred, an' the size of her crew . . ."

"I think he's right, sir," agreed Bryant, borrowing a telescope. The sea ahead was now free of mist and the chase, no more than a mile ahead, loosed all plain sail—but no stuns'l.

Houghton pursed his lips. To stand any chance of staying

with the chase he must soon spread stuns'ls abroad—a canny captain of the "frigate" would wait for the manoeuvre to complete, then put his own wheel over and go close-hauled, knowing that it would take some time for his pursuer to strike his stuns'ls and follow. But on the other hand, if they did nothing, the chase would draw ahead and disappear. "Mr Hambly, be so good as to see how the chase goes."

The sailing master found his sextant and measured the angle from masthead to waterline of their prey. A few minutes later he repeated the action. "We're dropping astern by as much as two knots, I fear, sir."

"Not worth our trouble," Adams said gloomily to Kydd. "We spread more sail, so does she—an' I've yet to find any two-decker can stay with a frigate. She'll be hull down by sunset."

The Frenchman was now visibly drawing away, disdaining even to set her own stuns'ls. Houghton took a telescope and trained it for a long time on the chase. Suddenly he snapped shut the glass. "Pass the word to Mr Bampton and Mr Renzi—we will yaw, and on command they will pepper the rogue with a full broadside."

The midshipman messenger touched his hat, expressionless. Even he knew that this was a last gesture after which the Frenchman could sail away over the horizon in peace. Houghton's action would hopelessly slow their advance in the light winds. The lad ran off smartly and from the rumbling Kydd could picture the long twenty-fours being run out, hand-spikes plied to make them bear as far forward as they could—and the talk around the guns as men peered out of open gunports to catch a sight of their target.

Houghton paced impatiently, waiting for the youngster to report back, his gaze fixed on the ship ahead.

Reported ready, it needed only the captain's order to complete their final, aggressive, act. Houghton gave a brief smile to the group on the quarterdeck, and said quietly to Hambly, "Larboard, if you please."

Tenacious sheered off slowly, giving the gun-captains time to lay their weapons, so when the order to open fire was given the guns crashed out almost together. Smoke rolled down lazily on their target and, seconds later, the sudden eruption of a forest of white splashes along the line of sight brought war-like roars from the gun-decks.

The wheel spun and, sluggishly, *Tenacious* traced her bowsprit back on target, and past. She steadied for a moment, and her opposite broadside thundered out across the calm seas. Again the gun-smoke, the close scatter of splashes—then the enemy's mizzen topmast fell in a graceful curve.

"Please, God . . ." breathed Adams. It was by no means a decisive hit, but the complete absence of square sail on the mizzen might be enough to hamper the vessel, allowing them to close and engage.

Activity died down as every man stared forward, willing the chase to falter, but it was not to be. Sacrificing his wounded topmast, trailing in the water alongside, the French ship ruthlessly cut it loose and continued on as before.

"O' course, she won't grieve over the topmast," Kydd said, glumly. "Going large, she c'n balance by tricing up the clew o' the mains'l one side. She knows all she has t' do is carry on and she'll lose us."

"That may be so," Adams said, "but what happens when she wants to go by the wind? Close-hauled she'd be a cripple."

"And why would she do that?" Bampton's acid comment from behind was nearly lost in a general growl of dismay at the sudden crump of gunfire and smoke issuing out from their quarry.

"She has stern-chasers," Adams remarked soberly. These guns, which could fire straight aft into a pursuer when there was no opportunity to return fire, would be a sore trial. At the next salvo Kydd heard the crack of the guns and, moments later, felt the slam of the passage of one ball over their heads. Several officers ducked automatically, then rose shamefacedly.

"Marines, go below. Stand the men down into the waist, Mr Bryant," Houghton ordered. Although these were only light six-pounders banging away, a hit would kill.

They kept up the chase for another twenty minutes, falling astern the whole while until the first lieutenant approached the captain. "There's no profit in this, sir—we shall have to give him best, I fear."

Houghton glared at him. "Damned if I will! Observe—he cannot run to leeward for ever. On this course he stands to meet the Nantucket shoals off Cape Cod before long. He must choose then between hauling his wind and going east about the Cape to slip into the Gulf o' Maine, or an easier passage west but directly into United States waters.

"I want to box him into the coast. Therefore I shall desire *Lynx* to lie to his starb'd and persuade him that this is his better course." The little sloop would thus stand between the enemy and a refuge in the wider reaches of the Gulf of Maine—but it would be a foolhardy move for the French captain to take on the little ship knowing that just one lucky hit from any of the sloop's sixteen six-pounders could deliver her straight into the clutches of the waiting bigger ship.

"Aye, sir."

Houghton smiled for the first time. "And when he has to bear away, he's under our lee and then we'll have him . . ."

In the early afternoon, the enemy was far ahead but, with *Lynx* faithfully to her starboard, the master was satisfied that they were irrevocably within the hook of the shoals, cutting off her escape to the east. "Tides o' five knots or more around 'em. Steep too, so sounding won't answer and if fog comes, it's all up with the ship," he added, with feeling.

The wind dropped further until it was a ghosting calm, favouring the smaller vessel, which glided a little further and out of range before ceasing movement. The three ships lay becalmed in the grey dusk.

Kydd came on watch: the position of the chase the same. In the night hours there was a choice for their quarry—to attempt a repair by the light of bunched lanthorns, or not show any betraying light and hope to steal away in the night.

She chose the latter: were it not for the quick-witted commander of *Lynx* she might have succeeded. As darkness closed in, the little sloop rigged a makeshift beacon for *Tenacious* of a cluster of lanthorns in a box beaming their light secretly in one direction only.

Through the night *Lynx* stayed faithfully with the enemy, her beacon trained; *Tenacious* lay back in the blackness. When the wind came up some time after midnight and the privateer captain made his move, Houghton knew all about it.

Coming round to the west, the Frenchman clearly wanted to put distance between him and his tormentor before he struck for the open sea, but dawn's grey light showed her the flat nondescript coast of an outlying island of New England to the northeast and two men-o'-war of the Royal Navy to seaward.

Houghton was on deck to greet the dawn, sniffing the wind's direction. "We have him!" he said, with relish. "He can't show much sail forrard with this wind abeam and no square sail aft—we can try for a conclusion before noon, I believe." He looked at the group on the quarterdeck with satisfaction. "It will be a good day's work for all today."

Tenacious bore down, guns run out. With land to leeward and two English ships to weather, the Frenchman's only course was west, the wind veering more southerly. To maintain a reasonable westerly course it was necessary to balance fore and aft sail: with no mizzen topsail the logical thing was to reduce sail forward to compensate and accept a loss of speed.

However, from her cro'jack yard canvas appeared. It was not a sail-bearing spar but the French had lashed a sail along its length, loosed it and secured its clews. They had a drawing square sail aft. Kydd shook his head in admiration; admittedly the "sail" blanketed the poop, silencing the chase guns, but she could keep ahead of her pursuers.

"I'm not concerned," said Houghton, in tones that suggested he was. "There's Long Island Sound ahead—he has to go about or he'll be trapped, so it's there we'll have *Lynx* waiting."

Kydd's first sight of the United States, therefore, was the nondescript sandy scrubland of Block Island ahead, then the low, forested New England coast to the north.

"Sir, I must point out that these are American waters." There was no response to Adams's concern, Houghton keeping his gaze on the fleeing ship ahead. "They're well known to be jealous of their sovereignty, sir—"

"I know that, damn your blood!" Houghton said. But the Frenchman showed no signs whatsoever of putting down her helm and proceeded to pass Block Island, entering the closed length of Long Island Sound.

"They're mad! They've no way out—what do they—"

"Mr Hambly! Quickly! What's the distance across the widest entrance to the sound?"

"Er, to nor'ard—that's betwixt Matunuck and Sandy Point on th' island—and it's . . . seven miles."

"We can do it. North about it is, Mr Hambly. Have a care you stay exactly mid-channel—the Americans claim one league from the low-water mark, which by my reckoning leaves just a mile breadth for our peaceful passage."

"Aye aye, sir," said Hambly, eyeing the Frenchman, who

seemed to have no notion of such niceties.

Leaving Block Island to larboard, *Tenacious* entered the capacious arm of the sea; there could be no escape now—with both English ships to windward and able to close with the Frenchman if he turned back, it was only a matter of waiting.

"He's wasting time," snorted Houghton, impatient.

"Sir, recollect: the French have been friends to the Americans since their support for them in the late war." Renzi had come up from the gun-deck in curiosity.

Bryant sneered: "Pah! Nonsense! They've seen how the French conduct revolutions and want no part of such roguery."

"Then what is the meaning of his motions now?" Renzi answered quietly. The privateer had run up a huge tricolour, which streamed out to leeward and barely two miles ahead, and boldly put up his helm to pass through the mile-wide entrance to an inner expanse of water.

"One league, sir."

"Yes, yes, I had not forgotten." Houghton bit his lip as he eyed the scene. "Take a cast of the lead. I believe we will anchor. One league off shore precisely."

After one last look at the French privateer, just six miles away and, with calm impunity, preparing to berth in a tiny port, Kydd joined the others in the captain's cabin. Houghton was irascible. "Ideas?"

"Cut 'em out!" Bryant's growl was instant. "And be damned to any consequences. There's nought hereabouts but fisherfolk an' farmers—and the Americans have no navy at all that I've heard about."

"True," said Houghton, thoughtfully, "but I'll remind you that in law this must be construed as a combatant seeking refuge in a neutral port, and it would go ill with any who can be shown to violate it."

"And who's to know? Cloth over our name on the stern, boat's crews at night and you can't make 'em out—"

"I honour the ardency of your spirit, Mr Bryant, but I fear this would provoke extremely."

"Swimmers! Under cover o' dark, they go in with borers, sink the bugger where he lies—"

"Mr Bryant! I will not suffer such language! And, besides, they'll never pierce a copper-sheathed hull without fuss and noise."

The cabin fell quiet until Renzi spoke. "Under the assumption that the sympathies of the Americans must lie with the French, I rather feel they would not be over-nice in the laws applicable in cases of neutrality. We may find ourselves lying at anchor, waiting, for some considerable time. Therefore it would seem logical to sail away—with deep regrets, of course."

Bryant snorted but could find no riposte.

"And while we dally, the admiral is deprived of a major unit of his fleet, which is nominally under his orders . . ."

Houghton grunted. "Possibly, but consider—this privateer is big. Should we leave her to her foul plundering, she can take her pick of the largest prizes. We would certainly be held to account if we did not a thing."

"But if you are unable to effect a solution, by reasons of *force majeure,* your course is chosen for you. We must give up."

There was a lengthy pause. Then the captain said, "We have stores only for days. An extended voyage was not contemplated. I have no choice."

Bryant let out his breath like a punctured balloon. "To sail."

"Yes." The captain's voice was final. But then he added, "There is, however, one small chance."

"Sir?"

"I will send an officer ashore to parley with the Americans.

They can't object to that. Try to get 'em to see where their interests best lie, bit of law, that sort of thing. It's possible then that they'll throw the Frenchy out to where we'll be waiting for him."

"A long shot, if I may say so, sir." Pringle's languid voice came from the rear of the group of disconsolate officers. "Did you have anyone in mind?"

"That is a matter that exercises me. If I send my first lieutenant there will undoubtedly be a confrontation, which is devoutly to be avoided." Bryant's splutter was ignored. "Any officer of eminence will confer too much consequence on the affair with the local authorities, whoever they may be in these backwoods.

"I rather feel that the name of Lieutenant Kydd suggests itself."

CHAPTER 9

"Mr President, the Minister Plenipotentiary of Great Britain. Sir, the President of the United States." The aide ushered Liston into the broad room, then departed.

"Robert, so kind in you," said John Adams. He was standing by the tall marble mantelpiece and advanced with outstretched hand. "Sit down, man."

"Thank you, Mr President." Liston took an armchair before the fire with a gracious inclination of his head. "May I know if Abigail is happy in Trenton? It's a wise precaution to depart Philadelphia before the sick season."

"She is indeed, God bless her," said Adams. In the absence of any others at this meeting, he poured the sherry himself. "Your health, Robert."

Liston waited, watching the President over the rim of his glass. Adams, a short, chubby man who looked like a country squire, was not to be underestimated. The two of them had seen much together of this new country's spirited political struggles and personally he wished it well, but this was not a social call. He had come in response to a diplomatic summons.

Adams set down his glass and steepled his fingers. "This cannot be allowed to continue, this stopping and searching on the high seas. Congress and the people will not tolerate it. Your

Navy provokes by its high-handed actions, whatever its rights in the matter. Impressing men from the very decks of United States merchant vessels—it's insufferable, you must understand, and now the British courts in the Caribbean are condemning United States merchant ships seized by the Royal Navy as prizes."

Liston murmured an acknowledgement. It was an old problem, and there were well-rehearsed rejoinders, but he chose another tack. "Mr President, this, I can appreciate, is your immediate concern—but you will understand that here we have a clash of belief and therefore law. You will have your country's position set in law—but we, sir, have had ours since the 1756 Rule of War and it is accepted by the world. Why then should we change it so?"

Adams picked up his glass and smiled. "That is well known, Robert, because it favours the Crown so disproportionate."

"And the French," continued Liston evenly, "with their demands of equipage and new decrees—"

"We will firmly abide by our treaty obligations of 1778."

"Sir, the point I wish to make is that unless these three systems of law are brought to an expression of harmony, your country's trade is in continued jeopardy. It would seem therefore but natural that, if only to restore a balance in world affairs, a measure of amity be enacted between our two nations prohibiting these excesses—here I do not exclude the possibility of an alliance."

"Against France? I think not. The country would never countenance it."

"Sir, consider, the French have been all but swept from the seas. What more practical way to safeguard your ships than have them watched over by the most powerful nation at sea, under flags in amity?"

"Minister, we shall look after our own. We have no need of a foreign power's intervention."

"Without a navy?" said Liston gently.

"Sir, this discussion is concluded." The President stood up. "Have you any other matter you wish to lay before me?"

"Thank you, Mr President. While we are in an understanding, may I be so bold as to refer you to the intolerable actions of French agents in arming bands of Indians on the Canadian border?"

That night the minister made his excuses to his wife and retired to the little room where he was accustomed to gathering his thoughts and rendering them lucidly for his master. Another hand would cipher the despatches.

He tested the nib of his quill, his mind ordering events into neat aggregations, then analysis to their natural heads. It was the least that was expected by Lord Grenville, King George's noble and demanding minister for foreign affairs.

Liston considered carefully: he had been ambassador to the United States for Britain in all but name during many of those turbulent years following the revolution and had acquired a respect for the colonials that bordered on liking. They had followed up their revolution with a constructive, well-considered constitution, which had humanity at its core; the French, even with the American example, had resorted to blood and chaos in an age-old lust for world domination.

There would be no elaborate salutations: Lord Grenville wanted meat in his despatches, personal observations and opinions unfettered by the delicacies of diplomatic language.

The first subject? The likelihood of intervention by America in the titanic world struggle that was reaching its peak. In Europe there was not a single nation of significance, save England, that still stood against France. America remained outside the fight, and as a neutral she could afford to; she was profiting immensely by trading across the interests of the belligerents—there would be little to gain in taking sides.

Yet the French were growing confident, arrogant even, in their dealings. New decrees had been issued by a victorious Directory in Paris that required all merchant ships to carry papers covering their cargo signed by a French consul if they were to escape being taken as a prize of war. There was even talk of an out-of-hand condemnation if British goods of any kind were found aboard.

If the French had the means to enforce this at sea it would have a devastating impact on the Americans. Without a navy, they would have no choice but to bow to French demands. In the end, though, Paris would find it never paid to bully the United States.

But would the Americans see this as cause for war? Some were still sentimentally attached to the British, and others saw French power as a threat that needed balancing. But there were those who remembered France as an ally closely involved in the birth of their nation and would never sanction an aggressive act against her.

Liston sighed. In the end, as always, it came back to politics and personalities in this most democratic of nations. He respected the bluff President, standing four-square for his country, plain-spoken and direct, even with his resolute opposition to British influences, but making no secret of his loathing of the French regime.

But he was increasingly isolated: his party, the Federalists, were the patricians, old landowners staunchly in favour of central government—and generally took the British view. His opponents were the Republicans under Thomas Jefferson, who had no love for England and were mainly new money, naturalised immigrants and strongly pro-French.

The two parties were locked in bitter political strife, which Liston could perceive Adams was badly placed to handle. In this odd system his own Vice President, Jefferson, was leader of the opposing party and privy to who knew what murky political secrets. And he was gravely handicapped by the extremist Hamilton at his elbow, splitting his party and draining confidence from his administration.

It was a fevered time: mobs were marching at night, shattering windows; newspapers were full of wild rumour and acid attack. He wondered briefly what Adams would say if he told him that such was his concern, the great George Washington himself was in secret communication with London. From Pennsylvania a deputation had even demanded clarity on the matter of Mr Adams, son of the President, who was said to be betrothed to a daughter of the King of Great Britain and thereby for the same General Washington to hold the United States in trust for the King.

There was an even chance of an alliance—but as the French depredations increased so must the Americans' grudging tolerance of British measures at sea. If the Royal Navy could be induced to grasp the delicacy of their position, there was a chance . . .

With a large white flag streaming from a halliard, *Tenacious*'s pinnace sailed towards the shore, Lieutenant Kydd in the sternsheets, Midshipman Rawson at the tiller.

It was unfair: Kydd knew next to nothing about the United States and even less about the international law with which he had been told to threaten the local authorities if they did not drive the French back to sea. He was dressed in civilian clothes and unarmed, in accordance with convention when visiting a neutral country. In fact, he had been obliged to don his best rig, the dark green waistcoat and rust-coloured coat that Cecilia had taken such pains to find in Guildford. He held his light grey hat with its silver buckle safely on his knees.

As the low, wooded coast drew closer, Kydd saw the masts and yards of the French privateer beyond the point; it was clear that she was securing from sea. Further in, he made out a timber landing area, and around it a scatter of people.

The sprit-sail was brailed up and lowered, the oars shipped. "Head f'r the jetty," he growled.

Only one of the figures seemed to wear any semblance of a uniform but a number carried what appeared to be muskets. Kydd braced himself: he was going as a representative of his country and he would not be found wanting in the article of military bearing.

A couple of hundred yards from shore Rawson put the tiller over to make the final run in. Suddenly there was the unmistakable report of a flintlock and a gout of water kicked up sharply, dead in line with the bow.

"Wha'? God rot 'em, they're firing on a white flag!" Kydd spluttered. "Keep y'r course, damn you!" he flung at the midshipman.

The people ashore gesticulated and shouted. One levelled his gun in Kydd's direction. "S-sir, should we—" hissed Rawson.

"Take charge o' y'r boat's crew," Kydd replied savagely. Ashore the weapon still tracked Kydd and then it spoke. The bullet spouted water by the stroke oar, followed by a wooden thump as it struck the boat below where Kydd sat.

"Sir?"

"Keep on, damn y'r blood!" snapped Kydd. Even these ignorant backwoodsmen would know they'd be in deep trouble with their government if they caused loss of life by firing on a flag of truce.

More long guns came on target. There was a flurry of shouting, then the weapons were lowered slowly. Grim-faced, Kydd saw the waiting figures resolve to individuals.

"Garn back, y' English pigs!" yelled one, brandishing a rifle. Others took up the cry. Kydd told Rawson to hold steady and lay alongside. The shouting died down, but a dozen or more people crowded on to the jetty.

"Oars—toss oars," Kydd told the midshipman.

The crowd grew more menacing, one man threatening them with a pitch-fork. The boat drifted to a stop. "Bowman, take a turn o' the painter," Kydd ordered. The boat nudged the timbers of the landing-stage; hostile figures shuffled to the edge.

Kydd stood up in the boat. "I ask ye to let me land—if y' please." Nobody moved. "Then am I t' take it you're going to prevent by force the landing on the soil of the United States of America of a citizen of a nation, er, that you're not at war with?" It sounded legal, all but the last bit.

"We don' want yore kind here. Git back to yer ship or I'll give yez a charge o' lead up yer backside as will serve as y'r keep-sake of Ameriky."

"Get his rope, Jeb—we'll give 'em a ducking." Hands grabbed at the painter, rocking the boat.

"Hold!" The crowd fell back to where a well-dressed man waited on horseback. He dismounted and walked to the jetty edge; malice hung about him. "Can you not see you're unwelcome, sir?" he called evenly to Kydd.

"Am I so fearsome the whole town turns out t' oppose me?"

"You're an Englishman—that's enough for these good folk. And Navy too. There's many here who have suffered their ships taken as prize, youngsters snatched away by the press—they have reasons a-plenty, sir." There were cries of agreement. "Therefore I'd advise you to return whence you came." He folded his arms.

Kydd lowered his head as though in resignation, but his eyes were busy measuring, gauging. He placed a foot on the gunwale, leaped across the gap of water, heaved himself over the edge of the jetty and ended up next to the man. "I thank ye for your advice, sir, but as you can see, here I am, landed." He dusted himself off. "L'tenant Kydd, at your service, sir."

The man's reply was cold. "Schroeder. Christopher." He did not hold out his hand.

Kydd bowed, and looked around at the crowd. "I thank ye most kindly for my welcome, and hope m' stay will be as pleasant." When it was clear there would be no interchange, he leaned over and ordered his crew to throw him up his single piece of baggage. "Proceed in accordance with y'r previous orders, Mr Rawson," he added, and the boat stroked away to sea.

He was now in the United States, and very much alone.

Kydd set off down the path into the village, which he knew by the chart was the tiny seaport of Exbury in the state of Connecticut. It was a pretty township, barely more than a village with square, no-nonsense wooden houses and neatly trimmed gardens—and, to Kydd's English eyes, unnaturally straight roads with their raised wooden sidewalks. It also had a distinct sea flavour: the resinous smell of a spar-maker, the muffled clang of a ship-smithy and what looked like a well-stocked chandlery further down the street.

Women carrying baskets stopped to stare at him. The men muttered together in sullen groups. "Can you let me know where I c'n get lodgings?" he asked one, who turned his back. When he located the general store to ask, its keeper snapped, "We'm closed!" and slammed the door.

Kydd sat down heavily on a bench beneath a maple tree. It was a near to hopeless mission, but he was not about to give up. He had no idea what had turned the town against him, but he needed lodgings.

A gang of rowdy youngsters started chanting:

... And there they'd fife away like fun
And play on cornstalk fiddles
And some had ribbons red as blood
All bound around their middles!
Oh—Yankee doodle, keep it up
Yankee doodle dandy ...

Kydd missed the significance of the revolutionary song and, nettled by his politeness, the youths threw stones at him. Kydd shied one back, which brought out a woman in pinafore and bonnet. She glared at him, but shooed away the urchins.

He picked up his bag and set off towards the other end of town. As he passed the houses, each with their doors and windows all closed, a man stepped out on to his porch. "Stranger!" he called sternly.

Kydd stopped. "Aye?"

"You're the Englishman."

"I am, sir—Lieutenant Thomas Kydd of His Majesty's Ship *Tenacious*."

The man was thin and rangy, in working clothes, but had dignity in his bearing. "Jacob Hay, sir." Kydd shook his hand. It was work-hardened and calloused. "Your presence here ain't welcome, Lootenant, but I will not see a stranger used so. If it's quarters ye're after, I'm offerin'."

"Why, thank you, Mr Hay," said Kydd, aware of several people muttering behind him. Hay glanced at them, then led the way into his house.

"Set there, Mr Kydd, while we makes up a room for ye." Kydd lowered himself into a rocking-chair by the fire. "Judith, find something for Mr Kydd," he called, through the doorway. A young woman entered with a jug and a china pot. She did not lift her eyes and left quickly.

To Kydd, Hay said, "There's no strong drink enters this house, but you'll find th' local cider acceptable."

Kydd expressed his appreciation and, proffering some coins, added apologetically, "I have t' tell you now, sir, I don't have any American money for my room."

"Put it away, sir. That won't be necessary." Hay pursed his lips and said, "I don't mean t' be nosy, but can I ask what business is it y' have in Exbury? Somethin' to do with the Frenchy, I guess."

"I—have to, er, enquire of the authorities what they mean t' do in the matter," Kydd said cautiously.

"To do? Nothin' I guess. Frenchy is here t' fit a noo mizzen and be on her way, and that's all—we let him be."

"It's the law, Mr Hay."

"Law? No law says we has to send him out fer you to take in that two-decker o' yourn," he said coldly.

"I have t' hear the authorities first, y' understands," Kydd said. "Who would that be, do ye think?"

Hay's coolness remained. At length, he said, "That'll be Mr Dwight or Mr Chadwick. Selectmen fer Exbury." Seeing the blank look on Kydd's face, he added, "Magistrates, like. Call th' meetings, run th' constables."

"I'd like to call on 'em, if y' please," Kydd said politely.

"Time fer that after supper." The aroma of fresh-baked bread filled the air. Hay sniffed appreciatively. "An' if I'm not wrong we're havin' steamed clams."

". . . and may the Lord make us truly thankful. Amen."

While Mrs Hay set about the dishes, Kydd tried to make conversation. "M' first time in the United States. I have t' say, it's a good-lookin' country." Hay regarded him without comment.

Kydd smiled across at Judith, who hastily dropped her eyes. He turned once more to Hay. "I'd be obliged if ye could find your way clear t' tellin' me why I'm not welcome, Mr Hay."

Hay's face hardened. "That's easy enough. We live fr'm the sea by fishing 'n' trade. We're a small town, as ye can see, and when a ship is built an' vittled for tradin' there's a piece of everyone in her when she puts t' sea. Life ain't easy, an' when a family puts in their savin's it's cruel hard t' see that ship taken f'r prize by a King's ship an' carried into a Canadian port t' be condemned."

"But this is because you've been caught trading with the French—the enemy."

"Whose enemy?" Hay snorted. "None of our business, this war."

"And if the French beat us, then you don't think they're going to come and claim back their American empire? They have most o' the rest of the world."

Hay grunted. "Eat y'r clams, Mr Kydd."

The atmosphere thawed as the meal progressed. Eventually, after apple pie and Cheddar, Hay sat back. "If you're goin' t' see a magistrate, make it Dwight." He wouldn't be drawn any further and Kydd set off alone. At the substantial gambrel-roofed house, which Hay had previously pointed out, he was greeted by a short, tubby man wearing a napkin tucked round his neck.

"Er, I need t' see Mr Dwight."

"Himself," the man said, in a peculiar, rapid delivery. "I guess you're the English officer. Am I right?"

"Aye, Lieutenant Kydd. Sir, pardon me if I seem unfamiliar with y'r ways, but I need t' find the authority here in Exbury—the public leader, as it were, in your town."

Dwight raised his eyebrows, but motioned Kydd inside and closed the door. "I'll shake hands with you in private, if you don't mind, L'tenant. Now sit ye down, and here's a little rye whiskey for your chilblains."

Kydd accepted it.

"Sir, if you're lookin' for our leader, I guess I'm your man.

Selectman o' Exbury. It's about as high as it goes, short o' the governor in Hartford. Now, how can I help you?"

"Sir, I come on a mission o' some delicacy. No doubt you're aware that a French privateer lies in your port—"

"I am."

"—which we surprised in the fog in th' process of takin' a merchant ship of the United States goin' about its lawful business."

"Don't surprise me to hear it, sir."

"Oh?" said Kydd, prepared only for disbelief and scorn.

"Sir. Let me make my position clear. I'm known as a plain-speakin' man and I'll tell it straight.

"I'm a Federalist, same as the President, same as General Washington himself. I won't try your patience in explaining our politics. Just be assured we stand for the old ways and decent conduct, and we don't hold with this damn French arrogance and ambition. We're opposed by a bunch o' rascals who think t' sympathise with them on account of their help in the late war—saving y'r presence, sir."

Kydd began to speak, but was interrupted. "I said I'll speak plain, and I will. We've been taking insults to our flag and loss to our trade, and we'll not have it. There's going t' be an accounting, and that soon.

"But, sir, I'll have you understand, because we take the same view, this does not mean we're friends."

Kydd gathered his thoughts and began again: "What we seek, sir, is an indication how you mean to act." As smoothly as he could, he continued, "You have here a belligerent vessel seeking a neutral haven f'r repairs. According to international law, he must sail within two days. Do ye mean to enforce the law?"

Dwight sighed. "Philadelphia is a long ways off—the law is as may be. Here, it's what the citizens say that counts."

"Does this mean—"

"If I tried t' arrest the Frenchman with my two constables, I'd start a riot—*and* be thrown out of office. This town has just lost a ship t' the British and two lads to your press-gang. And I'd run smack dab against Kit Schroeder."

"I believe I've met the gentleman," Kydd murmured.

"Owns three ships and the store, knows how t' lift a cargo with all the right papers to see it past the British an' then on to a French port. There's most folks here do business with him and don't want to see him interfered with, y' see."

"So you're saying that there's nothing you c'n do? You mean th' Frenchy to lie alongside as long as he wants?" For the sake of local politics the privateer was to be left untouched; *Tenacious* would be forced to sail in a few days, releasing the vessel to continue her career of destruction. Resentment boiled up in Kydd.

Dwight held up a pacifying hand. "Now, I didn't say there was *nothing* I could do. I'm a selectman an' you have come to me with a case. I'll be letting the governor in Hartford know—but that'll take some time with the roads as they is. However, I'm empowered to, and I will, issue a warrant for a town meeting to consider, um, whether the committee of public safety should take action to prevent there being a hostile action on our soil. Requiring the Frenchman t' take himself elsewhere, say. No promises, Mr Kydd, but you'll get to say your piece and—"

He broke off and cocked his head. Indistinct shouts sounded in the night, rhythmic thuds like a drum. Dwight crossed to the window and pulled the shutter ajar. "Trouble," he said, in a low voice. "Republicans. Don't like you being here, I guess."

Kydd peered out. Flickering torches were being borne along towards them, and in their light he saw marching figures, gesticulating, shouting.

"Had 'em here before, the wicked dogs. Here, lend me a hand, sir." They moved over to each window and secured the folding shutters, the smell of guttering candles in the gloom of the closed room now oppressive.

A maid came from the rear, hands to her mouth. "We'll be quite safe, Mary," Dwight said, and pulled open a drawer. Kydd caught the glint of a pistol. "They're only here 'cos they've had a skinful of Schroeder's liquor—they'll be away after they've had their fun."

He eased open the shutter a crack. "See that? They're wearing a tricolour cockade in their hats! Republicans do that so there's no mistake who it is they support."

The noise grew close. A drum thudded in an uneven rhythm, while harsh shouts and laughter came clearly through the closed shutters. Suddenly there was a sharp thud and tinkling glass, then another. Dwight stiffened and swore. "Breaking windows. I'll have Schroeder's hide—no need f'r this."

But, as he had prophesied, the influence of drink faded and the small crowd dispersed. "I'm truly sorry you've been inconvenienced, Mr Kydd," Dwight said, with dignity, "but in my country we value free speech above all things. Good night to ye."

Kydd did not sleep well and was up at cockcrow, pacing along the single cross-street to get the stiffness from his limbs.

It did not take long for the gang of youngsters to find him and begin chanting again, but Kydd grinned broadly and gave them a cheery wave. They soon tired of the sport and darted away. After a few minutes one returned and took station next to him. Kydd guessed he was about ten.

"Are you English?" the boy blurted out.

"Aye. I come fr'm Guildford, which is in Surrey," Kydd said.

"What's your ship's name?"

"Oh, she's His Britannic Majesty's sixty-four-gun ship *Tenacious,* an' I'm her fifth l'tenant, Kydd, so you have t' call me 'sir'!"

"Yes, sir," the boy said smartly. "I'm Peter Miller." They walked on together. "How do ye keelhaul a man, sir?"

"What? No, lad, we don't keelhaul sailors. We flog 'em, never keelhaul." Kydd chuckled.

"Have you ever bin flogged, sir?" Peter asked, wide-eyed.

Kydd hesitated. It was not an admission he would make in polite company. "Yes, a long time ago, before I was an officer."

Peter nodded seriously. "I want t' join the Navy like you, but my pap says we ain't got a navy," he added defensively.

"We have Americans in the Royal Navy, lad. Ye could—"

"No, sir!" Peter said with spirit. "I'll not serve King George. Er, that's any king a'tall, not just your king, sir."

Kydd laughed, and the boy scampered off.

He reached the end of the street, turned the corner and found himself heading towards the French privateer alongside the commercial wharf. At the thought of seeing the ship at such close quarters he quickened his pace. There were idle onlookers standing about on the quay taking their fill of the novel sight; Kydd could see no reason why he should not be one of them.

A shout came from behind him. "There he is—the English bastard! Come t' spy on our friends." He recognised the voice of a hothead who had been at the boat. Several men hurried towards him, one hefting a length of paling wood; an authoritative-looking figure watched from the foredeck of the privateer. Kydd stiffened. There would be no help from the spectators by the vessel: they were too busy gawping and the few looking in his direction seemed disinclined to intervene.

Kydd stood his ground with folded arms. He knew he could probably make a good account of himself, but he would not be the first to make a move.

"Spyin' dog! Y' knows what happens t' spies?"

"Are ye as chuckle-headed as y' look? I'm no spy, skulkin' around. I've got just as much right t' take the air here as—as y'r Frenchy there."

One of the bystanders came up. "He's right, y' knows. Both

furriners, stands t' reason y' can't pick one over the other."

"Hold y'r noise, Darby." Schroeder strode across. "You, sir!" he called at Kydd, standing aggressively between him and the ship. "Will you account for your presence as an officer of a belligerent power at the lawful mooring-place of a ship of the opposing nation? Or shall it be spying?"

Kydd held his temper. "No."

Schroeder started. "You're saying—"

"I said, 'No,' which is to say I do not have t' account to you or any man for what I'm about on m' lawful business on a public highway."

Schroeder's jaw hardened, but Kydd looked past him to the privateer. Scores of men were pouring on to the wharf, scattering the onlookers.

Kydd waited. Surely they would not dare anything in broad daylight, before witnesses. But then they spread out in a line and moved towards him. Kydd tensed, the features of individual seamen resolving, alien chatter quietening to a purposeful advance.

Kydd stood firm. They came closer and stopped in front of him, undeniably seafarers, but with their sashes, floppy liberty caps and Mediterranean swarthiness, there was something distorted and menacing about them. They shuffled together to form a barrier, and when Kydd moved to go round it, they blocked his way again. Kydd spotted the figure on the foredeck and bellowed, "Let me pass, y' villains!" The officer shrugged and called out an unintelligible stream of French. It was stalemate: there was nothing for it but as dignified a retreat as possible.

Kydd stalked off, seething at being outwitted by the French. At the very least he had hoped to report back on the ship, her state for sea, guns, anything he could see. Now he would have to admit he hadn't been able to get close.

He forced his mind to focus on the situation and by the time he'd reached the cross-street he had a plan: he would see the other side instead. That implied a boat; the tide was on the make, which would allow him to drift past and take his fill of the scene.

Kydd found the young lads playing in the same place and he called across to Peter, "A silver sixpence wi' King George's head on it should you tell me where I c'n hire a fishin'-boat."

The dory was double-ended and handy. In borrowed oilskins, Kydd set the little boat drifting along, an unbaited line over the side.

The privateer, the *Minotaure de Morlaix,* was big. Work was going ahead on the mizzen, a new spar chocked up ready on the wharf, but there appeared to be no hurry. Kydd scanned the vessel: her clean lines meant speed but also implied limited sea-endurance, given the large crew.

His attention was caught by a peculiar break in the line of bulwarks with their small gunports. A whole section amidships had been lowered on hinges—inside Kydd glimpsed the astonishing sight of the black bulk of a long gun, mounted on some sort of pivot, another barely visible trained to the other side of the ship. But this was no ordinary gun: it was a twenty-four-pounder at least. The armament of a ship-of-the-line on a near frigate-sized vessel.

This must have been the origin of the sound of heavy guns that had mystified *Tenacious* at sea earlier, and although there appeared to be only one on each side, it would be enough to terrorise any victim and certainly give pause to a similar sized man-o'-war; a grave threat let loose on the trade routes of the continent. It was sheer chance that had placed the only other ship-of-the-line in North America across the Frenchman's path.

After returning the boat and gear he walked back along the tree-lined road, deep in thought, but the only conclusion he could come to was the impossibility of his situation.

A man in an old-fashioned black tricorne hat stopped him. "Are you Lootenant Kydd?"

"I am."

"I'm a constable o' Exbury township," he said importantly, "an' I'm instructed by the selectmen to advise ye that a warrant fer a town meetin' has been issued concernin' you."

"Ah—does that mean they wish me t' attend?"

The constable looked aghast. "No, sir! Only citizens o' this town c'n attend a town meeting. Mr Dwight jus' wants ye to know that y'r matter is being looked into, is all."

Kydd turned to go, but the constable pulled at his sleeve. "Yon Frenchy is goin'—make sure an' be there as well, L'tenant. Th' meeting house is round the corner."

People from all parts of the town were making their way to a small building whose lines reminded Kydd of the Methodist chapels of his youth. Several greeted him openly; others glared. Schroeder arrived in a carriage and was handed down by a black man. He ignored Kydd and waited; a little later a French officer arrived and the two fell into discussion.

Kydd found his eyes straying to the tall, elegant figure he recognised from the morning's events. By the inscrutable logic of war, he was being granted sight of the man who, as his king's enemy, was his duty to kill.

The discussion stopped. The two turned in his direction and Kydd felt the intensity of the Frenchman's glare across the distance; he hesitated, then withdrew his gaze. When he dared another look, they were walking away.

"All attendin' please enter!" bawled the constable. The latecomers and Schroeder entered, leaving Kydd and the Frenchman alone.

Should he follow the dictates of politeness that required he notice the man and introduce himself, or was there some form of defiance required that he had not the breeding to recognise? The Frenchman was tall, mature and had a languid elegance in his mannerisms that made Kydd aware of his own origins. His feelings of inadequacy returned and he stared back at the man with dislike.

There were bad-tempered shouts from inside, then a head-to-head crescendo. The Frenchman looked across at Kydd and raised his eyebrows in a gesture of refined amusement, but Kydd was unsure of himself, wanting no part in any kind of engagement, and turned sharply away.

Unexpectedly the door to the meeting house opened and Dwight appeared. "Gentlemen," he called, looking carefully between them, "the meeting recognises that this is an, er, irregular situation, and wishes you each t' state your case now."

There was a hush in the audience, and heads turned as Kydd followed the Frenchman up the aisle. At the simple table at the front there was no provision for extra persons. "We have t' ask ye to stand, if y' will," Dwight said apologetically.

The rows of faces that looked back at Kydd seemed either impassive or hostile, and anxiety rose in him at the thought of a public humiliation from the worldly Frenchman.

"Citizens o' Exbury, it's my duty to present—*Capitaine* Hercule Junon of the French ship *Minotaure*." The French officer inclined his head graciously. "An' this is L'tenant Kydd, of the English ship *Tenacious*." Kydd inclined his head also, but feared the gesture had turned out as a nod.

"In view of Captain Junon bein' French as he is, and just to be fair, is there any man present can translate for him?"

Schroeder immediately stepped forward. "I can."

"Then let's begin. We have here a request from our English guest that it might be better to hear fr'm him direct. L'tenant?"

Kydd's palms moistened. He took a deep breath and turned

to address the meeting. "You have a French privateer alongside, here in Exbury. He has every right t' be here, to repair an' refit as he needs. But the law says he must leave in forty-eight hours. I request that th' United States do then enforce the law an' make sure he does. Er, that's all."

There was a disturbance at the back of the hall and a distant voice shouted, "Y' mean, send 'em out to just where y'r waiting for 'em?"

Another voice cut in, yelling at the first, and Dwight rapped sharply with his gavel. "I'll have order in the meeting. Now, Captain Junon?"

There was an exchange in low voices, then Schroeder faced Kydd. "Captain Junon understands L'tenant Kydd's duty in this matter and approves his spirit, but begs to be informed, what is this law of which he speaks? He has no knowledge of such a one."

Kydd tried to remember Houghton's hurried words before he left. "Ah, Captain Junon needs remindin' of the Rule of War of 1756. This specifies clearly—"

There was an urgent mutter from Junon, and Schroeder nodded impatiently. "The Rule of War of 1756 is, of course, an English law and has had no jurisdiction in the United States after 1776—and, since the lieutenant apparently requires educating, deals with the opening of trade to neutrals and really has no bearing whatsoever on this affair."

Scattered titters came from the audience. Kydd stared back stubbornly, but could think of no rejoinder.

"And while we are discussing rules, by what laws do the British press men out of American vessels and take their ships prize on the high seas?" Junon allowed an expression of injured pride to appear while Schroeder pressed home his words. "Are the British so careless of the sanctity of a nation's flag that they dare attempt to demand from the citizens of a neutral country—"

Kydd glared at Junon. "I saw y'r ship firing on an American flag vessel not two days ago."

A rustle of interest was interspersed with occasional shouts. Junon allowed it to die away before he made his reply to Schroeder. "Regrettably there are occasions when Captain Junon's government requires him to confirm that a vessel is not conveying contraband—there are some whose conscience is not clear in this regard and attempt to flee. It is sometimes a necessity to deter."

"And is this the action of a friend to America, I ask the captain?" Kydd said hotly, incensed at Junon's facile delivery.

A burst of clapping provoked angry shouts from another quarter and Dwight called for order again.

Kydd's face burned. "We also have our treaty!" he lashed out. "And in it—"

"Sir!" Schroeder called, in mock outrage. "You must recall that yours was not a treaty of friendship—not at all. This was, dare I say it, the vanquished accepting terms from the victor!"

A storm of mixed protest and cheers broke out, obliging the constable to intervene. Dwight stood and waited for the uproar to diminish, then spoke firmly: "Will the strangers now withdraw?"

Outside, Kydd paced rigidly, avoiding Junon's amused glances, as they waited for the meeting to come to a decision. It was not long before the hoots and shouts died away. After an interval the constable summoned them back.

"L'tenant, we have voted on the matter of your request," Dwight said importantly. "The township of Exbury has considered it, and as selectman I have to tell you your request is denied."

Kydd's expression tightened, but he tried to put the best face on it, remembering to turn and bow to the people of the town.

"The business of this meeting is now concluded."

The gathering broke up noisily and people streamed to the

door. Dwight fiddled with his papers and, in a low voice, said to Kydd, "I'm sendin' a rider to Hartford. This should be gov'ment business."

Jacob Hay came forward with his hat in his hands. "Jus' like t' say sorry it came out agin you, Mr Kydd, but as ye can see, the people spoke." He put out his hand and Kydd could see that it was genuinely meant.

Outside, people were still in groups, some in animated discussion. Kydd could not remember when he had felt so isolated. A roar of laughter drew his attention: it was Darby, one of the hotheads of the morning's events at the French ship.

Kydd's blood rose as the man approached him. "Y' lost yer vote, then," he said loudly. Kydd could not trust himself to reply, but then Darby clapped him on the shoulder and said, "No hard feelin's? I'd take it kindly if you'd sink a muzzler with us, friend."

Kydd could not think what to say, but a surging need for the release of a drink and the rough companionship of a tavern overcame his wonder at American generosity of spirit. "Aye, I would," he said, and allowed himself to be taken to the Blue Anchor. The weatherboard tavern was already alive with humanity, and Kydd began to feel better. There were odd glances at his clothing, but Darby loudly announced his presence. "What'll ye have?" he asked genially.

"Er, a beer?"

"Beer? That's spruce, birch, sassafras?"

A nearby toper closed his eyes and chanted, "'Oh, we can make liquor t' sweeten our lips—of pumpkins, o' parsnips or walnut-tree chips.'"

"Aye, well, it's the sassafras, then."

It was the strangest-tasting brew. "Er, what do ye mix with this'n?" Kydd inquired carefully.

"We don't *mix* anythin', Mr Englishman. That's straight beer, it is, bit o' y'r beet tops, apple skin, roots all boiled in, gives it taste, o' course."

Kydd downed it manfully, then called for something different. Darby slipped a china mug across to him. "Flip—now there's a drink f'r a man." Kydd lifted the creaming brew doubtfully and was not disappointed at the strength of the rum that lay within.

"To th' American flag!" Kydd called.

There was a surprised roar and Kydd found faces turning his way. The reddest called across to him, "Well, I can't drink t' your king, friend, but I can t' your good health."

The drink was doing its work and Kydd beamed at his new friends. In the corner a pitch-pipe was brought out and after a few tentative whistles two young men launched into song.

Come, join hand in hand, brave Americans all,
And rouse your bold hearts at fair Liberty's call;
No tyrannous acts shall suppress your just claim
Or stain with dishonour America's name!

"Let's hear an English song, then!" Darby demanded, grinning at Kydd and shoving another flip across.

"I'm no sort o' hand at singin'," protested Kydd, but was overborne. He thought for a moment, recalling what had most stirred him in times past. "Well, this is a sea song, shipmates, an' we sing it around the forebitts forrard—an' I warn ye again, I'm no singer."

Come, all ye jolly sailors bold,
Whose hearts are cast in honour's mould;
While English glory I unfold
On board o' the Arethusa!

He found his voice and rolled out the fine old words heartily.

And as he sang his mind roamed over the times and places where he had enjoyed the company of true deep-sea mariners in this way, beside him his shipmates through the gale's blast and the cannon's roar, and in all the seas over the globe. As he never would experience again.

Tears pricked and his voice grew hoarse, but in defiance he roared out the final stanza:

And now we've driven the foe ashore,
Never to fight with Britons more,
Let each fill a glass
To his favourite lass;
A health to the captain and officers true
And all that belongs to the jovial crew
On board o' the Arethusa!

Something of his feeling communicated itself to the tavern: not a soul moved and when he finished there was a storm of acclamation. Even the pot-boy stood entranced and the tapster abandoned his post to stand agog.

"Ah, Mr Kydd—he'll have a whiskey o' your best sort, Ned," one man said, and when Kydd had taken it, he raised his own glass and called, "T' Mr Kydd an' his Royal Navy!"

The morning was a trial. With a throbbing head, he had to endure an icy, disapproving silence at breakfast. "Guess you'll be on y'r way now," Hay said meaningfully.

He left after breakfast for a walk in the cool morning to consider his situation. It was obvious that he must admit defeat. He would display the noon signal that would have the boat return to take him off.

At the end of the cross-street he went to turn down the road but, catching sight of the French privateer, he decided to go the other way. As he did so he caught a fleeting glimpse of a figure slipping out of sight. He frowned and continued, but stopped sharply and turned, to see the figure behind duck away again.

This might be a French agent on his trail or a crazed citizen seeking revenge on an Englishman—and Kydd was unarmed. He remembered the trees where he had met Peter. He walked on rapidly and, at the end of the road, turned the corner, then sprinted towards them. He heaved himself up among the leaves and on to a branch overlooking the path by the road.

His shadower swung round the corner and stopped, looking baffled. He moved forward cautiously but did not appear armed. Kydd waited. The man increased his pace and came nearer, treading carefully. Kydd tensed and, when the man passed beneath, dropped on his shoulders. The two fell in a heap, but Kydd was faster and wrenched the man over, gripping his throat one-handed in restraint.

The man ceased struggling and stared up at Kydd, who slowly released his hold. "Er, if you'd kindly let me up, I'll try to explain." The voice was American, polite and apologetic.

"Do, if y' please." Kydd had never heard a footpad so well-spoken, but did not drop his guard.

The man dusted himself off and smiled ruefully. "My name's Edward Gindler—Lootenant Gindler—and this kind of work is not t' my liking, I'll have you know."

"Lieutenant—Army?"

"Navy."

"Don't try t' gull me—the United States doesn't have a navy."

The visitors had left. Liston climbed the stairs painfully to his private room, ruing the onset of age with its aches and pains, but he knew his duty.

He sat down and reached for paper, then selected a pen

abstractedly. A woman's hand placed a glass of brandy by him, and her lips softly touched his hair. He twisted round, reached for her hand and kissed it tenderly. "My dear," he said softly.

His wife said nothing, just looked down at him for a long moment. Then she left, closing the door behind her.

Liston sighed and collected his thoughts.

In respect of the biggest question of the moment—would the United States enter the war against France—there was no answer . . . yet. Liston smiled grimly as he penned his appreciation of the difficulties faced by the beleaguered President.

Following the commercial success of the contentious Jay treaty of two years before, the French had retaliated by insisting on the letter of the law in their own treaty, which granted free passage to any vessel carrying a French *rôle de l'équipage*. Now a vessel without it would be subject to seizure.

The consequences to the expanding trade of the young country had been nothing short of catastrophic. Liston picked up Pinckney's *Congressional Report on European Spoliation of American Trade* to refresh his mind on the figures.

It was staggering—worse even than the dire predictions of the fire-breathing Hamilton. In the Caribbean, worst hit, no less than three hundred ships had been taken and, counting the dangerous waters on the approaches to war-ravaged Europe since the Jay treaty, nearly a thousand American flag vessels had hauled down their colours and been carried into French ports; ship, cargo and crew.

Liston could barely credit that the proud Americans would submit to such intolerable and cynical actions by a so-called ally—but they had. President Adams had stoutly resisted all attempts by Liston and even his own party to be embroiled in a European war, whatever the provocation, but there had to be limits.

Even so, Liston could see his difficulty. The opposition

Republicans were led by the astute and learned Jefferson, talked about as the next president, who would never allow him to declare war on an ally. In any case he did not have the means: he had only a few frigates that had been left part built after a brief alarm over Algerine pirates nearly half a dozen years ago.

Yet something had to give. In the last few months, insurance rates in the Caribbean had soared to an impossible 25 per cent of ship and cargo value.

The French were defeating whole nations; coalitions against them had crumbled and they were clearly about to break out of Europe to the wider world. It had made them arrogant and confident, but Liston felt that the latest act was beyond sufferance: envoys of the United States in Paris, attempting to negotiate an amelioration of French attitudes, had been met with a demand for two hundred thousand dollars as a pre-condition for any kind of talks.

This incitement to naked bribery had appalled the Americans, and when it had leaked out there had been outrage. For the first time it appeared President Adams would have to move—to declare war? And with what?

Liston dipped his pen and began to write.

CHAPTER 10

"MAY I CORRECT YOU, SIR? We *do* have a navy," Gindler said, with an ironic smile, "As of a week ago. Might I explain?"

It seemed that there had been congressional authorisation for a "naval armament" since the Algerines trouble, but this had been a War Department matter of the time. Now Congress wanted the reality, and had therefore recently established a Department of the Navy to act like the British Admiralty and was to appoint a full secretary of the Navy.

"So, our navy is born." Gindler had an engaging smile, but Kydd detected a harder layer beneath his cheery manner.

Kydd's head was still muzzy after his visit to the Blue Anchor, and he tried to concentrate. "Y' don't just *say* you'll have a navy— you now have t' find ships, officers. How are y' going t' do that? And dockyards, victualling, slops . . ."

He looked at Gindler—and felt that this vigorous new country might just find some way. "Wish ye well of it, Mr Gindler," he said sincerely. Then he added, "But I'd be obliged now, sir, if you'd explain what you were doing."

"Certainly. I was spying on you, Mr Kydd."

"Wha'?"

"We need to know what a British officer is doing on our soil, you'll agree?"

"Then why th' skulking about? It's no secret why I'm here."

"Ah. This is not to do with your own good self, I do assure you. It has rather more to do with our democratic way, Mr Kydd. If the citizens of this town, living as they do in Connecticut, find out that I, as an agent of the federal government, am poking around in a matter they conclude is theirs, then I'll soon need a fast horse out of Exbury."

"Oh? Have you got what you came for, then?" Kydd thought the whole thing sounded more than a little far-fetched.

"Shall we say, sir, that I'd rather like to be shaking hands with an English officer as he steps into his boat to return to his ship?"

"Aye. Well, thanks t' y' citizens, the Frenchman lies here untouched an' my ship must sail away. Have no fear, you'll have y'r wish, Mr Gindler. At noon I throw out my signal and the boat will come to take me and my English carcass off." He smiled wryly, then added, "But do walk with me until then, an' tell me more of y'r plans for a navy."

Kydd retrieved his baggage from Jacob Hay and stood with Gindler on the small jetty. *Tenacious* was approaching and would heave to on the three-mile line for a space while telescopes spied the shore for Kydd's signal. If there was none, she would fill, stand out to sea and return on the following day.

"If it's any consolation, my friend, it grieves me as much as it does you," Gindler said, in a voice low enough not to be overheard by the ragged crowd that had come to see the defeated Englishman leave.

"Oh?" said Kydd bitterly. He was in no mood to be consoled.

Gindler was spared having to answer by the thud of hoofs. The constable hove into view and pulled up his horse. "Mr Dwight sends 'is compliments an' hopes you can pay him a call before y' leaves."

Kydd bit his lip. It was within half an hour of midday, and if he missed the time to display his signal flag, *Tenacious* would stand offshore for another day.

The constable leaned down. "Noos!" he said hoarsely, and winked broadly.

Dwight was businesslike. "It's none of your business, o' course, Mr Kydd, but you'll find out anyway—I've had word from the governor in Hartford, an' he takes his advice from Philadelphia. Seems they've had enough o' the Frenchies and I'm to serve an order on their captain that they've just twenty-four hours to quit United States territory." He stuffed papers into a desk. "I guess this means you'll be about y'r business then, Mr Kydd," he added, holding the door open.

Kydd had minutes—if he could make his signal . . .

A wily captain like Junon could play it well; he would use all his twenty-four hours to fettle his ship for any circumstance. Then, no doubt, he would sail slowly and directly to the edge of territorial waters, luring *Tenacious* towards him. When the English ship was committed to his approach he would throw over his helm to one side or the other and, hoisting every possible sail, break out with his superior speed into the open sea.

Gindler was waiting curiously at the jetty. "*Minotaure*—she's t' sail within twenty-four hours," Kydd said quietly, catching his breath, watching the main topsail of *Tenacious* brace sturdily around as she made to heave to.

"Well, now, you leave like a hero."

"Perhaps not—I have t' think," Kydd said, distracted. True, the *Minotaure* was forced to sea, but what was the use of this if the privateer could slip away past her pursuer? It was damned bad luck that their sloop, *Lynx*, would not yet have returned from alerting the admiral of *Tenacious*'s dispositions, for the two together had a chance of hounding *Minotaure* to her doom. Could anything be done?

Desperate times meant desperate measures: Kydd had heard of a drag-sail being used to reduce speed; a disguised ship would pretend dull sailing to lure a prey. Perhaps he could stay ashore and tie a sail secretly to *Minotaure,* slow her enough to catch. He soon realised that before the privateer had gone any distance her captain would want to know why she was slowing and discover the trick.

"Mr Kydd!" Gindler pointed out to sea where *Tenacious* was bringing round her main topsail yard.

Kydd pulled the red number-one flag from his pocket and hurried to the front of the gaggle of spectators, spread it wide and let it hang. His news would surely set the ship abuzz.

There appeared to be little activity on her quarterdeck: the daily run inshore had lost its novelty, no doubt. Then topmen began mounting the shrouds and in a smart display the main topsail came around and filling, at the same time as the main course was loosed—and *Tenacious* gracefully got under way for the open sea.

Kydd held the signal high in the forlorn hope that someone was looking back on the little township but, her sails sheeted home, *Tenacious* made off to the horizon amid the sniggering and laughter of the onlookers.

Kydd stood mortified. Not only was he left stranded but he had failed to pass on his vital news. Even if he could find a boat quickly no small craft could catch a big square-rigger in full sail. The only certainty was that *Tenacious* would return the next day.

And where could he lay his head that night? He knew he could not go back to Hay. "Er, Mr Gindler, if y're familiar with this town, do you know of any lodgin' house?"

"No, sir, I do not. That is, I don't know of one fit for a gentleman." He smiled. "Come now, I can't have an English guest take back a poor notion of my country. You shall stay with me, Mr Kydd."

"Why, Mr Gindler, that's very kind in you."

Gindler patted him on the shoulder. "And it keeps you safely under my eye . . ."

"I always try to make New England for the summer, a prime place to rest the spirit—and it is here that I stay." It was a retired fisherman's cottage by the edge of the water, complete with its own boathouse.

"Do you fish, Mr Kydd? The halibut and cod here, fresh caught, will by any estimate grace the highest table in the land. We shall try some tonight."

Kydd tried to take an interest, but his mind was full of the consequences of his inattention at the jetty. The only glimmer of hope was that if *Minotaure* made use of her full twenty-four hours, *Tenacious* would have returned in time to try to catch her prey.

"We shall have to make shift for ourselves, sir," Gindler said apologetically. "The hire of this cottage does not include servants."

"Oh? Er, yes, of course, Mr Gindler."

"This is American territory, Mr Kydd. Be so kind as to address me by my first name, Edward—that is, Ned."

"Thank you, sir—I mean, Ned, and pray call me Tom."

Kydd went out on to the little porch and stared out to sea. Gindler joined him with pewter tankards of cider and they sat in cane chairs.

"If you can believe it, you have my earnest sympathy, Tom," he said. "Damnation to the French!" he added.

"But aren't they y'r friends?" said Kydd, startled out of his dejection.

"They've caused us more grief and loss than ever you English did, curse 'em, and I have that from Secretary of State Timothy Pickering himself."

Kydd's spirits returned. "So it wouldn't cause you heartbreak to see this corsair destroyed."

"No, sir. It would give me the greatest satisfaction."

Kydd grinned savagely. "Then let's get our heads together an' work out some way we c'n bring about that very thing."

Gindler shook his head. "We? Recollect, Tom, that this is the territory of the United States. Should I act against a ship of a neutral flag while she's lying in our waters I'd be hoist by both sides."

"So I'm on my own again."

"And I'm duty-bound to oppose any action against a neutral—especially in one of our ports, you'll understand."

Kydd slumped in his chair.

"Tell me, Tom, are we friends?" Gindler asked.

Surprised, Kydd agreed.

"Then my scruples tells me it is no crime to help a friend. What do you think?"

An immediate council of war concentrated on one overriding thing: unless *Minotaure* could be slowed there was little chance that *Tenacious* could catch her.

"Then we're th' only possible chance," Kydd said morosely.

"It seems that way. How about a drag-sail?"

"It would easily be discovered, soon as they put t' sea and felt its effect. Perhaps I could cut half through a brace or somethin' that will carry away at the right time," Kydd said, more in despair than hope.

"With the barky alert and swarming with men? I don't think so."

It seemed ludicrous to contemplate two men against a frigate-sized ship, but Kydd persevered. "There is another way . . ." he pondered. "To slow the Frenchy's one thing t' bring him to us, but there's his steering as well."

"Steering? Helm and tiller ropes?"

"His rudder."

"You do anything with that and he's sure to know just as quick."

"Not so, if m' idea is sound." It was years ago, but the image was as clear as yesterday. An English frigate careening at a remote island in the south Pacific Ocean—and, in the balmy oceanic winds, the crew scraping and cleaning the vast rearing bulk of the hull. He had been at work around the stern, overawed by the hulking presence of the thirty-foot-high rudder at close quarters, and had gone to inspect its working.

"Ned," Kydd said cautiously, "may I quiz you on y'r understanding of how rudders are hung?"

"By all means."

"A pin—the pintle on the rudder, going through the eye of a gudgeon on the hull. Now I ask ye to agree this. At the last extremity o' the hull is the sternpost."

"Yes, this must be so. The underwater run of the hull coming together in a fine upright sternpost."

"And the rudder fits to th' sternpost with your gudgeons and pintles. Now I particularly desire ye to remark the gap between the forward edge of the rudder and the after edge o' the sternpost. The thickness of the rudder in a frigate would amaze you— it's every bit of a foot or more, as must be th' sternpost, and I mean t' thrust a wedge between them."

"A magnificent scheme, but pray how will you apply this wedge?"

"Er, we'll discuss that part later. F'r now, we have to settle some details. First, th' gap is only an inch or two wide. No wedge this thick c'n stand the sea forces of a rudder. But—and this needs y'r verifying—there is a very suitable place. At th' point where the pintle meets the gudgeon the shipwrights cut out a space in th' rudder below it, or else we cannot unship the rudder. This they call th' score."

"And how big is your gap there?"

"Above six inches—so now we have two flat surfaces a foot long an' six inches apart. A wedge that size has a chance." Kydd grinned boyishly. "Just think, Ned, the Frenchy goes t' sea, sees *Tenacious* coming for him an' throws over his helm t' slip by one side, but his helm is jammed. Before he has time t' work out the trouble he's kind enough to deliver himself straight to us."

"Congratulations—but of course—"

"Well, yes, there is th' question of how t' get the wedge in there, I'll grant ye."

"And what sort of ship goes to sea with jammed steering?"

"Ah, I've thought of that."

"I'm gratified to hear it."

Kydd gave a dry smile. "This is callin' for something special, and here it is. We screw an eye into one end of th' wedge and secure a line to it, which is passed through our gap. If you tug on the line it brings the wedge whistling up an' smack into the gap. But it won't be us that's tugging . . ."

"I stand amazed. Who will?"

"Ah! Your old friend a drag-sail. It's only a small piece o' canvas rolled up and secured to the opposite end of the line, and when it opens it does the tugging."

"How?"

"Well, we need the helm t' jam only at the right moment—so we must find a trigger to stream our drag-sail just at that time. And here it is—we bundle the canvas up with twine and when we want it to open an' start pulling the wedge we break the twine."

"Which is . . ."

"Yes, well, this is a long piece of twine, and if you look f'r a discreet little pick-up buoy astern o' the Frenchy, then that's the end o' the twine."

Gindler didn't say anything.

"Well?" asked Kydd anxiously.

"I can only . . . I have two objections."

"Oh?"

"Who is going to affix the device? And who is going to find our wee buoy—maybe under gunfire?"

"I'll do both," said Kydd solemnly, but he had no idea how.

The boathouse provided all they needed. A woodworking bench, try-plane, saws—it would be a straightforward enough task. Kydd blessed the time he had spent in a Caribbean dockyard working for a master shipwright.

"Ned, I want some good wood for m' wedge."

Gindler fossicked about and, from a dark corner, dragged out what looked like a small salvaged ship frame, dark with age. "This should suit. It's live oak, and very hard. Capital for hacking out a wedge."

"Aye, well . . ."

"And it damn near doesn't float."

"Done!"

The try-plane hissed as Kydd applied himself to the work, watched by an admiring Gindler. Indeed, the wood was extremely dense, and Kydd sweated at the task. Gindler had already found the twine and was snipping round a piece of dirty canvas; then he rummaged for a screw eye.

Kydd realised he needed to see the French ship again in the light. The big privateer still lay alongside the commercial wharf but with a renewed, purposeful air, loading sea stores and working at her rigging. As he looked across the little bay at her, it became clear that there was no easy way to get close: there were sentries on deck and quay, and the ship was alert.

Kydd scanned the shoreline: the wharf was set on timber pilings. If he could get among them . . . and there, at the end, he saw a spur of light grey rocks extending into the sea.

Back in the boathouse a lanthorn glowed. "I believe I have a chance," Kydd told Gindler.

"Yes, Tom. When will you go?" Gindler was indistinct in the evening shadows but his voice had an edge to it.

"It has t' be before midnight. The tide is on the ebb and her gunports'll fall below the level of th' wharf before then." He picked up the neat piece of canvas Gindler had prepared. It was rolled tightly together with sailmaker's twine, to which a stronger line was securely fixed.

"How long will you have this?" The coil of light line seemed a lot but was probably only fifty feet or so.

"I think all o' that," Kydd said. The longer it was, the safer the task of picking up the buoy and yanking the line. "And th' last thing—our buoy." He cast about for an object that would serve and found some duck decoys: one of the ducklings would suit admirably. He secured it to the light line—and all was complete.

In the blackness of night they stood at the edge of the woods where they were closest to the privateer and had a front-row view of the ship. Lanthorns in her rigging cast bright pools of light on to the wharf; figures paced slowly along the dockside. Work had ceased. This would not be the case if an early-dawn departure was planned.

"Well, here we are," Gindler whispered, "and it's here that we part, my friend. I cannot in all conscience go further, but I'd like to shake the hand of a brave man."

"Let's be started," Kydd muttered. He tucked the precious bundle of canvas and rope tightly under his arm and slipped down to the water's edge, careful to stay in the shadows of the spur of rock.

There he paused, safe for the moment, and listened to the quiet chuckle and ripple of the calm evening sea. The ship was over a hundred yards away—and when he stepped round the spur there was a dozen yards of open beach before the shelter of the wharf piling. For that distance he would be in plain view of the ship.

The single thing in his favour was surprise. They might expect a rush by an armed party, but never by a lone, unarmed man. It was small comfort, but it also seemed the height of absurdity to be going into battle against a heavily gunned privateer armed only with a lump of wood and a piece of dirty canvas.

In the shadow of the rocks he stripped down to his long underwear and stockings, awkward and vulnerable. He laid down his clothes carefully and stumbled over to the inky black sea. He could not risk the forty feet of open beach; the only alternative was to wade off into the outer blackness.

The water was fearfully cold and his heart nearly failed him. He forced himself to continue, his feet feeling the sharp stones and shells on the rocky bottom. Deeper he went—the cold biting into his legs then his waist, leaving him gasping for breath. Out past the end of the spur, the ship was now in plain view and as he turned to round the end he lowered himself into the numbing water to his neck. Past the rock, the bottom turned mercifully to the softness of mud and he leaned forward, shuddering with cold, pushing on parallel to the beach and praying he could not be seen.

Minotaure was bows to sea, her carved stern towards him. There was a light in the captain's cabin, a dim gold point through the mullioned windows. A couple of figures stood together on her after deck and Kydd could see the occasional red of a drawn pipe, but the rest was in shadow.

There was the odd scurry of unknown sea creatures at his feet, the stubbing of a toe against an invisible barnacled rock—

and what seemed an eternity of knifing cold. At last he saw the edge of the wharf piling resolve out of the darkness.

Gratefully he entered the safety of the overhang with its concentrated sea odours and stood upright. A mistake. The tiny evening breeze was now a searching icy blast that stopped his breath. He lowered himself back into the water, which was almost warm by contrast.

Stumbling along in the darkness he passed between the heavily barnacled and slimy piles, clutching his bundle until he came abreast of the looming black vastness of the privateer. Turning towards it he moved forward and felt the slope of the sea-bed suddenly drop away. He pulled back in alarm. He was an awkward swimmer and, encumbered with his device, he could not possibly do other than move upright.

With a sinking heart he realised it was logical to build the wharf for larger ships where the water was deep enough for them to come close in—*Minotaure* would draw fifteen or twenty feet. Far out of his depth. His frozen mind struggled and he looked around wildly. Past the stern of the ship, tucked in just under the wharf edge he saw a low, elongated shape, a ship's side punt used by sailors to stand in as they worked their way down the hull caulking and painting.

He pulled the little raft towards him, hoisted his bundle in, and hanging off one end, he thrust out. The punt glided towards the black bulk of the ship's hull and finally bumped woodenly against it. Kydd's feet dangled in the freezing depths.

A mix of terror and elation washed over him at the physical touch of the enemy; he worked his way along the hull, sensing noise and movement within until he reached the curved overhang of the stern. Here he would be out of sight from above while he set his trap, but any boat coming down the other side of the hull would burst into view just feet from him without warning.

He took the bundle, his hands shaking as he prepared it. The motionless rudder was lost in the shadows but Kydd could hang on to the rudder chains and be guided down to it. He would have to work by feel. Near the waterline would be the lower hance, a projecting piece at the trailing edge of the rudder; with its hoisting ring plate he could not fail to find it. He felt the barnacle-studded fitting and pulled himself to it. The final act: to thread the line through the score, the inner gap.

He let his hands slide inwards. The pintle strap led to the pintle itself going through the gudgeon eye—and there was the score. A gap just below the waterline and big enough to put his whole fist through. Excitement surged through him. All he had to do now was put the line through with the wedge one side and the rest the other.

He pushed the line through easily enough, then had to bend it on the wedge. His hands were numb but he fumbled it through the screw eye. But when he tried to tie a simple one-handed bowline his stiff fingers could not obey. He scrabbled at the line helplessly, aware that if he lost his hold on the wedge it would sink down for ever into the black depths. He couldn't *feel* anything! Nearly weeping with frustration he tried again and failed. Then, with one last effort, he rested his elbows on the edge of the punt, leaving both hands free. Clumsily he managed to manipulate the sodden line.

Letting the wedge hang free by its line he tested it, then let it sink slowly toward the sea-bed. Moving to the other side of the rudder he freed the bundle of canvas and let the pick-up buoy float away. The little bundle, weighted with a fishing lead, sank also, and all that was left of his night's work was a shabby little duckling floating nearby.

Gindler was waiting behind the rocky spur and when Kydd staggered up from the dark waters he threw a blanket round his frozen body and rubbed furiously. "Mr Kydd, you're the maddest son-of-a-gun I've ever heard of!" he whispered. "Now let's get something hot into you."

It was King's calibogus, spruce beer stiffened with New England rum, a drink to which Greaves had introduced him; taken hot in front of the log fire, it was medicine indeed. While Kydd recounted his tale, Gindler threw clams and chunks of cod into a pot, with onion and bacon, and crushed biscuit for thickening, then let the mixture simmer and fill the snug cottage with an irresistible aroma.

"Er, do pardon me the liberty," said Gindler, after the chowder pot had been satisfyingly scraped empty, "I can't help but observe that your character is so—different from your usual King's officer, Tom. You never hang back when there's a need to soil the hands, to bear a fist directly—and you speak plainer, if you understand me."

"Aye, well, that could be because I come fr'm a different land. I came aft through th' hawse, as we say. But now I'm a gentleman," he added doubtfully.

"You are indeed," Gindler said sincerely.

"How about your folk, Ned?" Kydd asked, cradling another calibogus.

"My mother's family came over with the *Mayflower,*" Gindler said proudly. "Settled in the north, near Boston. Pa runs a business . . ."

A grey day broke, and Kydd's sleepless night was over at last. Today would end in a flurry of gunfire and a captured privateer— or failure. Any one of those barbarous small rocks that had left his feet so sore could snag the line and part it, and they would be left with a useless end. So much could go wrong: even as they breakfasted, a crew member might look over the side of *Minotaure* and raise the alarm, and then it would be over before it started, or the ship might sail at dawn when *Tenacious* was not in the offing.

Kydd sat on the porch, brooding. "What do ye say we take a walk through th' town? Perhaps we—"

"You must stay here, my friend. Your presence near the vessel at this time could be . . . unfortunate." Gindler got to his feet. "I will undertake a reconnaissance."

He returned quickly. "They're ready for sea near enough, but there's a little duck taken up residence under her stern."

The morning dragged by; Kydd tried to learn a card game but it quickly palled. In the end they sat on the porch and talked, eyes straying out to sea.

"I believe we must take position now," Gindler said lightly. "We have our smack ready at hand."

The craft was not big but had a single mast stepped to a forward thwart, and with a light spritsail took the morning breeze with a will. In nondescript fishermen's gear Kydd and Gindler saw they were one of a handful of boats chancing the day for sea-bass.

The entrance to the inner sound was no more than a couple of miles across and the one league boundary a half-mile beyond. Gindler eased sheets and steered for the northern point.

"There she is!" cried Kydd exultantly. HMS *Tenacious* under topsails was calmly approaching from the north. All the players were now converging and it was only a matter of time before the final act.

Minotaure had to sail by noon; her captain was waiting for the last possible moment and, as a consequence, would have to face *Tenacious*. But he would have been told about the midday signal arrangement—why did he wait and risk the confrontation?

Then it dawned on Kydd. Junon was both confident and cool. He *wanted* the English ship to present herself: he knew he could out-manoeuvre the big ship and in this way could establish where she was and therefore be free of the threat of an unpleasant surprise later.

The privateer's fore topsail rose: she was about to proceed. Kydd's heart beat faster. Her headsails fluttered into life and, as he watched, her bow detached from the wharf. The French tricolour was lowered from her ensign staff but reappeared at her mizzen peak. Other canvas made its appearance and *Minotaure* stood out into the sound.

Her actions were not lost on *Tenacious* whose battle-ensign soared up to the mainmasthead in answer. Kydd pictured the frenzied rush to quarters and was torn between the desire to be back aboard his ship in action and the knowledge of what he had to do.

Tenacious stood squarely across the entrance at the edge of the boundary, heaving to in the slight winds, while the privateer advanced cautiously towards her under just topsails, not giving the slightest indication of which side she was going to pass.

Kydd's admiration for the coolness of the French captain increased as he noticed that the wind's direction had *Tenacious* hove to with broadside towards, normally a battle-winning raking position, but the bigger ship could not in any circumstances open fire into United States waters and certainly not risk shot ricocheting into the town. Therefore *Minotaure* could move forward in perfect safety.

"We need t' get under her stern," Kydd growled. Gindler sheered the boat round and edged more into the sound, keeping safely to one side. The privateer drew nearer and Kydd visualised the wedge and the little bundle bumping over the mud of the seabed, hopefully then to stream out behind—or they might already have been torn off.

Kydd spoke, more to himself than to Gindler: "When she makes her move, she'll loose sail t' crack on speed and only then

choose her side an' put over her helm sharp. Therefore our signal will be when she looses more sail." *Tenacious* would have
little chance of reacting in time, being stationary in the water with only the chance of a fleeting shot as the faster vessel
surged past.

The privateer came on, seeming immense from the little
smack. Her upper decks appeared full of men and her gunports were open. Gindler eased away the sail and let the big
ship come down on them, jockeying to be as near as possible.

"Wave at 'em!" Kydd said urgently. Answering waves appeared up at the deckline. They were very close now, every raw
detail of her timbers and gun muzzles plain. Gindler put over
his tiller and the boat spun about to face the same direction,
jibbing and rolling in the side wake of the privateer. *Tenacious*
was precisely dead ahead—still no indication. Kydd waved
again, anxiety flooding him at the thought of what hung on
the next few minutes.

Gindler jockeyed the boat about, slipping back until the
stern windows of the ship came into view then sidling up
behind. "The duckling, find th' duck!" Kydd gasped. They
searched frantically astern of the ship—but there was no sign
of a buoy.

"No!" Kydd cried harshly.

Gindler kept on behind the rearing stern then pointed.
"Th-there!" he whooped. Kydd leaned over and saw, in the
roiling, bubbling wake, a jaunty duckling bobbing vigorously,
much closer to the stern than he had planned.

"Get us in there, f'r God's sake!" he yelled hoarsely, careless of anything but the final task.

Hardening in the sheets Gindler brought the smack closer
but startled faces appeared over the stern high above. "Snag
the bastard, quick!" he hissed. The boat was bouncing around

in the uneven wake and the wind around the looming stern was fitful and chancy.

Clear and positive over the noise of the tumbling water came the sound of a boatswain's calls—to man yards and set sail. Kydd leaned far over the bow, reaching, scrabbling for the duckling. There would be no second chance now, and shouts were coming from above.

He touched the painted wood but it bounced out of reach then skittered back. He grabbed at it with the furthest extremity of his reach—he had it, pulled, but it jerked from his grasp. Kydd cried out in frustration.

The shouts above turned angry, demanding, dangerous. In despair he glanced back at Gindler, whose pale, set face took on a look of determination. He yanked on the sheets and the little boat responded, going right under the stern of the big ship. Kydd fell over the thwarts trying to keep with the buoy but at last he seized it in both hands.

Gindler instantly let out sheets and the smack fell back. Kydd was ready for it and crushed the little duck to him as the soaked line tautened unbearably—then fell slack. It was over.

Near sobbing with relief, Kydd fell back into the boat, still with the duckling clasped to his chest. He looked up—*Minotaure* was receding from them and, indeed, was loosing sail from every bare yard. She was still heading for *Tenacious* and waiting until the sails drew, gathering speed for the vital turn.

Kydd held his breath until it hurt—there was no sign, no hint that he had achieved anything: *Minotaure* was poised for her turn, all ready . . . and still no turn—

He had done it! Incredibly, unbelievably, it had worked! The privateer's steering had locked, to the bewilderment of her crew and now, as he watched, confusion and chaos overtook as orders for setting sail were reversed, panic and fear flooding in as the ship delivered herself into the arms of a ship-of-the-line.

It was over in moments. A disbelieving *Tenacious* had seen *Minotaure* come straight at her and sent a challenging ball under her bow. There was nothing any sane captain could do when brought to, helpless under the threat of the broadside of a two-decker—her colours came down slowly and HMS *Tenacious* took possession of her prize.

CHAPTER 11

THE PRESIDENT LIFTED ANOTHER ROSE in his cupped hands and sniffed it. "Perfect!" He sighed, raising his eyes to meet those of his new secretary of the Navy, Benjamin Stoddert. Then he straightened and said softly, "I'm right glad you accepted, Ben."

There was a moment of shared feeling. This was not the red-blooded hewing of a vision from the chaos of the revolution twenty years before: it was a time for hard-headed recognition of power and reality in a world at war.

"I fear we may be too late," Stoddert said. "It came all of a moil so quick, John."

The lines in Adams's face deepened. "I don't want war with the French—understand that of all things! I loathe their system and their arrogance, but I'll be doing anything I can think of to prevent an alignment of the United States with one party or the other."

Stoddert followed Adams to the next rose-bush. "Agreed—but we must stand up for ourselves. No one in this world will stand up for us."

Adams straightened. "Ben, I've abrogated the treaty we've had since 1778 with the French. I've swallowed insults from Jefferson about my reasons and finally pulled Congress into line. You have your navy. Leave it to me to take care of the rest of the world."

"Yes, sir." Stoddert saw no reason to dilute a response to French actions, but knew better than to debate Adams's moderate tactics. Besides which, Adams had a personal interest in the formation of this new navy: he had been the one to create the Continental Navy, the motley fleet of the revolution that had taken on the Royal Navy at sea. It had then been disbanded. This Federal Navy was going to be different, professional, and Stoddert had the honour of leading it into existence.

"You have your captains now." It had been a fraught business, the few experienced men available vying for positions of seniority and honour.

"I have. Truxtun, Nicholson, Barry, of course, and the lieutenants." It had taken the personal intervention of the ageing George Washington to settle the question of seniority.

"And the ships." Converted merchantmen to begin with, six frigate-class vessels racing to completion: *Constitution, Constellation* and others.

"And your budget," Adams said finally. Congress had voted it through, complaining bitterly at the cost of the new vessels, and the Republicans had fought against it as irrelevant to a continental power with no enemies, but now it was going to happen.

"Ben, be careful, my friend," Adams said quietly. Both understood the political risks that were being taken. "Well, I won't keep you." He plucked his rose with a sigh, then turned back to Stoddert. "One thing interests me. How will you forge a—a way of doing things, a spirit of the sea, if you will?"

Stoddert pondered. "It seems to me we acquire it in the same way as we have our common law. We take what we want from the English and cast away the rest." He pursed his lips. "After all, it's the Royal Navy, the first navy of the age."

The main sticking point was Gindler. He had begged Kydd not to mention his part, arguing that for him to have taken an active part in operations against a neutral might cause an international incident. But without Gindler's corroboration his account would not be believed—especially the latter stages, which would have been impossible without an accomplice. He could imagine the polite contempt with which his claim would be met at the wardroom table, seen as a shabby attempt to embellish his experiences. No—he could not risk that.

There was nothing for it but a bald statement of his treatment ashore, his urging of a town meeting and the final instructions from Hartford. He had reported as much verbally to the captain, who had generally approved his conduct, understanding his encounter with the odd notions of democracy obtaining ashore. It would take a lot to put the captain out of humour with such a prize meekly astern, and no doubt this report would be passed on to the admiral with suitably warm words.

Kydd was proud of what he had done and chagrined at having to keep it quiet—Renzi had agreed to go over the report for him before he handed it in, but afterwards Kydd had promised him such a tale as would keep him tolerably entertained.

Halifax had seen ships come and go in wartime, and this occasion was not noticeably different. *Tenacious* anchored in the bosom of the fleet, salutes were exchanged and Captain Houghton, in sword and decorations, went aboard the flagship to make explanation of his prize—and the consequent accession to the admiral's own purse.

By return new fleet instructions were sent to her signal lieutenant, the effective date three days hence.

Kydd groaned with vexation. Signals and their meanings were a prerogative of the admiral commanding the station and were buried in the *Fighting Instructions,* detailed prescripts from the admiral for the precise manner in which he wished his ships to engage the enemy. Admiral "Black" Dick Howe, who had brought the fleet mutiny at Spithead to an end the previous year, had done much to standardise operation of flag signals and Kydd saw that these from Admiral Vandeput were similar.

There were ten signal flags, then the preparative, and the sub-stitute—pennants and wefts, differences of meaning depending on where hoisted, night signals, recognition procedures, signals for individual ships, divisions, fleets. This was the system that had resulted from so much practice over years of sea warfare. It had gone into battle with Howe on the Glorious First of June; only the previous year Jervis had signalled Nelson at St Vincent, and Duncan had used it with such effect at Camperdown.

Now Lieutenant Kydd had inherited this accrued wisdom and must prove himself worthy of it. He took the signal pocket book, which had been owned by his dead predecessor, as a model and with scissors and patience set about constructing the *vade mecum* that would stay with him while he was a signal lieutenant.

The flag-lieutenant himself brought the summons: Lieutenant Kydd to wait on the admiral immediately. Kydd flinched when he recalled his previous summoning. What *could* be the rea-son now? It was astonishing. He was a mere lieutenant—and so many commanders would slay to be noticed by a commander-in-chief—and there was no apparent reason for it.

Kydd bawled at Tysoe in a fever of anxiety: only new stock-ings and faultless linen would answer. Decorations? He had none. Sword? The plain hanger he had bought in Halifax would have to do. He pulled on his breeches, watched by half the ward-room.

A gig was brought alongside and Kydd descended the ship's side and sat bolt upright in the sternsheets. The bowman cast off with an excess of flourishes and the midshipman in charge set the men to pulling smartly.

The flag-lieutenant led the way wordlessly to the great cabin. "Lieutenant Kydd, sir."

"Enter!"

Admiral Vandeput advanced to meet him. "Well, now, is this the officer the fuss is all about?" He regarded Kydd keenly.

"Sir?"

The white-haired admiral spoke in an easy manner; this could not be a carpeting.

"Please sit, Mr Kydd." He went round his desk and found a paper, while Kydd perched on the edge of an elegant Windsor chair. "This is a most particular request, not to say direction, and it comes from Mr Liston. Our minister to the United States, that is—what you might call an ambassador." He laid the paper on the table and Kydd glimpsed the cipher of the Court of St James at the top.

"In it he desires me to release an officer for a particular service to a foreign power—as you probably know, we have had officers seconded to the Swedish Crown, St Petersburg, other countries. This is not unusual. It is a little odd, though, that you have been named, and that you are so damn junior." His quiet chuckle took the sting from his words. "It seems the United States is conjuring up their own navy and they have asked Mr Liston for an observer from the Royal Navy, if possible a Lieutenant Kydd. He feels that it would be right at this time to be seen co-operating with a neutral nation.

"There! What do you think of that, Mr Kydd? You're noticed diplomatically." His genial smile grew wider and he stabbed a finger at Kydd in emphasis. "And I'd wager more went on ashore in that backwoods village than ever found its way into your report, hey-hey?"

"Er, sir, I—"

"Never mind. Whatever it was, you did right. Now, let's talk about what you'll be doing. They've got together two or three frigates—built 'em themselves, damn it—and I've seen the gunboats their Revenue runs. Calls 'em their 'treasury navy.' Now, you'll probably be shipping in one of their frigates—they're fitting out now. Your status will be supernumerary for the voyage—a passenger, any Christian would call it—and you won't be called upon to serve a gun if it comes to fighting."

"Er, who will be their enemy, sir?"

"Well, that's a little difficult to say, but . . ." he tapped his nose ". . . I've been hearing that the French have overstepped their position, making hay with American trade, and they don't like it. In any event, they'll probably tell you about it themselves.

"Now, I know you'll comport yourself as a gentleman should, marks o' respect to all the proper persons, flags and so on. But I think what they're probably after is a correct steer on how things are done in our service. I don't see any reason why you can't tell 'em anything reasonable they want to know. Must be hard to start from nothing," he reflected sombrely. "You go in plain clothes, will be victualled by the, er, United States Navy, and I don't suppose you'll be away from us for long. There's a brig leaving for Philadelphia shortly—it's their capital, where our Mr Liston is expecting you. Good fortune, Lieutenant!"

Kydd took in the sights as the brig rounded Cape May for the long trip up the broad Delaware. This was quite a different land from rugged grey rock-bound Nova Scotia or even pretty, forested Connecticut. Here there was well-settled land on either bank, farming and orchards, settlements and roads. The sails of coastal shipping thronged the river as it narrowed towards the capital. Kydd was impressed. No mean colonial sprawl, Philadelphia was a fine city that stretched for miles along the river, as busy as any he had seen in England.

Kydd followed his baggage ashore and looked to see if someone was there to meet him. A ferry loaded noisily and a market
stretched away into the distance, improbably occupying the middle of a wide road.

"Mr Kydd?"

He wheeled round. "Aye?" he said cautiously.

A well-dressed young man inclined his head. "Thornton, secretary of Legation."

"How—"

"Please believe, it's not so hard a task to spy out a sailor, Mr
Kydd." He raised a beckoning finger and a coachman came for
Kydd's baggage. "So good in you to leave your wooden world
at such short notice. His Excellency is returning from Mount
Vernon and hopes to make your acquaintance tomorrow. I trust
you'll find our accommodation congenial."

With a growing sense of unreality Kydd boarded a high-
wheeled carriage and the debonair Thornton pointed out the
sights as they made Walnut Street at a fast clip. "Minister Liston
keeps unfashionable hours, I fear. Can you find it in you, dear fellow, to appear at nine tomorrow morning? It seems he's anxious
to see you."

"Of course."

"Should you like theatre, I have tickets for this evening."

"Thank you," Kydd murmured, his head spinning with the
pace of events.

"Mr Liston," Thornton said softly, ushering Kydd into a small
drawing room and closing the door noiselessly as he left.

"Ah, Mr Kydd," said Liston, finishing a letter. "Pray be seated,
I won't be long."

While Liston sanded and sealed the missive, Kydd had the feeling that he was under discreet observation.

"Very well. To business. You will be aware by now that this

country has seen fit to begin the creation of a navy, arising from the grievous nature of the depredations of the French on their trade. For details of that you will no doubt have your professional sources." He paused significantly. "There are many elements of delicacy in this situation, and in a way I would wish that you were of a more elevated, senior character, but in this I am constrained by their very firm petition for your own good self to undertake this service. Therefore I will be plain. The United States has done us the signal honour of embarking on a characterisation of their navy that is in the greatest measure our own. This is gratifying to us, of course, as it presupposes an alignment of purpose consequent upon a convergence of practices. This, naturally, has put the French out of countenance, for the Americans have turned their back on their traditional ally in this."

Liston paused, considering Kydd. "And in this, as in all things, you will consult your honour as to how on foreign soil you will best conduct yourself in furtherance of your country's interests."

Something in the smooth flow of words alerted Kydd and he listened warily. "I will, sir, be assured."

"Then if this is your prime motivation I can rely on your loyalty to the Crown?"

"Sir."

"Then let me lay out the issues before you. You are in a unique position to allay the fears of your government on certain matters concerning the effectiveness of this armament . . ."

"Sir!" Kydd said tightly. "You're askin' me to spy on th' Americans?" The warmth of a flush spread, but he did not care. Spies and betrayal, this was not how he saw his duty.

Liston's face tightened. "Have a care, Lieutenant! Recollect you hold the commission of King George. And in it you have sworn certain loyalties that cannot so easily be cast aside. What I am asking is no more than any officer of honour is bound to do when on foreign territory, whether on parole or any other basis—simply to keep his eyes open." The crack of aristocratic authority in his voice remained as he went on, "And if I might remark it, you appear surprisingly deficient thereby in your understanding of the bounds of gentlemanly conduct."

Kydd stiffened, then dropped his eyes.

Liston's tone softened: "We're not asking you to report back on the number of ships and guns and so forth, if that is your scruple. It is something of far more significance. I desire that you will return to me with an opinion as to whether you believe the United States is determined in this matter, has resolved to establish an armed force of credibility, or is merely embarked on a ploy to deter the French." He fixed his gaze on Kydd. "And if you conceive that they are in earnest, your professional opinion as to their effectiveness at sea. In short, whether they can fight—should the world take notice."

Kydd returned the gaze steadily. "I will do that, sir." It was not an act of spying: it was an opinion.

Liston relaxed a little. "Then as we seem to have come to an understanding, would you care to join me for coffee? The American bean is generally accounted superior, and we have the remainder of this hour before your hosts make their appearance."

Twenty minutes later there was a firm knock on the door. Thornton appeared, with an indistinct figure behind him. "Sir, a gentleman for Mr Kydd." It was Gindler.

Outside they shook hands gleefully. "Well, this must be the strangest coincidence of the age," laughed Gindler, but his knowing look gave the game away.

"So, what has the American Navy in store for poor Lieutenant Kydd?"

"Ah, the United States Navy is what we call it—you English

will have reason to remember the Continental Navy of the revolution; this is now the Federal Navy but some take exception to the term."

"Noted."

"And you are now talking to L'tenant Gindler, third of the United States Frigate *Constellation,* Captain Truxtun, now fitting out in Baltimore." He smiled wickedly. "And *I* am talking to the mysterious supernumerary on our first voyage . . ."

Kydd laughed but his interest swelled fast. This was not to be a pettifogging political appointment but a real seagoing situation. "When—"

"Not so fast, good sir. I'm instructed that our new secretary of the Navy wishes to make your acquaintance before we hazard the briny deep."

"Do excuse this mare's nest of a room—my wife has not yet arrived in Philadelphia to take charge of my household." Stoddert made ineffectual attempts to clear a space at one end of a plain table where a stout chair stood. His manner was distracted but his gaze direct as he greeted Kydd.

"Secretary Stoddert has only recently arrived in the capital," Gindler murmured, standing clear of the welter of papers and furniture.

"Thank you, Lieutenant. Pray call on me before you leave Philadelphia. I may have something for Captain Truxtun." Gindler bowed and left.

"Now, you are Lieutenant Kydd of the Royal Navy."

"Sir."

"And you must be wondering why you are here, not to say concerned."

"Aye, sir," Kydd said, uneasy at yet more attention from on high. Stoddert lowered himself into his chair. "Then, first, the wider issue. We are in the process of creating our own navy. We have chosen to follow the example and traditions of the Royal Navy as a starting point for our own. It would be of the utmost value to us were an officer of that illustrious service to signify to us our success in this endeavour. As to why your own good self, Mr Gindler was good enough to render me a full and satisfying account of what transpired in Exbury—in confidence, of course. There can be no question that the United States is implicated in any way."

"I understand, sir."

"But more to our liking are Mr Gindler's remarks upon your character. Let me be candid, sir. The Royal Navy is a proud and ancient service, but there are many of its officers whose superior attitude is both lamentable and abhorrent to us as a nation. It is a trait that regrettably seems to appear more prominent with seniority, and this is why we have chosen to request a less senior officer.

"Mr Gindler tells us that your conduct ashore was circumspect and respectful to the feelings of the people even to the point of joining the merriment in a tavern—in short, sir, you have the common touch, which we as a people do prize so much." Stoddert rose, gripping the edge of the table and wincing as he did so. At Kydd's concern he gave a low chuckle. "Ah, this. A souvenir given me by the English at Brandywine Creek."

He drew the chair to a more confiding proximity. "Let me be frank, Mr Kydd. Your position as a King's officer in a warship of the United States Navy is anomalous, not to say irregular, and there are those who would put the worst construction on your presence. Therefore you are entered as a supernumerary on board, specifically a friend of the captain. You haven't yet the pleasure of an introduction to Captain Truxtun, but he will be advised of you, and will be encouraged to take full advantage of your knowledge and experience of the Royal Navy. I'm sure he will appreciate your assistance." He leaned forward further.

"Before you go, I should like to make it very plain that on your return I would deeply appreciate your sincere appraisal of our efforts. Do you think this will be possible?"

"Sir." Kydd felt resentment building at the way so many seemed to be treating him like a pawn in a higher game.

"Then, sir, it only remains for me to wish you God speed on your voyage. You will find Lieutenant Gindler waiting in the drawing room below."

"Was all that necessary?" A figure moved out from behind a covered escritoire.

Stoddert closed the door. "I think so. The military of any race should not be overburdened with considerations of politics." At times Murray, his political agent, could be insensitive to the perceptions of others.

"Be that as it may, Mr Stoddert, you didn't warn him of the Republicans—he should have been told."

"That we have an opposition in Congress so lost to honour they would stop at nothing to ruin our navy for crass political gain? Jefferson has done his worst to try to prevent America reaching for a sure shield against the world—how can I explain that to a man whose country continues to exist only because of her own power at sea? I cannot. In any case, this talk of subverting crews and so on is probably from unreliable sources and should be discounted. What most concerns me are my captains. A prickly, difficult bunch, Murray. Especially Truxtun."

"A fighting captain," Murray interposed strongly.

"Oh, indeed. But as a privateer. And pray bring to mind the fluttering in Congress there was during the English war, on hearing how he set John Paul Jones himself to defiance over some notion of which ship was to fly some pennant. Not one to be led easily—and too damn clever by half. Did you know he was once pressed by the Royal Navy?"

"Indeed?"

"But that's by the by. Here is my main hope for L'tenant Kydd. He has no interest in politics. He's a tarpaulin mariner and cares only for his ropes and sails. He must be intelligent, he wouldn't hold a commission else, so he'll be able to tell me exactly what I want to know . . ."

Nothing could convey better to Kydd the continental vastness of the country than the overland coach journey with Gindler to Baltimore. From as fine a four-horse conveyance as any in England, they admired the spring-touched verdancy of the deciduous woodland that had replaced the northern conifers, the glittering lakes, rivers and blue-washed mountains far into the interior.

At stops to change horses, Gindler added to Kydd's impressions: he pointed out that beyond the mountains to the west the land was wild, stretching for more than sixty degrees of longitude; an unimaginable distance, more than the Atlantic was wide, and no one knew what was within it. Unsettled by the effect of this enormity Kydd was glad when they met the cobblestones of Baltimore.

"She'll be lying in the Patuxent river," Gindler said. "We're nearly ready for sea." There was no delaying: a fast packet on its way down the Chesapeake to Norfolk had promised to call at Patuxent and their ship.

The sight of naked masts and yards towering above the low, bushy point made Kydd's pulse quicken. The packet rounded the point into the broad opening of a river and there at anchor was the biggest frigate he had ever seen.

"A thing of beauty," breathed Gindler. "Don't you agree?"

Kydd concentrated as they neared the vessel. She was distinctive and individual; her lines and finish owed nothing to the conservative traditions of old-world shipwrights, and there was an alert purposefulness about her. There was much in her that a sailor could love. Nearly half as big again as the lovely *Artemis*, she seemed well armed. "Twenty-fours?" he asked.

"Indeed! I'd like to see any frigate that swims try to come up against the old *Connie*," Gindler said proudly.

"Old?" Kydd said wryly, observing seamen applying a tar mixture to the last remaining raw timber of the bulwarks.

"Well, I grant you she's newborn, but I have the feeling you'll be hearing from us in the future, my friend." His glance flicked up to the flag with its stars and stripes and he added softly, "I promise you that."

Kydd had seen far too many ships fitting for sea to be concerned at the turmoil on deck. He followed Gindler aft to the captain's cabin. Gindler knocked and an irritable bellow bade them enter.

"Mr Kydd, sir," said Gindler, and when the captain looked up in incomprehension he added, "Our supernumerary."

The captain's gaze swivelled to Kydd. Intelligent but hard eyes met his. Then the man grunted, "Mr Kydd, y'r service," and turned back to his papers. "Berth him in the fourth lootenant's cabin. He won't be sailing," he ordered, without looking up.

"Aye, sir," said Gindler, and withdrew with Kydd.

Picking their way through men at blocks and ropework—some seaming canvas, others scaling shot—they headed for the after hatchway. "I fear I must desert you now, Tom, duty calls. I'll take you to the wardroom, and I'm sure Captain Truxtun will want to see you when less pressed."

"Welcome back, Lootenant!" a fresh-faced seaman called, with a grin, to Gindler and waved a serving mallet.

"Thanks, Doyle," Gindler threw back. At Kydd's raised eyebrows he added, "A mort of difference from a King's ship, I think. Remember, aboard here every man jack is a volunteer on wages and, as Americans, they're not accustomed to bending the knee."

Kydd did not rise to the bait and privately wondered at their reliability in action when instant obedience was vital.

The wardroom was almost deserted. A black messman glanced at him curiously and left. Kydd looked about him. The raw newness had not yet been overcome to bring individuality. At the same time there was an alien air. The unfamiliar wood graining, the slant of the munnions—even the smell: striking timber odours, the usual comfortable galley smells subtly different, no waft of bilge.

He crossed to the transom seat. Reassuringly, it was still the repository of the ephemera of wardroom life and he picked up a Philadelphia newspaper, the *Mercantile Advertiser*. While he awaited Truxtun's summons he settled by the midships lanthorn and opened it. There was no ochre tax stamp and the paper was of good quality. He scanned the front page, which was given over to a verbatim setting out of a newly enacted statute. The next page, however, was vigorous and to the point: a growing feeling against the French gave colour to the local news and trade intelligence. Further inside there were advertisements and notices.

"Mr Kydd? Cap'n wants ye." He folded the paper, tugged his waistcoat into position and followed the messenger, apprehensive at meeting those hard eyes again.

Truxtun was standing, his back to Kydd, staring broodily out of the windows of his cabin. He turned and gestured to a chair. "Sit y'self down, Mr Kydd." He himself remained standing.

"I'll be plain with you, sir. Mr Secretary Stoddert thinks to provide me with an aide who'll tell me how they do it in King George's Navy. I can tell you frankly I don't give a solitary hoot how you do things—this is the United States Navy and I'm captain o' the *Constellation*, and I'll do things the way I want." His face had the implacability of a slab of oak. "Therefore your presence aboard is a waste. For Ben Stoddert's sake, I'll carry you these few days, but I'll have you know, sir, that I'll be giving orders that no United States officer or crewman shall hold converse with you—I don't want 'em getting strange ideas agin mine about how a ship o' war should be run. I'd be obliged if you'd keep your views to yourself.

"In return, you're welcome to sit at vittles in the wardroom and the fourth's stateroom is yours. You'll know to keep out from under while the ship's being worked, and should we meet an enemy you'll stay below. Have I made myself clear, sir?"

It was going to be a hard time for Kydd. He was not introduced when the wardroom sat for dinner. He was passed the condiments when he asked, but none caught his eye. Desultory talk went on about progress in the final run-up to sea trials in the morning, a few lame attempts at humour—this was a wardroom that had not been long together but would coalesce around individuals as the commission went on.

In the morning he caught Gindler, now a taut-rigged lieutenant, about to go on deck. "I'm sorry it has to be this way, Tom," he said softly. He touched his hat and left for the nervous bustle above.

Kydd hesitated: he could see down the length of the deck to the cable party readying the messenger; the tierers were moving down the hatchway for their thankless task at bringing in the cable.

He decided against making an appearance and returned to the wardroom. Although it was galling to be left in ignorance below decks, this was a first voyage with a new ship and a new company and he felt it was not altogether fair to witness the inevitable mistakes and dramas. He found a dog-eared copy of the *North American Review* and tried to concentrate, but the long tiller up against the deckhead began to creak and move as the man at the wheel exercised the helm. Then piercing calls from the boatswain and his mates told of the hoisting of boats, all suffused with the age-old excitement of the outward bound.

Rhythmic singing came from the men forward, and he felt a continual low shuddering in the deck that was, without doubt, the capstan at work. A sudden clatter and flurry of shouting would be a fall running away with the men while heavy thumps against the ship's side were the boats being brought in and stowed. The noises lessened until there was silence. They were ready to proceed.

Constellation's deck lifted and moved. In a deliberate sway it inclined to starboard, a heel that paused then returned and steadied to a definite angle, which had only one meaning: they were under sail and moving through the water.

Kydd threw down the newspapers—it was too much. He had to catch a glimpse of the sea. There were no stern windows in the wardroom, so the nearest place to see the ship's position was from the captain's cabin above.

He hurried up the companion and through the lobby. To the sentry loosely at attention outside the great cabin, he muttered, "Have t' see out." If he craned his neck, he could just glimpse the coastline of the Patuxent slowly rotating; a discernible wake was disturbing the water astern and the frenzied squeal of blocks could be heard even below decks.

He nodded to the marine and returned to the wardroom.

He knew vaguely that they should shape course south down Chesapeake Bay to the sea, but without sight of a chart he was in the dark. The angle of the deck lessened, then he heard another volley of faintly heard shouts, and there was a brief hesitation— they must be staying about.

At the right moment the tiller groaned with effort as the wheel went over but after some minutes there was no corresponding sway over to larboard. They had missed stays. Kydd cringed for the officer-of-the-deck as the unmistakable bull roar of Truxtun erupted; he was grateful to be out of sight. He picked up the *Review* again and flicked the pages.

After an hour or so the motions were repeated but this time in a smooth sequence, the frigate taking up on the opposite tack. Again the manoeuvre and again an easy transition. Dare he emerge on deck? He waited for a space; the angle of heel increased gradually and he guessed that more sail was being loosed. Kydd could stand it no longer. He made his way to the aft companion and mounted the steps to the quarterdeck. In the tense scene, not a soul looked his way. Groups of men were at the bitts, the base of the masts, the forecastle, all looking aft to where Truxtun stood with folded arms, staring up at taut canvas.

"Stream!" he snapped, to the men at the taffrail. One held the reel of the log high while the log-ship, a triangular drag piece, was cast into the sea astern to uncoil the line from the drum. It hurtled out at speed and when the sand-glass had run its course a lanky midshipman called, "Nip," and then, "Eleven knots an' a hair over."

Truxtun's expression did not change. "Not good enough. I'll have the lee stuns'ls abroad immediately."

The spring breeze whipped the tops from the waves as Kydd edged his way behind Truxtun towards the wheel and binnacle. Under the unblinking eye of the quartermaster he got what he wanted—a sight of the compass. South-south-east, wind from the west with a touch of north in it. Ideal blue-water sailing for a frigate: no wonder Truxtun was letting her have her head.

They were passing a broad river mouth to starboard with small vessels of all kinds converging at the confluence. "Potomac," hissed the midshipman behind him.

"I beg y'r pardon?" Kydd said, taken off-balance.

"The river—Potomac." He busied himself preparing the log for another cast.

"Thank ye," Kydd said quietly.

With stuns'ls drawing and royals atop each mast, *Constellation* foamed ahead. It was remarkable for a new vessel to have achieved such speed so soon. The log went out and the excited midshipman yelled, "A whisker less fourteen!" It was nothing short of extraordinary—and exhilarating. If Kydd was not to be an active participant at least he could enjoy the sensation.

Truxtun's eyes darting aloft, then aft, caught Kydd's eye. Kydd smiled broadly in open admiration. "She goes like a racehorse!"

"Aye—like a Yankee racehorse!" But there was no rancour in his voice and his grim expression had eased. It would be a gratifying thing, thought Kydd, to be in command of a frigate that, with her twenty-four pounders, could outfight any other and, at the same time, run or chase as she chose.

In the darkness of late evening they came to single anchor in the shelter of Hampton Roads, within sight of the broad Atlantic. The wardroom was abuzz at the splendid showing of their ship and it seemed only right to invite their captain to a hearty dinner.

Kydd sat at the furthest remove from Truxtun's place of honour at the head, but he was grateful to be present, hearing the happy talk about him, seeing friendships being forged and strengthened that would stand by them all in the ocean voyages ahead.

The talk roamed over the chance of war with France, seeing *The Glory of Columbia* at the Chestnut Street theatre, the right way to treat a halibut—it was just the same as his own wardroom . . . but different.

The dishes came and went, and the cloth was drawn. Blue smoke spiralled to the deckhead, glasses were raised and confidences exchanged. The chatter rose and fell. Into a chance silence Gindler's voice was raised: "Ah, Mr Kydd, you must have seen some sea service in your time. Pray tell us of it."

Glances were shot at Truxtun but he gave no sign that he objected.

"Aye, well, I had th' good fortune to take a cruise around th' world," Kydd said, thinking quickly. "A frigate, nearly as fine as this." He saw this was received well. "Setting a parcel o' philosophers on a rock, an' keeping the cannibals in their canoes at bay . . ." He told them of the adventure, and when he concluded with the sad wreck of *Artemis* on the Azores, there was a general stirring of sympathy.

Midshipman Porter leaned forward and exclaimed, "Have you b' chance seen action?"

"A little—Camperdown, which was where I got m' step."

Kydd wouldn't be drawn on the experience and tried to move on to Venice, but Truxtun himself interrupted: "Your fleet were in bloody mutiny before then." A ripple of muttering showed that the dreadful events had been shocking news here as well. "How did that affect you?"

The warmth of the evening fell away as he forced his mind to deal with the sudden release of memories. "It—my ship mutinied, but I was not hurt."

"Would you say the sailors had just cause?"

"At Spithead they had their reasons, and the Admiralty granted most and gave a pardon. But at the Nore . . ." He felt his face redden.

"Yes?"

"At the Nore, where I was, their cause was understandable but they went about it the wrong way."

Truxtun growled, "There's no treating with mutineers, ever."

The next day a small convoy had yet to assemble, so the dark-featured First Lieutenant Rodgers was sent ashore to the settlement of Norfolk to open a recruiting rendezvous to bring in more volunteers. Kydd saw Truxtun hand him silver at the gangway, saying, "Get some music going and grog for all hands—indulge their humour in a farewell frolic." Rodgers grinned and went over the side.

From forward came the dull *blang* of scaling charges as they cleared the cannon of rust and debris. Men squatted on the foredeck as they made up paper cartridges for the small arms, while others had the hatches off for the last of the sea stores still coming aboard.

By the early afternoon activity had died away. But Truxtun was not satisfied. He beat to quarters, and for two hours had the great guns exercised. Big twenty-four-pounders given resplendent names by their gun crews, Thunderer, Volcano, Murderer, and all plied with ferocity and resolution.

That night Kydd did not sit down with the wardroom. Captain Truxtun had requested the pleasure of his company and he entered the great cabin with some apprehension, for they were alone. Through the stern windows Kydd could see dim specks of light on shore; a tawny gold issued from the windows of a vessel anchored nearby, prettily dappling the water.

They passed pleasantries while they took a simple meal, and the steward swiftly removed the dishes. Kydd's wariness grew with Truxtun's politeness. "Do take a chair," Truxtun said, gesturing to a comfortable one near the stern windows. He found a cedar box in his writing desk and drew out a cigar. "Do you indulge, Mr Kydd?" At Kydd's declining he put it away again.

"You'll pardon me, Mr Kydd, but you're the darnedest Royal Navy officer I ever clapped eyes on." His frank gaze was unsettling. "I can tell a smart man when I see one. Don't have the airs of a King's man but I'll guess that's because you come from the people." He pondered for a moment. "So, do you hold it right to press men from under their own flag?"

"Sir, if these men are British they have a duty to—"

"They are American, sir."

"They say they are."

"They hold protections to prove it—and these are spat on by English officers."

"Yes! Th' rate for an American protection by your consul in Liverpool is one guinea and no questions asked."

Truxtun smiled. "We each have our views." The smile disappeared. "It's insulting to our flag for our merchant ships to be stopped and submit to search on the high seas. What do ye think of that?"

"Sir, Britain is a small island," he said carefully. "Trade is all we have. To survive we have to protect it, and—"

"You're right—and damn wrong. Do you know that most of the trade out of Nova Scotia is your cargo in our bottoms, on its way to ports of the world only a neutral can reach? You stop an American and you sink your own trade."

Kydd flushed. "You asked for views—I don't know y'r details but this I do know: if you're doin' the same for the French you're makin' a hill o' money out of it."

Truxtun's expression hardened, then a glimmer of a smile showed. "Well, as to that . . ."

It was the first that Kydd had heard of the true extent of the French attacks on American shipping and Truxtun's tone left no doubt of his feelings. "If we don't stand on our hind legs and fight 'em we deserve to be beat."

He looked directly at Kydd. "You're wondering why we don't declare war. So am I!" He glowered. Suddenly he got to his feet, crossed to his desk and abstracted a folded paper. "I'll show you this," he said, in an odd voice. "It came in today."

It was a single page, and bore the seal of the President of the United States. Kydd looked up in surprise. "Don't worry, the whole world's going to know about this tomorrow," Truxtun said heavily.

It began, "Instructions to Commanders of Armed Vessels, belonging to the United States, given at Philadelphia in the twenty-second Year of the Independence of the said States . . ." Truxtun leaned over and stabbed a finger at the second paragraph. "There!"

"WHEREAS, it is declared by an Act of Congress . . . that armed Vessels, sailing under authority or Pretence of Authority from the French Republic, have committed Depredations on the Commerce of the United States . . . in violation of the Law of Nations, and Treaties between the United States and the French Nation . . ." Truxtun snorted. "And what must we do?" He tapped the last paragraph: "THEREFORE, and in pursuance of the said Act, you are instructed and directed, to seize, take and bring into any Port of the United States . . ."

"You see? It's on. A shootin' war against the French."

Kydd stared in astonishment—everything had changed. "But—"

Truxtun interrupted him: "But it's not. We haven't declared war, the French haven't. What kind of peace is it that requires me to fire into a Frenchman on sight? Some sort of—of quasi-war?"

Kydd was in no doubt. "Any kind o' war is fine. This is thumpin' good news—and c'n I say, sir, if we both have the same enemy then we must be friends."

"No! No—I didn't say that. I didn't say that at all. We just has the same enemy, is the truth of it. I'll be doing my duty at sea and you'll be doing yours as you see it." He took back the paper. "If it's any clearer," he said gruffly, "I mean to say I hope we meet at sea one day—as equals, Mr Kydd."

The convoy was finally ready to sail. Showers blustered in from the north in curtains of white, vivid against the sullen grey of the sky, and lines of foam-crested waves advanced seaward.

A sullen thump came from forward—the signal gun for departure; two cutters moved about the dozen merchantmen cajoling, threatening, shepherding. It was so similar to Kydd's sailing from Falmouth, yet there was a difference: the lift of a head, the ringing shouts of the petty officers, the brazen size of the flag at the mizzen peak, the length of the pennant at the mainmasthead. This was a unique experience: to be aboard the first frigate commissioned in the United States Navy, and the first to put to sea on a war cruise.

Kydd stood out of the way, to the side, buffeted by the wind and with rain dripping from his hat brim. He was in no mood to go below. Although he was a spectator, he knew that no one would forget the day: a navy brought in just months from nothing to one that could execute the will of the nation. From helpless acquiescence to a sea force that would now go against the country's enemy—and conceivably within hours.

He looked forward. Gindler strode ahead proudly, disdaining oilskins over his lieutenant's uniform. To starboard the square, lofty lighthouse of Cape Henry lay abeam. With *Constellation* in the lead, the convoy left the haven of Chesapeake Bay and sailed for the open ocean to the east and all that lay beyond.

Standing out to sea the frigate lifted to the swell, new men staggered to the businesslike roll, while others sniffed the wind as if eager to be out to sea—or was it in anticipation of bloody action? The merchant ships bunched together close to the American frigate: there had been talk ashore of a pair of big privateers lying in wait and self-preservation was a strong motive for keeping station.

The weather moderated as they made their offing, although *Constellation* needed only double-reefed topsails to stay with her labouring convoy. Kydd walked forward, keenly appreciative of the motion of a frigate once more and interested indeed in the weatherliness of the American.

After the sociability of the dinner he was now greeted with cautious nods and the occasional smile—even the intense Lieutenant Rodgers touched his hat to him at one point.

When the land had been sunk and a tossing wilderness of empty ocean had been reached, the convoy dispersed, some to the Barbadoes, others to Dublin and London, thousands of miles of hard sailing with small crews, with the constant fear of sighting the sails of a predator. But *Constellation* was free now to soar.

"Mr Kydd." Truxtun snapped, as though struck by a sudden thought. "We shall be cruising south tomorrow." The rest of the quarterdeck was listening intently. "Therefore I believe it would be most expedient for you then to take your leave from this vessel. I shall stop a Philadelphia packet for your convenience, sir."

Kydd had taken to standing beside the lee helmsman, willing the ship on, feeling her motion through the water, and turned in surprise. "Er—why, of course, Captain." It was a disappointment not to see the frigate at her best, and despite the circumstances of his passage, there was something about this ship and her crew . . .

In the dog-watches, as the ship shortened sail for the night, Kydd lingered on deck, then went below for his last dinner aboard the *Constellation*. He went to his accustomed place at the end of the table, but found a black steward there. "If y' please, sah," he said, and pointed to the head of the table, where all the American officers stood with glasses, grinning at him.

"Come 'n' set, Tom," one called. Kydd did as he was asked, and took the chair normally occupied by the first lieutenant, bemused.

"Just wanted t' wish you God speed, Mr Kydd," Rodgers said, proffering a glass.

Kydd took it and lifted it to them. "Your very good health, gentlemen," he called, touched beyond measure.

The group broke into warm conversation, and as dinner was brought he found himself talking as amiably as any. More wine, more dishes: Kydd felt a rush of feeling that came out as hot words of admiration for their fine ship, their spirit, their future.

He sat with flushed face and beamed at them all. No cool talk of the London Season, not a word about fox-hunting or estates in the country, this was good sturdy conversation about horses, prospects of prize money, scandalous theatre gossip—here he could safely say his piece without fear of being thought a boor.

"Fr'm Kentucky, friend, you'll hanker after this . . ." Bourbon whiskey was added to the list of Kydd's American experiences.

"Did I ever tell ye of Gibraltar? Now there's a rare place, one thunderin' great rock . . ."

Happy and muzzy, he did not notice that Truxtun was in the wardroom until he suddenly saw him sitting at the other end of the table. He froze—but Truxtun raised his glass. "Ye share the same forename as me, Tom, and I'd like to say that, should you find it in your heart to become an American, there could be a berth aboard *Constellation* if you choose."

Kydd turned in to his tiny cot, unable to control his whirling thoughts. An American? Thomas Paine Kydd, citizen of the United States, gentleman of the land and lieutenant of the United States Navy? It was not impossible—he had no ties, no wife and family back in England.

Excitement seized him and his eyes opened wide in the darkness. Why not start a new life in a country where there did not seem to be any difference between gentleman and commoner, a nation that seemed to have so much land and so few people—opportunity unlimited?

But he held the King's commission. Would he be betraying his country in her time of need? What about other officers in foreign navies? Well, they had been allowed to resign their commissions to take service, and was there not one in the Russian Navy who was now a grand duke? And, above all, if he were in the American Navy he would be fighting the King's enemies even if it was under another flag.

And there were so many English seamen already serving—he had heard aboard *Constellation* the accents of Devon, the North, London. He could always be among his countrymen if he felt lonely. They had made the choice, even if many had chosen desertion. Could he?

He tossed and turned until finally sleep came mercifully to claim him.

It seemed only minutes later when he jerked awake. He knew that he had heard a cannon shot and sat up. Almost immediately the urgent rattle of a drum beating to quarters set his heart hammering.

Kydd dropped clumsily out of his cot and reached for his clothing. Nearby, thumping feet sounded urgently. He struggled into breeches and shirt, flung on his coat and raced barefoot up the companion to the upper deck.

In the cold of daybreak, out of the thin drifting rain ahead, the dark shape of a ship lay across their path. *Constellation*'s helm was put up to bear away. Even in the bleak grey half-light it was plain that they had come upon a man-o'-war, a frigate, who had instantly challenged them.

"Get out of it, damn you!" Truxtun bawled, catching sight of Kydd. "Get below!"

There was something about this enemy frigate—Kydd knew he had seen her before.

"Now, sir!" Truxtun bellowed.

It was the characteristic odd-coloured staysail, the abrupt curve of her beakhead. But where? Her colours flew directly away and were impossible to make out; the two signal flags of her challenge flickered briefly into life as they were jerked down and, her challenge unanswered, her broadside thundered out.

In the seconds that the balls took to reach them Kydd remembered, but before he could speak, Truxtun roared, "Get that English bastard below, this instant!"

Shot slammed past hideously, gouting the sea and sending solid masses of water aboard. One slapped through a sail. Kydd urged Truxtun, "Sir, hold y'r fire, for God's sake—she's a British ship!"

Incredulous, Truxtun stared at him. "She fired on the American flag! She's got to be a Frenchman, damn you!"

"That's *Ceres* thirty-two, I'd stake m' life on it!" But how fast would *Ceres* take to reload and send another, better-aimed, broadside?

"An English ship!" Truxtun's roar carried down the deck and pale faces turned, then darkened in anger, menacing growls rising to shouts. "I'll make 'em regret this! Mr Rodgers—"

"Do ye want war with England as well?" Kydd shouted. Livid, Truxtun hesitated.

"Hoist y'r white flag!"

"Surrender? Are you insane?"

"No—flag o' parley." All it needed was for one over-hasty gunner on either side and the day would end in bloody ruin.

For a frozen moment everything hung. Then Truxtun acted: "White flag to the main, Mr Rodgers," he growled.

"He'd better be coming with an explanation!" Truxtun snapped to Kydd, as a boat under a white flag advanced, a lieutenant clearly visible in the sternsheets.

"Sir, be s' good as to see it from his point o' view. His private signals have not been answered and as far as he knows there *is* no United States Navy with a ship o' this force. You have t' be a Frenchy tryin' a deception."

Truxtun gave an ill-natured grunt and waited for the boat. When it drew near Kydd saw the lieutenant stand and look keenly about him as the bowman hooked on. As he mounted the side angry shouts were hurled at him by seamen, which Truxtun made no attempt to stop.

"Now, before I blow you out of the water, explain why you fired into me, sir," Truxtun said hotly, as the lieutenant climbed over the bulwark.

He had intelligent eyes and answered warily, "Sir, the reason is apparent. You did not answer my ship's legitimate challenge and, er, we have no information about an American frigate at sea. Our conclusion must be obvious." Before Truxtun could answer, he added, "And remembering we are under a flag of truce, sir, I believe I might respectfully demand that you offer me some form of proof of your national status—if you please."

"Be damned to your arrogance, sir!" Truxtun punched a fist towards the huge American flag above them. "There is all the proof anyone needs!" Shouts of agreement rang out and seamen advanced on the quarterdeck. The lieutenant held his ground but his hand fell to his sword.

Kydd held up a hand and stepped forward. "L'tenant, a word, if y' please."

The lieutenant looked in astonishment at Kydd's bare legs, his civilian coat and breeches, soaked and clinging to him. "Er, yes?"

Drawing him aside, Kydd spoke urgently. "I'm L'tenant Kydd of HMS *Tenacious,* supernumerary aboard. I have t' tell ye now, this is a United States frigate true enough, and no damn Frenchy."

The lieutenant's disdain turned to cold suspicion. "You'll pardon my reservations, sir," he said, giving a short bow, "but can you offer me any confirmation of your identity?"

Kydd pulled his wet coat about him: a great deal hung on his next words. "Very well, I can do that," he said softly. "Off Devil's Island not a month ago, *Ceres* was there when *Resolution* hangs out a signal to tack—in succession. *Tenacious* makes a fool of herself. *I* was that signal lieutenant."

The lieutenant stared, then smiled. "I really believe you must be."

He turned to Truxtun and removed his hat. "Sir, you have my condolences that this unhappy incident took place, but cannot concede any responsibility. This will be a matter for our governments to resolve. Good day, sir."

The furious Truxtun did not reply, glowering at the man as he solemnly replaced his hat and went down the side to his boat, followed by yells of defiance.

What if it had been *Tenacious* instead? Kydd's thoughts raced—a ship-of-the-line thundering out her broadside? How could two proud navies cruise the seas without it happening again? They were at war with the same enemy—that was the main point. All else was pride.

"Sir." Truxtun drew a deep breath and Kydd went on quickly, "Be so kind as t' honour me with a minute of y'r time—in private."

Truxtun turned to Rodgers. "Stand down the men." He stalked over to Kydd and stared at him. "Very well—and then, for your own safety, sir, I'm confining you to your cabin until you're off this ship."

"Thank you, sir." Kydd felt he was being carried forward in a rush of destiny that could not be stopped, yet his mind was protecting him from the enormity of what he was contemplating by an odd detachment from reality.

"If I might go t' my cabin for a moment." He was back quickly and went with Truxtun into his great cabin, closing the door behind him.

"*One* minute."

"Sir. Captain—this is a madness. We must fight t'gether, not each other. So I'm now going t' trust you with my honour, an' I know it's not going t' be misplaced." He could read nothing in Truxtun's stony face.

"Sir." He gulped as he felt in his coat and withdrew a small pocket book. "Sir, this is a copy of our secret signals. If you are challenged by a British ship you may safely reply with the correct private signal of the day, here, and at night challenge and response, here.

"Take it, sir, an' I know you'll protect its confidentiality with your own honour." If the enemy ever got hold of its secrets, the ships of the Royal Navy would be at their mercy.

Truxtun stared at the book and then at Kydd. "God rot me, but you're a brave man, Mr Kydd," he said softly. He took the book and slipped it into his own coat. "It'll be safe with me." He held out his hand. "I hope you do not suffer for this, but what you've done . . ." He clapped his hand on Kydd's shoulder. "An honour to know you, sir."

Chapter 12

KYDD HAD BEEN ABLE TO REASSURE STODDERT with what he had seen, and Liston had listened to his account of a new player on the world maritime stage with grave attention, accepting his considered opinion of the new navy as an effective force. But now Kydd must face his day of reckoning and his return to Halifax was charged with dread at how he would be received. He knew why he had acted as he did, but the Admiralty might regard it as no less than treason.

Leaving the deadly Sambro Ledges well to leeward, the packet he'd caught back finally rounded the grey rocks of Chebucto Head for the run in to Halifax harbour. He had been away only days but it seemed like months.

Soon Kydd was standing on Water Street pier. He knew exactly what he had to do. He left his baggage at the shipping office and hurried down to the watermen's steps to hire a wherry to take him to the flagship at anchor.

The officer-of-the-day quickly got rid of Kydd to the flag-lieutenant.

"I have to wait upon the admiral immediately," Kydd said tightly.

"You have an appointment, of course."

"I'm just this hour returned from th' United States."

The officer snorted in contempt. "Good God, Mr Kydd, you know better than to come aboard hoping the admiral is at leisure to see you. Leave your reasons with me and—"

"L'tenant, unless you take me t' Admiral Vandeput this instant, you'll rue it, an' that is my solemn promise."

"Very well. Be it on your own head. What ship, you say?"

The officer knocked softly on the door to the admiral's day cabin. "Lieutenant Kydd, sir, HMS *Tenacious*. No appointment, but he seems monstrous anxious to see you."

Kydd entered.

The admiral was at his desk frowning, his secretary standing nearby with papers. "Yes?"

"Sir, I have a matter of th' greatest importance." Kydd's voice came out thickly.

Vandeput looked at him steadily, then glanced at his secretary. "Go," he snapped, then turned back to Kydd. "You're back from America. What is it?"

It took but small minutes to convey the gist of his experiences, ending with the final, shocking clash. "Therefore, sir, I saw that if it happens again there's chance f'r a mortal fight or . . ."

Vandeput's expression hardened. "And then?"

Kydd took hold of all his courage. "I gave Captain Truxtun m' own signal book, which has all th' private signals for your fleet."

There was an appalled silence, then the admiral said softly, "You're saying this American captain now has possession of all our secret signals?"

"Aye, sir," said Kydd, trying to keep the tremor from his voice.

"Well done."

"S-sir?"

"A good, officer-like solution, L'tenant. Always worried me,

Americans at sea in a ship o' force sharing the same ocean without we have a form o' co-operation. The politicos won't go at it
out o' pride, but now we've forced their hands. I can see how this
can go further, Mr Kydd. As I say, well done, sir."

Weak with reaction, Kydd swayed. "Oh, I see it's been a fa-
tiguing journey for ye, Mr Kydd," the admiral said solicitously.
"Do sit, and I'll ring for a brandy."

Kydd stared moodily at the town from the decks of *Tenacious*.
He had been welcomed back by a newly respectful wardroom,
but after a while conversations turned once again to the social
scene. The whole town was mesmerised by the impending visit of
the Duke of Schweigerei, elder son of the Archduke of Austria,
which would climax in a grand reception and banquet given by
His Royal Highness Prince Edward in the Duke's honour. In
view of the importance attached to the country for its role in
Pitt's coalitions, every officer would be expected to attend the
glittering occasion.

Renzi had tried to be interested in Kydd's adventure, but he
was clearly preoccupied with some personal matter, and Kydd
found himself once more at a loose end. The seductive thought
on his mind was of what might be—service in the new navy of
a vigorous young land. No more would he hear of lords and estates, fox-hunting and the Season.

Kydd stirred uncomfortably and noticed the master, with a
large notebook and folded chart, checking something over the
side. "Nothing amiss, Mr Hambly?" It was unusual to see the
master at work on deck in harbour.

"Nay, sir, nothing t' worry you on," he said. Then, seeing
Kydd's interest, he explained further. It seemed that the new
Admiralty hydrographic department had issued instructions to
all sailing masters that anchorages they might from time to time
visit should be surveyed by hand lead-line from a ship's boat with

a view to verifying the accuracy of charts now in the course of preparation in England.

"A fine and proper thing," said Kydd. Every mariner was at the mercy of his charts, whether dependable or false, and any endeavour that could lessen the fearful risks of navigation was a service to mankind. "Where are you going t' start?"

"Why, Mr Kydd, it's kind in ye to enquire. I thought t' try the Bedford Basin—there, through the narrows, an' you'll find a fine body o' water twice the size of Halifax harbour there."

A nearly perfect land-locked haven: a fleet could safely ride out a storm there. This was really worthwhile—an exercise of professional sea skills with a purpose. Kydd brightened. "Mr Hambly, I'd like t' do some of this work m'self. Would you be s' kind as to show me on the chart?"

Kydd had chosen to begin his first line of soundings across the widest point of the basin to establish some sort of bottom profile. It was satisfying work, and congenial to the spirit. Real skill was needed to hold the octant laterally to establish the bearings ashore and provide the exact position of the pinnace. Poulden, in the bows, would send the hand-lead plummeting down, singing out in cadence the exact depth of water told by the marks. Kydd noted the time carefully; later, there would be work with tide tables to establish the true depth, corrected for the state of tide, then referenced to the chart datum.

Kydd was so engrossed in the work that, for a space, he had forgotten his concern about the banquet. It had been heavily hinted at by Captain Houghton that every officer would not only attend but with a suitable lady. To those who had attained a degree of intimacy with the gentle reaches of Haligonian society it would be a matter of choice. For Kydd, who had not only been away but felt awkward and ill-at-ease in well-born company, it was a trial. He realised he would probably end up with the insipid daughter of the vicar, with whom he was on nodding terms, to the amusement of the more senior in the wardroom.

He forced his mind back to the task at hand. Surprisingly, their first traverse reached the twenty-fathom limit of a hand-lead less than a third the way across. Such deep water? Perhaps he should stay with the shoreline and first establish a forty-foot line of depth along it, this being of most interest to a big-ship navigator. It was not difficult to pick up the mark again, and astute reading of the characteristics at the edge of the shoreline soon had a useful number of forty-foot soundings carefully pencilled in. But for the unfortunate narrows at the entrance, restricting access to square-rigged vessels whenever the winds were in the north, it was spacious and deep enough to take the entire Channel Fleet at single anchor, an impressive body of water.

Something ashore caught Kydd's eye: a figure in white, standing, watching. He ignored it and continued with his work. They drew abreast; the figure was still there. As he watched he realised it was a woman, waving a handkerchief.

She waved again, an exaggerated movement. "Someone wants t' speak, sir," Poulden volunteered.

"Aye. Well, perhaps we should see what she wants. Oars, give way together."

The boat headed inshore. The wooded slopes leading down to the water looked immaculately cared for, and they saw the edge of a building peeping out from blossom-laden trees. Closer in, Kydd noticed a discreet landing-stage and headed for it. The woman made no move to descend to it, still standing and watching from her vantage-point.

Cursing under his breath, Kydd threw a rope ashore and pulled himself up to the little jetty. He was hardly dressed for meeting ladies in his worn sea uniform but he clambered up to where she was waiting.

"Yes, madam?"

"Oh. I was watching you, you see," she said, her voice soft and prettily accented with French.

Kydd remembered himself and snatched off his hat. Dressed for the garden, she was in a white gown and beribboned straw hat. She was also strikingly beautiful, her large dark eyes adding an appealing wistfulness.

"And I thought 'ave you lost something—you look for it so long." She seemed a touch older than him and had a disconcertingly worldly-wise air.

"Not at all, madam. We conduct a hydrographical survey o' the coastline." She was probably one of the sad band of royalist refugees who had settled in Nova Scotia, he conjectured, although apparently from a wealthy family. "Oh, er, might I present m'self? L'tenant Kydd, Royal Navy."

"*Enchantée,* Lieutenant." Her bob coincided with Kydd's sturdy bow. "Then you do not know me?"

"No, madam, er, you have th' advantage of me."

She contemplated him, then said, "I am Thérèse Bernardine-Mongenet and zis is where I live." She gestured gracefully up the slopes.

At a loss, Kydd bowed again.

"I was taking refreshment in ze garden. Perhaps you would care to take some lemonade wiz me, and tell me about your hydrog-cally, Lieutenant?"

Kydd accepted graciously: the boat's crew would be reliable with Poulden and would not object to an hour's leisure. They walked together up a winding path, past little summerhouses with gilded latticework and bells tinkling on their pagoda-like roofs. It was the most enchanting and sumptuous garden Kydd had ever seen. Atop a bluff overlooking the water, cunningly nestled among trees, there was a two-storey wooden mansion, vaguely Italian in style, and on the grass lawn below a cloth-covered table with jug and glass.

"A moment." She summoned a maid and spoke rapidly in French to her, then turned back to Kydd. "So, tell me what is it you are doing."

Kydd was uncomfortable in his old uniform but he thawed at her warmth, and by the time the maid returned with another glass and a cake stand he was chuckling at her misapprehensions of the sea service. "Rousin' good cakes," he said, having sampled one of the tiny, lemon-flavoured shells.

"Ah, ze *madeleines,*" she said sadly. "The old King Louis, 'is favourite."

It did not seem right to dwell on past griefs, so Kydd said brightly, "Have you heard? The Duke o' Shwygery is t' be honoured with a banquet, an' we're all invited to attend. Your husband will have an invitation, o' course?"

"I am not married," she said quietly.

"Oh, I'm sorry, madam," he said. "Ah—that's not t' mean I'm sorry you're not married at all. I—er, please forgive . . ."

"Forgiven, M'sieur," she said gently.

"Will I see you there?" he asked hopefully.

She looked at him steadily. "I have not been invited."

Kydd's heart went out to her, so elegant, beautiful and serene. No man had begged her hand for the occasion, unwilling to risk the mortification of being declined—indeed, in the normal way he would never be noticed by a lady of such quality. It was so close to the event it was more than probable there would be no more offers forthcoming and she would be obliged to stay at home. Any gentleman . . . "Madam, I am not engaged for the occasion. It would be my particular honour t' escort you, should ye be inclined."

There was a fraction of hesitation, then she smiled. "I would be delighted to accept, Lieutenant," she murmured, and the smile moved to her eyes.

• • •

"What do ye think, Nicholas?" said Kydd, rotating in his new full-dress uniform coat. The white facings with gold buttons against the deep blue were truly magnificent and he looked forward to making his appearance in it.

"Dare I enquire, dear fellow, if you have a lady of suitable distinction marked out for the occasion?" Renzi asked doubtfully.

"I have." Kydd was going to give nothing away before the night; all he had to do was take a ship's boat to the landing-stage, then make his way to the house. Thérèse had said she would find a carriage.

"It *is* at Government House," Renzi stressed, "and although we shall not be prominently seated you do understand we *will* be under eye, possibly of the Prince himself."

"Thank you, Nicholas. I will try not to disappoint. And y'rself?"

"I have my hopes, dear fellow."

The day of the banquet arrived. Captain Houghton addressed his officers in the wardroom as to the seriousness of the occasion, the honour of the ship, the correct forms of address to the Prince and to an Austrian duke and duchess and the probable fate of any officer who brought shame to his ship.

Later in the day Tysoe jostled with others to begin the long process of bringing his officer to a state of splendour: a stiff white shirt topped with a black stock at the neck under the high stand-up collar of the coat, gleaming buckled shoes over white stockings, and immaculate tight white breeches. It had been shockingly expensive and Kydd had borrowed heavily against his future prize money from *Minotaure,* but he was determined to make a showing.

One by one the other officers departed, some to share carriages, others to walk up the hill. Renzi left, with a troubled glance at his friend.

Kydd trod the same path as before, the early-summer evening tinting the garden with a delicious enchantment. A footman waited and escorted Kydd to an open carriage. "Madame will attend you presently," he intoned.

Thérèse emerged and Kydd was left struggling for words: there must be few in Halifax who could possibly reach her heights of fashionable elegance. He took refuge in a deep bow as she came towards him in a full-length, high-waisted ivory gown, perilously low-cut and trimmed fetchingly in blue, her elaborate coiffure woven with pearls and a single ostrich feather sweeping up imperiously.

"*Bonsoir, mon lieutenant.* An' such a clement evening, *n'est-ce pas?*"

With the footman holding open the door of the carriage, Kydd helped her up, her long gloved hand in his. It seemed so unreal, and all he could think of was that he must not let down Cecilia after all her patient tutoring on gentility.

The chaise lurched into motion, keeping to a sedate pace. Kydd sat bolt upright next to his lady. Thankfully, the grinding of the wheels made conversation an effort, and he concentrated on the journey, imagining the effect on his shipmates when he and his lady were announced.

As they approached the town he was given a measure of what to expect by the reaction of passers-by. Some gaped, others pointed. Kydd swelled with pride—they must make a striking couple indeed. The carriage clattered along the streets and headed for a large building between two churches, illuminated in every window, and with the sound of fine music coming from within.

They drew up outside among the crowd of sightseers and Kydd was gratified once again by the impression he and his lady made. He bowed graciously this way and that, then hastened to assist Thérèse down. He offered his arm, and they swept into

Government House through a lane of gaping onlookers. His confidence soared.

Inside he glimpsed the *levée* room, packed with glittering personages in animated talk, jewellery sparkling in candle-light, and a military concert band in full flow in the corner. A bewigged major-domo at the door hesitated. "Er, Madame Thérèse Bernardine-Mongenet," Kydd said importantly—it had taken hours to learn, "And L'tenant Thomas Kydd."

The man looked petrified; possibly this was his first important occasion, Kydd thought. Nevertheless, he coughed and bawled resolutely, "Lieutenant Thomas Kydd and—and Madame Thérèse Bernardine-Mongenet." With her hand on his arm, Kydd stepped into the room. If only Cecilia could see him now!

Every face in the room turned towards them: conversations died, the band's efforts faded uncertainly. Kydd's head was spinning. This was what it was to be in high society! "You will introduce me?" Thérèse whispered.

Overflowing with happiness and with the broadest smile, Kydd turned to his left and approached the nearest group, who started with apprehension. He bowed deeply to the elderly gentleman and made a grand introduction. The man's wife curtsied, staring wide-eyed at Thérèse. Kydd moved on graciously, trying to think of suitable small-talk.

He knew he would never forget the night—or the effect of a truly beautiful woman on society. Around them conversations stopped, then picked up again as they progressed down the room.

To the side, he saw Houghton staring at them as if at a ghost. Next to him stood Bampton, clearly in shock. "My captain," Kydd said happily to Thérèse, as they approached. Houghton seemed overcome at the introduction, gobbling something indistinct, but Thérèse, clearly delighted, bestowed on him special attention and offered her hand to be kissed. As he watched his captain grovel before a grand lady, Kydd believed the evening could promise nothing more satisfying.

Prince Edward stood in the centre of the room surrounded by aides-de-camp, courtiers and military men in gleaming regimentals. Kydd summoned every ounce of courage and led Thérèse over to him. "Y'r Royal Highness, may I be allowed t' introduce Madame Thérèse Bernardine-Mongenet?" Thérèse's graceful curtsy was long held. "An' myself, L'tenant Thomas Kydd, o' HMS *Tenacious*." He bowed as low as he could.

"Lieutenant, tell me true, have you been in Halifax long?" The Prince had an aristocratically hard face; Kydd had heard stories of his unbending attitude to military discipline, his early-morning parades and merciless justice.

"Not long, Y'r Royal Highness, an' much o' that in the United States."

"Oh. I see. Well, I wish you a pleasant evening, Mr Kydd."

"Thank you, sir," Kydd mumbled, remembering to back away. He had survived, and he turned to grin at Thérèse.

A fanfare of trumpets sounded from the other room, announcing the banquet. An immediate move was made towards the connecting door, but Kydd remembered to keep clear: as a junior officer he would certainly be bringing up the rear. He stayed to one side, nodding pleasantly to those whose eyes strayed towards him and Thérèse until eventually he judged it time to enter.

The room was huge. In the distance a long table was raised on a dais, the centre occupied by the Prince and honoured guests. Behind them two servants gently fanned the principal guests with enormous ostrich feathers, tastefully coloured in red, white and blue.

Lesser mortals occupied the long tables in rows from the front and, as he had suspected, he was shown to one near the rear. To his delight he saw Renzi seated there. Next to him was a voluble woman with pasty skin and a profusion of cheap jewellery who tugged incessantly at his sleeve. Renzi looked up at Kydd, and stared, stricken, at him as if the world had been turned upside-down.

Gleefully Kydd made his introduction, indicating to Thérèse that this was his particular friend, but when he made to seat his lady, he was interrupted by a courtier. "Sir, His Royal Highness commands you and Madame to join him," he murmured, discreetly indicating the Prince, who was beckoning.

Heart thudding, Kydd turned to Renzi and muttered his excuses. He wended his way with Thérèse through the tightly packed tables, feeling all eyes upon him, hearing animated murmuring following in their wake.

They mounted the dais and approached Prince Edward, who leaned back to speak. "Ah, so kind of you to join us." His eyes did not move from Thérèse as he continued, "I don't think you've met *Hoheit Herzog* Schweigerei, his wife the *Herzogin* Adelheid. Sir, Lieutenant Kydd and Madame Thérèse Bernardine-Mongenet."

The evening proceeded. Over the wild duck Kydd found himself explaining sea service to the Prince; the saddle of mutton saw him recounting his American sojourn to the sharp-featured Duke. While he was helping Thérèse to another pompadour cream he looked out over the massed tables below them. Somewhere in the hazy distance Renzi, Captain Houghton and the rest were looking enviously to the dais at Prince Edward, Thérèse Bernardine-Mongenet—and Thomas Kydd.

At last the banquet drew to a close. The Prince rose, conversation stilled, and there was a sudden scraping of chairs as everyone stood up. One by one the members of the high table descended, following the Prince as he processed out affably, nodding to the bobs and curtsies as he passed. Looks of admiration and envy shot at Kydd, who smiled back lazily.

In the foyer the Prince turned to Kydd. "Lieutenant, you will

no doubt be returning to your ship. Pray do not stand on ceremony for Madame—I will personally see she returns home
safely." With a wry smile, Kydd bowed. "And, Lieutenant, I will
not forget your service to me this night!"

Thérèse looked at Kydd. She crossed to him and kissed him
firmly on both cheeks. "*I* will not forget this evening. *Bonne
chance, mon ami.*"

They left. Kydd watched the Prince's carriage depart, Thérèse's
last glance back and fond wave. The rest of the guests issued out
noisily, and it seemed the whole of Halifax wanted to meet him,
make his acquaintance, be seen with him. Captain Houghton appeared, staring wordlessly at Kydd and shaking his head slowly
before he moved on; Adams came up and insisted on taking his
hand. "Damme if that wasn't the finest stroke of the age!" he
said sincerely.

Finally Renzi emerged. Full of the deepest delight Kydd said
casually, "Then was she not a suitable lady?"

"Brother, we must walk for a spell." Renzi did not bother to
introduce the lady with him, who pouted at the slight. "Into your
coach, m'dear," he said firmly. "I shall follow." When they were
alone on the street Renzi turned to him. "My dear fellow," he began, then stopped. "My dear chap. Where can I *begin?*" He paced
about in frustration, ignoring the admiring glances passers-by
were throwing at Kydd. "In polite society—in the highest society—damn it all, what you did was either inspired deviltry or the
purest ignorance! And all Halifax believes it the first."

"Nicholas, you talk in riddles. If you're just envious—"

"Tom—if you must know, this is what you did. You invited
the Prince's mistress to a banquet hosted by the Prince himself."

"Thérèse—Julie?" Kydd fell back in dismay. The flush drained
from his face. At the very least it was the ruin of his career, a
spectacular end to his promising beginnings. After the exaltation
of earlier it was agonising.

"Not at all." Renzi struggled for the words. "The world believes you knew that Julie appears at lesser occasions, the Prince having a particular taking for her, but at affairs of state—foreign potentates—she must not be seen. To the Prince's great pleasure you produced her for him at this occasion under the unimpeachable courtly pretence of not knowing her situation."

He gave a low laugh. "There must be many haughty matrons of Halifax who have been put sadly out of countenance tonight—but many more gentlemen whose admiration for you is unbounded. Just consider—you now have the ear and attention of a prince of the Blood Royal. You are made in society, you—you have but to claim the fruits of your cunning."

"Where's Renzi?" It was late morning in the wardroom and he had still not appeared. Kydd had put it down to over-indulgence, but his friend's cabin was empty.

"Renzi? I do believe he must still be at Manning's tavern—he was well away when I saw him," Pringle drawled.

A tavern? Kydd threw on his coat and clapped on his hat. In all the time he had known Renzi he had never once seen him in liquor. Surely he was not a spurned lover. The woman whom he had seen at the banquet? Impossible!

Manning's was often frequented by officers but Kydd could not find Renzi in the high-backed chairs of the taphouse or in any of the more secluded public rooms. Discreet enquiry yielded that he was still in his room and furthermore had sent for two bottles since midnight, and was unaccountably alone.

Disturbed, Kydd went up the stairs. Knocking at the door several times did not produce a result. "Nicholas!" he called softly. "I know you're there. Let me in, brother."

About to knock again he heard Renzi's muffled voice, "Thank you for your visit, but I'm indisposed. I shall return aboard—later."

"If bein' tosticated is what ails ye, then it's a poor shab as won't see his friend."

There was a silence, then a rattling, and the door opened. Kydd nearly laughed at the frowsy bleariness of his friend but kept a grave expression and entered. He sat in a chair next to the bed. "Can I be of service to ye?" he asked neutrally.

Renzi glared balefully at him. Then he groaned and lolled back in the other chair. "I'm all undone, I see. You shall have the truth of it—but first a drink."

Kydd sat up, alarmed, but Renzi reached for the water pitcher on the dresser and up-ended it, gulping the water noisily. He wiped his mouth and tried to grin. "Ah, let us say I have been the unwitting sport of Venus, the plaything of Cupid. In fine, I have to admit to being gulled in full measure."

"Aye?" said Kydd, trying not to show his considerable interest.

"A charming nymph, a young sprig of society, whose name will be known in the highest reaches of Haligonian gentility, she it was who—who has refused me."

"That—that woman at the banquet?" Kydd said, appalled.

"Not her," said Renzi testily. "A mere *quicumque vult*, a Cyprian taken up for the occasion. No—I speak of a young woman of grace and talents, a perfect specimen of spirited maidenhood. I met her at the admiral's rout and since then have been seen in her company at many a polite occasion, a sparkling companion. Then, the sap unwonted rising high, I pressed my attentions on her, would not be denied . . ." He trailed off, staring disconsolately at the wall.

"And then?"

"It grieves me to say it, but she—she . . ."

"Yes?"

"It seems that the young lady is—how shall we phrase it? Of

the Sapphic persuasion." At Kydd's blank look he added wearily, "This is to mean that she prefers the company of women to that of men, in all its forms."

"Then—"

"Quite so. For her I have been but a toy, a necessary social ornament. It has been a—salutary experience."

"Nicholas, I—"

"And is now most firmly a thing of the past," Renzi concluded bleakly.

Kydd subsided. It explained Renzi's distraction, his absences. And it was certain he would appreciate neither sympathy nor pity.

Renzi drew a deep breath and leaning forward said, "Therefore we shall speak of your transmogrification."

"My . . . ?" said Kydd carefully.

"You're clearly not fully aware of what has happened, and by that I do not mean simply your appearance with Madame Thérèse." He held his head and closed his eyes for a space. "Consider this: your action in bringing Julie to the banquet is seen as a very clever piece of theatre to bring yourself to the attention not only of society but of Prince Edward himself, a coup that has all Halifax abuzz.

"Now what that is telling the world is that you must be accounted a superior player in the arts of society, and it would go well with any who can boast your acquaintance. This is my wager with you—you'll have more invitations in the next week than you can possibly accept in a year."

"But I don't—"

"Let me continue. This is a triviality, a vaporous nonsense compared to its true significance." He took another pull at the water pitcher and, looking directly at Kydd, continued, "Tom, dear chap, what is signified is that the forms of politeness, so well expressed by John Locke, however requisite in the salons and courts, must always yield to that of true character in polite company.

"*In vino veritas,* then. I was wrong. I freely admit it. You are your own man now, with a character and reputation that will only grow. You don't need airs and my clever words—and neither do you need to bandy empty talk about fox-hunting or the Season, for you've established a manly character of your own, which, dare I say it, is above such nonsense.

"My dear fellow—go forth and conquer. Know that you can match any gentleman for wit and reputation and at last take your place in society."

Renzi closed his eyes. "And leave me to die in peace."

Kydd rose noiselessly and tiptoed away.

Renzi was right. Invitations arrived by the dozen for Lieutenant Kydd in the days that followed. At one point Captain Houghton came to him personally with a mumbled request that he grace an evening with him at the attorney general Uniacke's, known like Cunard for his four daughters, and a power in the land. Fortunately Kydd found his diary free for that night.

And Renzi was right about the other thing: the wardroom continued to talk country estates and Vauxhall Gardens, but when Kydd came in with an appreciation of the new United States Navy or a light observation on signals he was listened to respectfully, getting laughs in all the right places.

It was a heady discovery that he was free at last. Free of the demons of inferiority, the fear of being seen as socially gauche, the oaken-headed tarpaulin, an embarrassment. Now he could hold his own in any society.

"Nicholas, are you at liberty tonight? It would give me th' greatest pleasure to sup with you—at Pontac's at seven?"

Kydd was determined to do his friend proud. "Do have more o' the roast lark, they're so particular in the cooking here," he said. "And I hope the Lafite is up to your expectations," he added anxiously. He piled Renzi's plate high and insisted on pouring the wine.

Renzi was unusually silent, which Kydd put down to his recent experience. It needed all of an hour before he finally spoke his mind. "There is an observation I feel obliged to make, Thomas, bearing as it does on our long friendship." He weighed his words carefully. "An unkind observer might remark that in our lower-deck existence we had a peculiar need, one for the other. I—that in my term of exile there was one of intelligence, uncommon good sense and enquiring nature to lighten my durance. You—my trifles of philosophy and intellectual penetrations could enable you to rise above the limitations of your surroundings. That same observer could then say, in perfect truth, that those needs are now concluded. You have succeeded in all the accomplishments of gentility and the sea profession, so I am no longer needed."

Kydd slammed down his glass. "Stuff 'n' nonsense, Nicholas!" He saw Renzi's eyes glitter—it seemed it was costing him much to speak as he had.

"And I," Renzi continued, with some difficulty, "I have had my choice of wranglers in reason, the company of my peers in breeding, the sweets of society, but in cleaving to these it grieves me to recall how I have so shamelessly neglected our friendship—all for the sake of the evanescent. Is this then an end to our association? Logic is a stern mistress and pronounces that, with the extinction of need, we must necessarily part, go our own ways—"

"A pox on y'r damned logic!" Kydd said angrily. "As a philosopher you're nothin' but a double-barrelled, copper-bottomed fool! Do ye think I don't still want you as a friend, share the laughs 'n' pains o' life, enjoy while we can? Raise up y'r glass, Nicholas, an' let's drink to friendship."

Renzi lifted his head. A reluctant half-smile spread and he replied, "I will—but this time it's a friendship of equals."

Glasses clinked. When they had regained composure Kydd fumbled in his coat. "Er, Nicholas, I'd value y'r opinion. Which o' these invitations do ye think we should accept?"

Author's Note

A question I am often asked is how long does the research for each book take? That is a difficult thing to quantify because in some ways I suppose I have been unconsciously doing it all my life—during my time at sea absorbing the universals all mariners hold dear, and ingesting material from countless maritime books, both fiction and non-fiction, that I've been drawn to since a very early age.

The proportion of my time now devoted to research must come close to fifty per cent. But I have to say, it's an aspect of being a writer that I *particularly* enjoy.

Research for the Kydd series has provided an opportunity to go down many fascinating paths in search of some arcane fact or other—and this book has proved no exception. I found myself corresponding with Dr David Green at the USDA Forest Service about the specific gravity of swamp oaks; this enabled me to send Kydd on his night-time sabotage mission against the French frigate. A chance discovery of an old pilot book of Kydd's time in a Falmouth museum had me enquiring of the august Royal Institute of Navigation. One of their members, Dr Mark Breach, confirmed the antique rule-of-thumb about the moon's meridian that saved Kydd and his boat crew in the fog.

And while on the subject of chance, what were the odds of

my coming across a signal book actually belonging to a lieutenant on the North American station at exactly the time when Kydd learns his craft as a signal lieutenant? Retired Paymaster Commander William Evershed generously extended a loan of the precious family relic for me to study.

Research has enriched my life in another way, too. It has made me many new friends who also are irresistibly drawn to the sea. Two, in particular, have a special connection with *Quarterdeck*. I first met ship modeller Robert Squarebriggs when I visited Canada's Maritime Provinces in 2002. He shared his love of the boreal wilderness, and I hope in this book that I have done justice to his infectious enthusiasm for his native land. Tyrone Martin is an erudite scholar of the dawn of US Navy history, and a former captain of *Old Ironsides*. His many insights into this fascinating period will again be invaluable when Kydd returns to North America, which he assuredly will.

I feel some degree of guilt in not being able to acknowledge everyone I consulted in the process of writing this book, but they all have my deep thanks. However I could not omit mentioning the three wonderfully professional women in my life—my wife (and creative partner) Kathy, my literary agent Carole Blake, and my editor Jackie Swift. Between them, they contrive to keep the hassles of the modern world at bay, allowing me to give full rein to my creative juices, ready for the next adventure . . .